PENGUIN BOOKS

Shiang

Empire of Salt: Book Two

Praise for *C. F. Iggulden*

'A must read. Iggulden is clearly having fun pitching his various heroes and villains into bloody combat' *SciFi Now*

'An old-school fantasy novel, strong on character, in which readers can immerse themselves' *SFF World*

'Iggulden is in a class of his own' *Daily Mirror*

'A master storyteller' *Sunday Express*

'Iggulden tells an absolutely cracking story' *The Times*

ABOUT THE AUTHOR

C. F. Iggulden is one of the most successful authors of historical fiction writing today. He has written three previous bestselling historical series and two standalone novels: *Dunstan* and *The Falcon of Sparta*. *Shiang* is the second novel in his epic fantasy series, Empire of Salt.

Shiang

Empire of Salt: Book Two

C. F. IGGULDEN

PENGUIN BOOKS

PENGUIN BOOKS

UK | USA | Canada | Ireland | Australia
India | New Zealand | South Africa

Penguin Books is part of the Penguin Random House group of companies
whose addresses can be found at global.penguinrandomhouse.com

First published by Michael Joseph 2018
Published in Penguin Books 2019
002

Set in 12.15/14.4 pt Garamond MT Std
Typeset by Jouve (UK), Milton Keynes
Printed and bound in Great Britain by Clays Ltd, Elcograf S.p.A.

A CIP catalogue record for this book is available from the British Library

ISBN: 978–0–718–18677–7

www.greenpenguin.co.uk

To all those who will not
bow their heads.

Acknowledgements

I must first thank my wife, Ella. She has been a rock, like Feist's Tomas, while Valheru storms surge all around. I could not do this alone. I also have to thank Jillian Taylor of Penguin Random House, whose delicate midwifery played such a part in bringing this trilogy into existence.

Lastly, I would like to thank David Gemmell, for his influence on me from the earliest days. I only wish I could do it in person. I used the grey fields of Homer's Hades in this book, just as he did – though I dare say not as well. Finally, I am grateful to anyone who ever loved one of mine: *Caesar, Genghis* and *The Dangerous Book for Boys*, or *Tollins, Dunstan* and *The Wars of the Roses*. All I ever wanted was to tell stories. Thank you for walking the path.

Conn Iggulden

PART ONE

Nature has left this tincture in the blood,
That all men would be tyrants if they could.

Daniel Defoe

I

Slave

The swordsman made no sound as the bandages came off. With distaste, Taeshin saw they had yellowed. There was a sharp smell in the room, of herbs and corruption. He found he was breathing shallowly and had to concentrate to bring calm once more. His slave Marias held a mirror up for him to see, averting her own gaze so that he had to guide her.

'Up a little. Your left hand forward. No, the other — there. Hold it there. Look away, Marias. I order you.'

It was an effort to keep his voice steady. Taeshin could barely contain his own revulsion when he looked on the rippling black skin that stretched from his armpit to his navel. It looked like a line of spider bites, somehow risen from within, in a way that terrified him. Taeshin glared at the shining bulges, controlling a desire to draw his knife and cut them out. He felt fouled, invaded, as if some strange plant had laid seeds in him. Just brushing his fingertips across the darkened band made pain soar. In the presence of his slave, he clamped his lips and breathed through his nose until it had passed. Despair touched him then. He could not train; he could not fight. In truth, he could barely stand straight, his body in a constant war with his will.

He shuddered, waving Marias away. She knew better than to risk a look at him after he had forbidden it. Taeshin took his responsibilities seriously. The literature of Shiang warned of the dangers of letting a slave go unpunished. Entire households could be ruined by a master too weak to command obedience in his own home. Like every other free man in the city, he kept a short whip on a nail by the front door. He had used it on the day he had brought her back from the slave market, to establish his authority. Later that first night, she had read the page in his pamphlet on slave ownership that suggested it.

Taeshin had not enjoyed striking a woman, she had observed in private wonder. He was used to facing opponents of enormous skill and strength, Mazer masters with steel swords and armour. The experience of chastising a female slave had been slightly humiliating in comparison. That had been a revelation to Marias. To spare Taeshin, she had worked hard not to give him cause to take the whip down again. She didn't think she could bear the gruff awkwardness and throat-clearing a second time.

'Shall I ask for Doctor Elman to attend, master?' Marias asked at the doorway, looking down at her pretty bound feet.

He glanced up, suspicious of mockery. Taeshin hated the feeling of weakness, the knowledge that even Marias could have overpowered him in that moment. It was hard to endure the touch of bandages – the thought of someone actually striking the black lumps was appalling. Death would surely follow. He could not defend himself, never mind complete his duties at court. He was a lord's guard who could not fight. Yet he had nothing else, no family, no savings. Taeshin had borrowed heavily to buy a house more suited to his status. If he lost his place at court, he would simply starve on the street. He might sell his armour to one of the younger men, but it had been his father's and he thought he would prefer to die before that. Taeshin wondered how long he would keep that sense of honour when he was weak with fever and the need to eat. Some men could, he knew. Others seemed strong, but they were hollow vessels, liable to break at the first great test. He was not certain which he was.

'Doctor Elman cannot help me with this.'

Taeshin felt sudden tears come and was grateful the girl stared resolutely at the polished floor. He felt a sense of peace steal over him as he made a decision. He would go into the hills around the city and find a quiet place to sit, where he could see for many miles. He would wash himself and clean his weapons, one by one. He would compose a final poem to be read by those who came looking for him, placing it in a wax-cloth fold with his work contract and the deed to his house. He was not a wealthy man. Marias would be returned to the market with the rest of his household goods, to be sold. He shook his head as he watched her.

His parents had died years before, when he was still a little boy. The aunt who had raised him had always been weak, beset by fevers that left her oyster-eyed and help-less. Whatever restless ambition he owned had come from within, rather than anything that had been imposed on him. He made his own way and took pride and even iden-tity from that. The old lady had clung to life just long enough to see him to adulthood. She had been found cold a few days after he'd been accepted into a noble house.

Taeshin imagined his home being sold without anguish. It was actually a relief not to have to think about such things any longer. He felt lighter, just for having made the decision to die.

He had not dismissed Marias, so she remained, one foot placed before the other, with her head lowered, perfectly still. Taeshin contemplated the roll of clean bandages at his side, ready to bind him. The thought of the pain he would have to endure to put them on was enough to make him hesitate. It would be easier with Marias to help, but then she would know how the disease had spread. He bowed his head, feeling calm flood through him. This was his last day.

'Marias, look upon me,' he said.

He waited until she raised her head, watching closely as her eyes widened and her face grew pale. He hid a wince of discomfort as he rose to his feet and held out his arms.

'No ordinary wound, Marias. It comes from within. It grows . . . worse.'

She came forward as if drawn on a thread, unaware of her own steps as she stared at the black flesh. Her hand rose to touch him and he had to struggle not to step back.

'We could petition Lord Ran to examine you . . .' she said faintly, shaking her head. 'Taeshin, you should not have kept this hidden. How long?'

It was the first time since she had entered his household that she had used his name. Taeshin blinked at her, unsure how to reprimand a slave who took such a liberty, yet whose eyes glittered with tears that were surely proof of some affection. He could not understand her. Marias had been a bargain at the slave market, which he'd thought

6

might mean she was a danger to her old master, or perhaps to his children. There were some slaves who grew only more sullen when they were punished. Yet she was all he had been able to afford and there was no wife or children in his household, nor even a dog to guard his door. He smiled at the thought of his innocence and that tiny room above a bakery. He'd risen, like the bread that had warmed his first floor. He'd passed the trials to serve Lord Hong, beating two thousand others in the Mazer steps. His master demanded and paid for the best, so that all lords might fear his soldiers. Only six months before, Taeshin had been selected for the lord's personal guard. His new home reflected that rise, with six rooms and fine, polished wood. He was twenty-four years old and he had expected to take a wife in the new year. He remembered telling Marias of his plans, excitement filling him. It seemed an age before, when he had been immortal, his flesh still unmarked.

'I thought it was bruising,' he said, craning his neck to look down. 'You know I train every day – I am always in pain. Bruises or cracked ribs are nothing. No physician can treat them, either way. They always say to rest, which I cannot do, so I bind myself up and wait to heal.'

He could feel sweat trickling down his cheek, another sign of weakness that brought with it a touch of anger. He was as fit as it was possible to be. His legs and arms had endured ritual beatings with canes from a young age, forcing bone growth that made them stronger and more dense. In armour or without, with a weapon or unarmed, he was one of the elite warriors of the city of Shiang. To be made weak felt like a failure of will. He had devoted himself to excellence, and in that devotion there had been moments of perfection. They shone like jewels in his memory, when in his strength, he had moved like silk through the fingers of the world. Before his flesh had swelled into buboes that made him gasp and ache.

A voice called from the street outside, making them both freeze. Taeshin knew the impatient tones of his master's son and he reached for his armour like taking a breath. Her hand stopped him.

'Bandages first. Sit straight and I will wrap and knot them.'

'Anjin has a key,' he murmured. 'He will not wait outside for more than a second.'

'Then we will have to hurry.'

Her hands moved swiftly as she wrapped clean bandages around him. To reach, she had to come in close, bumping her face against his chest almost as an embrace. It was not an unpleasant sensation, if he hadn't been expecting his master's son to appear in the doorway.

He hissed when she drew the strips tight. Marias apologised under her breath as Taeshin rose to his feet, already reaching for the tunic lined with silk. She tugged that over his head and then heaved the armoured jerkin from where it rested on the back of a chair. That piece split along one length in a strip of buckles, so that he imagined a clam closing on him as he put his first arm through.

'Taeshin! Where are you? Will you make me come in?'

The voice was imperious, as the father's never was. Taeshin admired Lord Hong, but the man had been cursed with an eldest son he did not deserve. Still, it was not the place of a lord's guard to question, only to obey. Taeshin was as ready as he could be, with sweat running down his face, and his side feeling as if he had been speared, but upright and in armour. He reached for his sword and groaned aloud. Marias took hold of the scabbard and belted it to him. Once more, he found he was enjoying what felt like affection from her. She sensed his interest and snorted.

'Concentrate, my lord and master. If your illness is revealed, I will be sent back to the slave market. I prefer your household! So stand straight, Taeshin!'

He blinked at her, though both of them heard the key turn in the lock and he did not reply.

Lord Anjin entered the house with his gauntlets in one hand. The other held a bunch of keys like a landlord. He was scowling and flushed as he came in like a gale wind, scattering a stool across the floor. He halted when he saw Taeshin standing at the bottom of the stairs, in armour. The young lord was not to be denied his anger so easily, however.

'I know you heard me, Taeshin! I have five men waiting in the street – and they all heard you would not come. Are you so weary of my father's service? Is that it? Shall I release you from your oath?'

The younger man had come further in as he spoke. Anjin was no swordmaster, but he was still young and fast. When he caught a flicker of movement on the steps above, he drew his sword and dropped to first position, ready to be attacked. He flushed when he saw it was only the man's house slave.

Anjin glanced at his father's warrior, seeing only a dark seriousness. Taeshin was not fool enough to be caught laughing at his master's son, no matter how he had been startled. It was a reminder that Taeshin was actually one of the better ones. Some of his father's guards would have spread the story of Anjin drawing his sword on a young woman all over the markets and teahouses.

The nobleman sheathed the blade with a flourish. He glanced once more at the slave now kneeling on the uppermost step, with her head down. He considered having her killed while he was attending his father and Taeshin was busy with his duties. Women gossiped, unfortunately. It would be for his father's reputation as much as his own.

He told himself he would decide on the way to the palace.

'Come, Taeshin, you have kept me waiting long enough!'

As his father sometimes did, Anjin clapped the swordsman on the shoulder. The young lord did not see how colour drained from Taeshin's face, nor the slight stagger before he righted himself to follow.

At the top of the stairs, Marias watched them go with a dark expression. She detested the arrogant little lordling, so full of his own importance that she thought he might burst. Anjin held the power of life and death over Taeshin, as much as any slave. In that at least, they were the same. It was in her interest for Taeshin to thrive and grow well, she told herself. There was no conflict in wanting him to rise. Yet she was also in love with him, which complicated matters. She thought again of the ugly marks along his side and shuddered. The sound of hooves and jingling mail had moved away outside. She only hoped Taeshin would be able to conceal his weakness for another day. She bit her lip at the thought of what she must do.

*

The royal palace had been built at a junction of four main roads that stretched across the city, so that each quarter of Shiang met in the household of the king. A thousand years before, it had been a mere fortress on a hill, protecting the lives of those who gave an oath to the first lord to settle in that place. Even the hill had been eaten away by time and labour. The original palace had increased in size every generation, growing down through the earth until it rested on bedrock in layers of cream stone. Where once had stood the homes of farmers, paved streets ran through the administrative hub of the entire region. Within a thousand paces of the palace, a man could purchase a marriage licence or have his taxes assessed, or find himself facing magistrates who might take a limb or fine him everything he had. There were no drinking houses there, no raucous crowds. A civil service of thousands made their way to work each morning. By noon, schoolchildren trotted in snakes from museum to statue to courthouse, chided by furious tutors if they stepped out of line or whispered. The Hub was a place of order and work, without frivolous decoration for almost a century, since the current ruling family had taken the throne. King Yuan-Choji might have been a younger version of his father and grandfather, though he was just eighteen years old and had been king for barely a year.

His father's death had brought the city to a halt for weeks, but the changeover had been smooth and without serious unrest of any kind. Mazer warriors had stood on every street and corner, watching for rebellion. Shiang thrived best on continuity and calm, after all. The dynasty of Yuan provided the same sense of peace as a man might experience with a rope around his neck, waiting for the floor to drop away.

Lord Hong approached the palace with six guards trotting in pairs behind his horse. His rank was proclaimed by the number of armed men accompanying him and he sat straight as he rode alongside his son, Anjin. There were only six families in the city so trusted as to bring swordmasters onto royal grounds. Lord Hong was related to all of them, by blood or marriage. Only the royal house stood above them, and he had been delighted to see a healthy young heir ascend the throne. When Yuan-Choji took a wife and sired sons of his own, the house of Yuan would be secure for another century.

Lord Hong smiled to himself as he approached the outer gates of the royal precinct. Guards stepped back so that he and his men could enter. Lord Hong felt his son's gaze flicker to him, wondering at his mood. The boy was a disappointment, but he was still young. Some men came late to their maturity, so that they left a string of failures behind but still went on to achieve greatness. Lord Hong could only hope Anjin was one of those. Others, of course, would have been better left as carrion for wild birds, useless as the day they were born. It was hard to be sure which way his son would go at that point, but the gods had given him only one, so there was little choice.

He brought his horse alongside four steps set alone in a yard, so that he could dismount and walk down without ruffling his dignity. Anjin threw a leg over and leaped clear, of course, but that was a young man's display and nothing more. He had been born late, after a host of daughters, to delight Lord Hong in his old age. At least at first. The older man inclined his head to the royal steward. He said nothing to his guards as they fell into step beside him. As well as their skill with weapons, each of the six had attended a thousand meetings and grand occasions. The duties of his personal guard were nine parts social and one part violence – if that. Lord Hong hoped never to see swords drawn in anger in his presence. Such things, like youth, were behind him and he had come to appreciate the perfect calm of the palace and the Yuan family.

His son strode at his side and the old man wondered if it was mere imagination that Anjin lengthened his steps so that he drew ahead. His son chafed in his obedience; Lord Hong understood that. He had been the same with his father, though he would never have risked a rebuke in such a way, not in public.

The steward led them along a cloister Lord Hong knew well. When he saw his son's impatience had placed him a full stride clear, he stopped at one of the rose bushes that lined the cloister, where it opened out into gardens. They were in fine bloom as it happened, but it also served to remind his son which of them set the pace. His six guards spread apart slightly as the nobleman bent to inhale the fragrance, alert for attack from any quarter.

'Such a beautiful flower, Anjin. Come and smell this.'

Lord Hong made sure he did not see his son raise his eyes in frustration. Anjin came forward and took a quick sniff at the rose, nodding as if he could hardly believe how his time was being wasted.

'It is a yellow-blend tea rose, my lord,' the steward said. 'The . . . peace rose. Shall I have cuttings sent to your estate?'

Lord Hong smiled.

'Is there anything you don't know, Master Chen? Yes, thank you. That is very kind of you.'

The man blushed and bowed, delighted by the praise.

'It is my duty to know things, my lord.'

'Still, if you ever tire of the palace and feel you would prefer a life on the tea plantations, with servants of your own, I hope you will consider my offer.'

'Of course, my lord,' the man replied, bowing once again. Both of them knew it would never happen. It had become a routine over the years for Lord Hong to try and poach the best royal servants. In truth, the king had a fine eye for staff, like his father before him. If one of them had ever said yes, Lord Hong would have been overjoyed.

Having rebuked his son in a manner which had almost certainly been wasted on him, Lord Hong continued on past anterooms to a hall that never failed to steal his breath as he entered. The ceiling stretched far above them in ribs of stone that spread like white fans. The floor was a miracle of polished black granite, reflecting the world above and in particular the great columns that held the roof. They were Lord Hong's private joy. He had loved wood since he'd been a child and each of the thirty-two columns was unmatched in the realm. They stood two hundred feet tall and had been carried by ship across half a world. The richness of colour was a pleasure every time Lord Hong entered the room. It did not matter that he knew very well the room was designed to impress visitors and put them at a disadvantage. Lord Hong felt pride in a royal house that could create such things – he felt he was made greater rather than reduced by it.

He was announced in ringing tones ahead and he strode forward, picking up speed as he saw the other men gathered around the king's throne at the far end. His son Anjin had to hurry to catch up and Lord Hong had the sense of one of his swordsmen moving awkwardly. He dismissed the thought from his mind. He was in the presence of the king and he had to watch everything with his most perfect awareness. In that place, more than any other, a mistake could very easily cost him his life.

Tea

Wrapped in a shawl, Marias knew a sort of freedom once more. The harvest market was a busy place, where household slaves and free women mingled, making a thousand purchases. The stallholders were mostly men, who called and joked with those who bought from them, keeping up a stream of cheerful banter.

Marias had removed all trace of paint from her face before setting off. With her hair bound in simple clips, she knew she looked like any other wife or young mother, out to buy vegetables or a length of cloth. Yet she was aware even so of every second glance, as if something in her bearing might still cry 'slave'. It was hard not to flinch from the gaze of men who might suddenly shout that she had no chaperone, or that she had run. The punishments for that gravest of sins were meant to be terrifying. That was their purpose.

As she passed through the main market and on to the tiny streets beyond, even more crammed with stalls and doorways than the square, she could feel the brand on her thigh. It seemed to ache again in remembered pain. She dared not look down, in case it gleamed through the cloth. She was sweating freely, though she told herself it was just the crush of the market and the warm air, rather than her own fear. Taeshin was not a cruel master, especially compared to her first household. Yet he was as oblivious as any of the ruling lords when it came to his food and clothing. He expected a meal to be there on the table when he returned from training. He probably thought his undergarments grew unbidden in the drawers by his bed, like mushrooms in the dark. Marias found herself smiling at the thought. She had greater concerns that day, but it helped her to think of him as she navigated through the press. Worst was when a sly hand pinched at her. A free woman might have slapped it away or shouted in outrage. Marias dared not accuse a Shiang free man. At the first sight of a slave mark, she would be whipped for such insolence.

She had been introduced to the market by a neighbour from the first house she'd known with Taeshin. Amoy had been a slave as well, of course. There was not much call for paid domestic servants in Shiang. Yet the woman knew her own worth and had settled into a gentle relationship with a man and woman twenty years younger than her, looking after their children and managing a small household that might have been poor if not for the status of owning a slave. Marias had admired the older woman for her humour and stoicism, seeing in her a model for accepting the unbearable.

As she pushed through a busy junction of four alleys, Marias remembered walking the same tiny streets with Amoy, through clouds of cooking smoke, always guarding their bags from the hands of thieves. Marias had learned early to beware of wonders – while one child played with a monkey, another would snatch an earring or a coin and vanish into the crush.

Amoy had introduced her to the family businesses, long established – those who owned a reputation they would not willingly see destroyed. Such things mattered to the great nobles like Lord Hong, but they mattered just as much to the stallholders who traded on their word. Most of them, anyway.

Amoy's young master had died of some fever or other, Marias recalled with sadness. It seemed he had run up great debts in pursuit of a fortune. His wife and children had been sold into slavery themselves and, of course, poor Amoy had been sent back to the market blocks by the creditors. Marias remembered the way her cheeks had flushed as she walked streets where she was known – and the fear in her eyes. Marias had told herself then that she would never forget she could be sold on a whim or a debt, that she could be gambled away or given as a gift. If Taeshin killed her, he might be reprimanded or fined, depending on his status. The life of a slave, perhaps one accused of disobedience or laziness, was not held to be any great loss.

Marias stopped by a door she knew. Amoy had taken her there twice before, to see the old woman who made a living in that place. Marias raised her hand, but hesitated, afraid to knock. She breathed all the way in, steadying herself. Before fear could strengthen its grip on her, she twisted the handle and went straight in.

The parlour was bright and warm, with pine dark as honey all around, from the floorboards and the beams above to the table and chairs. A single log flickered in the grate, as if close to going out. Marias bowed to the old woman straightening from the task of prodding it with a poker of black iron.

'Mistress,' Marias said, giving her the greeting of a slave to a free woman.

'I know you,' the old lady replied. She came around the table and peered up at her, taking Marias' hands in hers. She smelled of woodsmoke. It was a hard gaze to meet.

Marias could see no change in the years since she'd last stood in that room. Little Mung was as wrinkled as a palm, with deep seams and skin mottled with flaps and growths. Yet her back remained straight and her brown eyes were clear. When she smiled, her face folded on itself, as it did then. Marias felt tears come, though she could not have said exactly why. Perhaps it was the warmth of the room after the cold wind outside.

'You came here with Amoy, is that right?' Little Mung said. She was a tiny figure, though Marias could feel the strength in the hands that still held hers. She nodded mutely and Little Mung sighed. 'Yes. I was sorry to hear about her. The spirits can be cruel, or perhaps men can be cruel. The result is the same.'

'Have you heard from her since she was sold again?' Marias asked.

The tiny woman looked away as a shadow crossed her face.

'I heard she died. A new household and a new master who left her out in the rain as a punishment – at her age! She took a fever and went like that.'

Little Mung released one hand to snap her fingers, her eyes glittering. The old woman turned away then, leading her visitor to the table where a pot of tea and two old cups steamed. Marias frowned at the sight. Had they been there when she entered?

'Were you expecting a guest, mistress?' she asked.

'I would be a poor seer otherwise,' Little Mung said with a touch of smugness. 'Sit, dear. Let me see if I can read the leaves for you. We'll take what comfort we can.'

Marias lowered herself to a seat and accepted a mug of tea, watching in amazement as Little Mung poured milk and sugar into hers until it was a shade of muddy brown. The old woman sensed her appalled glance and chuckled.

'I prefer it so. Would you like to try it? Or I have lemon. It makes no difference to the leaves, Marias.'

Marias was flattered to be remembered. Had she said her name? She did not think she had, though perhaps the old woman had remembered it from before. It felt, somehow, as if the usual rules had been suspended from the moment Little Mung held her hands. With a start, she realised she could no longer hear the noise of the street traders hawking their wares and she began to rise from her seat.

Little Mung reached across the table and touched her arm. The grip was surprisingly warm.

'Don't worry, Marias! We'll ask. There's no harm in asking. We'll see what there is to see. Just sit and sip. Let the tea warm you.'

Marias nodded, feeling tension drift away. She accepted milk and saw how tea leaves swirled on the surface. The drink was sweet and comforting. She felt some part of her fear ease.

'There we are, dear,' Little Mung said, cheerfully.

She patted Marias on the arm and they sat in companionable silence until the tea was drunk. Marias put her cup back on the golden wood, and when Little Mung spoke, she heard the voice almost as a breeze, from far away.

'Ask your question. Hold the cup as you speak and then hand it to me. I'll see if there's an answer. You might be lucky. I feel strong today, dear.'

'I want to know how to heal my master, Taeshin. He has black lumps on his side, like nothing I've ever seen.' Marias held the cup and spoke dreamily, then handed it over.

Little Mung bit her bottom lip at the question, though she said nothing. A slave fool enough to fall in love with her master would know more pain than anyone should endure. Little Mung could see the girl's adoration in the way she said his name.

The old woman sighed to herself as she swirled the leaves three times clockwise, then peered into the depths. Marias had a kind heart. If the world had been a different place, there might have been better times ahead, amidst all the sorrows and disappointments. Yet Shiang could be a hard place, especially for a young woman, especially for a slave. There would be no justice for her, Little Mung was sure. She stared at the patterns of leaves in the bottom of the cup. They seemed reluctant to settle into shapes she could interpret. The young woman's gaze was on her and so she closed her eyes and began to mutter a charm. Tea leaves could not tell the future, of course. Tassomancy was merely a way of drawing on the spirit, of using other eyes. It did not hurt to use the ordinary eyes she had been given, either.

Little Mung stiffened suddenly. Marias leaned closer as the old woman's sinews tightened, so that they stood out like wires in her neck and forearms.

'No . . .' Little Mung said sharply. 'No, he must not!'

Her eyes flew open and Marias saw them clear and

refocus in the room, as the old woman came back from wherever she had been.

'Did you find an answer?' Marias whispered, dreading what she might hear. 'Can he be saved?'

Little Mung stared at her, looking suddenly older and exhausted.

'Oh, my dear,' she said. 'I'm so sorry. I saw a great darkness.'

'Have you no herbs for him then, no medicine? Please!'

'I saw only death,' Little Mung said. 'There's nothing more I can do.'

The hands that raised her cup were shaking visibly, a tremble that made her teeth click against the porcelain. Marias stared at her, unable to accept it. The old woman rose to her feet with sudden briskness. She ushered Marias up and back to the street door as if the young woman had brought contagion into that house. It seemed mere moments since Marias had entered it, but she found herself out in the weak sunshine, blinking and overborne by grief. As Little Mung turned back to the gloom of the interior, the old woman hesitated.

'Forget about him, dear, if you can. Death rides him. Look to yourself now.'

The king's father had been an impressive man, Taeshin remembered. The son might eventually grow into the same authority, but at eighteen, Yuan-Choji's cheeks were smooth and unlined. At times, he seemed almost a boy, though he held power over every man, woman and slave in that hall. It was not a comforting thought on that day. In the past Taeshin had found it exhilarating to be held to the highest possible standards, his own life as the stake. He had not known weakness then, nor the sense of being slowly eaten from within by some blind and champing worm.

Taeshin marched alongside Lord Hong and his son, his hand resting on the hilt of his sword. He knew the men around him as well as brothers, after thousands of hours of practice and sparring. He knew, too, that he was no longer able to hide his pain from them. They moved forward at double time, a jingling lope in a phalanx around the two noblemen they served. In the same way Taeshin could have read the slight hitch in step of a torn muscle, the personal guard of Lord Hong felt something was off in him – and in turn, he sensed their discomfort. He steeled himself, though pain radiated from his side and brought nausea flooding through him. The idea of vomiting in that hallowed place, in front of not only his master but the king and all the other lords, made him light-headed with fear. Lord Hong would never live it down, Taeshin knew. He was suddenly aware that he had put his master in danger by hiding his illness. Lord Hong had too many enemies who would delight in his humiliation.

The ritual of approach was deliberately noisy. There could be no sense of armed men stealing into the king's presence without his knowledge. The rattle of armour and weapons came to a halt only long enough for Lord Hong to call out his arrival.

'In honour, the house of Hong attends His Highness!' Hong roared.

Though he was approaching sixty years of age, the man still had a voice to fill that vast hall. Echoes rippled back from the web of arches far above and every other party froze. Taeshin felt the urge to smile in pride. Hong was a good family, well respected in the realm. Taeshin had chosen them carefully as a house where he could rise quickly to a position of authority. There were richer families of course, with armies of Mazer swordsmen in their service. Taeshin had considered those as well, indeed been courted by them after his trials. He thought he'd made a clever choice back then. He had planned for three or four years with Lord Hong, then a transfer to a senior role, perhaps to command a hundred for another house. Some preferred to remain in the same family, while others bartered their contract like any other object of value. Both paths were understood in Shiang.

Taeshin's life had been laid out, ready to be plucked. Yet he stood in perfect stillness in the king's court, trying to breathe while a red-hot bar touched his ribs.

'Hong estate! Hong estate! In peace of realm, on pain of death, approach!'

The king's seneschal had lungs to match even Lord Hong as he bellowed back. Conversations ceased as he made the ritual reply, then went on as soon as he had finished. Taeshin gave a small grunt as the small party of armed men lurched into movement again. He saw his master turn just a fraction at the sound, identifying it as a concern, or more likely in rebuke. Lord Hong missed nothing, especially when it came under the scrutiny of the young king.

The practice of being allowed to approach the king and other lords as if for war was ancient – the bond of trust and honour that kept the families of Shiang together.

Taeshin had read of dynasties where no man was allowed to carry a blade in the king's presence. The idea was ludicrous, not least because there were so many weapons that could be concealed. He wore a number of them himself, fitted imperceptibly into his armour and belt.

Honour bound them all, so that the gathering of lords looked more like a war camp than a peaceful discussion – and was all the more polite for that. No one raised their voice where loyal swordsmen watched for the slightest insult. Taeshin had actually seen two men of opposing houses excuse themselves from the king's presence just a few months before. They had left with perfect dignity, but only one had returned and the point was considered settled between their masters.

The young king came to greet Lord Hong and his son, as if they were not surrounded by fanatically loyal swordmasters. Yuan-Choji wore white leggings and a long tunic cut square at the neck in some sort of gold silk. Taeshin took his hand from his sword hilt as his master and Lord Anjin dropped to one knee with bowed heads, their armour creaking. In that moment, Taeshin was the eyes of the house. He could feel sweat dripping cold from his armpits. In normal times, he did not enjoy the king's immunity. No other adult male could approach Lord Hong without his guards being ready to attack.

The king exchanged a few words with Lords Hong and Anjin, making some light comment that had them both smiling as they rose. Taeshin's pain was only growing, blossoming through his stomach and making his heart pound. He knew he was sweating as if he had trained all morning and come straight from the yards. Once again, he felt Lord Hong's gaze flicker past him. The old man gave no visible sign of disapproval, but there would be trouble later – a reprimand or even worse.

The king strolled to the benches with father and son, leaving the personal guard to stand down on their own initiative. Taeshin nodded to the most senior of the group. Though he disliked Xian, he could admit the man was competent. At Xian's whispered order, the six guards took station in a single rank, settling into a statue stillness they might have to maintain for hours. In the past, Taeshin had prided himself on his physical control at such times, though it was in part a relaxation of thought, a placidity that allowed the body's itches and twitches to die away. He sought that perfect calm and instead felt his side burn so savagely he had to stifle a cry of pain. He felt his eyes fill with tears and actually spill down his cheek as if he wept! It was appalling.

The king rose to address a dozen of his most senior lords, not twenty paces away. Taeshin stood with other files of guards. Some wore ornate armour that resembled huge, scaled beasts, for show rather than function. He was grateful Lord Hong preferred the simple armour of the battlefield that allowed a man to move and breathe.

Taeshin felt the room sway around him and he fought against panic. The king's seneschal was calling out the arrival of another house and he focused on the crash of voices and the jingling armour as they approached. He saw the king walk over once more, bringing the lords out of the armed group as if plucking seeds. The young man looked relaxed and cheerful, with no sign of tension. Taeshin envied him, for the agony he did not feel.

'My lords,' the king said. 'I have found my dear uncle, at last. I was not even born when he broke faith with my father. Indeed, I believe it was that betrayal that hastened my father's death and cost me years of his guidance. I doubled the reward my father offered, then doubled it again. Yet nothing came of it until this month, when two monks returned from a pilgrimage into the west. They came home with a dozen stories, my lords, of fighting in the streets of a city, of unrest and treason – and a report of Mazer steps being taught to children.'

That caused a ripple to go around the entire hall. Even Taeshin felt the room steady for a moment as the import struck him. The steps were taught as a secret craft, never to be shared with outsiders. The knowledge had kept the realm safe for over a thousand years, with every child trained and only the very best selected. It was the heart of Shiang, and the thought of it given freely to the citizens of another nation was a blasphemy.

The young king patted the air for silence.

'I see you share the outrage I felt on hearing the news. It is my thought to send a small group of warriors to fetch my uncle home. Men of experience and judgement. We do not seek a war. We seek only the return of what is ours. My uncle will be an old man by now, but who knows what allies he might have bribed. He took my mother from my father's side, after all. Tellius was always said to be a *persuasive* man.'

He sneered the last as if the words were acid on his lips. Another murmur went around his lords, though there were assessing glances as well at the mention of warriors.

'I ask then that you put your best men forward,' Yuan-Choji said. 'Decades of dishonour have already passed, gentlemen. I do not wish to lose the man to old age or a winter fever. Select . . . four masters of the sword – those you can all agree are without peer. I will lend my own First Sword to the enterprise. Perhaps it would be fairest to say you should select three from among your own.' A dutiful chuckle clattered through the noble lords. 'I will send them west with one instruction: enter the city of Darien and bring home the one who was called Tellius, who was once my father's most trusted brother.'

He paused for a moment in thought and then nodded, making the decision with all the quick certainty of a young man.

'I do not know how many he has taught, but if it is just a few, perhaps that knowledge can yet be pruned back before it spreads.'

He might have gone on then, but the voice of his seneschal bellowed out once more. Taeshin knew better than to turn his head like some gaping slave. Instead, he counted the banners arrayed ahead of him. Only one was missing, as the seneschal confirmed. Lord Ran had come into the king's presence. The king's Lord of Trade was not one of the old families. Neither was he particularly successful in trade, so city gossip had it. Lord Ran had accepted the title as a reward for his research, but showed only disdain for such worldly concerns.

'Lord of Trade, Lord Ran of Shiang!' the seneschal roared. 'In peace of realm, on pain of death, approach!'

The man's steps were audible because he approached without guards at his side. Taeshin kept his gaze forward, but could not resist watching the one some called 'Lord Ruin', for the way he ignored his responsibilities. Taeshin had never been able to understand why the king endured him.

'Highness, I crave an audience with you,' Lord Ran said, dropping to one knee. He carried a number of scrolls under his arms, which crumpled and rustled as he dipped down.

The king's mouth was a tight line as he came forward and raised the man to his feet. Taeshin was close enough to hear the words the king hissed to the older lord.

'Really, Ran? I agreed to hear your plan after this meeting, did I not? Unless it is the same foul business as before. I will not allow you to risk the lives of free men. Use slaves if you must, my lord. I will not waste a single guard on such things.'

Rather than accept the rebuke, Lord Ran's eyes were bright with possibility.

'Highness, you said you wanted to send swordsmen after your uncle. If I am right, I can make those men immune to hunger or thirst. I can make them faster and deadlier than anything we have ever seen. Yet I have only the one stone, Highness. I dare not waste it on slaves.'

The king grew more pinched as the man kept speaking. Taeshin heard himself gasping as the room seemed to lean back above his head. He felt his jaw loosen so that he gaped like a village idiot, with a line of spittle drooping from his lips. He saw the king turn to him, the man's gaze drawn by unfamiliar movement. Lord Ran began to turn to see what had caught the king's attention.

Taeshin fell out of line with a crash that echoed right

across the hall. He was unconscious before he hit the floor, so that he did not put out a hand to save himself. Instead, he lay on the polished stone, his eyes rolled up to show the whites, as he began to shudder and kick in a great fit.

3

Mercy

Taeshin opened his eyes to see the face of Lord Hong looming over him. His master looked as stern as Taeshin had ever seen him. He thought he saw a glimmer of concern in the dark eyes, but no doubt he had imagined it. Lord Hong was famous for two things – the quality of the men who served him, and the way he counted every renminbi coin he spent. The nobleman's book-keeping was meticulous and if Taeshin saw strain in his master, he suspected it was at the thought of all the training costs he had clearly wasted.

As Lord Hong slipped from sight, Taeshin saw the ceiling was very low. He was no longer in the royal hall, but had been removed to some basement, where beams of polished oak were set in white plaster. He searched his memory for an explanation, but there was nothing. He had been listening to Lord Ran speak to the king and then . . . he was here, feeling as if he had been beaten to within an inch of his life. He felt his face heat with humiliation. The room smelled of antiseptic and . . . sweat, or urine. Something sour. He blinked, his thoughts tumbling slowly, like ice in a deeper sea.

Lord Hong was saying something and Taeshin tried to sit up. He could not rest like some slothful child while his master addressed him! The pain in his side returned instantly, a flame held to his skin. That was at least something familiar. Fear surged as well when he found he could not move. Thick straps of leather held the wrists that turned in them, probing automatically for weakness. He could not even crane his neck to see the cold band pressing against his throat. Taeshin felt panic then, the sort of swallowing horror that would make him a wild animal if he gave in to it, his humanity lost. He clamped down, his will surging through the confusion.

'He is awake, Lord Ran,' his master called.

Taeshin could turn his head a fraction in the restraint. He saw the king's Lord of Trade approach him, peering down with detached interest.

'You did the right thing, bringing him here,' Lord Ran said as he peered and examined Taeshin's side.

The swordsman blinked up at the ceiling. He imagined Lord Hong was furious he had not been told about his illness before, but there was relief too – and still fear. Lord Ran was said to experiment on animals in his workrooms by the river. The sluices that ran into the passing waters sometimes drew children in delighted horror. At the right time, a great gush of blood and entrails, even whole limbs, would slide out and disappear beneath the surface. In times of famine, the poorest river-workers waited for that harvest like fishermen with hooked poles. Yet some of the things they caught for their families were not for eating. Lord Ran concerned himself with the dead.

'Is Doctor Elman here?' Taeshin tried to ask. His voice had dried and he had to repeat himself twice before they heard him.

Lord Hong looked steadily down at the man who served him.

'We thought you had fainted, Taeshin. I asked for you to be taken from the royal hall to another room to recover. The king's own servants removed your armour to give you air. They found . . . well, you know what they found. You are very lucky Lord Ran looked in on you. He says he has seen such things before. He believes he can cure you.'

'Why am I restrained, my lord?' Taeshin asked. He tried to keep a tremor from his voice, but it was there and he knew his master heard it.

'In case you thrashed around and injured yourself. You are not a prisoner, Taeshin. Here, let me remove the strap on your neck.'

Taeshin stared up at the ceiling as Lord Hong tugged roughly at a buckle he could not see, then pulled a strip of golden leather away. He breathed more deeply, as if he had not been able to before.

'Will you free my hands as well, my lord?' Taeshin asked.

In response, Lord Hong called across the room.

'Lord Ran? Is there any reason my man should be restrained? Now he is awake?'

Taeshin watched the hollow-cheeked Lord Ran return to stare down at him. He repressed a shudder under that gaze. In the youth barracks, some of the boys told wild stories of Lord Ran. It was hard not to imagine others who had seen his cold expression in their last moments. The man resembled a cadaver himself, Taeshin thought. A cadaver with a scalpel and a detached interest that was somehow more frightening than anger.

'I'm afraid so, Lord Hong. At least for the moment.' Lord Ran leaned further over Taeshin. 'Young man, I believe I can excise those lumps without killing you, but please understand, the most likely outcome is that you will die on my table. Can you hear me?'

Taeshin nodded, struck dumb. He could still feel the wrongness in his side. It lurked there, always in his awareness. He hissed in a cold breath as Lord Ran drew some pointed thing from his pocket and probed at him. He seemed to reach almost inside. Taeshin felt tears come to his eyes, the pain so sharp and sudden that he made a sound like a child.

Lord Ran tutted and shook his head, turning to address Lord Hong once more.

'It is well advanced, as you can see. I have never seen such a fine specimen. Perhaps if he had come earlier to me ... I do not hold out much hope, my lord. Nor should you.'

'Has Doctor Elman seen him?' Lord Hong said.

'That charlatan? He is forbidden entry to these chambers, my lord! I do not let fools and gawkers in where they are not welcome.' Lord Ran flushed at some memory and his entire face tightened.

'If you wish to take your man to see Elman with his powders and useless ointments, you are, of course, welcome to do so. I say only that my door will be barred to you when you return! I will not waste a day waiting for you to make the right decision, Lord Hong. It is my opinion that the only chance is with surgery. Even then, it is almost no chance at all.'

Taeshin listened to the assessment with a calm that

surprised him. He had decided to find a place on a hill with his swords just that morning. Had it been that morning? He had a sudden memory of waking before and raving in delirium.

'My lords, how long have I been here? How long has it been since I stood in the royal hall?'

'That was two days ago, Taeshin,' Lord Hong replied more kindly. 'You were screaming. If you do not remember it, I can only say that is a mercy.'

Taeshin had a sudden memory of drinking something bitter, half-choking on it. His sense of how much time had passed expanded. The room seemed familiar because he had been there for periods of waking. His groin ached and he wondered if his bladder and bowels had released in that time. Somehow, he could not make himself care.

'Has he drifted off?' he heard Lord Hong asking. 'Taeshin? There. Lord Ran has dosed you with something for the pain, but it is a kind of poison. There is a limit to how much you can be given before it kills you as surely as that . . . thing in your side. Do you understand me? Lord Ran has been working night and day to prepare his surgery. He has some contraption he says will help control the flow of blood during the . . . operation, was it?'

Lord Ran could not conceal the contempt that twisted his mouth as he replied.

'Indeed, Lord Hong. I have worked to prepare my "contraption", yes. As every hour counts, I have worked through the night to gather tools . . .'

His voice trailed away as he bent to examine the black lumps. Taeshin heard the tall lord hiss to himself.

'I think it is time, Lord Hong. If these buboes burst,

they will carry their foulness into his blood – and that is the end. If you have anything else to say to your man, I suggest you say it now. I will knock him out in a moment. After that, well . . . we can only hope.'

Taeshin tried to sit up, but it was as if he had no stomach muscles. Weakness and fear left his senses swimming and he could only gasp and stare, his eyes blurry with tears that shamed him. Lord Hong grimaced at the sight. Taeshin felt the man's callused hand pat him on the shoulder.

'Good luck . . .' he said gruffly. 'You are a fine young man. I have every confidence in you.'

It was so transparently false that Taeshin chuckled through his pain and tears, though the action made him feel as if he might pass out. He heard Lord Hong's steps grow quieter as he left. Taeshin became slowly more aware of the room around him, of a faint bubbling and the hiss of a gas jet. He wished for madness then, so as not to feel whatever lay ahead.

With no warning, Lord Ran tugged some mechanical lever and raised the whole top half of the bed. Taeshin cried out in shock. He clenched his eyes closed and felt tears dribble down his cheeks.

To distract himself, Taeshin looked over a place he had heard about only in whispers. The laboratory was long and airy, but a dozen narrow tables lined it. Each was of mahogany and supported something that snagged at his attention. On one, a monkey sat with shining rods through its joints. It was held in place by them and yet remained conscious. It looked back at Taeshin with red-lined eyes as he blinked in horror. This was hell, and he was in it.

He jerked his head back and forth, searching for the

comfort of more familiar things. Instead, he watched pale flesh move under liquid, folding on itself over and over, in a glass case as large as a child. It rippled almost lasciviously as he watched, as if it sensed his gaze.

Lord Ran had placed his bed to face a pedestal of beautifully carved walnut wood. Thin strands of bare metal stretched from the tables around it, so that the item on the pedestal seemed suspended, held in all directions. Servants carried in massive chemical batteries, heaving them onto stands and attaching other wires as if there could be some sort of sense to the nest they made. The reek of acid became sharper, so that Taeshin had to struggle not to cough. He suspected he would pass out if he did and was suddenly desperate to remain conscious, despite the pain. He had never felt more helpless in his life.

A hand pressed against his forehead, without warning or sound of approach. Taeshin gave a shout of surprise, stifling it as Lord Ran stared into his eyes.

'You are running rather a high fever, Master Taeshin. I have given you another dose of opiate milk. The results will be delirium and hallucination, I have no doubt. That is why I have kept you restrained. Can you understand me?'

Taeshin nodded and the man looked impressed.

'You are very strong. I do not think I could have found a fitter subject, if not for your little passenger. Do you know how often the king has refused me permission to use live warriors? If I could have had healthy young men, I would have reached this stage a year ago. Instead, I am told to work with the dead, with monkeys, with men so old they die of shock on my table!'

Taeshin watched as Lord Ran grew red-faced in memory. A drop of spittle had appeared in each corner of the man's mouth. It clung to his lips, so that a horrified Taeshin watched it seep into a thin line as the lord grew angrier in his recollections.

'. . . more than eighty thousand warriors in the realm! Yet for want of a dozen, I am denied the materials for my work.'

Lord Ran seemed to realise Taeshin could not truly understand his concerns. He sighed and pinched the bridge of his nose with two spidery fingers. The others flared out and Taeshin saw old stains on them, of yellow and black. He hoped it was nothing worse than ink.

'Bring the others in,' Lord Ran ordered. 'I'll work with what I have been given.'

He tied a white cloth over the bottom half of his face and, as if at a signal, all the servants did the same. Taeshin felt his heart thump. He did not know if he could bear whatever they would do to him and keep his dignity, not any longer. Strangely, it was that which frightened him most, more so than actual pain – that other men would see him break.

Lord Ran's servants were all young and about as skeletally thin as their master. It was as if the work itself burned away flesh. They raced to do his bidding. Taeshin managed to turn his head when the doors crashed open and three wheeled beds were pushed into the cramped space, the layers of wires rearranged to allow them through. Each bed held a man, though Taeshin could see no common thread to explain their presence.

Two of them raved from the moment they saw Lord

Ran. They had been restrained with the same leather straps, though Taeshin saw there had been no kindly patron to remove the ones around their necks. They gibbered and cursed as the beds were halted and the wires draped over and through, many of them removed and reattached.

Taeshin found himself in a horrible intimacy with three strangers. He looked from one to the other, while Lord Ran and his servants ignored them all, fussing over the equipment. Taeshin felt himself trembling as if he stood in a freezing wind, though the room was warm and the air thick with chemical odours.

The two who struggled were painfully clean, their skin sore and pink with scratches, as if the dirt of years or decades had been scrubbed away without much care or pity. One of them had been shaved just as roughly, so that cuts and patches wept clear fluid as he flung himself against the restraints almost mindlessly. Taeshin waited for him to open his eyes, but when he did, it made Taeshin flinch. The sockets were not empty, but they had grown over with scarring that looked more like the inside of a cheek or a muscle. It was pink and marbled-looking, foul in its appearance. Taeshin wondered how much the man even understood of his surroundings.

'Calm yourself, sir, if you can,' he said.

The man stopped his writhing on the bed, turning towards Taeshin like a dog catching a scent. It was a strangely unnerving experience as the sightless man leaned against creaking straps, trying to sense him.

'Help me! Help!' the man cried out suddenly. 'Please!' He began to shriek with astonishing volume.

Taeshin saw a group of the servants respond together.

39

They came with determination in their stance and Taeshin wanted to look away but could not. Two of them held the man's kicking legs. Another wrapped a piece of tubing around an arm until Taeshin could see a web of purple veins showing. That servant slapped at the arm, reddening the skin. He pulled back a cloth from the tray and revealed a plunger of metal and glass, filled with a white substance. Taeshin remembered Lord Ran had said something about milk and he shuddered as they pressed the thing against the man's arm and emptied the liquid into him. The result was almost instant, the man's wailing losing force. Taeshin watched as the blind man sagged, his pink eyes clearly visible without the strength to clench them closed.

Silence and the bubbling of acid returned. Taeshin looked to the bed of the other who had shouted, perhaps hoping for rescue. That man met his gaze easily enough, though he did not call out again. He had seen the fate of the first and didn't want any part of it. Taeshin saw he had the same scrubbed look, as if they'd all had years of filth removed. As if they'd been plucked from the gutters of the city for whatever Ran wanted. One was blind, the others . . . Taeshin felt the gaze of the third on him. The last man was watching him with something like suspicion or rage. He had more muscle on him than the two street rats, if that was what they were. The third had been scrubbed as brutally as the other two, but he bore other marks and scratches, as if he'd fought back every step of the way. When Taeshin spoke, it was to an equal, until he knew more.

'I gather you did not choose to be here,' Taeshin said.

The man shook his head, his eyes busy. It was clear he

still hoped to find a way out. That was either admirable or foolish, Taeshin was not sure. When he continued to stare, the man's gaze fixed on him in irritation.

'What do you want? Some lord's boy, are you?' he growled, suddenly.

'My name is Taeshin. Lord Hong is my master and patron. And you?' He thought the question would have no meaning for the fellow. Taeshin was surprised when it was answered.

'Samson Edo, last of the house of Ruijin.'

'Ruijin is an honourable house,' Taeshin replied, weighing the man anew.

'It was once, though it has fallen low these days.'

'You served a household? Truly?' Taeshin asked in genuine curiosity. He could not explain the presence of a swordsman in that place, though he supposed the same could be said of him.

'Until I was cut and the wound festered, yes,' the man growled back at him. 'I found out then what loyalty was – and how it stretched only one way, from us to them. I found out what I was worth then.'

He kicked at the blankets over his legs. As they slipped to the floor, Taeshin looked down. He blanched as he understood. One of the man's legs ended just below the knee in a pink and yellow bulge of muscle. It looked like a knot and Taeshin shook his head in pity.

'I am sorry to see that, Master Edo,' he said.

The man coloured at the courtesy. He twitched in such a way that Taeshin knew he would have waved the words off if he had not been bound. It was part of his craft to read the movements of other men and assess the threat in them. Taeshin saw anger in the way he sat, but despair in the dark eyes.

'Been a long time since I've been called that,' the man muttered. 'I'm not a master now, nor Ruijin. I just said it because I could see the scorn in you, the arrogance. You've never been cut, son. You've never watched anything of you hacked away. I have. They took everything from me. When they do it to you, perhaps in this place, you'll understand.'

Taeshin made himself look away from the malevolence. He did not know if the man had been treated cruelly, or if he was insane. Taeshin had even heard of men who claimed ties to noble families that bore no relation to the truth. That was a dangerous game, though. The houses of Shi-ang were harsh with those who undermined their honour and their names.

Taeshin sighed, shaking his head. He could not concern himself with the fate of strangers, no matter what Lord Ran was doing there. His side had been aching like a rotten tooth, but as he shifted on the bed, it flared up, making him grunt in pain. The servants seemed oblivious. Only the other three might have heard. He thought he saw the one who had named himself Samson Edo curl his lip in a sneer, but Taeshin ignored him. Some men carried too much poison in them to be restful. He sensed Edo was one of those – a bitter man. Taeshin had known others who had lost a leg or hand. It had not destroyed them, not in such a manner. The strong remained strong; the weak broke. That was the truth.

The second man smiled at him suddenly, making a hissing sound that might have been laughter. Taeshin looked back to a face that had creased in on itself, showing a few grey teeth in withered gums. The man was laughing at him, while all the time tears streamed from his eyes. He reminded Taeshin of the drunks who begged in the old city, their brains rotted away. As he stared back, the fellow raised his chin and spoke, though the words were little more than mush and the wheezing laughter began again. He had been driven to madness, or drunk himself to it, Taeshin could not be sure.

He looked around the gathering of broken men with new eyes. One was blind, one lame, the third ruined by drink or poverty. Taeshin considered his own lumps that promised death and agony unending. He looked up as Lord Ran returned, his eyes bright with anticipation. As Taeshin watched, the king's Lord of Trade peered and poked at each of them, careless of their dignity. When he came to Taeshin, the man pressed him back against the upright bed. Taeshin had no strength to resist, while his side spasmed and made him pant. He felt the man's fingers refasten the thick strap around his neck, holding him in place.

'There, that's better,' Lord Ran said. 'I have hopes for you, Master Taeshin. Of all these men, you are the most . . . whole. One of Lord Hong's chosen, no less! Only Edo here has known training and that was twenty years ago. You, though, are young and strong, perhaps strong enough to survive. If I had three more of you . . . but, no matter. Be brave now, sir. Endure. You have as good a chance as any.'

4

Cruelty

Marias knew she was breathing too fast, her heart beating like a hare's. She stood in the dwindling shadow of the city gate while hawkers, guards and workers streamed by, all busy with their lives. Those who kept moving had a sort of immunity, she saw, as if their bustle protected them from notice. She sensed the attention of others flickering past and then returning to her: a butcher opening his shop, a schoolchild eating a steamed bun filled with red bean paste. Just standing still brought her to the notice of those who knew she had not been there before. Marias did not want to be challenged. Yet what choice did she have? Taeshin had vanished two days before. She had no way of claiming his income, if it was still being issued in his name. No house slave would be allowed to collect a man's pay, even if she'd known which of the offices in the palace quarter was the right one. She bit her fingernails as she stood at the roadside, worrying at the tips until the skin was ragged and sore. Taeshin had not been a wealthy man, she knew that. He had paid late on occasion, using his status and name to make tradesmen wait. Yet he had not been seen since he'd collapsed in front of half a dozen noble families and the king himself. The news had spread as if it had wings. Those to whom Taeshin owed money had heard and come to bang on his door that very first evening. Warriors who became ill had no protections from such men. The obsequious manner she'd seen in them before had vanished, just as soon as they thought they had the upper hand. Marias had sat at the top of the stairs and hugged her knees to herself, watching angry shadows peer through glass.

They had not forced the door, at least. Some of Taeshin's creditors had left boys to watch the house for his return, or perhaps to be first in line if the property was sold at auction. Marias would have starved or frozen if she'd stayed inside, without a single lamp to betray her presence. Instead, she'd climbed out of the small window in Taeshin's bedroom and crept across the tiles.

That had felt like freedom, of a sort, above the heads of bustling men and women. They went about their lives below and, as far as she could see, hardly looked up at all. Certainly, she had not been spotted as she made her way out. No cry had begun, no chase summoned to recapture a running slave.

She clasped the good cloak close around her. Marias had never worn it before. She thought it had belonged once to Taeshin's mother and it still smelled of a faint perfume. Yet it sheltered her from the glances of those passing. On impulse, she held out a hand to beg for coin. That made her even less visible to the merchants and traders coming into the city. Her face was smeared with dirt and her hands were filthy from climbing around on green tiles. It was either a disguise or her new reality. For the moment, she chose to believe it was a disguise.

Taeshin used to keep spare coins on a round plate by

the door. It was bad luck there had been only a couple of renminbi there. She'd spent the last of the household wealth on bread and a handful of dried silkworm larvae, all the while listening to every conversation and asking questions like a gossip. She'd considered going back to Little Mung, but Marias was not that desperate, not on the first day. After another day and night with no sign of Taeshin, her certainties were slipping through her fingers and she was losing hope. She'd eaten the last of the food the previous evening and all she'd heard was the rumour that Taeshin had been taken in by the Lord of Trade. Marias imagined a kindly man, treating Taeshin's illness with poultices and doctors. None of the street sellers would tell her where that lord had his home. When she pressed them, they sensed her need was dangerous. They looked again at the dirt on her and they clamped their lips tight and waved her away.

Marias was certainly hungry enough to consider stealing, but was all too aware of what happened to slaves who did. She had decided to die on her feet rather than be stripped and hanged in the nearest square. A wave of dizziness swept over her, so that she reached out to the gatepost, brushing against a soldier coming out. He eyed her warily at first, then with more confidence as he took in her visible poverty. Something unpleasant kindled in his eyes and Marias turned away from it, only to have him grip her arm.

'You should come into the guardhouse, love, where it's nice and warm. We've got food in there – and wine, if you want. Come on.'

Marias yanked her arm from his grasp. She knew very

well what awaited her if she was fool enough to go with him, especially if they discovered her brand.

'Get away!' she snapped at him. Anger or perhaps hunger gave her the confidence. She was a free woman in that instant, gathering tattered dignity like the shawl around her.

The guard sneered, flushing. He was younger than she'd first thought and embarrassed by the glances coming his way. The butcher was watching the little scene, Marias saw. The guard didn't reach out again, but there was spite in him too and a desire to hurt.

'Go on, get away from this patch,' he said, his voice coarse and too loud. 'You'll not beg here, bitch.'

Marias felt her own face flush under the dirt. It stung, even after so many years. Yet she was pleased just to be able to turn into the crowd once more. It was the only victory she could have against the man and all he was: strong and violent, trained and clean and free. She wished Taeshin could have been there, to put the man across his knee and beat him like a drum. The thought took some of the pain from the encounter. She began to push her way through the passers-by, ignoring the touch of hands that felt for some hidden purse under her cloak. She had nothing to steal, nothing even to prevent her stomach croaking like a marsh frog.

Further along the street, cheering began. Marias stood on her tiptoes to see, holding on to a short stone post to keep her balance as more and more people swept forward to see what was coming. She clung there like a limpet, refusing to be dislodged from a place that would allow her to see which of the king's master swordsmen were riding through the gate. The city was alive with the rumour and she had convinced herself one of them would somehow be Taeshin. As mad as it was, she could not let them leave Shiang while she searched for her master, not without glimpsing their faces. The thought that she might have missed him in her weakness and hunger would torment her if she didn't look. That much was certain.

It was a modest group compared to some she had seen. Military processions could march along those main streets for hours: thousands of men in perfect ranks, with the banners of noble houses fluttering overhead. In comparison, those four horsemen might have passed through Shiang almost without notice. Yet the crowds thickened by the moment and Marias felt breath catch in her throat.

In a city that revered the craft of the sword, those who could claim true mastery were considered national treasures. Even Marias knew the name of Hondo, first swordsman of Shiang. He looked younger than she had expected, riding a shining brown horse with his hands lightly on the pommel. No group of the best swordsmen could be assembled without him, she imagined. Though he had to be fifty, he had won tournaments for thirty years, against all comers.

She did not know the names of the three riding with Hondo, though the crowd around her obliged by calling them at the tops of their voices. The twins Hi and Je could not be told apart, of course. They were identical warriors and were said to have achieved their mastery by training together every day, stopping only to sleep and eat.

Marias blinked as she discovered she did actually recognise the last of the four. Bosin was a huge man who rode a

48

horse more suited to pulling a plough than being ridden into battle. It was a beast that dwarfed even its master, who stood head and shoulders above the other three. God had given Bosin unusual gifts as a child, so that he was said to be able to lift any man above his head. Untrained, he would not have been a challenge for a Mazer swordsman. Yet he was as fast and deadly as any of the others – and far stronger. In normal times, he trailed admirers like a comet passing through the city. Marias had seen him twice over the years, both times when she'd glanced up to see who could possibly laugh so loudly. Bosin was a man of gold, far above the pettiness and frustrations of an ordinary life, at least as she imagined him.

Marias craned and peered for some sight of Taeshin amongst them. It surprised her to see such names travelling without servants or slaves to tend them. It was true their saddlebags were crammed full, but they would be lighting their own fires in the wilderness. Bosin's animal seemed to be carrying twice his weight with all he had brought. Yet Taeshin was not there.

Marias let go of the post and her space was immediately filled by those who desired a glimpse of the Shiang masters. Almost without effort, she was pushed back and back, retreating from the press of elbowing humanity as her strength faded. She turned for home, then changed her mind and headed to the market once more. At the end of each day, the stallholders threw away the food that had turned. She had seen the sick and the poor gather for that harvest the evening before, holding out their hands. She had not been ready to fight them then, but she knew she would be too weak if she let another chance go. Marias was not yet ready to give up. She wondered what it would feel like when she was.

Taeshin had not experienced electrical pain before. Part of his training in the Mazer steps was simply being hit, both in sparring bouts and as a separate procedure, to force his bones to grow stronger. Nothing trained the body for battle as well as actually being struck. He had lived with bruises and cracked bones from the age of seven, when he'd been taken to the boys' barracks for the first time. His bunkmates had welcomed him with a beating that had left him senseless and with two broken fingers.

None of that prepared him for the helplessness he felt in the long room. He had grown to fear the sound of the door opening as Lord Ran appeared and consulted his servants in quiet murmurs. The four men lying strapped to the tables no longer seemed to concern the nobleman as individuals. Lord Ran and his staff moved and prepared around them as if they did not stare and tremble. The blind man called for help, at intervals, as if the sound lay buried in him and bubbled to the surface. No one answered him.

They were offered water to drink. As the setting sun turned the windows to gold across the river, one of the servants even spooned a steaming mush of boiled vegetables into them, one by one. Taeshin was starving, but turned his head and refused even so, clamping his jaw shut. He had been hungry before. It felt like surrender to take charity from people who considered him just another ape tied to the bed.

When darkness came, Lord Ran's servants lit tapers, touching them to tiny jets of gas behind glass, so that light bloomed again in the long room. Taeshin had known oil lamps, but never anything that suggested pipes and contraptions hidden in the walls. He wrinkled his nose as the thin and toothless drunk urinated where he lay. The man was weeping, Taeshin saw. He looked for some expression in the servants, but as soon as they saw what had happened, they whipped the sheets away and brought clean ones, dabbing the man with cloths as best they could. Taeshin wondered if they would release his bonds if he emptied his bowels. He was almost desperate enough to try it.

Great vats of sulphur acid and metals he did not know still bubbled on the tables, a line of white mist standing above each one like a rain cloud. Taeshin shuddered as he tried to make sense of what had happened. Lord Ran had turned a circular knob of some dark metal and the results had been like sour magic in him. First, his muscles had tensed on their own, without his control for the first time in his life. Taeshin had seen ridges stand up in his forearms, and he could still feel his jaw and neck ache from where they had been tensed for so long. Yet it seemed that Lord Ran had no particular accomplishment in mind when he worked the machine. It was as if he was still setting up and testing each part of his equipment. Taeshin had watched the men on the beds arch, one after the other, giving him a chance to see how he looked when the wires were attached. It was an ugly thing, he thought. The eyes of men could be made animal by pain. Taeshin felt himself twitch suddenly in the bed, though the wires had all been removed. That too brought a kind of fear, that they had taken some of his control away from him, a man who had worked hard to gain mastery of his flesh. It was one of the few things he owned and he sensed the machine could rip even that out of him.

No one had explained why he had been placed there, nor why the wires made his muscles tighten with an unseen hand. Lord Ran ignored questions as if he could not hear them, moving like a ghost as he checked every connection and read his notes aloud as he did, murmuring instructions to himself as much as his servants.

Lord Ran left the room occasionally, presumably to eat or rest. Taeshin still twitched and he thought he would not sleep, not in that place where every sense screamed to stay awake, to gnaw his way out if he had to. If he could have reached one of the wrist straps with his teeth, he would have tried it. All he could do was lean back and close his eyes.

'Taeshin, wasn't it?' a voice said.

It was the big man across from him, the one whose leg was missing. The servants had not replaced the fellow's blanket, so that Taeshin could still see pink ropes and bristles along the stump. He had stared at it when the man had leaned back and closed his eyes. It was a fascinating thing to a young man, especially one who knew anatomy. Sword-masters were trained in the structures of the body. It made them better able to cut a man apart.

Taeshin nodded.

'Do you know what they're doing with us?'

Taeshin looked up. The long room was quiet, as if the staff slept. He had no doubt one of the servants would come through in a moment, but they were alone, no matter how briefly.

'I thought I might be healed. All these wires, though – I don't like the look of them.'

'Torture, I thought,' the blind man said suddenly.

Both Taeshin and the soldier looked to him, wincing at the pink growth where eyes should have been. The man seemed to sense their scrutiny and he leaned as far forward as he could against his throat strap. The sinews in his neck stood out like wires under the skin.

'Take a good look, boys. That's what acid will do to you. I know that smell, I've known it before. We'll not live through this, I'm telling you. I'd make your peace, if I were you. Never thought I'd get caught twice, but I couldn't see them coming, could I?'

He began to laugh and Taeshin thought it a cold sound. He wrenched against his bonds then. The black lumps in his side flared their agony, but for a time he was almost mindless, yanking and tugging, throwing his whole strength against the straps. He was only dimly aware of the servants rushing in and holding him still with cool hands against his skin. They checked the straps and nodded to one another.

Little by little the long room came back to life. The peaceful gloom of the small hours was replaced by morning brightness as they turned down the jets of the lamps. Taeshin was exhausted and in pain. He spent a time wondering what would happen to Marias. She would not know where he had gone, he realised. No one would think to tell her. The thought of not being there to protect her was an oddly discomfiting emotion.

The servants lined up on either side, their mouths covered with clean cloths tied behind. They stood in silence for an age and the only sound was the weeping of the thin man and the whispered cursing of the soldier. The one with no eyes did not speak again and seemed to have retreated into his own personal hell. Taeshin spent the time looking back over his life and seeking forgiveness for every sin and moment of cruelty. That was all that mattered, his father had said. It would not concern God that he had killed a dozen willing opponents. They had chosen their fate and risked their lives to stand against him with a sword. All that mattered was when he had been cruel, when he had deliberately caused pain. Not carelessly, for he was not a saint – and not any of the times when he had apologised and made amends. By his count, it left only three occasions. Though he regretted them all, he considered it was not too high a tally for a man of the sword. Not in Shiang, at least.

As the sun rose, Lord Ran returned to the long room, looking refreshed. He was dabbing his mouth with a cloth and he had changed his clothes. Taeshin wondered if the man knew or cared that they had all emptied their bladders in the night and had sheets changed. It was a humiliation, but he sensed Lord Ran cared nothing for details of that sort.

The man smiled as dawn entered the room. He was clearly in a good mood.

'Gentlemen!' he said. 'Thank you for your patience. It will not be much longer, I promise you. Turn the gaslights right down, would you? Yes, off, I think.'

He said the last to a servant, who went around the room and twisted tiny brass knobs, until only sunlight brightened the walls.

Taeshin grimaced in remembered pain as the king's Lord of Trade attached wires once more to the backs of their hands. The enormous batteries were wheeled closer, so that Taeshin had to blink and breathe shallowly against the smell of acid biting at his throat.

'Lord Ran, would you please let me go?' Taeshin said firmly. He had promised himself he would, as soon as he saw the man. The soldier across from him perked up at the words and added his own voice.

'Me too, my lord. I'd like to call it a day here.'

The drunk and the blind man said nothing, sagging in the straps and their own damp clothes.

Lord Ran shook his head.

'I am sorry it has taken so long, gentlemen. You have no idea how delicate these arrangements are, how careful I must be. I have one chance to prove my assertion. If I waste it for lack of care, I will never forgive myself – indeed, I may never get another. Rest assured, my intention is to heal you. For some of you' – he inclined his head to Taeshin – 'I believe it is your only hope. Have faith then, gentlemen, in science and in magic. Have faith in me!'

'Please, my lord. I would prefer not to risk it,' the soldier said again.

Lord Ran ignored him, though his colour deepened and the good mood evaporated.

'Put the stone in place,' the lord called to his servants.

They brought in a box and removed a stone about the size of a man's outstretched hand, or a little longer. It was a creamy white, flecked with gold that caught the sun streaming in through the windows. Taeshin could not look away from it. He saw a similar reverence in Lord Ran as he rested his hand on the surface.

'Is it not beautiful?' he murmured, though the question

was not directed at the men on the beds. He smiled more gently then, his irritation eased by its presence.

'It is a source of magic, gentlemen, if it can be tapped and used. My instruments suggest a vast reservoir of power in this white stone, but until recently, I could not find a way to draw it out.' He gestured to the batteries with a sweep of his hand.

Taeshin began to struggle again, almost mindlessly. He could not stop them placing the stone in the tangle of wires, nor could he pull free the ones they stuck to his side, though tears of agony and terror rolled down his cheeks. The men on the beds were draped in thick braids of metal and cloth, made almost into machines themselves. Taeshin felt bile come into his throat and burn him as Lord Ran checked the entire assemblage once again.

'Stand clear,' he said to his servants. 'Do not touch these men now, on pain of your lives.'

He stood with his hand on a dial and Taeshin could only stare. Lord Ran nodded to them all.

'Ready yourselves, gentlemen. It is time.'

Taeshin saw the hand turn and he felt a jolt of strain enter him, then swell impossibly, so that he arched against the straps. Lord Ran was shouting something and the servants were scurrying around. The men on the beds twisted and writhed. Taeshin could see light burning in them, behind their teeth and in their eyes. The whole world seemed to flare into whiteness and he knew he walked with death.

5

Into Dust

It was hard to recall the taste of things, Gabriel thought. He remem-
bered lemons as bitter, but saying the word no longer had any real
meaning for him. His memories had lost the concept, as if all the
colours had seeped out.

He had half-expected death to be nothingness, but it was not.
When he had died and woken in surprise on a cold plain, he had
hoped for Valkyries, or even angels. Instead, he had found himself in
armour, standing in grey dust. The armies of the dead had formed
around him, accepting him. Orders had been roared up and down the
lines and it had been familiar, almost comforting. He had fought, for
ever, seeing souls vanish as they were cut down. If they were souls; he
did not know. He fought because there was nothing else on the plain —
and because it was what he had known best when he was alive.

It was always the hour before dawn there, when the air was chill
and hands were numb and stiff. He tramped and fought, and when
the battle was at an end, they sat and stared and even slept. Then the
souls returned and the ranks rose once more. They did not seem to
mind the repetition, but every time it made him want to roar out his
frustration. They had not killed him, though, not once in countless
years. He had that much pride left amidst the dust.

There was a hill by the battlefield, a gentle rise in the land that
Gabriel had always told himself he would explore. Yet each time he
awoke rolled in his blanket, each day he was called, he just stood and

brushed himself down. He could not leave the line, the men around him. So he spat on the ground and clicked his neck and took up a brass shield from where it lay at his feet. Sometimes in the fighting, he would glimpse the hill on his left and tell himself he would not answer the next call. Yet he always did – and some part of him howled, knowing he would answer for ever.

On that morning, as Gabriel stood and made ready, he looked over the plain as he had so many times before. It would be a hard day, with his courage put to the test. Of that he was certain. As he raised his head, he saw a light appear high up on the hill, a grain of gold in the distance, as if a bonfire burned on the peak. In awe, he stood still and shaded his eyes.

'What is that?' he said, turning to the man next to him.

They had fought side by side for years but Gabriel did not know his name. He realised he had not spoken a word to any of them before that day, as if his mouth had been sewn shut without him knowing. The stranger had a cruel face, his teeth sharpened into points. Gabriel had heard of such things in warriors. Fear was as much a weapon as a sword.

'I have not seen it before,' the man said.

His voice too seemed unused, almost a croak. It was the voice of a dead man and Gabriel took fresh stock of those around him. Most of them were preparing for the day's battle, as they had done every morning for longer than he could remember. Had they always worn such an array of armour? There was no pattern to the styles. Even the swords were a dozen different lengths and shapes.

In the ranks nearby, two others stopped checking their kit and readying themselves. They raised a hand to peer at the hilltop, remembering they had to shade their eyes from the sun. One of them looked at Gabriel.

'Are you going to see what it is?'

'Yes. I am,' Gabriel said, making the decision.

He wondered if he could, but as he hesitated, the battle lines formed around them and a great mass of men began to march towards the enemy. None of the four went with them. They stayed behind and the entire army moved away. Gabriel expected one of the officers to roar his name and summon him back, but they were facing forward, intent on the enemy as they had been for . . . He shook his head. For too long.

He looked at the other three. They were young and strong-looking, with serviceable weapons and armour. The first to have spoken wore a set of plate as ornate as anything Gabriel had ever seen, with designs and swirls etched on the metal. The other two wore simpler kit of leather and brass or bronze, with short swords he knew very well.

'Will you follow me?' Gabriel asked.

He had led thousands in life, he remembered suddenly. He had lived for blood and conquest, so that he had carved an empire out of forests and plains. He did not understand why he had been left to march and fight every day in the grey place, but he felt no special anger at his fate. Like the taste of lemons, anger was a thing he had forgotten.

'I will follow you,' the first man said, suddenly.

'And I,' the other two added.

Gabriel smiled, though it was a strange expression in that place.

He gestured and they walked together towards the hilltop and the gleam of light there. Behind them the army trudged on, the officers roaring orders and formations. This would be the day they finally won. They had been promised victory and they would gladly give their lives if that was the price.

Yet Gabriel and the others walked away, their faces turned towards the golden eye that had opened above the plain. After a while, *they began to fear it would close before they reached it. Though they could not have explained the sense of urgency, all four began to run.*

Lord Ran groaned and picked himself up from the floor. He hadn't been punched in the face since he was a boy, but the feeling was instantly recognisable. His lips were swollen and crushed, so that he could taste blood in his mouth. His servants were scattered around the long room. One of them was pressing a hand to his face as if he had been struck with something. As Lord Ran watched, he saw a line of blood dribble between the man's fingers. He shook his head and felt the room spin crazily. His fingers probed a lump at the base of his skull, making him wince. He'd fallen badly, that much was obvious. The air was thick with the smell of acid and fire, and in the middle of it, the four wheeled beds lay around the Aeris Stone, festooned in wires.

His heart thumped in sudden hope and he jerked forward, to see. It was an instant of perfect anticipation and it lasted just long enough for him to reach the beds and look down on the same miserable figures he'd been given. He sagged at the sight of open mouths and lolling tongues. The blind eyes were still blind. Nor was there any mistaking the stub of a leg that twitched even as he stared at it. Lord Ran sighed as he examined them. It was a failure. Perhaps the connections to the stone had not been of sufficient thickness. He saw some of the wires had heated as they passed over bare flesh, so that they'd burned lines of red onto skin. The woven cloth covering the terminals had smouldered and gone black in places. He shook his head, following the length of the wires to the pedestal and the source he'd tried to tap.

The white stone looked subtly different as his gaze reached it. Lord Ran froze, instantly afraid. The surface had been a smooth and creamy white before, flecked with gold. He'd spent hundreds of hours working with it. He knew the Aeris Stone as well as his own hands. It invited the touch and he had stroked it or patted it a thousand times. Yet that perfect surface had grown pitted somehow, as if acid had scorched it.

The men forgotten, Lord Ran made a choking sound and bent close enough almost to touch the stone with his nose. Had the battery acid splashed over it? His heart was in his mouth as he reached out, his fingers trembling. At the first touch, the stone collapsed into white dust, finer than flour, so that most of it became smoke or vapour.

He let out a great cry of anguish as his most precious possession was reduced to worthlessness. Lord Ran leaned both hands on the pedestal and supported himself on locked arms, head bowed in grief. The stone had cost him a great part of his family fortune. He'd almost bought it for next to nothing, but then Lord Wen had bid against him on a whim, just for spite. The resulting price had forced the sale of his summer home. Worse, Ran had spent years researching the thing, seeking some way to employ the forces he was sure lay within. He had neglected his public position in his obsession, letting the noble families get on with their pointless games of trade on their own. And it had all been for nothing. He knew the people of the city called him the Lord of Ruin, whenever they blamed him for some poor harvest or when the docks needed to be dredged again. For the first time, the name suited his despair.

'My lord . . .' one of the servants began. 'Is the stone . . . ?'

'Gone. Just get out,' Lord Ran said.

He brushed pieces of dust and glass from his coat as the servants left the room, some supported by others. He was alone then with the smell of burned flesh and the pieces of four years of his life all over the floor.

He stood looking down on the dead men he had brought as prisoners to that place. Perhaps if the king had allowed him to use healthy young subjects, the experiment would not have failed! He closed his eyes in sudden worry. Lord Hong would expect word of his man. If the king found out he'd gone ahead and used the beggars, despite the royal command . . . Lord Ran glanced at the metal sluice that opened out onto the river. It was nothing more than a polished metal slide. It would be bloody, unpleasant work, but if the king learned he had disobeyed an explicit order, his family connections would not be able to save him. Lord Ran winced at the thought. The servants could be sent home. No doubt they were waiting nearby in case he summoned them once more. He could dispose of the bodies himself, into the river. What vanished beneath the surface was gone for ever. Unless one of those foul fishermen hooked it back, he thought sourly. He'd have to drive them away first.

He reached down and raised the eyelid of the swordsman with a thumb, shaking his head. Lord Ran suddenly became very still, not daring to believe. The pupil had contracted as he'd exposed it to the light, he was sure of it. With a shaking hand, he raised the other lid and saw it happen again. The chests did not rise or fall. The four men were as still and waxen as the dead, but if the eyes reacted, there was yet life in them.

'Attend me, here!' Lord Ran roared.

He pressed his ear to the chest of the blind man and was rewarded with a distant thump, then silence for an age before he heard it again. They were alive. In such a deep sleep it was barely a whisper from death, but alive!

His servants came back in at speed, seeing their master point at the four subjects.

'Get these straps off them. Rub their limbs and work the arms and legs to bring back the movement of blood. They sleep, merely. They may yet die, but not for lack of will. Not for lack of our labour! Move!'

He had trained them well. In pairs, they freed each of the slack figures and began to pump the arms and legs and bow them forward and back. He saw the results in the faint flush that returned to the pale cheeks, the sweet colour of life's triumph over death.

The drunk was the first to make a sound, though it was a groan of pain. Perhaps because he had survived a thousand nights of vomit and pain and unconsciousness, he struggled back before younger, stronger men.

'This one is alive, my lord!' a servant said.

Lord Ran watched as the old drunk held up a hand and peered at it as if seeing it for the first time.

Lord Ran actually smiled when the blind man began to cough into his hand and swung legs over the side of the bed. After the drunk, he was the second, but the heavyset man was only moments behind him. That old soldier cleared his throat as if something itched him, making a grating sound. It was all too clear that his leg remained a stump, the proof of failure every time it caught the eye.

Lord Ran's brow creased suddenly. All the tests he had

63

made indicated a huge reservoir of power in the Aeris Stone. If the thing had a purpose it could only be as a sort of battery, though it would have been a battery the size of a king's palace. Yet it sat at the centre of that little group in that moment as a pile of dust. Where had the power gone, if not into the men?

One of the servants was rubbing the chest of Lord Hong's swordsman with some foul liniment that reeked like ammonia. The young man began to cough as the fumes reached him, pressing the servant away. Lord Ran smiled, despite his despair. He knew some of his colleagues thought he was unfeeling. Indeed, he prided himself on his lack of sentiment. If he had been asked to choose between the lives of the four men, he would have had no difficulty judging one more valuable than another. There were some clerics who bleated how all men were equal, though a mere child could see they were mistaken. Some men ran faster than others. Some created knowledge where there was none before – or just tantalising hints in the oldest books.

If it would have healed one of them, Lord Ran would have happily seen the others die. Yet in defeat, he was pleased the price had been less than he'd thought. The king would have no cause to close his laboratory as he'd promised he would. Lord Ran would just have to find another source stone like the Aeris. If that one had taken him a lifetime and a fortune, perhaps the next would come more easily.

Lord Ran glanced up when he heard a moan of pain from the servant with the liniment. Lord Hong's swordsman had reached out and grabbed his wrist, crushing the bones against one another.

'Sir!' Lord Ran said. What *was* the man's name? He had been told it, but he was not good with names and it would not come. 'Sir, you have not been harmed. The experiment is at an end. You see? In the name of Lord Hong, release that man immediately.'

The hand that held the servant closed convulsively, so that the fellow's wrist broke as easily as chicken bones. The servant shrieked in agony, falling limp. Even then, the swordsman didn't let him go, but stood, dragging the poor man upright as he did so.

'Who . . . what is this place?' the swordsman demanded.

'Taeshin!' Lord Ran blurted as it came to him. 'You are safe, sir, I swear it. The experiment is at an end.'

He saw the young warrior take a step forward, with the groaning servant still gripped in his hand. An expression of pain crossed Taeshin's face then and he opened the hand, touching it to his side. Freed at last, the servant retreated like a beaten dog, whimpering.

The swordsman looked up in confusion. He pressed his hand into the black lumps that ran down his side and made a soft sound that turned into a growl.

'Well, this won't do,' Gabriel said. 'Who is this Taeshin? Is this Shiang? My god, am I home again?'

Lord Ran blinked. He saw the blind man slap hands away from him and rise to his feet. One by one the others did the same.

'I have no eyes,' the blind man said.

'My leg has gone,' said the other. 'I cannot stand.'

'I can see, brother,' Gabriel replied with satisfaction. 'I can stand.'

*

Marias raced through the market, wrapped in her cloak. It broke her heart to find the seer's house empty and cold. The single window below and above in that rickety terrace was covered by a shutter and held by a wooden peg on a nail. It looked abandoned, somehow. Marias peered through the cracks and hammered on the door but no one came to open it and she slumped in defeat. She put her back to the door and slid down until she sat on the thick doorstep, facing the street. The buyers and sellers pressed past without even glancing down at her and a light rain began, so that her tears vanished as fast as they came.

She turned at clicking hooves and scrambled up at the sight of the old woman swearing and gesturing for someone to get out of the way of a tiny dog-cart. It seemed a fragile thing, pulled by an ass with long ears. Yet Marias saw it was piled high with bales and cloth, all tied down with twine.

'Mistress!' Marias called.

She jumped higher to be seen over the heads of the crowd, waving and calling until the seer known as Little Mung spotted her. The donkey did not want to stop and Little Mung was red-faced with effort by the time she had reined him in, some ten paces past the door.

'You found me then, dear. Did you also find your master?' she called over her shoulder.

Marias shook her head and she saw a look of compassion touch the old woman's stiff features, softening them.

'I wanted to ask you to try again. But . . . you're leaving?' Marias asked.

She watched as Little Mung considered her reply, pausing only to curse someone who complained she was blocking the road with her cart. The certainty was clear in her. Marias felt her spirits sink even lower. She knew so few people in the city. It hurt to see the old lady abandoning Shiang.

'You should go as well, dear,' Little Mung said. She bent down to murmur and Marias came to the edge of the cart and stood on her tiptoes to hear. 'Something terrible has come to Shiang. These fools don't have the sense they were born with, but I do. Look to the seers, dear. If they start leaving a city, it's time to run.'

6

First Sword

Hondo watched his companions as they prepared to sleep under the stars. The twins, Hi and Je, worked almost as one. There was a nagging familiarity about the two of them that had eluded Hondo for two days until it came to him that evening. His parents had been just as comfortable with one another. Seeing the twins prepare a meal had made Hondo feel almost like a little boy again, half a century before. As one of the brothers reached for a knife or a pouch of spices, the other would hand it to him, without needing to look up. Hondo recalled operas he had seen in Shiang, where a kitchen scene had the same air of rhythm, almost of music. The two young men seemed quietly disciplined in all things, so that the meal they made for the camp was delicately flavoured and presented in clean wooden bowls. Hondo had also seen them fight in demonstration bouts a dozen times. He knew the silent brothers were fearsome opponents, in part because of that intimate understanding.

Bosin was a different sort. To Hondo's eye, the enormous black shire horse was as ridiculous as the man who rode it. Hondo had felt himself flush with embarrassment as they'd passed through the first villages and towns near Shiang. Of course the people there had come out as soon as the swordsmen were sighted. Some seemed to know Hondo from his black, lacquered armour, or the twins for the identical blades they wore, with hilts of gold. In a realm that revered masters, all four were famous names. Hondo had ignored the calls and children held up for him to bless. He and the twins had kept a cold face as they rode through. They were on Crown business, after all, a most delicate task given to them by their noble masters and, through them, the direct command of the king himself.

Hondo shook his head a fraction in irritated memory. They'd had no need of directions or supplies, as close as they had been then to Shiang. They'd desired only to put the first miles and perfectly tended fields behind them. Yet Bosin had performed for the villagers. There was no other word for it. That enormous swordsman had stood up on his carthorse and walked the length from neck to tail. In its own way, the animal was as much a behemoth as Bosin himself, a beast with a back like a polished dining table. It was, of course, uncut. The creature's parts were in proportion and dangled as they travelled west. Bosin seemed to enjoy the blushes of maidens as they glimpsed what swung beneath. He was not above calling ribald comments on the subject either, leaving them staring in shock or laughter.

Hondo clenched his jaw. A man chose neither family nor travelling companions, so went the old saying. Yet the thought of months on the road with Bosin was almost beyond endurance. They would come to blows, Hondo was certain. He had not lost a bout in thirty years, but the great size of the man still worried him. It was too easy to imagine Bosin falling on him like a tree. It would be difficult to stop such a man, Hondo admitted grudgingly. At least without killing him. Yet even the greatest heart could be pierced by a sword. That was the sword's purpose.

Bosin finished the meal the twins had prepared. He used a handful of grass to wipe the bowl and passed it back, but his gaze was everywhere as he looked for more. Hondo raised his eyes in exasperation. It had been bad enough on the night they'd taken rooms at an inn. The sword saint had watched aghast as Bosin ate enough for three and drank so many cups of clear spirit that the entire tavern had come to a halt to watch him. Some of the locals had counted aloud each time Bosin emptied a cup and banged it back on the boards. It had been a rough place, but a great cheer had gone up when the enormous swords-man finally waved his hand in surrender. With an amiable grin at them all, Bosin had staggered to a chair by the fire-place, where he'd snored all night.

Hondo had wondered then how they would fare when such a man found himself in the wilderness, without serv-ants or slaves to feed him. It seemed the answer lay in irritability, like a child denied. Hondo could feel Bosin's gaze swing around as he looked for someone to distract him. In response, the sword saint of Shiang closed his eyes and sat cross-legged rather than observe further. He needed no friends. In truth, he needed no companions.

Hondo wanted time to consider the king's actions. By sending the other three with him, was His Majesty Yuan-Choji signalling the end of a career? It would be a subtle move for such a young king, but Choji was not without guile. Hondo was fifty-six years old and no man, not even a saint of swords, could hold back time for ever. He was still strong and frighteningly quick. He practised the

70

Mazer steps each day and ran for hours if there was an opportunity. He was both lean and supple, the master of most men. The trouble was that he was neither as fit nor as fast as he had once been. For all his talent that year, his younger self could have carved him into pieces – and only one of them would have been sweating at the end. Hondo thought he might surprise that younger version of himself with a trick or two, but he also knew age stole more than just speed. The mind itself became less flexible, less able to react to a new factor.

He recalled the time, six months before, when a pigeon had clattered into his face as he'd practised in his gardens. It was not that the bird had startled him. The creature could have blundered across his path at any stage of his life. Yet his younger self would have drawn and cut it from the air. Instead, Hondo had stepped back, falling into a defensive stance. He had told himself it was the mark of experience that he had not swung the blade. That was true, but it was not all. Part of the truth was that he'd also been a touch too slow to take the bird before it was out of range. He'd almost strangled that little moment of disappointment when he'd finally understood it. If he had not reflected on the event and made himself relive each . . .

'You are meditating, aren't you?' Bosin said, suddenly. 'I could never manage it. I kept falling asleep. No matter how I tried to stay awake. I would empty my mind and think of nothingness, but then I'd be snoring and the masters would send me for another beating. They beat me like a rug, Master Hondo. Oh, they beat me like an egg.'

Bosin chuckled in memory and pleasure at his own description. Hondo gave up his internal examination and opened his eyes. He reminded himself he had a long time ahead on the road. It was always correct to maintain politeness. He had to ignore the little voice that told him he was polite in part because he was afraid, that Bosin was like a bullock and about as mindless. Hondo put the thought aside to be examined later. He did not like to feel afraid, if that was truly what it was. Fear was an animal spirit. It made him angry and he preferred to be calm.

'I have ridden twelve hours today, Bosin. I believe we have covered fifty miles and I find I am weary. Now that we have eaten, I would prefer to meditate and then to sleep, but I am willing to take first watch if you want.'

'Oh, I won't be able to sleep tonight,' Bosin replied, cheerfully. 'I'm too used to beds! Now, when I was a boy, I could sleep anywhere. I could sleep in a tree, even, if there were wolves about. But not now. Now that I'm thirty, the ground resists me and I can't sleep for hours. I think there is something alive in my jerkin that keeps biting. Would you take a look?'

'No. I will not take a look,' Hondo replied, already nettled by the man. Only thirty! The news was galling. How fast his hard-won sense of peace seemed to shred when Bosin started flapping his lips! It was extraordinary. Hondo wondered if he had become too used to the respect of others. Even noblemen were usually careful not to offend him. Most men walked gingerly around one who could make them look like a child or take their life at a whim. They told themselves they honoured the title of 'sword saint' that he had won. Yet there was always fear there, too. It seemed Bosin did not share that sense of caution.

'You are not afraid of me, are you?' Hondo asked. He

had trained himself not to avoid a difficult question merely because he might not like the answer. He spoke the words as soon as he felt the first desire to stifle them. He allowed no dishonesty, in himself or anyone else. It was a cancer to a man's peace.

Bosin blinked slowly at him, looking as if he thought he was being mocked. He frowned heavily and Hondo could almost see thoughts crashing against one another.

'Lord Inijui came to me and said I had been chosen from among many . . .' Bosin said slowly. 'He said it was a great honour that I would be accompanying you – and these silent lads as well. He did not say I should be afraid, Master Hondo, of anyone. Why would I be afraid? I saw you fight for the old king twenty years ago, when I was a little boy. I saw you then and I said to myself that I would become a master. It was a great day for me. I cannot fear my childhood hero.'

Hondo found himself smiling at the big thug's earnestness. He had heard the same story, or some version of it, a thousand times.

'Would it please you to spar with me?' he heard himself ask. He regretted the offer as soon as it was made, but there was no taking it back. To his surprise, Bosin shook his head and lay down, tugging a blanket into place and folding his hands across his chest.

'I don't want to hurt you, Master Hondo. You were younger then. I haven't sparred for years, anyway. There were too many accidents. I'll take second watch, if you want.'

Hondo watched in astonishment as the enormous man settled himself. Bosin's mouth sagged open after a time.

Despite his previous certainty, the man seemed to pass into sleep as easily as a child, with no sign of cares or worries. Hondo watched the twins exchange a glance and settle into their blankets by the embers. The night would be cold. He folded his own blanket into a square rather than let sleep take him unawares. Hondo rose from that spot and went away into the trees to empty his bladder and practise his forms. He tried not to hear the snoring that echoed after him.

Gabriel flexed his hands and forearms, pleased by the muscle and condition. If not for the lumps that ruined his side, it would be as good a body as the one he had known in life. Yet even as he had the thought, he realised he could not quite remember his old frame. Identity seemed linked to flesh, more powerfully than he had ever understood. Already, he had no idea if he had been shorter or taller in his previous existence. Even the memories of the grey plain were fading, though he understood he had escaped. He and the other three had been wrenched back into the world.

He raised his face to the sunlight streaming through the glass, where the river ran beyond. Warmth touched him, true warmth, for the first time in an age. Morning had come, at last, in all its glory. He let out and drew in a long breath, delighting in every sensation.

There was a man talking. A man who moved to block the light that washed over him. Gabriel understood most of the words, though they sounded strange to his ear, as if the speaker was from a different region. Some were mere gibberish. Without thought, Gabriel reached out and

74

gripped the man's neck, holding tightly enough to bring silence.

The entire room froze, Gabriel saw. The servants revealed themselves by their cringing demeanour. The man he held was the master in that room – or he had been.

'What is your name?' Gabriel asked.

The fellow was terrified, he could see that. He began tugging at Gabriel's fingers, but they might as well have been cast from bronze for all the effect. Gabriel frowned a touch, then raised his arm higher, so that the man was made to stand on the tips of his toes. Lord Ran made a gurgling sound.

'Be silent,' Gabriel said. This body . . . no, it was more than mere muscle. He was stronger than he could believe. When he had reached for the throat, it had been like a rattle-snake striking. His eyes had barely followed his own movement, yet the tendons had not snapped, the muscles had not torn. Gabriel felt alive and aware, so that the entire world flooded in on him.

He let the choking lord go and fell to his knees, holding his head in his hands. He could taste the air! He could smell sulphur and vinegar and, dear God, he could smell violets and river water and excrement, blended into one great pulsing hymn of life. There had been *nothing* on the battle plain except darkness and pain. He had bound wounds a thousand times, only to see them healed or scarred by the next morning. Yet it had not been life. A hundred years of it had not been as vivid as a single moment in that long room. It was a second chance.

He rose to his feet once more, looking at the pale figure still trying to talk.

'. . . Taeshin, you are very ill. Can you hear me? Do you understand what I am saying?'

'You speak like a peasant,' Gabriel said with a grin. 'Is this Shiang? What reign is this? Who sits the jade throne?'

He watched the man pat the air as if to calm him down. Gabriel counselled himself to be patient. He knew only one thing. He would not go back without a fight. It did not matter if this stranger spoke to him like a child or a madman. He needed to learn all he could, as quickly as he could, to protect the miracle.

'King Yuan-Choji sits the throne, Taeshin, as you know. You saw him just a few days ago, do you remember?'

'The Yuan? They are potters, aren't they? Was Shiang invaded or something?' Gabriel demanded.

He saw a look of incomprehension cross the face of the other and tried to speak slowly.

'What year is it?'

Lord Ran looked at him in confusion and genuine fear. He answered with great care, as he could still feel the bruises on his throat. He'd heard his vertebrae creak under that grip and he had not managed to dislodge a single finger. His life had rested on the whim of another and he was still shaken by the experience.

'It is the second year of Yuan-Choji, Yuan two hundred and four.'

'Further back,' Gabriel said in frustration.

'The city . . . Shiang is said to have been founded eleven thousand years ago. Is that what you mean, Taeshin?'

'Be silent,' Gabriel said. He swallowed as he understood. If the trembling fool was correct, he had been dead a long time.

'What were you doing here?' he said suddenly. 'These men, who are they to you?'

'Are you all right? Are you hallucinating?' Lord Ran asked.

He stepped forward to examine Taeshin's eyes and Gabriel slapped him with extraordinary force, far more than he had intended. The Lord of Trade sank to the floor, his eyes glazed by the impact. Gabriel spat an old curse in frustration. Denied answers, he lurched into movement around the room, looking at the wires and coming to rest at the white dust that seemed the heart of it.

'This thing . . . what is this?' he said to the room at large.

The servants gaped at him, but one of them thought it best to answer a man who could strike Lord Ran in such a way.

'It was the Aeris Stone,' he said. 'Lord Ran hoped to make greater warriors with its power. He told the king it was for healing, but he wanted enhanced knights to protect Shiang. It did not work, but the stone became dust.'

Gabriel thought of the golden eye that had opened on a hillside. He had been drawn through, with three others. He thought too of the friends and generals he had known when he was alive. If he could bring them back, how pleased they would be.

He could not finish the thought. The pain in his side was growing more and more insistent. He had felt an agony like it only once before – the day he had first opened his eyes on that grey plain. He grunted as flames ate into him, feeling a tear trickle down his cheek. Not all the paintings and sculpture he had witnessed in his life brought such joy as the sensation of weeping. To be alive was pleasure beyond sensation, now that he knew what lay beyond. He thought suddenly of a lemon and felt his mouth flood with saliva and pucker at the mere prospect. The sensations were simply overwhelming, but the pain was deadly. He forced himself to concentrate on it.

He tore the shirt that covered his chest and whistled to himself at the black and shining lumps revealed. They quivered like something alive. He thought it was in time with his heart, which raced in that moment. If such foul things had reached his beating heart, he would surely die.

The thought was a different kind of agony. He had forgotten life. To have it thrust into his hands once more – and then taken – would be its own special hell. He placed his hand on the lumps and felt something shift within him, as if his balance had changed. He frowned, closing his eyes. Warmth came to his fingers and then faded as he lost it again. It was maddening, like picking up a thread on a piece of glass. He plucked at something internal, over and over, and then suddenly he held it. Warmth flooded through his hand into his side. He opened his eyes as the servants crowded around, drawn by awe even greater than their fear. The lumps were shrinking back into the flesh. Veins appeared and disappeared as maps of purple wires, like nets coming to the surface only to sink again. Gabriel felt himself choke as something lodged in his throat and then he was vomiting, pouring acids onto the bed where he had lain.

Lord Ran came back to consciousness and stood up. He saw Taeshin standing, panting and bare-chested, wiping his mouth with his hand. The servants were all staring at a thick, pink lump that glistened and stained the sheets of

78

the bed with watery blood. There was no sign of the buboes on the young warrior's skin.

'How is this possible?' Lord Ran said, forgetting the strangeness of before in his excitement.

Gabriel ignored him. He held up his right hand in a sort of dazed wonder. The blind man had remained on his bed, his eyes hollow. Gabriel felt the warmth surge in his hand and as it became almost too hot to bear, he stepped around the bed and pressed it to the man's face. The blind man shrieked, but it was in shock rather than pain. When Gabriel took his hand away, eyes of hazel looked back at him. The man fell back, shaking his head and blinking tears he could not shed before.

'What is your name?' Gabriel asked him.

'Thomas,' he said.

In a daze, Gabriel stepped across to the one-legged man, power roaring through him. He had never known such a feeling in life as in that moment. He was a god in a heartbeat, beyond life.

He gripped the stump of the man's leg and heard him groan. Gabriel leaned in and visualised the leg growing back, tendons and muscles wrapping around one another, bones growing like coral through the air. When he opened his eyes, a foot was still forming. He stared in wonder, then suddenly with a sense of doubt.

The ocean that surged in him was less. He could feel it, as he might have felt an arm grow numb, or a sense of weariness. He was not a god. Whatever had brought him back was finite – and he had wasted too much of it on strangers. He pulled his hand back with a curse. The man on the bed cried out, reaching to him as a child might.

'Finish the job, brother! Please.'

The foot was indeed unfinished, without toes. It ended in a mass of tendons and veins, all coiling. As Gabriel stared, they fell limp. After a moment of stillness, they began to bleed.

'I cannot risk more,' Gabriel said. 'Finish it yourself, if you have the strength. I have given you all I can.'

He watched as the warrior closed his eyes and struggled to complete the work. The veins and tendons twitched half a dozen times, but they would not rise up and knit themselves into flesh, not as they had done before. Gabriel wondered if stepping first through the eye had given him more, or whether his training had made him better able to harness those forces. It did not matter. Now that he had discovered there was a limit, he would spend his coins more carefully.

The fourth man had not struggled against the straps that bound him. Gabriel had never known his name, but there was little sign of life in the fellow who sagged on his bed.

'So,' Gabriel said. 'One of us was blind and one lame. I had some foul thing eating at me.' He looked to the man whose throat was still darkening with bruises. 'And this one? Was he a leper? Where did you find him?'

Lord Ran looked at him in quiet awe, unable to explain what had happened.

'He was a drunk,' he replied. 'His mind is gone.'

Gabriel peered closer, trying to remember which of his companions of the battlefield had found himself in such a pitiful carcass. As Thomas had been blind before, someone was trapped in a mind rotted almost to nothing. Gabriel shuddered. It would be its own torment, perhaps. Yet he

80

could not spend more of what had revived him. He had already given too much.

Gabriel cursed his excesses, though he had been drunk on life, intoxicated and made mad. He had burned too bright for a while. Yet his judgement and his control had returned.

'I see. There's nothing I can do for him now. Take us to the palace, Lord Ran,' he said. 'I would like to see this Yuan potter king with my own eyes.'

'Taeshin?' Lord Ran said. He still could not believe what he had witnessed, nor whether to be afraid or pleased.

'Call me Gabriel,' he replied. Gabriel felt a whisper of protest within him, as if something sat poorly in his gut. He belched into his fist. His mother had named him for an angel, he recalled. Well, he would be the Morningstar in Shiang. He would be the light returned.

7

Tiger

Tellius avoided the eye of the king's royal crier, Morbon. The man was red-faced and beady-eyed, huge of chest and with an almost pathological delight in the volume of his own voice. Lady Sallet had plucked Morbon from the markets just a year before, where his low price for fish could be heard over all the others. Morbon had been taken in and examined for some sort of magical assistance. It had turned out to be a natural talent, as was his ability to talk his way into a job. Within a month, Sallet and even royal proclamations were being read aloud on city squares and street corners by the man.

Tellius heard Morbon had been beaten up twice on some of the narrow streets closer to the river. That explained why he went everywhere with two guards in royal livery. Yet despite Morbon's inflated chest and sense of importance, Tellius didn't want to hear the news that kept him hot on his heels.

To say Tellius' life had changed in the previous two years would have been an extraordinary understatement. While the city had suffered an attack by its own legion, led by one of the Twelve Families, an old man from the east had found the love of his life. He hadn't even been looking. In all the bloodshed and chaos and wild magic, Lady

Sallet had held his life in her hands more than once. To his surprise, she'd resisted the urge to make him disappear. She had never been one for the easy solution.

He knew her rather better after two years than he had then. For all her tendency to push through life like a ship, Lady Sallet had been lonelier than even she had realised. In his more contemplative moments, Tellius understood that he had been as well. Men are made for partners. He had hardened himself against the world – a sadder, much colder man when he looked back. He also appreciated a fine-figured woman, there was no point denying that. It was not just a spiritual union of lonely souls. Lady Sallet had a very deep chest, his mother might have said, as if describing furniture. The truth was that Win Sallet delighted him and was part of the reason he had wrought his own changes. Though he was perhaps a little shabby in places, Tellius wore a decent tunic of dark green velvet and he was only two days clear of a razor, with white bristles barely visible.

The city ran like a clock around the two of them, which Tellius felt in part was his doing. The new king was a quiet and obedient lad, seemingly proud of the relationship between Tellius and Aunt Sallet, as he called them. The boy Arthur had been crowned two years before, in the wreckage of civil war. There were still many in the city who believed he would grow into the seat. Tellius knew he actually would not, but that was something that would reveal itself over time. There was no hurry. The people of Darien lived with magic in their daily lives. They would accept a child golem as king once he had overseen a few more years without all hell breaking loose. Peace was the key, Tellius told the lads of the old crew, whenever they met for a beer at the Red Inn. People wanted to be left alone. Unless they were actually intent on butchering strangers with a cleaver, that was the best the king and the Twelve Families could do for most of them – to just stay out of their way.

As an untitled companion to the head of House Sallet, Tellius was content to live well and privately, without ever troubling anyone or going hungry again. Life had rewarded him and he was not about to disappoint it by scorning the gift. At his age, one bad cold and he'd have seen his last winter anyway.

Tellius saw Morbon had spotted him and was making his way through the visitors to the royal park, not quite in pursuit. Tellius increased his pace. He considered his daily walk around the royal park and estate grounds a chance to order his thoughts in peace. Really, the man had no right to seek him out. The fellow might have been a bullfrog for his ridiculous chest. No man should be preceded into a room by any single part of him.

Tellius snorted to himself. Something to tell Win. Lady Sallet had a surprisingly broad sense of humour, which was just one of many unexpected things he had learned about her in their time together. A man should not be so blessed, he thought, lengthening his stride and beginning to breathe harder. Let the bastard sweat.

'Master Tellius!' he heard called behind him.

Tellius went faster. Too much good fortune invited misfortune, though he hoped he was perhaps a little immune after so many years of misery and exile. If there was anything like balance in the world, Lady Sallet was his reward. He had told her that once. She'd laughed and proved it.

He could hear Morbon panting like a pair of old bellows as he came up behind. Tellius felt his deeper thoughts pull apart, the threads lost. He halted, staring into the distance as the royal crier reached him and rested his hands on his knees. Morbon was pink as a salmon, which was a dish Tellius had only experienced since taking rooms on the Sallet estate. He and the lady of the house had kept a polite fiction of separate households for almost a year before he'd forgotten himself and been discovered fast asleep, laid out across her bolsters.

Tellius rubbed his chin as he stared into the distance, giving Morbon time to recover his breath. The whiskers were old-man white and Win said they made him look like a vagabond. Perhaps it was time to shave once more, or more accurately to be shaved by the army of attendants who made the Sallet household run. They were very protective of their mistress, he had noticed. Perhaps that was why he did not trouble the barber too often, a man who held a long, shining razor to his favourite throat.

'Master Tellius, I called out . . .' Morbon broke off, appearing to need still more time.

'Ah, Morbon! Were you looking for me? I had no idea. I walk out here sometimes, to watch the new palace going up. I think it will be an extraordinary building when it's finished, don't you?'

The man's colour was fading a touch, shade by shade. Tellius relented.

'Is it Lady Forza again?'

Morbon nodded, his eyes bulging.

'You know, Morbon, you should walk this path each morning, at a good brisk speed. Not when I do, you understand.

Earlier, much, much earlier. You'll find you won't puff quite as badly. You need those lungs to work, don't you?' In truth, Tellius was feeling a little cruel for making the man follow so far in his wake. It was not the crier's fault that Lady Forza was so insistent.

'Yes, Master Tellius. Lady Forza has refused to leave until you agree to listen to her.'

'I have listened to her, Morbon. Many times. It achieves nothing.'

The crier had regained his breath and stood taller, looking disapprovingly at the old man who had led him such a chase through the royal grounds. He knew it was deliberate.

'Nonetheless, sir. Lady Sallet asked me to insist. She said she would prefer not to entertain Lady Forza quite so often and would you please treat her with some courtesy.'

'Lady Forza is a daft old hen, Morbon.'

'Sir! Please!'

The man was scandalised. Tellius was tempted to remind him he had been bawling the price of fish just a year before, but that would have been cruel. There were no airs like the ones in those recently raised, he thought. He supposed he might consider himself in the same rare group. The thought was somewhat uncomfortable and his collar seemed to chafe suddenly, so that he ran a finger around the inside of it.

'I have spoken to Lady Forza before, Morbon. I believe I left strict instructions not to be disturbed by her again. My life has too few years left to waste another hour of it on Lady Forza's tea leaves and fortunes.'

'She brought her stone with her this time, sir,' Morbon said.

Tellius bit the inside of his lip as he thought. He could not deny he was interested to see the thing. As the great treasure of her house, Lady Forza had never allowed it out before.

'Lady Sallet said to insist, did she?'

'Very clearly, sir. She said I was not to allow you to escape.'

'I hear her tone there, Morbon.'

'That is very likely, sir.'

'Damn it,' Tellius said. 'Very well. Lead me to another wasted afternoon. Could I at least prevail upon you to call me away to an urgent meeting after a little while? That has worked before.'

Morbon still streamed with sweat. He dabbed a handkerchief over his face, using it to wipe the pink folds. His eyes showed a flash of malice as he replied.

'Of course, sir. I am at your service.'

Tellius glanced at him and grinned suddenly.

'Good for you, Morbon. You won't be coming to fetch me, will you? There'll be no urgent call.'

'Oh no, sir,' Morbon admitted. He smiled as he spoke and tucked his handkerchief into the pocket of his waistcoat. Tellius chuckled as he turned back.

Lord Ran walked almost in a trance through the streets of Shiang. Try as he might, he could not understand what had gone wrong, nor how he had come to be leading the four men he had embroiled in his experiments to the king's palace. Whenever he paused or demurred, he felt himself prodded in the back by the one who called himself Gabriel, whom Lord Ran had known as Taeshin, one of Lord Hong's swordsmen. They wore no swords, in a city where swordsmen were treated with elaborate politeness and caution. Insults were not forgiven in such a place, whether a man was armed or unarmed. Lord Ran staggered on, wondering if he was a prisoner. His mind still reeled. The experiment had succeeded in some sense. The entire power of the stone had been drawn out, but still, three of the men had been healed. The last pitiful creature staggered in their wake. Gabriel had tied a piece of rope to the fellow's neck and drew him along with them like a pet. Lord Ran saw no light of understanding in the eyes. He had looked back only once and shuddered at the man's slack expression.

The streets were busy at that time of the morning, with half the city heading to work or already bawling their wares and prices to passers-by. For a time, it seemed the way would constantly clear before them. There was something not quite right in the small group that strode so purposefully along the western avenue, something that jarred against the normal rhythms of the city and its commerce. For those with eyes to see, it was enough of a warning to take a step back and watch with silent scrutiny until whatever it was had passed. A man did not live long with a tendency to ignore his surroundings, at least in Shiang. There were just too many willing to take offence – and too many swordsmen capable of enforcing instant reprisal. On a normal day, the politeness of strangers could be an art form as elaborate as a royal ceremony.

Lord Ran came to a halt when a group of Mazer

warriors remained in the centre of the road. Six young house guards cast glances at those bearing down on them, but they saw no threat in the small group. Even the man on a leash was not too unusual in the city, where slaves could be punished in a multitude of ways.

A young woman was coming down the last steps from rooms far above. Lord Ran assumed she was the mistress of some noble son, flaunting his men and his power in the street for her neighbours. The six men had brought a litter to that place and even laid a path to it. She blushed under their attention as she walked across clean rushes.

Gabriel stepped forward to see why they had stopped. He saw Lord Ran cringe and ignored him, surveying the scene and particularly the woman with open appreciation.

She felt his gaze and faltered. It was not common for a man to look so openly, especially with swordsmen in attendance. Lord Ran saw her mouth purse in irritation as Gabriel looked on, a slight smile on his face.

One of the six swordsmen glanced at whatever had caught her attention. The young warrior frowned and nudged the one next to him, exchanging low words. Lord Ran groaned.

'Gabriel?' he said out of the side of his mouth. 'These men will kill us all if they are not shown more respect. Please avert your eyes from the young lady.'

'No, I don't think I will,' Gabriel said.

The beauty on the rushes had ensnared him, though he did not know if she was truly a vision, or whether it was part of his reaction to being alive once more. He could feel a fleck of black mud on his cheek with a shiver of excitement, so he suspected he was still unbalanced. He had been too long in the grey land, perhaps. They said the best sauce for any food was hunger. Perhaps all women were queens to one who had once been dead.

He felt his cheeks flush and experienced a physical reaction that might have embarrassed him in a previous life. Another of the swordsmen had seen the way a stranger stared. That fellow bristled and cried out in anger, calling some command across the heads of the others. Gabriel dragged his gaze at last from the young woman and fastened it on the one who stepped forward in challenge. The house swordsman wore fine panelled armour and had a slightly curved scabbard on his left hip. Gabriel smiled. He had held such a blade just the morning before, though it had not come with him. His hand remembered too many years of war and his fingers twitched to feel the weight of rippled steel again.

He waited a beat then, but it was already too late. Under that infuriating smile, the swordsman came rushing at him, drawing his sword in a motion Gabriel recalled as well as his own breath. He moved aside from the first blow, so fast that he was able to watch the man's eyes widen. Gabriel laughed. He had never been as quick before. He did not know if it was centuries of fighting every day or the stone that had drawn him back, but even a house swordsman seemed slow to him. He touched the man's outstretched arm as he swept past, not to hurt him, but lifting it a little to prevent the tip of the sword touching the ground. It was a lovely weapon and Gabriel did not want to see it damaged.

The man recovered, though he was off-balance. Dropping low, he brought the blade back in a short, chopping motion. Gabriel hit him on the side of the head and he crumpled instantly, knocked dead or unconscious. The sword fell from nerveless fingers and Gabriel snatched it up, swishing it through the air with delight. Every breath he pulled in was different! He felt the giddiness of it, as if he were drunk on air alone. He had been blind and deaf and mute before, his senses dulled in the grey place. Here, he was more alive than he had ever been.

The other warriors watched in disbelief as their officer was taken out with a single blow. They attacked as they had been trained to do, to remove the stain of dishonour and to bring instant justice. Gabriel moved amongst them, stepping in much closer than most men wished to be, so that it was almost a dance of lovers, though drops of blood spattered the air. He laughed with each blow, steeped in dark delight.

In just moments, the street was quiet and the last of them fell onto the stones to bleed. Gabriel wiped two fingers down the blade and knelt to untie the first man's scabbard. The young woman began to scream until he glanced up at her. He held her gaze then and she was still.

'Come, my dear,' he said. 'I am going to the palace. Would you like to meet the king?'

He reached out and, in a daze, she took his hand. Gabriel smiled at her.

'Ah, "She walks in beauty like the night". To know such a thing again . . .'

He turned back to the small group he led. The one called Thomas was watching him with a certain tension. At his side, the half-foot soldier had already bled through the bandages that wrapped him. It was as if he wore a boot of blood and he looked as pale as death and about as resentful. The man on the leash stared and breathed and seemed unaware of anything. Of the three who had returned, he was by far the most restful companion. Gabriel shook his head, raising his eyebrows to Lord Ran.

'These were truly the best you could find?' he said.

'I was not allowed to choose healthy men,' Lord Ran said. 'Nor even these. You should all have been dead.' He said the last as a mutter, but Gabriel heard.

'I have been,' Gabriel said. 'I do not recommend it.'

Lord Ran blinked. He had been stunned and disorientated from dawn. He could not recall being so terrified of anything before, but there was something about the one who called himself Gabriel that inspired a constant and exhausting fear. It was as if Lord Ran's life rested on a coin toss in each heartbeat, so that it could be snatched away at any moment. He wondered how long he would survive.

As Gabriel turned to the palace quarter ahead of them, Lord Ran touched the knife that was hidden in his belt. Part of the buckle, it was a coward's weapon, but he might bring an end to the horror of that day if he could cut Gabriel's throat. He could not escape the sick sense that even that might not be enough.

He saw the man who had been Taeshin turn back to him. It was as if the sun returned.

'You look nervous, Lord Ran. There is no need to be. You understand the stone and the wires – everything I need to do it all again. Believe me, you are safer than anyone else in Shiang at this moment. Perhaps I will make you king.'

'I . . . my lord . . . there was only one s-stone. I have no other!'

As he spoke Lord Ran cursed himself for being a fool. The madman was telling him he had value and there he was, throwing away the thing that made him useful!

Gabriel raised his head further and drew in a breath, as if he sniffed the breeze.

'No, it was not the only one, brother. Power calls to power. There are other stones in the world. Stones I can use. Now, strip these men of their armour, my lord. Take two more swords and present them to Thomas and . . . you. What is your name?'

The man whose foot was only half formed growled his response.

'Sanjin. If you would finish healing my foot, I would be more use to you.'

'That is your test, Sanjin,' Gabriel said. 'I have shown you it can be done. So finish my work. Show me you are worthy to follow me, or bleed to death.'

Lord Ran hesitated only a moment. If he was as valuable as Gabriel said he was, he could not be killed for refusing to strip the dead. Yet before he could say as much, Gabriel pushed him forward, so roughly he fell onto his hands and knees in the slop of the road.

'I gave you an order, my lord. I have restored a blind man before. Would you have me take your eyes? Your tongue? I suggest you obey me.'

Lord Ran choked down his fear and began tugging at the panels of armour, passing them back to the men he had brought into the world. The nobleman was filthy with blood and mud by the end, his face smeared with all sorts of foul muck where he had wiped sweat.

Gabriel, Thomas and Sanjin eyed one another in the armour. They had not bothered finding a weapon or a coat for the fourth, who hissed softly as he breathed and understood nothing.

'It feels right, brothers, does it not?' Gabriel said. 'To stand here?'

The young woman began to sob and he turned to her, so fast it made her flinch in her tears.

'Do not cry, my dear. Tonight, you will share the bed of an angel, perhaps of a king – or a god. Does that not please you?'

She shook her head and the sobbing only intensified. Gabriel scratched the underside of his chin and made an exasperated sound. Yet the day was too perfect to be angry for long. He smiled at the faces watching them from every window that looked down on the street.

'I tell you, Lord Ran, there will be others weeping before I am done. It is good to be home.'

He took the young woman by the hand and at first she tried to pull away from him.

'Do you see this man who wears a rope on his neck?' he said. 'Would you have me lead you in the same way?'

She shook her head, her eyes huge in her despair.

'Then walk at my side, my dear. Take my hand in yours and walk like a queen. Who knows, if you please me, you might become one.'

The presence of armed strangers approaching the royal precinct did not go unnoticed. Gabriel and Lord Ran passed the line of dark stone that marked the royal grounds and were immediately challenged by the guards of a royal tax office. Those four men had stood to perfect attention like mannequins for the first hours of the morning. They moved a little stiffly to halt the progress of strangers who had no right to be strolling onto Crown property.

The outermost buildings were of a previous age, with great columns thicker than a man in white stone and doors apparently designed for cavalry to ride through without ducking their heads. If the swordsmen who guarded collectors of taxes and royal archivists tended to be a little past their prime, they were experienced men nonetheless. They stepped into the street, fanning out across a pinch point that had been designed with exactly that purpose in mind.

The sight of a young woman marked by tears did not assuage the tension that showed in their stances. Nor did the hissing man held with a rope around his neck. The four guards exchanged glances, with the most senior raising his flat hand. He was not worried by what he saw, though it interrupted an otherwise peaceful morning.

Gabriel drew in a breath, but it was the one called Thomas who spoke first. The man who had been blind stepped ahead of the little group. His hazel eyes were strangely piercing and he smiled as he kept moving. He pressed his chest against the outstretched palm held up to stop him, leaning onto it as if testing the man's strength.

The guard captain frowned at the bravado. He had served the royal family with distinction for some thirty years, before accepting a lesser post to take him quietly to retirement. He opened his mouth to speak sternly to them and then recognised Lord Ran. His manner changed immediately.

'My lord, I did not see you. Please accept my apologies. May I assist?'

'Lord Ran needs an escort into the palace,' Gabriel said smoothly. 'He has an urgent matter to discuss with the king.'

The guard's eyes flickered across to the speaker and his eyes widened.

'Taeshin? I thought you had fallen ill . . .' His confusion cleared as he recalled Lord Hong's man had been taken to the Lord of Trade to be healed. It appeared to have been a success. 'I am glad to see you have recovered.'

The guard jerked his head to the other three and they took their hands from their sword hilts and returned to their posts at the tax house columns without another word. Gabriel looked slightly disappointed.

'I will take you to the king's seneschal, Lord Ran,' the captain continued. 'I cannot say when His Majesty will see you, of course.'

'I don't . . .' Lord Ran began. Gabriel spoke over him.

'Lord Ran must see the king now. Run ahead and announce us. No business of the court is more important than this.'

The guard frowned once more. He could not understand why Taeshin was giving such orders, especially to one of his seniority. Yet he had obeyed that tone for thirty years and so he bowed low and clattered away. The small group followed at a more sedate pace.

'My lord Ran,' Gabriel said softly. 'If you call out in warning, I will not kill you, I swear it. But I will visit

suffering upon you. Until you are broken. Do you understand me?'

Lord Ran nodded, miserably. He rubbed his nose with
one hand, finding that it smeared his hand in blood. A
nosebleed. He was lost, a confused and battered old man.
A gentle rain began above them, making the air into damp
mists as it struck and leaped from the cobbled ground.

8

Forza

Tellius entered a chamber that had a ceiling thirty feet above his head. Half the rooms of the Sallet estate were hung with ropes of plaster as decoration. In the greeting hall, they formed great ribbons and loops on the walls, painted gold over a sage green. Tellius had discovered green was very common in Sallet holdings. Frankly, it had begun to wear on him. He knew the colours were meant to both soothe anger and remind guests of the noble stone that had raised the Sallets to one of the foremost families in the city of Darien. To his eye, it had an acid look. For all he knew, that was intended. Green could be spring, fresh salads and grassy meadows. Or it could be bile, and mould, and bitter as gall.

Tellius felt his heart sink at the sight of the old lady waiting for him. Though she must have been eighty, Lady Forza had the manner of a bird, with quick movements and sharp eyes. He smiled even so and dropped to one knee as she turned her head.

Her expression was so relieved, Tellius felt a stab of guilt for having led Morbon such a dance to avoid being called, though he quickly hardened his heart. He'd endured two previous meetings with no clear purpose. He knew Win wanted him to take an interest in the business of

House Sallet. It boded rather well for their relationship that she wished to demonstrate her trust in him, especially in public. He believed too that she told the truth when she said she valued his particular judgement – how could she not? He had led an interesting life. There were times when he felt a little like the fox let loose among the chickens for a day.

The noble houses tended to employ hard men to be suspicious on their behalf. Perhaps the original families had been men and women of iron. Yet behind the walls of their estates, some of their descendants were as innocent as babes. A less moral man might have taken terrible advantage, Tellius thought with a sigh. Sadly, those days were behind him. Only a fool would foul his own nest, no matter which shade of green it was.

As he bowed deeply and braced himself to be kissed on both cheeks, Tellius could not help glance at the box that rested on a table of onyx and iron at Lady Forza's side. He knew that box had not been present in the room on any of his previous visits. It was a dark blood red for a start, as out of place in that room as he sometimes felt himself.

'Thank you for seeing me, Master Tellius,' Lady Forza said.

She wore jewelled earrings, he noted, as he kissed her in greeting. Rather fine-quality rubies, like tears of blood. He had desired such symbols of wealth for much of his adult life, though mostly because breaking them up and selling them meant he could live warm, that he could eat and work uninterrupted in the little workshop he'd owned. He tried to remind himself that it had been a lord much like Lady Forza's late husband who'd forced the sale of that shop, rather than letting him manage the debts at a slower rate. Tellius had barely hung on to the attic above it and made a second life for himself, of a sort. He had certainly not bathed then as often as he did these days, though the thought was not without a strange sort of regret.

'Dear lady, I am only sorry I can't do more for you,' he said.

He took a seat across from her and tried hard not to show how intrigued he was by the box. She knew very well what had brought him back to see her, of course. That was why she had risked her family heirloom on the open streets. It explained why he'd seen guards in Forza colours on the grounds as well. Favours had been called in, which made it all the stranger. Tellius found his curiosity prickling. He was surrounded by interesting women. As curses went, it was not such a poor fate.

'Oh, I know you think I am just a daft old hen, Master Tellius,' she said.

He began to protest, but she held up her hand and tutted at him, her eyes bright with amusement. He had the uneasy feeling that she had somehow heard his earlier comment to Morbon. Was that possible? Of course it was. He cursed himself and flushed.

'Mine is a wealthy house, Master Tellius. I do have a few little items of use to me.' Her hand flicked one of the earrings, making it swing. 'My late husband never spoke of our . . . advantages, but you see? I trust you now with that knowledge. I came to Lady Sallet with just the vaguest of fears that first time. I was impatient – at my age, impatience is not such a strange thing. If you scried and saw Darien destroyed, would you not act? Would you sit and drink tea in a blaze of late autumn sunshine and do nothing about what you had seen? Or would you seek out the house with the closest connection to this strange new boy-king of ours?'

'Lady Forza, I am sorry if I have not taken your warnings seriously. The very fact that you have brought your house stone here makes me re-evaluate your intent. Does that satisfy you?'

The old lady closed her eyes in relief. She sagged slightly as she sat there, as if even her straight back was an effort almost too much to bear. It was an instant of weakness, present and gone, as she straightened once again. Yet he had read her and he bit his lip once more.

'My lady, how long do you have?'

In reply, she smiled, so that her eyes almost vanished.

'I was told you were sharp, Master Tellius, just like Win. She wanted me to prove I was serious. She wanted me to bring this stone, or she would not have made us both sit through our previous meetings. Oh, do not look so surprised, Master Tellius. The lady who shares your bed is as cunning as her figure is baroque. I would be astonished if she could not hear us now. But wait, here are my bona fides.'

She picked up the red box and passed it to him. He saw the weight was a little more than was comfortable. He liked her in that moment and wished he had not been such a fool before. Already, the previous meetings belonged to a different life. Lady Forza had revealed herself and he in turn to her. Their eyes met as he took the box and he nodded, sealing a pact that needed no words.

He opened the box and gazed on a red stone the length of his outstretched hand, rounded on one side and flat on the other. It was flecked with gold that drew the eye deeper, just as the Sallet Stone did. Tellius had some sense of what it was and he saw his breath mist the surface in quiet awe.

'It is very beautiful, Lady Forza,' he said.

'Thank you, I have always thought so. It is . . . Now wait a moment, dear. I suspect the lady of the house . . .'

Lady Forza looked to the door as it was opened by two servants. Lady Win Sallet swept in, her dress making a swishing sound on the carpets.

'Lady Forza, I am so sorry. I have treated you with less courtesy than you deserve. I have many calls on my time, but I did not understand this was one of the important ones. Please accept my apology. Speak now and I promise you, I will listen.'

The old woman looked in surprise from Tellius to perhaps the most powerful woman in the city. She nodded to herself as if she had confirmed something she'd only suspected before.

'How lucky you are,' she murmured a little sadly. 'To have found one another.'

Lady Sallet took a seat, smoothing the folds of her dress when they threatened to rise up before her. She did not even glance into the Forza box. Lady Forza had acted with honour and trust. No further confirmation was required after such an extraordinary gesture.

'Please call me Win, Lady Forza.'

'In that case, dear, I would like you to call me Elizabeth.'

The two women smiled at one another. Tellius shut the box lid with a snap, making them both jump.

'You spoke before about a vision, Elizabeth,' Tellius

said. Neither woman replied and Tellius sensed a slight coldness. 'What? Am I to call you Lady Forza, then?'

'Tellius, Elizabeth and I are equals,' Win said. 'As widows, we are the heads of two of the Twelve Families of Darien. Please understand this.'

Tellius let a beat of time pass. Had he been a young man of twenty or even thirty, he knew he might have stormed out, provoking them both with some acid comment that would take days to smooth over. As he was some years past sixty, however, he took a deep breath and mastered himself. It was perhaps the only comfort of old age, that understanding of what mattered – and what truly did not. Half the battles fought by young men were as forgettable as breakfast.

'Of course. Please go ahead. I will do my best not to shit on the carpet.'

He closed his eyes in frustration. Apparently, he had learned nothing over the years.

When he opened them again, Lady Forza was holding a cloth to her mouth and her eyes were streaming. Win looked mortified. Tellius sighed and shook his head.

'I am sorry, Lady Forza. I forget sometimes that the language of the street lads is not heard too often around here. It was my error. I will excuse myself.'

'No, please stay,' Lady Forza replied. 'I said you were a sharp one and you are. My husband would have enjoyed that. Now, let me tell you what I have learned.'

She leaned forward, though a slight wince crossed her face as she did so.

'Are you so ill?' Win said softly.

Lady Forza chuckled.

'How well you suit each other. Yes, dear. My doctor tells me I will not see another spring. My son, Reno, is ready to be head of Forza. I do not doubt he will call on you at some point, to introduce himself. Until then, I remain the voice of my house. Now, no more interruptions, Win! If tea should happen to arrive, I would not say no, however.'

Lady Sallet rang a tiny bell and passed on the order to the servant who entered. Lady Forza began to speak as the doors closed once more.

'I came before to see the king, when I still believed poor Johannes was the voice of the throne. When he died and the city came under attack, I thought that was surely the disaster I had seen. Yet the dreams kept coming. It is true, I am old woman who is rather unwell. It was not so strange to be disturbed in my sleep. Yet I saw a great dark liquid splash against the walls of this city – and rise over it, like a wave crashing against the shore. I thought first it was the Aeris legion attacking the walls, but it is two years since that terrible night and still they come. I began to take the family stone to bed with me, to rest under my pillow. I have had some success with it in the past, when it came to advising my husband in his investments.'

'One rumour confirmed,' Lady Sallet murmured.

The older woman inclined her head.

'As you say. It was never reliable enough for certainty, but I was right enough times to build a great fortune. The Forza are the richest family in Darien as a result. I say this not to be immodest, but to establish my own history. In my family, when I have a strong sense of the future, we listen.'

She looked from one to the other and seemed satisfied by their attention.

'I cannot say what form the threat will take, but I saw snow and trees in ice. I feel danger threatening and I think it will be this winter.'

'Not the next? Or the one after?' Tellius said.

Lady Forza shook her head.

'I will not see the next winter, Master Tellius. I believe it has to be this one, before you, and my son, know spring again.'

She took a deep breath and clenched her jaw, so that he could see tiny sparrow muscles move beneath the skin.

'Open that box again, Master Tellius. I have trusted you both with the honour of my family by bringing it here. I will not hold back now from the rest. Give me the stone.'

Tellius glanced at Lady Sallet and saw her hesitate and then nod. They both knew the family stones were sources of power, though few others in the city shared that knowledge. The Forza Stone Tellius lifted out was, in its own way, as dangerous as any artefact of power. It may have been centuries, even millennia, since the stones had been properly understood. So they believed. It occurred to Tellius that such knowledge might have been guarded as jealously as every other secret in Darien. He formed the thought as he passed it into the gnarled hands of Lady Forza.

She cradled it like a child almost, holding the thing in the crook of one elbow and stroking it with the other hand.

'It gives me comfort to touch it, you know,' she said, almost dreamily. The sharpness in her voice had gone and she looked younger and less anxious than before. 'To know my mother and father touched it, and all my sisters and brothers. We all put our hands on this, just as my children will when I am gone. Perhaps they'll feel my love for them when they do. I hope so.'

'What do you wish to show me?' Lady Sallet said softly.

The question seemed to bring the old lady back to where she was. She sat up and nodded.

'If you would both touch the stone with me, I swear you will not be harmed. It is the only way to see what I would show you. For you to know I have not lost my mind, at least not yet.'

Lady Sallet's expression had hardened.

'You ask a great deal, Elizabeth,' she said. 'Hold a moment, while I summon my personal guard.'

'It is unnecess . . .' Lady Forza began, then gave up. It was not her decision to make, not in the Sallet estate. In moments, two swordsmen in lacquered green armour had entered the room. Tellius was only pleased Win had not summoned the enormous figures known as Sallet Greens, who had played a vital part in the defence of the city two years before. Those monsters remained in their silent rooms by the outer gate, waiting for her most loyal servants to step into them and bring them back to life.

The two who entered showed no surprise to be called, though Tellius saw them look for a greater threat to their mistress than one tiny old lady in a dark red coat and glittering rubies.

'Lady Forza has asked us to place our hands on the stone of her house. It is a great honour,' Lady Sallet said to the two men. 'However, if something should go wrong, it will be your task to save my life – or to avenge it. Is that understood?'

Both men nodded and drew their swords. They took up a stance that was passive, but ready to strike in a number of directions. Tellius vowed to make no sudden movements until those men had been stood down. He had no desire to lose a hand that morning.

Lady Forza seemed unperturbed by their presence. She rested the stone on the red cloth of one sleeve and touched her fingers of the other hand to the polished surface. Without another word, Lady Sallet did the same.

Tellius watched her eyes unfocus and her breathing grow shallow, before he put his own hand beside Win's. He had been ready to knock the stone aside. It was strangely hard to reach out and touch the thing. In that instant, it reminded him of meat, but then his hand was on it and he felt its slickness and a surprising warmth.

Lord Ran shook his head in rising anger, at himself, at the madman who called himself Gabriel, at the blood of innocent men running through the gutters as the rain intensified. The king's seneschal was dead, with half a dozen clerks who had tried to come to his defence. Royal guards had come running at the sound of fighting and Gabriel or Thomas or Sanjin had killed them.

With the pillars of the gatehouse ahead of them, passers-by ran with squares of bamboo held above their heads, or wax-silk umbrellas if they were of some noble house. They scurried in fear, not daring to look at the wolves who had come amongst them.

Gabriel seemed either unaware of the rain, or was

somehow revelling in the touch of it. He stood in the street with his face raised slightly and his eyes closed. He had let the young lady's hand go and she stood trembling, her dress soaked through. Yet she did not try to run. There was a beatific expression on Gabriel's face, though it was not peaceful. Lord Ran dreaded the moment he would open his eyes once more.

Ahead of that small group, armoured ranks of swordsmen waited in a silent line, bristling with weapons. Word had spread quickly of violence on the street. Cries of alarm had gone up and raced ahead of them. Like a portcullis coming down, the way forward had been blocked. No man could approach the king's personal quarters with a red blade and rain streaming off him. Not Lord Ran, not the king's most trusted friends and family. The commander of the royal guards had decided to stop the strange group there and apologise later if he had overreached.

Lord Ran breathed through pursed lips, almost a hissing sound to match the lackwit staggering along with them. It was the right decision.

Thirty-six men faced them in the narrow street. Lord Ran knew the Mazer swordsmen trained in twelves, so that they could split into groups of three and four and six and two without a moment's hesitation. It simply gave them more formations than groups of ten. He shook his head to clear it, wondering if he could use the sound of the rain to cover his retreat and just creep away. He did not want to be part of whatever was coming.

Lord Ran glanced over his shoulder and his heart sank. More men were jogging up behind them in full armour, carrying shields and drawn swords. Rain was a cruel foe for steel, Lord Ran knew very well. Every swordsman there would be furious at having to draw a blade in the wet. Hours of oiling and drying lay ahead of them. Yet Lord Ran could see arrogance in the way they stood. This was merely duty, some group of peasants running mad with stolen swords. Not one of them considered the little group a true threat.

Lord Ran swallowed. There was no retreat for him. He realised he was going to die in that place. His only chance was to drop to the stone road and pray.

Gabriel opened his eyes. He flicked rain off the sword he held with a jerking motion. It shone with oil as he turned it, watching drops bounce and scatter from the steel.

'Put up your blades,' an order came. This guard captain was one Lord Ran knew. The man had won a laurel for himself – and promotion – in two city contests.

'You are under arrest for unlawful killings, in the king's name. There will be no further warning. Lay your swords on the ground and live to your execution. Or die here, in the rain.'

The man's voice changed, becoming gentler, as if he sought to persuade.

'Come on. Whatever it is, have your moment in court to say your piece. Don't make me kill you.'

'Sir, please!' the young lady said, her voice breaking. 'I am a prisoner.'

Gabriel smiled. Thomas, who had been blind, stood on his left. Sanjin, who stood with a puddle of red water around his half-foot, bared his teeth, his hair like rat's tails. The last of them made his hissing sound, as if he laughed through missing teeth.

'We fought every day, for the passage of ages,' Gabriel said. 'And I am . . . faster now. Come on, sir, if you wish. Test us.'

The officer shrugged.

'Take them,' he snapped.

Lord Ran threw himself down and covered his head with his hands. The young woman shrieked in terror and dropped into a crouch. Before and behind, rows of swordsmen charged the tiny group who stood against them.

Tellius was on the wall of Darien, with a great gale blowing hard against him. He looked to his right and left and saw Win and Lady Forza. Each of them was whipped about and tugged by wind that roared in their ears, too loud to hear anything else. He had always loved a good storm, but this was unnatural, as if some great movement of land had collapsed, moving a thousand miles of air in the direction of the city. The wind filled him hard with every breath, so that he had to close his eyes and lean into it.

'There! It comes!' Lady Forza called.

Tellius opened his eyes once more and felt his testicles try to creep up into him. A black wall stretched across the horizon, so that the city at his back seemed suddenly small and vulnerable. The wave rose and rose and there was thunder in it as well as the gale.

In an instant, the storm winds had gone and yet the wave remained. He stood with his gaze rising and rising until he saw the wave would not break before it reached the city, but would pass right over them. They would be washed away as if they had never been.

'No,' he said, but it was just a breath. It could not be stopped, any more than death could be stopped. He knew it in his bones.

The base of the wave stripped the ground as it came, dragging up the stones of the road. They stained the darkness like a ribbon

creeping up its surface. Tellius took Win's hand as it reached them —
and they were gone.

He snatched back his hand from the Forza Stone as if he
had been stung. Win too had pressed fingers to her lips
like a little girl surprised by nettles. Lady Forza was more
controlled, but she nodded to them. She handed the stone
over and Tellius was reluctant to touch the thing again,
then ashamed, so that he held it in a tight grip and put it
into its box. He sensed the smell of salt and seaweed in
the air as he touched it, so that it was hard not to flinch. He
did not want to see that again.

'There,' Lady Forza said. 'Now you have seen my dream.
Now you understand.'

9
Returned

Gabriel stood, surrounded by the dead. He could hear weeping, which was fitting enough. Blood was everywhere and somehow it overwhelmed him. There had been no blood in the grey place, he remembered suddenly. Mortally wounded men had cried out in despair, but vanished as they were trampled underfoot.

Here, bright blood mingled with the rain, seeping between road stones. Gently settling corpses lay sprawled and broken all around. Such things were older memories, from his first life. Gabriel could hear the sighs of dying men as they breathed their last, or as bowels released in death. The dead relaxed, he recalled. They slept like children.

The rain came to an end, though everything dripped and plinked and steamed as soon as the sun came out. It appeared first as a bar of gold across the gatehouse columns, then lit dead and living alike. The weeping sound turned to great sobs as the young woman stood up slowly. There was blood on her dress, he saw. Gabriel smiled at her.

'There, my dear. That wasn't too bad, was it?'

He could still not quite believe his own speed, nor the strength in him. He fought with his old instincts, and perhaps he and his companions had practised more than most men ever could, taking entire lifetimes to learn the trade of iron. Yet when he moved, it was like a shadow falling across a man. Those who stood against him barely had time to cry out before they were cut down.

It should have wrenched his joints apart to have moved so fast. It should have broken his bones. Yet whatever had opened a hole on the hillside of the grey place, whatever had allowed him to return a man's eyes and grow new flesh on old scars, it filled him still. It made him fast as thought and strong as hatred.

Gabriel turned in a full circle, seeing bodies and armour scattered on all sides. He had become the fallen angel, the story he had loved most as a boy. He was lightning – and he burned. He began to laugh, though he knew it was a kind of madness. He needed a quiet place, to rest and think. He looked up at the gatehouse that still loomed before him. Running footsteps and the clatter of arms were getting closer.

Gabriel took the young woman by the hand once more, though she tried to pull away from him, her beauty spoiled by fear.

'Come on,' he said. 'We should not give them time to consider a defence . . . I . . .'

He looked down and saw that some of the blood that dribbled down his legs was his own. A wave of weakness staggered him, bringing sudden certainty. No. He would set the world on fire before going back.

With an effort of will, Gabriel touched his bare left hand to his side. It took just a moment to seek out the great sea he had drunk, the torrent that still filled him. He could not help wishing back the greater ocean he had known on waking, that he had spent so carelessly on the other two. He turned to Thomas then and found the hazel eyes were steady as they watched him. At least the man was loyal. He was not as certain about Sanjin, who seemed to glower at the world and could not heal himself.

Gabriel waited a beat and the blood stopped. A little warmth had sealed the gash, though he thought then of crossbows and cannon. He raised the woman's hand and kissed it.

'It is just a little further, my darling. Stay beside Lord Ran, where you will be safe. There, don't cry! Did you think I would allow them to hurt you? Of course not. Now, do I need to ask if you will run?'

She shook her head, wide-eyed and afraid. Gabriel touched her cheek, feeling how cold she was.

'Good. Then take up the fool's leash and bring him with us.'

Gabriel strode on through the gatehouse, with Thomas on his right side and Sanjin limping behind.

Tellius paced up and down, so that the heads of some forty men and women followed his progress as one. The Twelve Families of Darien had not come there for him, of course, but for Lady Sallet and in particular at the command of the boy-king.

Arthur sat on a throne to one side of the man who had found him on the streets and taught him the Mazer steps. The golem seemed calm, but he was listening intently as Tellius laid out a plan. It was already clear from the expressions of the family heads that they were not happy. Arthur looked from face to face, seeing the ancient lines of men and women. He recognised some traits still surviving in the descendants of an older empire. Lords like Hart, with his mane of grey hair and the precious Blue Border. He had played a part in the defence of the city. The same could not be said of many of the others. While Lady Sallet and Lord Hart had been on the streets, risking their lives, where had the Regis family been hiding? Or De Guise, with his sword? Very few of the Twelve Families had covered themselves in glory that Reapers' Eve festival, two years before. Perhaps, Arthur thought, it explained why they were resisting Tellius then. Through argument, they reminded all the others of their authority – and so played a part. It was possible that Tellius was not completely incorrect in his assessment, Arthur could admit. As their king, he felt a responsibility for them all, but there really were too many fools in the world. In that room, certainly. Arthur had lost count of the times one of them had tried to pat him on the head. It had been tempting to take his sword and thrash them with it, but Lady Sallet had forbidden any display of that sort. A king employed men to preserve his dignity. He did not do it himself. Apparently. Arthur kicked his shoe against the leg of the chair.

'What you are asking . . .' Lord Bracken began. He rose to his feet to speak and Tellius looked sharply at him, speaking again before the man could go on.

'I ask nothing, my lord, beyond my responsibilities as a loyal citizen. The Crown asks this of you. The Crown and the Sallet family.'

'Yes, yes of course,' Lord Bracken continued. He was a large-chested man and the only one among that group who wore his family stone in the open. Deep purple, it rested as a bracer in gold on Lord Bracken's forearm. It was said he never removed it. More than one lord or lady eyed the stone, their gaze returning to it again and again.

The man himself reached down to fondle the ears of a large golden hound sitting upright by his knee. The animal's tongue lolled and it glanced around with the flickering interest of a young child, making some of the others look away. There were rumours about the animals in Bracken's household, as many as there were about the stone he wore.

Bracken tried again, directing his words to the boy on the throne and Lady Sallet, sitting over to one side. She was the only real power in that room, Bracken thought. After himself, and perhaps Regis and De Guise. The others merely played at power. He felt a gaze on him and looked down to Lord Canis. The man was watching him with the coldness of his particular clan. Bracken tugged his gaze clear with an effort.

'Master Tellius, I think perhaps "the Crown" has not considered the difficulties or the costs involved in what you propose. You would have us train the entire population as an army? To feed and clothe and arm them from our own treasuries? That alone is . . . No, I will come back to it. You suggested we send teams of engineers around the walls of the city, looking for ways to strengthen the defences. That is not unreasonable. I would be happy to put my name to such a suggestion. Yet you'd have us building trenches and traps and Goddess knows what else, tearing up farms and villages around the city for this wild scheme?'

'It is my understanding that the Twelve Families of Darien take their authority to rule from the defence of the city,' Tellius said suddenly. 'If you will not defend Darien, perhaps you should consider how that affects your primary role. Perhaps you should consider whether a city even needs a lord who will not . . .'

'Tellius,' Lady Sallet said softly.

He clamped his mouth shut rather than raise his voice further.

Lord Bracken looked to those on either side of him for support. He found only one or two nodding, though that was in part the instinct or the caution of many years. There were few alliances among them, unfortunately.

'What you have failed to consider is what will happen to the city while this is going on,' Bracken said. He deliberately left bombast and anger aside to reply, knowing it gave his words more force to speak slowly and clearly in that place. 'While men train as an army, they are not working. So food rots in the fields. Ships remain at anchor and are not unloaded in the docks. The entire economy of Darien comes to a halt for lack of souls to run it! What you are asking will mean poverty for tens of thousands, even starvation. The system runs, Master Tellius. It is a brave man who would put his hand into the wheels and cogs of Darien!'

Tellius began to pace again.

'Two years ago, my lord, the city was unprepared for an attack. No one saw it coming. We lost the king, and the Aeris legion was inside the west gate before anyone even understood the city was in danger. There are still things we do not understand about that night, but we were not ready. That much is certain.' Despite himself, he had begun to raise his voice in frustration once more.

'You are asking us to bring the city to a halt for a vision?' Lord Hart interjected.

Tellius knew the man was trying to be helpful rather than to undermine his points. It was still hard to reply calmly.

'My lords, no. I am not asking that. It is true Lady Forza saw an attack on the city, as I said. I believe . . .'

'This dark wave,' Lord Bracken interrupted, his voice full of disdain. 'Yet there are other seers in Darien, Master Tellius. Not one of them has come forward.' He sat down, as if the point was unanswerable.

'Not one of them has the Forza Stone!' Tellius said curtly. 'But that is not the issue at hand. The Crown desires his lords to prepare for an attack, to assess how well we could resist a major event like the one at Reapers' Eve. That royal request was prompted by the Forza vision, yes, but that is *not* the reason for it. The reason is that we should never be caught by surprise again! Everything you value, Lord Bracken, was almost lost two years ago. The Twelve Families – your own family – would all have been killed in the civil war. His Majesty asks only that we run drills across the city, to establish our readiness. To be prepared. His Majesty has asked the Twelve Families to review our strength. If it goes well, perhaps it will become part of our calendar, every four or six years.'

Tellius could see grudging acceptance in the room. More than a few of the lords were raising their eyebrows and looking to those they called friends in surmise. The idea had found its first roots.

Lady Sallet rose and Tellius sat down, mopping his brow where it shone. It was his turn to observe the noble crowd, to see where resistance might yet cause a problem. His first glance, though, was to where Win stood straight-backed before them. His instinct was always to protect her, but it was a pleasure to be reminded she could command the room.

'My lords, ladies,' Win began, 'His Majesty seeks a display, as you have heard. A review of the city defence. I think the common people of Darien will enjoy seeing the house guards march along the ring road – and many of them will welcome being trained. I have had a number of requests for citizen militias in the last two years. They fought well enough then, after all, as builders and carpenters and butchers. Without training, they fought for the city and for their own homes and families. It is reasonable to arm such men for the future, no matter what it holds. As Master Tellius has said, this may have been prompted by the Forza vision, but I believe it has sound foundations. It could be a great opportunity. Darien will surely face threats in the future, whether they come this winter or a dozen years from now. It is the merest common sense to be prepared for them.'

The mood altered slightly when Lord Canis rose to his feet. He was careful to observe the niceties of even an informal gathering, waiting in perfect stillness until Lady Sallet inclined her head and took her seat. She may have had the king's ear, but the Sallets did not stand higher than any other of the great families.

Lord Canis was thin and strong-looking. It was said that he practised swordsmanship for hours each day and that he found no pleasure in food or love. The Canis family were rumoured to take no pleasure in anything, a particular facet of the black stone they held. Lady Sallet shuddered as she considered their fate. The 'Dog Stone', as it was called after their name, could heal the most terrible of wounds. Lord Canis himself had been cured of a rotting illness that would have taken his leg as a child. The cost was in the strange coldness she sensed in him even from across a room. The stone took gentleness and warmth. There were some who whispered that it took a soul. Yet it remained, as a vital treasure in the city. No one would ever break the Canis Stone, not if they had loved ones.

'Your Majesty, my lords and ladies, Lady Sallet, Master Tellius,' Lord Canis began, bowing to the king. 'If we train the subjects of the Crown as soldiers, I wonder how long it will be before they have demands of their own. There is a great risk in this proposal, is there not? If the city is attacked, then, yes, there is merit in preparing stronger defences. If it is not, and yet we have given weapons to every adult male in the city, how long will we survive then?'

He paused, as if to invite objection. Lady Sallet spoke immediately.

'The people of the city are loyal to the king, Lord Canis. Less so to the king's lords, perhaps. That will not change.'

'My lady, we do not rule by consent, but by the capacity to destroy. Your green warriors, combined perhaps with the Regis shield, the De Guise sword, the Hart border. There is no wild mob who could ever remove us from power. Yet your proposal is to create a vast army, to train and arm entire regiments. Will you give them these new guns? How long before someone suggests arming them in such a way, instead of months or years of sword training? No, what you describe is a shift of power, my lady. Perhaps a fundamental one.'

The king cleared his throat, so that both Lady Sallet and Lord Canis sat down. Arthur stood and walked a few paces forward. He was dressed in white and he looked no older than a ten- or twelve-year-old boy. Very few in that room knew his nature, but they had accepted him while the previous king lay cooling, while the city was still strewn with rubble and bodies. He had done nothing to concern them from that day, for all there were some who considered he was in the control of the Sallets.

'My lord Canis, I believe you are mistaken,' Arthur said. 'I was there at the west gate during the assault by the legion. I watched from on high – and I fought on the gate itself. I saw the people of Darien rally to fight the invaders. I saw them take up what arms they had and strike back against trained soldiers. They gave no quarter. They did not run. It is true I saw no sign of the Regis shield or the sword of De Guise that day – though I did see the Sallet Green warriors. It is possible those artefacts could resist the murderous rage of an entire city. I doubt it, however. It is my belief that we already rule by consent – and that understanding is to be seen in every transaction. Or do you cheat your suppliers, my lord? Do you take their daughters against their will? Do you make slaves of their sons?'

Lord Canis looked away for a moment as he considered.

'Your points are well made, Your Majesty. I will consider them further.'

He sat down and a subtle tension went out of the group. Arthur smiled at them all.

'I have talked more today than in the last month. Lady Sallet and Master Tellius have my trust in this. I will leave them to arrange the defence of our city. Pray, gentlemen, ladies, that you never have cause to look back on this day and give thanks.'

Everyone in the room rose then to bow to the king of Darien. Arthur turned on his heel and left them to it. They waited until they heard the lock of the door being closed before they stood straight. The instincts of loyalty were ingrained, not least because their own status flowed from the Crown. Tellius sensed the shift in the room and nodded, pleased.

'So, my lords. It is time for a distribution of duties. Imagine for a moment that an enemy approaches Darien. How shall we send him running? How shall we bloody his nose for him?'

Gabriel led his little group into echoing marble halls, urging them along whenever Lord Ran or the young woman wanted to collapse. Glancing back, he saw they were leaving a trial of bloody footprints, like a wound.

He had lost count of the number who had come against them. His monstrous speed had not slackened, though he had been wounded twice more in a melee. As far as he could tell, the cuts were more by accident than any great talent in those he faced. The Mazer swordsmen of his day had been giants. Those he faced seemed a lesser breed, unless it was just that he had grown beyond them. He did not find that advantage unpleasant, at least at that moment. Discovering he was both faster and stronger than all his opponents was actually making him giddy with pleasure.

Ahead of him, two masters waited in stillness and apparent calm, their swords drawn. Gabriel saw their eyes widen and he felt their heart rates spike higher. He knew he was blood-spattered by then. He could feel it gum his fingers. That was one thing he had not missed, in the grey place. Blood was unpleasant stuff, the very essence of a man splashed out into the world.

'Thomas?' Gabriel said to his companion-in-arms. 'Would you mind?'

He gestured at the door and stopped to wipe something from his eye. His fingers came away red and he knew he would look terrifying when he entered the throne room of Shiang. The idea amused him. All men wore a mask. His just happened to be made of blood. Perhaps in its way, it was more honest than most.

The man called Thomas stepped forward, raising his sword in a guard position, as if about to begin a formal duel. His two opponents stepped in to meet him and Gabriel watched the man accelerate into a blur, his sword a silver streak they could not see to stop. With Gabriel's heightened senses, he was able to observe their expressions change, from determination to sudden disbelief and blooming fear.

They did not have long to be afraid. Thomas finished them quickly, with blows across the throat, each a hair's breadth above the armoured collar. Gabriel saluted with his blade as the man looked back.

'Well done, brother,' Gabriel said.

Thomas grinned and pushed open the doors to the throne room. They strode in together, with the woman half-hiding her face with one hand and Lord Ran stumbling and dazed as if he had lost his wits.

They had not stopped since passing under the shadow of the gatehouse. Gabriel still expected an army to be waiting for him in that room, but he had left a path of dead swordsmen behind on the way there. Blood dripped in a ring around him when he stood still. He flicked his sword and a spatter of it marked the polished floor.

At the far end, the young king rose from his seat and took up the sword of the Yuan dynasty. Gabriel could feel the power of the thing as he stalked down the length of the royal hall. It awoke a hunger in him and he remembered once again all those he would like to see restored to the world. Lord Ran knew the secret of it. All he needed was another stone.

'Your Majesty, you won't believe me, but this hall is just the same as it was a thousand years ago, more. You potters have maintained it well.'

Gabriel was moving quickly as he spoke, with Thomas like a leopard at his side. Sanjin was slower, falling behind with his half-foot. They left the young woman holding the leash of the fool and Lord Ran weeping behind them.

Gabriel lengthened his stride as he reached the king.

'I thought your swordsmen would be better, Your Majesty,' he said.

'We sent the best of them away,' the king replied.

He tried to move suddenly as he spoke, but Gabriel was ready for him. He watched the young man swing and lifted his blade to let them ring together. To his astonishment, the royal weapon passed right through his own, as if the steel was just clay. Gabriel had to pivot sharply on one heel to avoid the sweep of the blade ending in his ribs.

Yet whatever the magic of the sword, the wielder was still little more than a boy. Gabriel found himself holding the stub of a blade, just four inches from the hilt. With a shrug, he pushed it into the king's neck.

The young man stared at him in shock. Gabriel reached out and took the Yuan sword as the king's hand opened and life fled.

'Thank you. It is a fine blade.'

As Gabriel sat on the throne with the royal sword across his knees, he frowned to himself. It was oddly disappointing. The meeting hall was empty except for the few he had brought to that place. He shook his head, dissatisfied. He had been a long time in the grey land. Happiness was elusive. Still, he had to seek it out, like prising a sea urchin from a rock. Beyond the spikes and injuries, the flesh would still be sweet and good. He looked up at the thought, seeing the young woman he had brought to the great hall. She too was marked in blood, with spatters of it right across her dress. Her eyes were dark with horror at all she had seen that day.

Gabriel breathed out, relaxing into the chair.

'Come here,' he said. 'I will have the royal dressmakers replace that rag.'

He watched as she came forward, as if held by strings only she could see. As she reached him, she sank down on the steps, so that her dress spread around her. She sat with her head bowed.

Gabriel looked at her, seeing the beauty that had caught his attention on the street. His wife's name had been Laila, but that did not seem to suit her. He thought back to the queen of his day.

'I will call you Song,' he said. 'It was once a royal name, a royal house. Does it please you?'

She used the sleeve of her dress to wipe her nose and tears away. After a beat, she nodded. He smiled, satisfied.

'Good. This is the first day, my dear. You'll see some changes now . . .'

A note sounded and was gone. He hesitated. Neither Thomas nor Sanjin had reacted, but the fool on the leash had turned like a dog to its master. Gabriel blinked. It had not so much been a sound as a throb in the air, a pulse, or a call. It had come from the west, impossibly far away. He rubbed his face, suddenly weary.

'Thomas? Summon the court. I think I will speak to them before we eat. And send for a barber to shave me.'

10

Militia

Taeshin stood on a grey hillside strewn with loose rocks. Nothing grew in that place, while below on the plain, two vast armies clashed. He watched in awe and resignation. This then, was death.

Other men had been nearby when he opened his eyes. Without a word to him, they had walked down to join the ranks of the armies below, taking up fallen shields and swords. Taeshin did not know why he had not, nor why he still dreamed of the world he had known. He remained, unable to go on or back, in a place of grey dust, waiting. When he clenched his eyes and his fists, the sounds began to fade and he was no longer on that hill above the plain. If he strained until he trembled, he could sense another place in the darkness, where frightened eyes watched him walk back and forth.

Gabriel paced in the light of candles. Two hundred men and women had been rounded up in the night to stand before him. Some still sobbed, while the rest were silent and watchful, prepared to wait for whatever they would hear. Most people could not be shepherds, he thought. They were willing to endure hard work and cold winters to feed their families. That was who they were. It should not matter to most of them who sat on the throne, not beyond a few close friends and blood relations of the king.

'My name is Gabriel Hernan Cortez,' he said to them. 'I was once ambassador to this city, oh, beyond the memories of . . .'

He paused and waved the words away. They watched him like cows waiting to be slaughtered, he realised. He had seen that once, when he was a boy and slaughterhouses had run all day and night. The animals had stared in the darkness when he'd raised his torch. They had the blackest of eyes, he remembered. The people in that hall had the same look in the candlelight, as if they saw death.

'What matters tonight is that I defeated the Yuan in combat. However you choose your kings, that should suffice for most of you. I am willing to toe the line against any champion you wish to bring, but until then, I . . .'

He broke off again as he heard the same sound that had thumped through the air earlier that day. None of those assembled to hear him reacted to it.

'What lies in that direction . . . ?' Gabriel asked them.

No one dared reply and he was on the verge of losing his temper when the young woman kneeling at his feet spoke.

'The west, Your Majesty. The realm.'

He shook his head.

'Beyond that, further. I sense something far off . . . What lies beyond the realm in this age? Does Spain still stand? Or Rome?'

The names meant nothing to them and he frowned. The woman he had named Song could only raise her empty hands in confusion.

'My lord, what could lie beyond the realm?'

Gabriel blinked at her in disbelief.

'Truly? You have lost a great deal, my dear, whether you know it or not. Any of you? What nations are to the west?'

A man raised his head in the crowd, seeing the monster who had killed his king. He spoke with thick hatred.

'There is a city named Darien some thousands of miles west. A realm as great as this one, so it is said. Perhaps you should seek it out.'

Gabriel chuckled.

'Well done. I had begun to think there was no spirit of defiance in any of you! How the rest of you cower! I should make you my servant, boy.'

'I would not serve you,' the man replied. He stood with his hand on his sword, ready to be attacked.

Gabriel took a deep breath and released it, feeling all tension leave him.

'I have seen enough blood today. I summoned you merely to say this: go about your business. Make bread in the kitchens. Tend the royal horses. Make cloth, wash, mend – do whatever it is you all do in the royal household. But do it for me. There, I have said it all. Return to your duties.'

They began to stream out, their faces showing desperate relief. Gabriel watched them for a time and turned to Thomas and Sanjin. The latter's foot had been wrapped in fresh bandages, but it was already showing a red spot the size of a coin. He could feel Sanjin's anger as their eyes met. Gabriel knew very well that the man wanted him to heal it. It had become a test of will between them.

'Did either of you feel that, before?' Gabriel said.

Thomas shook his head and Sanjin shrugged.

'Where is the fool?'

Thomas jerked his head and Gabriel saw the last of the returnees had been roped to a choir stall like a dog. The fool's trousers were dark with urine and as he saw Gabriel looking at him, he beamed.

'His mind has gone,' Thomas said. 'I don't know if he could even be healed now. It might be better to put him out of his misery.'

The fool shook with laughter, making a 'shee shee' sound that echoed unpleasantly from the stone ribs above. Slowly, he raised his hand and pointed west.

Riding three hundred miles had brought Hondo a sense of mental clarity, if not peace. He watched the crowd with no sign of the turbulence that troubled him. The city of Shi-ang was a distant place to those who lived in those hills, made real by annual visits of tithe and tally men from the capital. Only the schoolteacher had been born near to Shi-ang, Hondo had been told. They seemed to think that was a mark of high status. The rest had lived and bred in those same farms and fields for the passage of centuries.

Their faces were a little longer than the people of home, the eyes deep-set and darkened by long lashes, so that a few of the women were almost presentable. Yet they had unfurled a woven image of the Yuan king and laid a long feast table in a meadow for his champions. They too were of the nation. Hondo only wished he could feel as they felt, without his constant need to reflect and examine. To live a simple, rustic life! Hondo knew he would envy them when he was a thousand miles away. At that moment, however, he found them intensely annoying.

Hondo sensed another villager turn to look at him in

delight, seeking out some shared joy. He had seen the same impulse at weddings and the births of healthy children. There was no harm in it, he reminded himself. Joy was a fragile thing, but it could overwhelm a man.

Whenever those seeking that connection actually met his eyes, they looked away immediately. It hurt him when it happened, like a sliver of ice pushed into his soul. Yet he could not pretend to fellow feeling he did not share! He could not laugh, not when he knew his eyes remained as cold as he did. Other men flinched from him if he aped their roars and bantering talk. They sensed a falseness, an awareness that watched them still.

He wondered if the twins felt the same, though as they hardly ever spoke, it was difficult to tell what those two thought about anything. Hondo had accepted them as travelling companions, but the pair were so self-contained that he thought he would never truly know them. It was a reserve he could respect. Some men were made for cold-ness, he thought. It was as much the nature of a man as desire in the presence of beauty. If anything separated man from . . .

Hondo's train of thought came to a halt as Bosin came around the corner with one of the twins on his shoulders. The twin clamped Bosin's head so hard with his legs that the big man had gone a bright red, but he still staggered on through the delighted crowd.

The village blacksmith was some way behind on the road, bearing his own twin and doing his best to catch up. Hondo sighed to himself. He had never met anyone quite like the giant swordsman before. He was not sure he was enjoying the experience. The crowd were chanting Bosin's name, Hondo realised. They had asked for a test of strength with the local man and Hondo had been framing a polite refusal when Bosin agreed and heaved one of the twins to his shoulders. It had been fairly chaotic after that, with the people of the village in fits of laughter as they set off.

The two pairs had run to a distant oak tree and back. Some of the village had gone with the staggering blacksmith to urge on their man. Hondo had seen with some surprise that at least as many cheered for Bosin even against their own. The big warrior seemed to invite laughter, but it was without rancour. Hondo shook his head. He would never understand it. Some men found each meeting with another took a certain effort, a slight strain that could exhaust them over the passage of a day. Others, like Bosin, seemed to be invigorated by the same contact with others. There was no artifice involved. Bosin liked people. They sensed it and liked him in return. That was all there was to it.

The finish line was a horse trough in the centre of the square. Hondo wondered if he should be pleased one of the royal companions was at least winning the race, but it was hard not to begrudge the morning they had lost. He watched as Bosin laid a hand in triumph on the trough. The twin on his shoulders leaped down and bowed to all points of the compass, punching the air and launching flying kicks to roars of the crowd. A great luncheon had been assembled on tables in the open air, ready for their return. The entire village had the air of a harvest festival, or a wedding. They would certainly not forget the arrival of the four masters. Hondo wondered if they would be able to recall his name when they told the story of the race for generations to come. Sourly, he rather doubted it.

Bosin and the twin – though whether it was Hi or Je, Hondo could not tell – went back to clap the blacksmith home. Bosin was still bright red in the face and pouring with sweat, but he roared and chanted with the rest, gesturing to the trough. The second twin was just as animated, pulling his legs up into a crouch and balancing on the blacksmith's shoulders like a monkey.

The poor villager was near dead on his feet from the run. A mile there and back with a man on his shoulders had been a fine test of endurance. Hondo admired the blacksmith's spirit when he straightened up and walked the last few paces with something like dignity, laying his hand on the stone trough to a great shout from the crowd. Hondo watched Bosin embrace the fellow and yell something into his ear as the second twin leaped down and turned cartwheels and somersaults.

Bosin headed for the feasting table. He had spotted a roast pig and felt as if he could eat the entire thing himself. He came to a skidding halt when he saw Hondo.

'There you are!' Bosin said.

Hondo had to steel himself not to step back as Bosin advanced on him. The man's sheer size never failed to make him nervous. To his horror, Bosin tried to reach around him and pick him up. Hondo had to strike with a knuckle into the elbow joint, hard enough to numb the entire arm.

To his astonishment, Bosin did not seem to notice and heaved him into the air like a child.

'Put me down, ox,' Hondo said, flushing. 'I will not be handled.'

'Let them see you!' Bosin said, laughing. 'This man is

the greatest sword of Shiang!' he cried to the crowd. 'The sword saint!'

Hondo gripped one of the hands that held him, turning it hard against the joint so that Bosin grunted with sudden pain and surprise.

'Put me *down*,' Hondo said.

The big man did so, rubbing his wrist with the other hand. Hondo saw the smiles fade around him and he was suddenly angry with them all.

'I wish to meditate in my room. Well done, Master Bosin. It was a fine race.'

To say a word more would be to unleash a bitter tirade, Hondo could feel it. So he clamped his jaw shut and bowed to his three companions. The twins looked crestfallen, he saw. That gave him some satisfaction at least.

Little by little, the crowd fell silent as Hondo walked through them. He felt a cold anger simmering in him at Bosin. The man seemed to have no sense of dignity, for himself or anyone else. In quieter moments, Hondo might have envied it. At that point, he felt nothing more than humiliation – and as every man knew, humiliation was brother to rage. He turned his back on them and tried not to hear when they began to roar Bosin's name once more.

Hondo had covered fifty miles that day and he was no longer a young man. He tried to meditate, but when the twins came back to their cots in the little room above the tavern, they found him snoring softly. Hi and Je looked to one another in private communication then, their eyes bright with the evening and with wine.

*

Gabriel woke to find the lady he had taken as his mistress trying on a new dress. It seemed Song understood how to make the palace servants leap to do her bidding. They ran at her command and pinned and stitched as she directed. From the king's bed, Gabriel lay and watched her, wondering what he had wrought. Taking her from her guards had been an expression of power rather than desire, at least at first. He'd been wary of sudden lusts after so long in the grey land. Yet she had come to his bed willingly enough the night before. He'd expected tears, but she'd surprised him, pressing him down and sitting astride. He'd let her pin his arms for a time and when he'd tired of that, he had been gentler than he'd planned to be. When he'd slept at last, it was with flashes of terror that he might awake in the other place, with all pleasures stolen and only eternity as a comfort. He'd clawed the air, he remembered, but been drawn down even so. As always, his dreams had been terrible. Yet the sun had risen and he had opened his eyes to industry and bustling servants. Song had brought something like order back to the royal rooms.

He raised himself up on his elbows and scratched his side, seeing flakes of dried blood come loose. Gabriel grimaced at that. He was not a savage. In his first life, he had always been a fastidious man, preferring to wash two or three times a day. Yesterday had been for death and killing. Today he would bathe and make love to his mistress. He would find a clean set of armour and take up the wonderful sword King Yuan-Choji had wielded. Perhaps he would ride in the royal gardens. It had been a long time since he'd known simple pleasures, or anything but war. Gabriel could smell grass and flowers, though such things . . . He jerked as he felt the pulse beat through the air once again. He knew the location of west in that moment.

His mood darkening, Gabriel leaped naked from the bed, ignoring the squeaks and scurrying of servants as they dashed out of the rooms.

'Lady Song, where is Thomas?'

'At your door, Gabriel,' she replied. 'I will fetch him.'

There was no fear in her then, but only a sort of slyness, like a cat with blood on its whiskers. Gabriel realised she reminded him of his first wife, who had run off with one of his captains. He wondered if this one would be more trust-worthy, or whether he had chosen poorly once more. A man had patterns, he thought. Good or bad, his patterns made him what he was.

He felt the pulse thump through him again, as if the air moved without sound. It was not a pleasant sensation. It was a summons, an awareness. Or an awakening. He felt a string being tugged in his chest, not as pain, but as if the very matter of him was being drawn away. He wanted in that moment just to set out. To take a horse and the Yuan sword and answer the note that called him.

Thomas entered and dropped to one knee. The man seemed content in his new role, though Gabriel could see he was a thinker. Not all men desired to lead. Some were happy to be second or third. He hoped Thomas was one of those. Gabriel did not want to kill him. And, of course, he was not completely sure he could.

'Thomas,' Gabriel said. 'Have you felt these . . . beats in the air?'

'I have,' Thomas said. Gabriel closed his eyes in relief.

He'd wondered if he was going mad, like the fool. 'Last night and just now. What do you think they are?'

'We were brought back with a stone, Thomas. Power calls to power.'

Gabriel knew he was correct as he said the words. Whatever the stone had been that Lord Ran had used, the threads of others lay to the west. Stones called to stones – and he and Thomas carried one within them. Gabriel sensed he could ignore it; the question was whether he wanted to.

'If I had another stone,' he said slowly, 'and Lord Ran to help me, I could bring back men I trusted in life.'

He spoke warily, testing the thoughts. He had returned to the world just the day before and he had been king for less than twelve hours. Too many things had happened quickly and he knew he needed time to settle and consider.

'Has Sanjin said anything?' he asked. 'He was behind you, when we came through. The fool came behind him. Perhaps it is as simple as that, Thomas. I came first, so I am the strongest.'

Gabriel shrugged. There was so much he did not know. For all his new speed and power, he was as a new-born child.

He and Thomas looked up as the royal tailor entered the room and knelt, ushering a dozen servants into Gabriel's presence. The new king of Shiang stood naked before them all, untroubled by it as he remembered a line of poetry he had once known. It was good to be alive that day . . . but to be young, oh to be *young*, was very heaven.

*

High on the walls of the city, the wind was constant and exhilarating. Tellius clapped a captain of the guards on the shoulder. The man had done well, though of course it was at the orders of his master, Lord Bracken. One thing Tellius had discovered about the Twelve Families – they could argue whether the sun set in the east or the west, but when they agreed, when they *moved*, they moved fast.

The defences of Darien had first to be broken before they could be rebuilt. All along the outer wall, stones were being gently prised apart, while new stocks came by river, on barges from the Woodville quarries. New fortunes were being made, with careful accounting of all of it, Tellius was certain. There would be new debts and favours owed by the time the king's review of the armed forces of Darien was at an end.

Tellius pressed his thumbs into his eyes, seeing green lights flash. He was weary and he was not a young man. Yet he had somehow become the foreman of the project, with a hundred different requests for attention and decisions that needed to be made reaching him each day. He looked along the crown of the great wall as it began to curve away in the distance. The truth was, the review was long overdue. It should have been something they'd begun after the attack two years before, but there was no point regretting that lapse then.

All across the city, defences were being catalogued and marked as obsolete, or missing, or in dire need of new funds and labour. The results had meant a fortune in gold coming out of the royal treasury, as well as every noble house. The king could draw on the Twelve Families to the limit of their wealth. That was the ancient compact that served them all, and if they grumbled, they could not deny the results of it, nor whisper that the money was vanishing in corruption. The new walls going up were those of a fortress in pale stone, with massive ridges and buttresses.

Not every citizen was delighted by the work, nor every head of the great houses. Those families who depended on trade made constant complaint as it was choked off in favour of supplies. Others had lost the labour of their key people while they were trained to fight outside the walls, on the great plain by the river. Tellius had begun referring to it as the Campus, after Lord Canis told him an ancient city had employed a field of war to train its citizens, a Campus Martius.

From that height, he could see them, the people of Darien, looking small against the vastness of the world. Yet they marched and halted and presented arms. Tellius shook his head in frustration as he recalled the influence Lord Canis had played in the choice of weapons. The men learning field tactics and battle commands on the Campus were armed with only swords and daggers, or long spears. They held shields in their hands and drilled with them as their forefathers had done. Tellius had pleaded for entire gun regiments, but that was the one skirmish he had lost, though it might prove the most important. The Regis family owned the workshops – and it seemed Lord Regis was a close ally of Lord Canis.

As Tellius watched, a tiny number of men revealed their weapons with a puff of white smoke and, some time after, a rippling crack of sound. He shook his head in irritation. It was not enough to arm small teams in such a way. He had seen the new guns actually used in a street battle, the air alive with bullets and stinging grains. In that moment, he had seen the end of swordsmen on the field, he was certain. The very idea that an army could approach another on foot now that guns existed was a sort of madness. He clenched his jaw. When challenged, Lord Canis had pointed to bows and crossbows, saying those would suffice for common men. Tellius had been forced to concede the point in open debate, as he was not allowed to strangle a lord in front of all the others. Yet he knew every single subject who could afford the rising prices had an order in for a pistol as a private purchase. Other workshops were opening to repair and service the pistols. More than a few were on the cusp of making their own – and it wouldn't be long before the Hart family entered the market. Whether Canis and Regis knew it or not, many in the new militia would be armed with more than blade or bow when the time came.

Looking away from those training, Tellius turned to the darker streets that ran below. He could see faces in the crowd as bustling men and women went about putting bread on the table each evening. He knew them, Tellius reminded himself. He was one of them. He did not always like them, but by the Goddess, he understood how they thought. Perhaps Lord Canis was right to fear the common use of guns, but that was a problem for the future. Tellius could still remember the slow horror of the wave that crashed against his city. He believed in the Forza Stone and what it had shown him. Nothing else mattered as much – not the sensibilities of Lord Canis, not even the unrest that might one day lie ahead. They had to survive till the following spring first. He recalled Lord Hart had said something about difficulties in securing finance for gun shops under his own name. The Harts were friendly with the Sallets and proud of the part they had played in the defence of Darien. Tellius nodded to himself. Perhaps he could persuade Win to cover a loan the banks would not. Odds were, it would be a good investment.

Shouts sounded on his left, so that Tellius turned and blinked at a sight that never failed to amaze him. Lord Bracken had fashioned harnesses for his dogs, so that they could carry the tools and equipment for the men working on the walls. As a new shift began, the animals appeared in a flood, racing along with jingling packs on their shoulders. That they were hunting dogs was not in doubt. It still took an effort of will for Tellius to pat one as it sat with tongue lolling, looking as if it laughed at him. They were muscular beasts with wide heads and powerful jaws, but Lord Bracken controlled them in some way with the stone he wore on his arm. It looked as natural as breathing to him, and Tellius could not deny the animals were useful. They were so fast! He had spent too many years on the wrong side of the law to ever be comfortable in the presence of such animals. It was just too easy to imagine them chasing one of the old gang through the streets.

As Tellius watched, the animals were relieved of their burdens and ran off once again, as if they raced one another. Tellius wondered if Lord Bracken's dogs enjoyed their lives. He suspected they did. Their owner was large and brash. Being accompanied by a yelping pack of hounds made him harder to dislike, in Tellius' opinion.

He made his way to the steps and looked across the city to where the Hart estate had its gates. He would see Lord

Hart that very evening to guarantee the loan, he decided, whatever was needed. Lady Forza would surely come in on the deal. Either way, it did not sit well with Tellius to have only the poorest denied the new weapons. He had been poor. Even if the new regiments still officially carried swords, it would not hurt to have a pistol on each belt as well.

'Master Tellius! One of the river barges has run aground. Lady Woodville says you must come.'

Tellius swore under his breath as the house messenger found him. There was another one in different livery racing along the wall. Damn them. He could not find a moment to himself.

'I will be there in an hour,' he called over his shoulder.

The messenger set his jaw and followed him down the steps.

'My mistress said I was not to let you out of my sight, Master Tellius. Lady Woodville says you did not come as you promised you would yesterday.'

'Lady Woodville can . . .' Tellius began. He forced a smile. 'She can wait a little longer, I am certain.'

11

Hondo

Hondo woke with frost pinning his hair to the ground. He blew air as a stream of vapour and sighed. He hated the cold. As a young man, he could not recall even noticing it, but after he'd turned fifty, winters had seemed to grow worse and worse each year, as if the world drifted further from the sun.

Away from civilisation, he had decided it was mere vanity to continue to shave and trim his hair. The straggling beard he'd grown gave him some protection from the wind, though it itched to the point of madness. Even so, it had been the right decision. His service to the king lay in how fast and how well he could complete the task ahead of him. Hondo had been given the name of a man who had offended the honour of the king's father. Whatever this Tellius had done in his years of exile, Hondo wanted nothing more than to see him at that moment, so that he could consider the journey at an end and begin making his way home with the prisoner.

He sat up to see white first light and a thick mist lying over tended fields. The boundaries had been marked by their owner with stone walls and neat fences. This was not wild land, but a farm in the middle of nowhere, perhaps a thousand miles from Shiang. Away to the west, Hondo had no way of judging how far they had come, beyond the vaguest of guesses. The first days of good roads, regular taverns and fifty miles a stretch were long behind. His first horse had gone lame and he'd replaced it with a farmer's mare of lesser quality. The man had been almost in tears, though the mount Hondo had left him was worth a hundred in silver, perhaps more.

Bosin, of course, had pointed in satisfaction to his enormous shire horse, still plodding on while weaker mounts fell behind. The idea made him insufferable for a time, until Hondo reminded Bosin of the temple dogs of Shiang. Those animals stood almost as high as a man, but lived just eight or nine years. Terriers on the other hand, lived twice that long. Bosin had been silent for days after that. Given that the twins seemed to need only their own company and spoke hardly at all, it had been a period of silent meditation that had left Hondo feeling quite rested and prepared for whatever lay ahead.

Shiang's influence had waned over the previous few days, though there had been no clear boundary. Hondo saw it in untended trees left to be a danger to travellers, as well as different crops in the fields. These farmers no longer sent their goods to Shiang. It was just too far to keep the food fresh. Perhaps that was the natural boundary of all cities, Hondo thought, as he stretched.

No one really knew how far Darien lay beyond. Hondo had seen maps of the world that showed it by another name he could not pronounce, though the king had been certain they were one and the same. Hondo had asked the twins about it and discovered neither had troubled to view the maps. The young appeared to lack the intellectual curiosity he remembered from his own youth. It was somehow less surprising that Bosin had not checked the maps either. Nothing about that man gave an impression of careful preparation. 'What if I were killed? How would any of you find your way then?' Hondo had demanded at the beginning of their trip. Bosin had just shrugged at him and pointed west.

Honestly, the man could be infuriating. Hondo sometimes spent days imagining the giant swordsman hanging by his fingernails off a cliff, or vanishing slowly into quicksand. Hondo enjoyed constructing the last conversations, over and over. He had developed a number of favourite variations on the theme. In not one of them did he manage to save the big man from death.

The world was rather beautiful when it was trapped in frost, he thought, as he ran through morning patterns with the precision of decades of practice. More importantly, a farm meant food somewhere nearby. Hondo brushed himself down, feeling warmth begin and fade in his chest. He began to shiver again, as soon as he was still. The night's cold had sunk right into him, as it never had when he'd been young. He slapped his hands back and forth and blew air harder. He was starving, but he would be able to buy eggs at the farmhouse – and a thick piece of bacon. Perhaps even a handful of onions, if he could keep them away from Bosin.

The twins had woken and were untying their packs, ready to start a fire from the embers of the night before. Hi, or possibly Je, nodded to the sword saint in acknowledgement. For once, Bosin's snoring was muted by his own bulk, as the cold had made him curl up into a ball. The morning was peaceful and Hondo was glad to be alive. He took joy in such moments of beauty, knowing that they would come to an end.

'Don't touch your sword and you'll live,' said a voice over to the right.

Hondo looked round in astonishment as a ragged group of men raced down the slope of a hill towards them. They were still some twenty yards off and Hondo cursed himself for his inattention. He'd been too long in civilised lands! The very idea of any citizen of Shiang creeping up on the sword saint was laughable. Yet the result was that he hadn't been wary of it happening.

Hondo crossed their little campsite and booted Bosin hard in the back, making the giant grunt and ask a garbled question in his sleep. Hondo kicked him again in a temper. He no longer felt cold, he realised. Perhaps he should begin every day by kicking Bosin awake.

The half-dozen men who approached their little camp spread out in a fan formation. Only one held a sword, though the blade was spotted black with ancient rust, resistant to all polishing. Three of the others carried long-handled axes, like woodsmen, while the remaining pair held only knives in their hands. Those two jabbed the air with them, as if they could intimidate the camp with sheer effort.

The twins were ready, Hondo saw, their hands resting on the hilts of swords worth more than the ragged men would see in a lifetime. Hondo wondered if they could even understand the quality of his own blade, made for his own hand by the greatest master in Shiang. Whenever he drew the sword, it passed between lips of brass that caused a note, as if a finger rubbed the edge of a crystal glass. In Shiang, the Ling or Bell sword was as famous in its way as the man who wielded it.

Hondo kept his hands loose. These men were not worthy to hear that sound. As they came closer, he and the twins took up positions on an arc. They left a place for Bosin as the giant sat up and smacked his lips, opening one eye at a time.

'When you are ready, Master Bosin, we are being robbed,' Hondo hissed at him.

'How many are there?' Bosin replied, looking around blearily. He was about as rumpled as his own blanket, with creases across his face from his own weight as he slept.

'Six men,' Hondo snapped.

Bosin lay down once more and rolled himself into the blankets.

'Then you do not need me,' he muttered, closing his eyes.

Hondo was tempted to kick him again, but now that Bosin was awake, he was not sure how the man would react. Also, it had been like kicking a tree. He thought there was a chance he had cracked a bone in one of his toes, as he could not clench it in his boot.

'Surrender your weapons,' the leader said. 'If you do it now, you will live.'

Hondo turned to face that one. The accent had been strange, so he spoke slowly and clearly in reply.

'Are you "roadmen"? Yes? You steal from travellers?'

The fellow was not used to being questioned so openly. He looked over Hondo's padded coat with a sort of longing. It was clearly warmer than his own. He saw too the

147

perfect black scabbard, with an orange tassel. The man who wore it was bearded and a little unkempt. There was frost in his hair.

The thief felt his confidence unravelling and his anger grew. He jabbed his sword at Hondo, inching closer. His ragged companions went with him, step by step, like a pack of dogs closing on prey. Hondo had rarely seen a more pitiful crew. He had been warned of such bands of brigands while he had been in Shiang. They were said to be a terror to travellers in the wild lands beyond the influence of that city. The reality was actually a little disappointing.

'Put that sword away, young man,' Hondo said. 'It will win you nothing from us. However, I am willing to pay you for directions to Darien. Earn a coin rather than steal one, yes? How close are we to the city?'

The leader of the thieves blinked at the offer, sensing that something was wrong. The man speaking as if to a child appeared quite unworried by the weapons they carried. The other two ... The thief saw they were twins. They were smiling in the oddest way, both dressed the same, like a mirror. And the last! Even curled up and grumbling about all the talking, the man was about the size of a brown bear. The thief had no interest in seeing him stand up. He made a decision.

'Very well,' he said. He sheathed his sword with a clumsiness that made Hondo wince. 'Pax in the camp, lads. We'll earn our coin this morning.'

'It won't be as much as they have with them,' one of the others grumbled.

Hondo lost patience. It was one thing to spare scavengers, just as he might ignore wild dogs. He was a swordsman after all, not a butcher. It was quite another to have to listen to them bicker as if he had not just granted them their lives. Hondo gestured to the twins and one of them strode forward through the thieves. The twin moved like smoke, startling them. For one who had never seen a Mazer swordsman before, it might have seemed like a cat running along a branch, a balance so perfect it could make a grown man stand in awe.

The fellow who had spoken was dead a moment later. The twin had drawn and cut him in a single blow. As Hondo watched in silent appreciation, Hi, or perhaps Je, cleaned the blade on the fellow's coat, then polished it with a second cloth before replacing it in the scabbard, protected once more. Even the touch of a bare finger could spoil the mirror finish of the steel if left untended. A blade was not just for a lifetime, but centuries, if treated with respect.

Hondo bowed to the twin as he returned, honouring his skill. The young man flushed, delighted by praise from the sword saint as he rejoined his brother. The rest of the thieves still stood transfixed and horrified.

'There,' Hondo said, as if the entire event had been merely an interruption. 'Now, without further argument, please. You know of Darien? You can direct us?'

The leader of the thieves had paled at seeing one he called a friend bleeding into the frozen ground. The frost vanished there as the blood touched it, he noticed. He seemed a little dazed, but when Hondo raised his hand, he babbled a response.

'My father knew it well. He met traders from the west. He said it lies six hundred miles past the mountains

149

there, on the banks of a great river. It's a trading city, my lord. Once you are across the highest peaks, you'll surely meet merchants who call it home.'

'Thank you,' Hondo said, though he had hoped to hear it was closer. Even so, he fished in his pouch for a low-value piece of silver and passed it into the man's hands. 'Go on your way now, gentlemen. Know that you have earned an honest coin.'

They trooped off like boys dismissed from class. Hondo watched them go and turned in irritation to Bosin as the man gave up on sleep and sat up. He saw Hondo's expression and shrugged.

'What? You won't say you needed me against a few skinny thieves?'

'It was not a matter of need, Master Bosin, it was a matter of discipline and my orders.'

'The king sent me to Darien, Master Hondo. He did not say I was to be your servant. I don't remember that. Do you remember that? You were there as well. Did he say that? Did he say, "Oh yes, don't forget, Bosin, Hondo is your master on the trip"? When was that?'

Hondo controlled his temper with difficulty. He was suddenly no longer hungry. Bosin watched the sword saint move stiffly to saddle his horse, anger in every gesture. The big man was already feeling guilty for what he had said, but he didn't know how to call it back. Instead, Bosin stood in sullen silence until Hondo mounted and rode on, clearly determined to leave him behind in his bad temper.

The twins looked nervously to Bosin as he stood there. He sighed and waved them after Hondo.

'Go on. Look after the old bastard. I'll catch up when I've had breakfast.'

Gabriel felt ill. There was no better way to describe it, as he had no words for the discomfort he felt. It was not quite a pain, but almost a sense of loss, as if he had watched a child die and each moment was the anniversary . . . He gave up with a wave of his hand. For weeks he had ruled a terrified populace in Shiang. At his order, the noble families and great estates had come to prostrate themselves before him. Those who had refused he had visited himself, leaving the walls of their homes daubed in blood. It had been necessary only twice, though he had made an example of a third in the city, so the Fool could have somewhere to live and be tended. The other estates had gone to Thomas and Sanjin, his gift to them.

Gabriel leaned on a balcony, looking out at the administrative buildings they called the Hub. He had thought he would have those cleared for the view, but he had planned many things that remained undone. He gripped the stone and felt the sill crack, so that his palms were marked with dust. He had been given much, but it came with a price that was driving him to madness.

Even as he had the thought, he felt a slight passage in the air, the beating heart that seemed to eat at his self-control each time he felt it. He'd read once of a torture that was no more than a drip of water landing on a man's forehead, while he was bound beneath and unable to move. Gabriel had laughed at the idea of it. He had known torture in many forms and when he compared the slow drip of water with his knives and irons and his room of little ease, he thought it a foolish thing.

The reality was different, he knew by then. Over the previous week, he'd even had an iron bed made to test the water-drop torture on a royal guardsman. So far, the man had lasted three days, but he'd begun screaming that morning and it did not look as if he would stop. All from a drop of water, or a call he would not answer.

Gabriel clenched his fist and felt a sting as a flake of white marble sliced his palm. He held it up in something like wonder, seeing the extraordinary brightness of blood against the paler dust. Blood was the only true red – and only then when it was full of life. It darkened as life drained away. It became brown and then black, then the dust of the grey land. Gabriel shuddered at the thought and then again, when the strange thrum in the air touched him.

How many times had it been that morning? His great fear was that they were coming more often. He told himself it was mere imagination, but if there was any truth in it, he knew he could not withstand the beats for ever. Like the water drops, each one was nothing, but together they would bring his walls down, he could feel it. Water wormed its way into foundations, so that castles and even cities fell.

He turned back to a room where his ministers waited for him. They included men and women taken from the street and made to wear the robes of a noble house. It had amused him to do it, to see the light of greed or just possibility come to their faces as he gave them more than they had ever dreamed. He thought those common men and women would be loyal to him, if only to protect what they had.

What a pleasure it was to lead! People were such simple creatures, in the end. They needed food and warmth and family. They wanted power over others. The men wanted a harem; the women . . . well, who knew, really? His first wife had said women wanted babies and security. Give them that and they would ask for nothing else. He wondered if that could be true, though. His new queen seemed not to need him at all, now that he had given her power. She had gathered an army of servants to tend her, seeking out old enemies around the city to lie in the mud and be walked upon. One of them had drowned just that morning, he'd been told. He liked her, but she could be vicious, there was no doubt about that.

'Gentlemen, ladies, I thought some sort of ball might entertain the families of Shiang . . .' He paused as the *thump* ran through him. Of course, they felt nothing, but just stared at him with bovine expressions or obsequious smiles. He gathered his thoughts and tried again.

'There are trading cities further to the east. I thought I might invite their ambassadors to my coronation here. The ball could be' – *thump* – '. . . an event to mark a new reign, and a new royal house.

'There are no riots any longer in Shiang. Now that I have brought back execution for treason in all its forms, there is no unrest against my rule. I trust that will continue. I thought to hold the ball at the new moon' – *thump* – '. . . Damn it! None of you feel that movement in the air?'

They looked at him in terror, he realised, with the whites

of their eyes showing. They already feared him, but this was the dread of the insane, of a different order entirely. He shook his head to clear it, forcing his thoughts back on course.

'It is my intention to make Shiang a great trading city once more.' *Thump*. 'We have too long looked inward.' *Thump*. 'Hellfire! What? Would you draw back from me? Perhaps you should be afraid! Thump thump thump! Can none of you hear it?'

'I hear it, brother,' Thomas said wearily from the doorway. 'Sanjin does as well now. The Fool is tormented by it. He does nothing but shriek at his servants like a cat caught in a trap. He gets worse each day. We all do.'

Gabriel raised hands like claws, showing the red blood that still seeped from one of them. He had not bothered to heal or clean it.

'It's getting harder to bear,' he said. 'Not stronger, but...'

'But more often, Gabriel, yes. There is no doubt any more.'

Both of them winced as the pulse went through them again, the tugging, deep in their stomachs.

'If I leave Shiang, they will forget me in a month,' Gabriel said. 'They will undo all I have done.' *Thump*. 'You know it.'

Thomas shrugged.

'I have enjoyed living as a lord, but I cannot go on like this. We'll win it back, perhaps, or find some other place. It is still better than the grey land, brother. Remember that.'

Gabriel nodded slowly. He looked around at the lords and commoners all staring at him.

'Very well. It seems I must leave my throne and this city

behind. Bring Sanjin and the Fool. There are horses here. I will answer this call. I'll *face* whatever there is waiting for me — and if there are stones, I will take them all.'

He and Thomas both tensed for the pulse, but there was nothing. They looked at one another in wild surmise. Thomas nodded.

'It seems you have made the right decision, brother.'

As the sun rose to noon, the king of Shiang rode along the west way to the great gate. Gabriel's horse bore packs of food and he wore the royal sword on his hip. Thomas rode at his side and Sanjin kept an eye on the Fool and Lord Ran as they rode behind, though he had complained bitterly at being given such a menial task. His foot still bled. Gabriel was so relieved to be heading west he had considered healing it, but changed his mind at the last moment. Perhaps he'd reconsider if Sanjin ever showed a little grace and good manners, instead of the constant scowl.

Few in the city knew they were leaving. Crowds began to gather even so as the horsemen headed for the gate and were recognised. One or two cheered, but most of them were silent. They would not jeer or call out, such was their fear of the new king. Yet they could glower and hope the man would know. That was all they dared to do.

Gabriel ignored the sullen crowd, riding with a straight back. His new guards looked nervous as he passed them. They had not been told the king was leaving the city and some of them feared what might happen when the news spread. Gabriel had employed some as executioners as well. They would surely be torn apart without his protection.

There would be violence and fire in his wake. The thought made Gabriel smile as he reached the gate.

'Taeshin! Oh, it is you!' Marias called.

A young woman stepped up to his stirrup and touched his boot as if she thought he had to be an apparition. Gabriel was tempted to kick her away, or just dig in his heels and ride on. Somehow, he could not bring himself to do it and drew his mount to a halt with a squeeze of the reins.

'I do not know you,' he said.

'It is Marias! Your slave, Taeshin! Oh, what have they done to you? Taeshin?'

Gabriel sensed a flash of awareness, there and gone in an instant. It frightened him and he wanted to ride on. Yet he was held in that spot as if rooted in stone.

'Let me come with you, Taeshin. Please. Wherever you are going. I thought you were dead. I was certain. Please, Taeshin.'

She began to weep. Gabriel closed his eyes for a moment and summoned his will. The young woman had clearly known the one who owned the body he had been given. Gabriel had hardly thought of him from the moment of first awakening. She was beautiful – and competent to have survived a month without her master. She would be useful to him on the trail, to cook and tend the animals. Gabriel shook his head once more, confused. He had left Song behind, to whatever fate befell her, but he would take a slave out of Shiang? It was madness.

'Get up behind me,' he said, his voice hoarse as if from lack of use.

Perhaps it was a whim, but he was heading out into the

wilderness and ... no, he had no explanation. Thomas and Sanjin looked at him as if he had lost his wits. The Fool made his 'shee shee' sound, though whether he laughed or wept was, as ever, hard to say. Lord Ran just looked stern, though he watched everything they did. At least the man knew by then that he could not run. Both Gabriel and Thomas were as fast across open ground as a galloping horse.

Gabriel felt the woman's hands slide around his waist and the pressure of her head on his back as she embraced him. It was oddly comforting as he rode through the gate and left Shiang behind. He was going to the source of the call that hurt him. He was going to Darien and whatever waited for him there.

Taeshin opened his eyes on the grey land, unchanging, though armies clashed below. He had been afraid to walk down the hill before. He had no desire to join those serried ranks that slaughtered one another and then reappeared each morning as the sky brightened. The sun did not rise in that place. There was nothing as joyous as warmth, nor even the bite of winter. Neither did he feel hunger or thirst, though at times he longed for those signs of life.

Grim and silent, he watched the armies gather. Officers rode up and down the lines on both sides, exhorting the men to greater efforts than before. Taeshin could hear them shout and answer.

It was not always the same, he had begun to see. Two great kings met on that field every day to fight. Whatever the result, no matter which side was triumphant in the evening camps, they still trooped out to fight again the next day.

He closed his eyes, but no colours came, no flashes of strange scenes he had never lived. Of Marias in the wilderness, of the tiger named

Gabriel who walked in his flesh. Taeshin shook his head, feeling once more a surge of anger that anyone could even consider hurting Marias. That was a true emotion, he realised, a part of himself that was not of the grey land. It warmed him like the sun rising would have done. He decided once again that he would not walk down to the battle, not that day.

12

High Pass

The funeral of Lady Elizabeth Forza took place a week after her death, while snow lay on the walls of Darien and winter drove hard across the city. Peals sounded in every church spire, muffled by cloth pads held to the bells, so the notes were as short as life. Dressed in black against the frosts, the funeral procession looked unusually sombre. The heads of the Twelve Families were present, including Lady Forza's eldest son, Reno. He was a stern and handsome man in his forties, with a touch of grey. Unfortunately, as they all knew, he might have inherited his mother's house, but he lacked the talent to use the Forza Stone. One of his younger sisters was working with it, but it might as well have been basalt or red porphyry for her. Lady Forza had written down all she had seen in her visions, but it was always some variant on the black wave breaking over the city. As Lady Sallet had noted wryly to Tellius, they were a long way from the sea. Whatever was coming, whatever destruction awaited, it could still be almost anything.

The coffin was carried by the heir and five other men Tellius did not know, all wearing matching black coats with dark red collars. The snow gave the scene dignity somehow, though he hoped they would not slip and drop a lady he had come to like. Tellius shivered suddenly as he followed them, wondering if her spirit had brushed past him, or whether it was just his own advancing age. He looked up as he and Win passed under a bridge packed with Forza staff, there to give silent honour to their mistress. The man he had once been could not help think it would be a good time for thieves to be about. One lad to cause a commotion, perhaps by dropping something from the bridge, then half a dozen more to dip and snatch. It would be almost too easy. No guard could chase thieves in the snow, not with a chance of catching them.

Nothing dropped from above as the procession of lords passed by. Tellius was almost disappointed. He could not lose the frown that had settled on him as they made their way into the church of the Goddess and bowed to her effigy. It was one Tellius had always liked, a rather benign version, more maternal than the usual young lover capable of leading a man to destruction as easily as joy. He nodded to her, exactly as he might have done to an old friend.

The city was quiet for the passing. Perhaps the snow and cold played a part in that, but Tellius knew Lady Forza had been respected, even loved. She'd used her wealth to invest in businesses – and one thing you could say, she'd had a flair for it. Even the new Hart gunsmiths looked like they would make a fortune. Her son would never be short of a few coins, once the full scope of his inheritance became clear. Tellius still hoped to retain Reno Forza as the primary donor for the new militias training across the city and the Campus outside it. The costs of feeding and equipping eighty thousand men were simply staggering. With a sniff, Tellius only hoped they would be enough.

He had not forgotten the sense of helplessness he'd felt as he'd watched the black wave break over the city. Whatever it meant, he would rather lose a fortune and six months of his life preparing for nothing, than be caught with his trousers round his ankles when the end of the world came. Put like that, it was not such a grand ambition. New Hart pistols were coming out of the workshops Sallet and Forza had funded, finding their way to the regiments and private customers in boxes of grease and straw. It made Tellius smile to think of it. Unlike Lord Bracken and Lord Regis, he did not fear the mob. In his heart of hearts, he was the mob.

Tellius did not sing with the others as music swelled over them. He had grown to manhood some thousands of miles to the east. He had no half-forgotten knowledge of old songs to dredge up. His childhood prayers had been to a different god, who saw all and seemed remarkably indifferent to any of it. Tellius was not quite sure if he believed in the Goddess of Darien, but he had learned not to cross a vengeful woman and it cost him nothing to observe the forms. A world without even an attempt at a better nature was a cold sort of place, as he knew very well. The journey mattered as much as the destination and he chose to take part. He enjoyed the hymns as well. Some of them were quite rousing.

When the service was at an end, the bearers gathered around the coffin once again, all serious men of matched heights. From the church in the city, Lady Forza's body would be loaded onto a carriage and taken to a tomb on their estate, a place Tellius had never seen, but which he imagined would be very grand. He said a silent prayer for

Elizabeth Forza, wishing her well and hoping she could hear.

'Sad day,' Lord Bracken said at his shoulder.

The man was taller than Tellius and seemed pleased about that. Tellius noticed too that one of the Bracken hounds had padded up, seating itself like a statue. There was something not quite right about the way those dogs reacted, Tellius thought. Whatever control Bracken exercised over them, Tellius could never relax in their presence.

'Very sad,' he replied. 'I came to like Elizabeth. I'm only sorry I didn't know her for longer.'

'Of course. Feel the same. Still, at least we were spared her prophecy coming true. Perhaps our building of walls and training of militias scared it off, whatever it was.'

'You don't believe it can still happen?' Tellius asked.

Lord Bracken frowned down at him as if he had said something stupid.

'Old Forza said it would come with the snow, didn't she? That was what I understood. And here it is. The whole city is shivering and logs are up to fourpence each in some places. I'd say whatever she thought was going to happen has passed us by, don't you think?'

Tellius saw the man wished to be reassured. Perhaps because he had lived a harder life, it did not occur to him to try.

'No, my lord. I saw it, when I touched the stone – guided by Elizabeth. It was something savage, something pitiless coming here. And yes, there was snow on the ground. So it could come today, or tomorrow, or any time you see snow over the next few months. All Lady Forza knew was that she would not live to see the spring. There's something

162

coming for Darien in the cold, my lord. I wish it wasn't, but this funeral doesn't change a thing.'

Lord Bracken lost his conspiratorial lean and stood straighter. Tellius had the impression the dog too was looking at him in a more hostile way.

'Perhaps,' he snapped, making the word just one syllable. 'Though I wonder if you aren't a little smitten by your new position in the Families. It doesn't hurt you to be able to talk of nameless threats and have all the old ladies fanning themselves and imagining the worst, does it? I suppose our new Lord Forza will be donating a fortune to the wall fund, now his mother has passed, or was that part of your arrangement with her?'

Tellius was certain by then that the man's hound was watching him with an unnerving scrutiny. He was coldly furious at what Bracken was suggesting, but he suspected the lord knew very well how feared his animals were. There was something unnatural about the Bracken Stone, even to the fact that it could be worn. Perhaps that went some way towards explaining his overbearing manner. Tellius knew the type well and loathed it. If he took offence, Bracken would claim it was all a misunderstanding, that Tellius was merely being too sensitive. Such men lived for victories of exactly that sort. The best defence was to go on the attack, instantly and without mercy.

'My lord, I've been meaning to ask. I remember the night the city was breached two years ago. I fought alongside the Sallet contingent, against Aeris soldiers. I was under fire for an age. I do not recall seeing you there . . . ?'

He waited, with his eyebrows raised, knowing the man

would take it as it was meant. Tellius could have crowed when Bracken began to bluster, pursing his lips.

'I was not in the city that night, sir, as I'm sure you are well aware. If I had been . . .'

'Oh, I don't doubt your pets would have been useful, my lord. I think, though, that those who were not there, who did not stand to protect the city, well, perhaps they feel sometimes that the battle must be fought and refought, over and over, if you understand me? For those of us who actually were there . . . we know our worth. We know what we endured together. It is a sort of brotherhood, my lord. Now, if you will excuse me, I see Lady Sallet wishes to leave.'

He turned away from the saturnine lord and his dog, the animal softly snarling as it mirrored its master's emotions. Tellius could not help smiling in response as he went lightly down the steps.

Lady Sallet saw his expression and that of the man he had left behind.

'I hope you were not measuring your length against Bracken, my dear,' she said.

Tellius felt his mouth drop open.

'That is a . . . surprising phrase, Win. Where did you hear that?'

She shrugged.

'My father used to say it. He was a naval man. I don't . . . Oh!' She blushed and put a hand to her mouth. 'I will not be using it again, then. Still, we need his support, Tellius.'

'He is a bully . . .' Tellius murmured as he reached over to kiss her cheek. 'And he annoys me when he relies on his dogs to growl for him. He had the nerve to suggest the danger of Elizabeth's vision had passed with the snowfall.'

'He wants to believe it, Tellius. He is not the first to say that aloud this morning, believe me.'

'What of the seers?' Tellius asked, still keeping his voice low.

'No word from them. Not one glimpse in Darien of a black wave, or the city under attack. I am half-tempted to pay for scryers of memory, Tellius. To have them confirm what we saw.'

'It would make us look weak,' he said, shaking his head.

She nodded, accepting his judgement where it was most sound.

'Bracken is not the only one to voice doubts. Lord Canis is still arguing against gun regiments, though it seems the merest common sense. Regis is openly dismissive of me. I think he distrusts women. Now that Lady Forza has gone, the direct link is broken. You and I are the only witnesses to what we saw – and they will believe we stand to gain, in power, in wealth, who knows? If those other seers were not just promises and wind, we'd have lit a fire under them all by now.'

'Not one of them has the Forza Stone,' Tellius said thoughtfully. 'I have no expertise here, Win, but could we arrange for one of them to touch it? At least to try?'

He saw her pale slightly as she considered. Tellius was content to wait, knowing she understood the games of the Twelve Families better than he ever would.

'I don't think you understand even now how rare it was for Lady Forza to bring her family stone out of her estate to mine. They are objects of veneration, Tellius, especially to the subjects. The closest I can think of would be to hand a royal crown to one of them, a crown that has seen a dozen famous kings and been worn in battle. Do you see? What you are suggesting is not a small thing. Nor can I order Reno Forza to do it. He is head of his house now. If he decides to keep the Forza Stone in a vault, that is his right. Not one lord will gainsay him.'

She brushed a hand across her lips and began to pace. Tellius glanced at the guards who waited for her, extending a flat palm to tell them not to approach. He knew them well and they had accepted him. Even so, they would not let anything happen to their mistress.

'If I persuade Reno Forza . . .' she went on, 'perhaps to allow a visitor to his estate, rather than asking to move the stone again. Yet if we put seer and stone together and there is no vision, we will have vastly undermined our case. Men like Bracken, Canis and Regis would petition the king to end the training of militias, perhaps even to cease work on the walls of the city.'

'A fraud would not arrange such a test,' he murmured. 'Those who believe we are exaggerating or have some other end in mind would see that.'

'But in turn, we run the risk of seeing it all stop,' she said.

Once more, her fingers brushed across her lips. He wanted to kiss her.

'Then wait as long as we can. If the other lords strangle the funds, or begin to pull their men out of the militias and the wall teams, then we can decide. If they merely grumble, we will go on. I know what I saw, Win. I will do anything to stop that happening.'

*

Bosin was not a man to suffer in silence, Hondo had discovered. A great part of the culture of Shiang was veneration of self-discipline. By the time they reached manhood, every boy and girl had been told a thousand tales of extraordinary sacrifice. Of men who had been tricked into giving their oath and yet gone to their deaths rather than break their word, of others who came back from hell to complete a promise to a king. Still more who carried word of a battle to the royal reinforcements, though they died as they handed over the orders, so fast had they run. Duty and discipline and self-control came above all personal considerations. It was the foundation and heart-stone of their culture.

The wind actually howled at that height, low and high notes together, so that it moaned or shrieked in their ears. It carried flecks of snow or ice that stung as they struck the bare skin of the four men. That was merely pain, though Hondo feared he would be made blind and walked almost with his eyes closed, sheltering his gaze with his hand whenever he needed to look further. The way ahead was through thick snow, to the level of his knees, so that each step was an effort and sapped his strength. The white surface might even have been beautiful if it hadn't been so damned cold. Ice swirled there in patterns of shining dust. He could not feel his feet, Hondo realised, with a stab of fear. He had seen the results of frostbite before in black toes and fingers. The pain was brutal before they came off.

Bosin could also not feel his feet. Hondo knew that because the giant mentioned it every couple of paces. The big swordsman had wrapped himself in blankets, so that he could see hardly anything. He staggered along like a bear lost in a snowstorm, complaining with every step. It was infuriating. Not for the first time, Hondo wondered if Bosin had been included in the group just to get rid of him. He imagined his patron lord had been delighted to volunteer the man's name for a task that would take him from the city for months, if he ever returned at all.

'I have not eaten since this morning,' he heard Bosin say suddenly. 'My stomach is groaning like the wind. My bowels are loose and fit to burst, but I dare not stop and squat in this snow. I would freeze my cock off.'

Hondo clenched his eyes shut. The man could be crude, appallingly so at times. Hondo had already discovered the depths of filth Bosin was capable of voicing when the man had slipped and barked his shin a few days before. There was little point in asking him to stop. The constant stream of complaint seemed almost unconscious. Hondo also suspected the big man was concealing deafness, though he was not yet certain as to the degree. It didn't matter what he said on Bosin's right side, anyway. There would be no response. If he gave an order from the left, he'd sometimes catch a startled expression. Perhaps it was just the noise of the wind or the terrible cold, but he hadn't noticed Bosin favouring one ear when they'd set out.

Hondo ground his teeth together. They had not prepared well enough to cross a high pass in winter. They'd purchased thick furs in the last village, but the reality was much worse than he had imagined. Everything was white or grey and the air bit at his lips. Hondo had listened patiently to the warnings from the village hunters, but they'd had no choice. That was something he had understood better than Bosin seemed able to. They had been ordered west to Darien. If the pass truly was closed, if the shovels they carried were not enough to get through to the other side, they would be found frozen in the thaw. They could not wait until spring, as Bosin had suggested at least a dozen times. The big man had tried what he thought was subtle persuasion on the other three. When that didn't have any effect, he'd said straight out that he would rather wait until the pass was clear. Hondo had reminded him then that he was not Bosin's master, that Bosin could wait in the valleys if he wished, while the others went on. For once, the twins seemed of the same mind and Bosin gave up, kicking a bucket over in a temper as he went to say goodbye to his horse in the stable. Being unable to take mounts through the pass seemed to anger the big man more than anything. He had become childishly sullen after that, refusing to speak to anyone.

Hondo glared at the great back. Bosin was a trial to his patience, a great shambling irritation. The man alone was big enough to intimidate an army. Wrapped in fur and then thick woollen blankets, he looked at times like an actual bear. Only the stream of complaint was definitely that of a man.

It had seemed reasonable to explain their duty to Bosin down in the village. The reality, of actually dying while the wind hooted and roared in his ears, felt rather more like failure and disgrace. Hondo dipped his head again and pressed on. His cheeks would lose skin, he was certain. He'd seen mountain men with strange marbled scarring from the heights they'd crossed. He would surely be one of those, if he survived at all.

'. . . I am no more than an icicle walking. They will find

me blue and stiff in the spring . . . I should prepare a pose, so I will be useful to them. Yes, I will point the way to weary travellers and they will say, "Look at that poor big bastard, who should never have tried to cross the pass in winter. I wonder which cruel sod insisted on it . . ."'

Bosin cleared his throat and roared into the wind as if in challenge. Hondo shook his head, until he understood Bosin was shouting distinct words.

'Horse skulls, Hondo! Horse . . . skulls!'

Hondo blinked in confusion, but then he realised the ground they walked on no longer sloped upward. He stopped, understanding at last. Horse skulls. They'd been told to watch for them.

Ahead, half-hidden by swirling snow, two rocks narrowed to a gap a single man could just about push through. It was the only pass for a hundred miles of hard country and there was no room for mounts. The narrow way had been discovered by a group of soldiers decades before. They'd killed their horses rather than leave them to starve, before passing through. Over the years, other travellers had taken up the skulls of the horses and put them on spears. They stood as a warning of the pass, in yellow bone.

Hondo looked up as Bosin trudged forward and fell to his knees to climb the packed snow of the slope. There was no true glimpse of the way ahead, just a white sky that seemed unending.

'Shovels!' Bosin called back. 'Twins, this is work for two young champions. Bring the shovels and dig us a path.'

To Hondo's surprise, Hi and Je stepped forward without complaint and began to dig.

'Slowly,' Hondo called to them. 'Your sweat will freeze and we have a long way to go.'

Bosin snorted.

'It's all downhill after this, remember? We are warriors of Shiang! We'll run down.'

Gabriel sat on a roll of blankets by the fire and licked blood from his wrist. As the day ended, stillness and the musty air of deep woods lay all around. He felt relaxed and – he searched for the word – content, for the first time since he had awakened in Lord Ran's long room. Gabriel glanced to where that man lay on a mat of dry pine needles, his hands bound once again. Lord Ran was not enjoying the experience, though it was hardly important if he did. Gabriel needed his knowledge. He'd told the man again that if he ran, he would take his eyes. The threat seemed to have worked. Gabriel wondered idly if the lord would gain a better understanding of the terror experienced by those he used in his experiments. Being truly helpless could mark a man for the rest of his life.

They had ridden hard until sunset and then made a fire in the woods, too far from the road to be spotted. Gabriel had seen a deer as he'd dismounted and gone after it like a wolf. It had been one of the most exhilarating experiences of his life, a moment of absolute joy, with the wind cold in his throat and, at the end, hot blood and meat.

The Fool made no attempt to remove the leash they had placed on his neck, though the flesh had grown raw there. He curled up by the fire and slept like a dog, or better than a dog, with no troubling dreams or anxieties. Gabriel almost envied him, though he was growing filthier by the day.

The pulsing thumps had started to come less frequently as soon as they were heading west. They had not faded, but Gabriel thought the slowly increasing tempo of the beat had been interrupted, or even reversed. He was grateful for it. Water could break even stone in the end.

Marias had served them all slices of venison on plates from the packs. Gabriel watched her cut pieces for herself, now that the others had eaten. She settled back and crossed her legs, leaning over the plate in her lap. Gabriel noticed Sanjin watching her as well. He frowned. A woman always caused trouble in camp, he remembered that much. Yet Gabriel was still uncertain why he had allowed her to come. Was there some part of him he did not own? Some fragment of soul that might yet steal back what it had lost? Having Marias in the camp was like probing a cracked tooth. He had to know why he had brought her. Or perhaps the one she called Taeshin would not let him send her away.

Gabriel shuddered, suddenly reminded he was not in his own body, but that of another. He had grown so used to the strength and speed, beyond anything he'd known before, that he sometimes forgot. When he caught sight of himself in a mirror at the palace, it always involved a shock of confusion. Who was that dark-haired young man glaring at him? With almond eyes and a hard, flat face? He already knew Taeshin had been a swordsman, which explained the grace and strength, though not the extent of it. That had come from the stone that had brought them all back.

Gabriel looked up as Sanjin rose from his place. The heavyset man still limped and wore a dark expression, but there was something else there as well, something more like lust in the firelight. As Gabriel watched, the man walked around the fire and took hold of Marias by the arm. He began to pull her away from the light of the flames, his intentions clear. She cried out in shock and fear, her feet kicking marks on the ground and scattering sparks at the edge of the fire. In anger, Sanjin took a better grip on her hair.

Gabriel stood up, his hand dropping to the Yuan sword. He hesitated, suddenly unsure of himself. What did it matter to him if Sanjin took the woman? Marias was not his slave, was nothing to him. He began to take his hand from the sword hilt and a voice spoke within him. *He challenges you.*

It was true. As soon as he had the thought, he knew it. Sanjin had been surly from the first moments in the long room, when Gabriel had interrupted the healing. His half-foot was a burden, but the man could have cauterised it in fire if he'd wished. Instead, he had kept it wrapped and bleeding, suffering constantly. Gabriel had sensed the man's resentment enough times.

'Put her down, Sanjin,' he said. 'You will not hurt her.'

Gabriel blinked at that last. He had not meant to add anything beyond the first command. He was not certain he had control of himself in that instant and the thought terrified him. He had come too far to be thrown out of his new life. He opened his mouth once more, but Sanjin was already coming at him. The limp slowed the warrior only a touch as he came round the fire.

Gabriel found himself fighting for his life, the Yuan blade flickering. He already knew it would not cut for him as it had for the young king of Shiang. The royal sword had been attuned to the man's blood in some way which

173

did not respond to Gabriel's hand. Still, it was a thing of savage beauty even so, the balance perfect.

The swords clashed a dozen times in succession, like bells ringing. He had the edge on Sanjin, Gabriel realised. Beyond the initial shock at the sheer speed of their encounter, he knew he was better. It was a heady feeling. They had fought side by side for an age in the grey place. There were no more experienced swordsmen alive.

Gabriel picked his moment and struck Sanjin's hand with the flat of his blade, hard as a hammer blow. The man's sword dropped from nerveless fingers and Sanjin stood with his chest heaving and his eyes wild, certain he would be killed.

Gabriel held up his sword in the guard position.

'Be still now, brother. Or would you be killed over a woman? Over a slave? Is your life worth no more than that?'

Sanjin took the opening he had been given and smiled through his bitterness.

'I'm sorry. I am always in pain . . . It is hard to be calm.'

Gabriel repressed a grimace. The price of peace was to be the man's foot, it seemed. He gritted his teeth.

'Very well, brother. I will try. But she is mine.'

He hid the shock that rippled through him as he heard himself say the last four words. There had been no intention to speak again, but he had done so anyway. Gabriel swallowed, feeling sweat break out beyond mere exertion.

'Show me the foot, brother,' he said.

He watched as Sanjin seated himself and unwrapped the bandages and the makeshift boot he'd had made in Shiang. On the other side of the fire, Marias was left alone to collect herself and wipe at her tears. She gathered up the plates and stayed away from the firelight. Gabriel did not look in her direction, preferring to keep an eye on Sanjin.

The foot was worse than he had expected, Gabriel saw. He could smell the rot before the last bandages were off and drew back from it.

'You should have seared the wound,' he said.

Sanjin shrugged, though now that Gabriel looked for it, he could see a tinge of sickness in the way the man sweated. His skin was slick with the rot. Perhaps that alone had given Gabriel the edge in their struggle. The thought gave him pause, but he had promised to try.

The place where toes would have been was a clotted lump of dried pus and thread-like veins. It seeped and Gabriel put Sanjin's blanket across his lap before he cradled the thing, trying not to gag at the smell. Darker lines reached up from the ankle and he wondered if it would be possible even to save the leg.

'I have said I will try, and I will, but you must know this is rotting. It might be best to take the leg off – to make a clean cut.'

'No. You gave Thomas *eyes*,' Sanjin hissed. 'You can heal this.'

Gabriel nodded. He breathed long and reached within for the ocean that lapped against the rocks of whatever he was. It was no longer infinite, if it ever had been. He wondered if he risked his existence by dipping into it once again. Gabriel closed his eyes as he felt the first tremble of power seeping through his fingers. He heard Sanjin gasp, though in pain or relief, Gabriel did not know.

When he opened his eyes again, the veins were writhing like worms. No. He did not have the strength to give.

He felt the man's fever withdraw, but as the ocean began to surge, Gabriel broke his grip and stood up.

'Finish it!' Sanjin said in desperation.

'Brother, I cannot,' Gabriel said. 'There is no more in me! Look, I have done all I could. Your fever has lessened. I will tell Lord Ran to help you sear the wound. At least then it will not become infected again.'

Sanjin nodded, anger clear in his face. Gabriel was pleased to see that frustration. Sanjin weak was dangerous enough. Sanjin whole would have been to invite his own destruction. The man was a snake.

Gabriel felt a pulse in the air. He twitched as it passed through him, seeing the same shudder in Sanjin and Thomas. The Fool whimpered and clasped his knees close. Only Lord Ran and Marias were unaffected. It was not a happy camp, Gabriel reflected.

At Gabriel's order, Lord Ran heated a horseshoe nail in the fire until it glowed gold and red. When he pressed it to sizzle against the veins of the half-foot, Sanjin began to scream. It was very loud in the darkness, with the forest silent around them.

PART TWO

But better down there in the battle
  Than here on the hill
With Judgement or nothingness waiting me,
  Lonely and chill.

John Betjeman

13

Forest

Hondo had lost the heel of his boot somewhere around the high passes, unnoticed at the time as he'd been in deep snow. It was such a small thing to cause him so much irritation, but each and every step was awkward after that. He was worried that his uneven gait would set off an old injury to his lower back and make him practically useless. An active man of his age always had parts that were weaker than the rest. His mastery of the Mazer steps had helped him recover from injuries that would surely have ruined others. Yet time rolled on for all men. Despite the talents of his youth, Hondo still had a right knee that twinged under load, and two sore spots on his elbows that never seemed to ease completely. Just about every joint ached as he trudged through forests, and the return of blood to his feet felt as if he'd put them in hot embers.

It did not help that his single broken boot seemed to amuse Bosin. The great bear had come through the mountains unscathed, of course, though he told the twins he was hungry enough to eat at least one of them. None of it would have mattered if they'd found new horses, or even a village with a half-competent cobbler to fix the boot. Instead, they'd come below the snows to trackless forest. Hondo had been forced to remove the other heel with his knife. It was not ideal, as his feet now seemed always to be wet, but it was better than his back going.

Hondo had said nothing when Bosin made a great play on how he had become shorter. He endured every weak attempt at humour with the same steady expression until the big man finally gave up.

They had trudged together for five days, low on food and spirit, when they crossed a logging trail, the first sign of man they had encountered since coming down from the high passes. It was nothing more than an old cart track, with the marks of wheels, but it meant they were returning to civilisation. With only the sun to guide them, the forest had seemed endless, as if some terrible curse or spell had been enacted.

Hondo stood and stared along the track in dawning delight as he understood. They were all bearded and filthy beyond description, he thought suddenly. The prospect of a return to the company of men brought back some sense of correct form. It had not mattered as much in the woods, nor in the snow.

'We should follow it,' Bosin said.

Hondo shook his head immediately, though he wanted to pat the ground, just to know it was real. The thought of leaving it behind brought an ache to his chest, but his old self was still there somewhere, beneath the scratches and the beard, beneath the shivering and the clotted muck in his hair.

'It runs north and south, who knows for how long. Look there, at the mosses growing in the wheel marks. This has not been used for a long time.'

'There'll be a logging camp somewhere close, though,'

Bosin went on, dropping his head and adopting his most mulish expression.

Hondo forced himself to speak calmly.

'Logging camps move on when they have cut the trees in an area. This is an old track. I see no clearings here. Our destination is the city of Darien, Bosin, by royal order. Now, I am as tired as you, as wet and cold as you, but I will not weaken. We continue west. If it helps, consider your body as a lazy animal which must be beaten. Your will is stronger than your ass, Bosin.'

To Hondo's surprise, Bosin snorted and almost bent over, growing red as he wheezed his amusement. He was actually ill, Hondo realised, listening to the tortured breathing. The man had endured a great deal without even his usual complaining.

'I hope so,' Bosin replied.

'Good,' Hondo said sternly. 'This is not a committee. I am continuing west. Come with me or not, as you please.'

He set off and the twins paused only to glance at Bosin. He raised his eyes and muttered an oath before following.

Hondo did not look back, though his stiff-legged anger faded after an hour. They walked as a group once more as the sun sank ahead of them, showing gold through the trees. On previous nights, they had made camp at about that time, but they'd crossed a newer track some way back and found the black embers of two old fires.

Before the light could go completely, they heard the noise of men ahead and came out of the brush onto a wider track lined with old branches. It led down to a large and muddy clearing, with a dozen dormitory shelters raised on wood piles above the clay and roots. Huge saws could be seen as the four men stood and looked. As well as enormous tree trunks, piles of sawn lumber rested on pegs, waiting to be taken back to the markets. Village tables and doors all came from that place. A fire crackled in a stone pit, but no one sat near it. The night was cold and the loggers had set no guards, so that the clearing had an empty, almost deserted air.

It was a rough-looking sort of place, Hondo thought. For all his delight in seeing the light of oil lamps and the prospect of shelter from the cold, he was aware that strangers would not be a common sight there, not so far out.

'Let me speak to them,' he said, eyeing Bosin. Hondo doubted the twins would start a fight in that place, but Bosin was a different matter. 'I have silver. I'll arrange to hire one of those huts for us, as well as some dry blankets and food.'

'A *lot* of food,' Bosin grumbled. 'I am starving.'

'Oh? Well, you should have *said* something!' Hondo snapped.

Bosin's astonishment was so comical that they both ended up grinning. The lighter mood was down to the prospects ahead of them as much as any warmth of feeling.

As the four swordsmen walked in, a bearded logger came staggering out of a building ahead. That place was bigger than the rest, with more light spilling from the cracks. The open door let noise out onto the muddy slush of the main yard. The man was laughing at something, but then he saw the four watching him. Almost without a pause, he spun on his heel to go back inside. As the door slammed shut, the men of Shiang could hear him yell a warning.

Hondo cursed under his breath. He'd hoped for a chance to explain, but he supposed they looked like thieves or wild men to the loggers, coming in unannounced as they had from the dark woods. He felt his temper fray as the door slammed open again. Hondo had endured snow and hunger, rain, frost and being unable to wash properly or shave. He had endured the company of Bosin. Hondo felt ten years older than he had in the peace of Shiang, where a man could bathe and was treated with respect.

The workers poured out of their rough tavern. They stumbled over one another to see the strange thing that had appeared in their camp in the middle of nowhere. In response, Hondo drew his sword. The bell note echoed across the camp, his action copied on the instant by the twins. Bosin looked at Hondo.

'This is talking to them?' he said.

Hondo did not reply. He waited with his sword held downwards, relaxing into a guard position. For those who knew the language of stances, it would signal his willingness to fight, without being overtly hostile.

The loggers kept coming. There had to have been forty of them in that single building, but even more came trotting over from various other shacks across the camp. They were, to say the least, a hard crew. Half of them had hatchets or axes to hand. The other half had drawn knives the length of a forearm at the mere sight of swords. Hondo was not worried by such untrained men. He did not doubt their courage, but he was the sword saint of Shiang. No professional is ever afraid of amateurs, as his first master had taught him. Hondo recalled the man had been trampled to death in a mob, which gave him pause. There were a lot of loggers and they were all armed. He should not underestimate them.

The first man to have come out had returned buckling a thick belt around his waist. A tool of black iron hung from each of his hips. Hondo frowned as he came to the front of the group. He wondered at the open stance the man presented to him. Though he carried no blade, the fellow was grinning, utterly unintimidated in the face of the four men of Shiang.

'You have no business here,' the man called. 'We ain't a village and this is private land. So move on and you won't find more trouble than maybe you expected.'

The accent was strange, but Hondo could understand the words well enough. He certainly understood the tone.

'I am Hondo, servant to the court of Shiang,' he said. He waited for some flicker of recognition, but there was none. The loggers just stared blankly at his little group. Hondo sighed. 'We've come a very long way and we are weary and hungry. All we desire is food and a place to sleep and wash.'

'A lot of food,' Bosin added.

In the gloom, Hondo saw the speaker's gaze flicker to the big man and remain on him, awed by the sheer size. The only light came from the tavern lamps and it had not been completely obvious just how big Bosin was. Hondo watched in irritation as the speaker turned a fraction in Bosin's direction – as if Bosin were the greatest threat, or the master of that group. It was infuriating – and disrespectful.

'Nice to meet you, meneer,' the speaker went on. 'My name is Vic Deeds and I'll say it one more time. This isn't a tavern for strangers and their pet bear, especially ones who walk in with swords drawn. So be on your way. Now, I won't tell you again.'

Hondo turned to his companions.

'Kill this one. Perhaps the next will be more cooperative.'

One of the twins stepped forward with the same unearthly grace he had shown before. The reaction was instantaneous. The speaker's hands blurred as he reached for the guns on his belt. Before the twin could strike him down, Vic Deeds had fired twice and reholstered the pistols as if he had never moved.

Hondo froze as white smoke billowed across him, tasting of gunpowder. To his horror, he saw the twin give a strange grunt and pitch forward. His brother ran to him with a cry of anguish and Hondo saw the one who called himself Vic Deeds reach again for the weapons he carried.

Hondo reacted at the speed that had made him renowned. His hand came up with the tiny blade he had palmed almost without thought, flicking it past the second twin as the man dropped to his knees by his brother. It passed through a small gap and sank into the side of the gunman, spoiling his aim.

Hondo had come forward behind his own blade, but his path was suddenly blocked by Bosin, who charged the loggers with a roar. Once again, gunshots sounded, over and over. Hondo saw Bosin smash one man down with a blow of appalling force, bellowing all the while. His sword killed another and then Hondo too was amongst them. Two men turned to flee and he put them down with quick strikes to the back, sliding his blade between ribs into the heart. The rest scattered and when he looked around, the gunman had staggered away, hunched over his wound.

Even as Hondo peered into the darkness of the camp for some sight of him, he saw a horse being untied and the man trying to get up into the saddle.

Without a thought, Hondo ran, making his legs work faster and faster in the thick mud. He made no sound as he came and Vic Deeds was frantic at the sight of a swordsman who moved like a rattlesnake coming at him, sword held low and clearly ready to cut his head off. There was no time to reload, not against those four. The reins of his horse had snagged on the holding rail and Deeds had to slash them with the knife he pulled from his ribs, though he cut his fingers as he did so. The leather parted and he leaped on. Even without reins, the horse sensed his panic and lurched into a run as he dug in his heels and gripped the neck with bloody hands.

Hondo skidded to a halt as the horse vanished into the dark, fixing the man's face and name in his memory. The sword saint was still trying to comprehend what had happened: the cracks of sound and the bitter powder smoke, the sudden collapse of the twin. Hondo felt a wave of dismay pass over him. He had not yet even reached Darien. He dreaded what he would find when he walked back.

None of the other loggers seemed to be carrying the weapons of black iron. He wanted to look at one and understand how a man could use such a thing to strike another down from a distance. The thought made Hondo swallow drily as he crossed back to where the crowd had scattered. He understood what such weapons might mean.

One of the twins lay in the road, held in the arms of the other. The one who had been shot was still and very pale.

'Hi is dead,' Je said hoarsely.

The young man held up his hand and Hondo saw the palm was marked with bright blood. The twin opened his brother's tunic to reveal two red holes. When they turned him, two more could be seen in his back. Blood dribbled from them, pooling in his brother's lap.

Hondo looked to where Bosin stood, rooted to the spot. The big man still wore his furs and yet he was breathing hard, as if he had run a long way. As Hondo stared, Bosin went down on one knee in the mud, his head dipping. With a visible effort of will, he pulled himself back to his feet.

'Were you hit as well?' Hondo asked.

Bosin nodded at him. There was anger in the man's eyes and Hondo wanted to look away from it. He had seen Bosin drunk and complaining. He recalled he had never seen him truly angry before that moment.

'Sir? Gentlemen?' a voice came.

Hondo was up in an instant, his sword held ready to strike. He looked into the terrified expression of a short man who had approached them with his hands held up to show he carried no weapon. The stranger could not quite believe how quickly Hondo had crossed the space between them. He held very still and Hondo could see he was shaking.

'Sir? That Vic Deeds is a drunk and a scoundrel. He's no friend to this camp. He don't represent us, do you understand? We do have a doctor here. If you want to have wounds looked at, he's a good man, I swear. We don't want any more trouble, sir.'

The man's gaze slid to where the bodies of four loggers lay sprawled in the mud. Hondo did not turn to see.

Instead, he chewed the bristles of his lower lip as he thought, folding them between his teeth. He was tempted to make an example of the men of the camp, but two things held his hand. Not only had the culprit already escaped, but Bosin was clearly hurt.

'Very well. I will see your doctor. We need food and a place to rest. If this . . . Vic Deeds returns, I would like to be told immediately.'

The woodsman glanced at Hondo's sword, shining like a bar of moonlight in the darkness. He was a senior man, however, and not one to push without him pushing back.

'I don't think he'll return here, sir. If he does, that is between you and none of my concern, if you follow me. The doctor and the food I can arrange. There has been enough trouble here tonight. We ain't soldiers, sir. We're working men, away from our families and homes to make a bit of money.'

'And where is home?' Hondo asked. He sheathed his sword as he spoke, knowing how fast he could draw it once more. 'When you are not in the forests, cutting trees?'

'Why, Darien, sir. The city. A hundred miles or so to the west, as the crow flies. Most of us are from there, or thereabouts.'

Hondo felt his heart thump faster. Despite the disaster, it still raised his spirits to hear that name spoken by another after so long.

Doctor Adams stank of old sweat, which did not endear him to Hondo. He could not help wondering when the man had last washed his hands, but there was no one else. The twin, Je, brought in his brother's body in his arms, laying him down on a table in the tavern and arranging his hands. Bosin was persuaded to follow, though he just stood and stared at nothing while the doctor was summoned.

Hondo watched the man carefully, noting the black bag he carried and the whiskers on his face. He supposed the wounds of a logging camp would always be serious. The man would have seen fingers or feet cut off many times, but perhaps not so many wounds of this sort.

The doctor went first to the body, but when he saw the wax colour of death, he looked to the giant who stood with glazed eyes, breathing hard. Hondo watched the man snap his fingers in front of Bosin's face. There was no response.

'This one's out on his feet, just about. I need to get these layers off, to see if he's been hit, or if it's just shock.'

'Shock?' Hondo said, raising his eyebrows.

The doctor glanced at him, registering him as another stranger.

'Some men freeze up when they see death, sir. It speaks to their own and they panic.'

'It is not shock,' Hondo said. 'This is Master Bosin of Shiang. He is an experienced swordsman. He has seen death many times.'

'Either way, these furs need to come off. Can you hear me, son? Can you lie down?'

Bosin winced suddenly. The pain seemed to revive him, so that he nodded and clambered up onto the largest table in that place, where some twenty men could sit to eat dinner. As might be expected in a logging camp, it was a great heavy thing, with planks as thick as a man's hand. Even so, it creaked alarmingly as Bosin lay back on it. The swordsman's face was bright with sweat. His breathing was audible indoors, a wheeze that sounded wet and heavy.

'He has a cold,' Hondo said, though he knew it was something more.

The doctor didn't look up, but busied himself cutting away the furs and the clothes beneath. Hondo winced at the grey flesh that was revealed, stained by damp and the dyes in the tunic. The doctor used a razor with neat strokes, and strips of fur and cloth fluttered down.

Three more of the red holes could be seen. The doctor put his finger into one and nodded.

'That's the one that hit his belt. Look there – the bullet is so close to the surface you can almost see it. I can get that one out.'

'What about the other two?' Hondo asked the man. He felt out of his depth, numbed by the sudden change in their fortunes. He had not expected Bosin to be badly wounded. The man was too large to be brought down by some small fellow, no matter what weapon he held.

The doctor wiped his hands with a cloth and shook his head.

'There's one in his side – so he'll be bleeding in there. The other sounds like it's in a lung. If I could roll him, I'd know whether it went through.'

They both looked at the man lying unconscious on the massive table. Rolling him was no small thing to contemplate.

'Will he die?' Hondo asked. The idea was ludicrous, impossible.

The doctor rubbed bristles with fingers still marked in Bosin's blood.

'He has one chance in three, something like that. I can take the one bullet out, but if the other two are still in him, he'll rot from the inside and there's nothing anyone can do, not here anyway.'

'Where, then?' Hondo asked, though he knew the answer even as he spoke.

'Darien, maybe. If he lives that long. I would not hope for it, sir, if you understand me. These are serious wounds.'

'But there are doctors in Darien, men who could heal him?'

Once again, Adams rubbed his chin.

'If he survives the trip, and if you have gold, he has a chance.'

'Fetch a cart to carry him,' Hondo said. 'And a man who knows the way.'

'It's the middle of the night, son. I think it would be better . . .'

Hondo placed the flat of his hand on the man's chest. He could feel the heartbeat quicken.

'I have lost two men since entering this camp. My patience is at an end. Fetch me a cart and a guide or I will burn this place to the ground.'

The doctor stared at the stranger who had brought violence and death to the logging camp that evening. He remembered too the bodies still lying in the mud outside.

He nodded.

'Very well. One of the lads is going back tomorrow. He'll take you.'

Hondo looked back at the figure of Bosin.

'Tonight. I will need blankets and food – and some men to help me lift him onto the cart.'

'I can't just let you take a cart, sir.'

'You cannot stop me,' Hondo replied. He said it with such quiet assurance that the doctor believed him.

'Even so. The cart belongs to the logging company. Take it if you want. But you and your mates killed four men. You have no friends here to help you. Not now.'

Hondo tossed a small pouch to the man, who caught it and glanced inside.

'I'll gather a few lads.'

As the doctor left, Hondo clenched his jaw, feeling himself sway. It was always the same after a fight, or it had been since he'd turned forty. He was exhausted and still cold. The room's warmth was making him sleepy, but he would not give in to it. Only Bosin's wheezing and the muted sobs of Je as he brushed the hair from his brother's forehead broke the silence.

14

Gabriel

Gabriel pushed them all hard. Sanjin suffered the worst, when the cauterised wounds on his foot took another infection. The man rode in constant pain, wincing at every jog and bounce. When they stopped, he limped around the camp, his foot always wet. Sanjin's eyes became red and sore from fevers, but they had no medicine and he did not ask Gabriel to look at it again. As the days passed, Sanjin's gaze seemed to turn within.

Gabriel watched the man sitting alone, holding his leg bent and searching for the internal sea that Gabriel had described. It was surely there, though Gabriel felt a perverse pleasure that Sanjin had no luck finding it. Each time the swordsman failed, he shouted in fury, a great blast of frustration. The rest of the time, Sanjin glowered, his gaze always drifting to Gabriel.

Gabriel understood that silent accusation, but ignored it. He was tempted to put the man down like a mad dog before he made trouble for them all. Yet Sanjin was still enhanced as a swordsman, remade by whatever part of the Aeris Stone had touched them. Even a mad dog could be useful.

Marias was a more intractable problem, at least to Gabriel. While Sanjin watched him, Gabriel watched her in turn, as a puzzle to be solved. There was no hiding her feelings for the one whose body he wore. They shone, whenever Marias met his eyes. She thought he did not notice, but he felt it, just as he sensed the rage in Sanjin. It seemed at times that only Lord Ran and Thomas were at all sane in that little camp.

Lord Ran was not doing well, Gabriel had to admit. He had not troubled to ask the man his age, but the Shiang lord was not young. The pace Gabriel had insisted upon might have exhausted a royal messenger of half his years. Gabriel himself seemed to need very little sleep, so he roused them all when they were still groggy and the dark was absolute. He made them ride horses to exhaustion and change mounts at every opportunity, so it was just the riders who grew slack and dull in the eye.

Thump. The pulse sounded as Gabriel gazed at the mountains rising before him. Winter had come, to be seen in spirals of snow caught in the wind. The village elders said the passes were all blocked by then, even the lowest, the one they called Horse Skulls. The headman assured the strange group that they could not cross alive, not until spring. He told them he had said the same to four other swordsmen just weeks before, but back then, there had at least been sun in the mornings. Winter had taken its grip on the peaks since they had passed. When it came, there was no mistaking it – and no release until the thaw.

Gabriel stood and thought. The sky was clear and he did not fear the cold. Whatever the stone had done to him to give him speed and strength, he knew he could walk where any other man would freeze. Even in that place, he stood wearing leggings and a loose shirt, while the villagers went wrapped in furs. Yet if he went on, Marias and Lord Ran would surely die.

He hissed an old curse to himself. He needed Lord Ran for his knowledge – and he could not abandon Marias. That certainty remained like a fishbone in his throat. His will was his own, but he could not leave her, so his will was not his own! Gabriel went round and round in his thoughts. This Taeshin retained some scattered sense of self, perhaps no more than grains on a threshing floor, drifting without purpose. There was no intruder in Gabriel's thoughts, no second voice. Still, he was not completely free, not to do as he wished.

Gabriel knew he needed stones. He needed power. He stared up at the mountains, willing himself across them as if sheer focus would see him taken to the other side. He had seen stranger things. He had come back from the dead.

'I have brought tea, Taeshin,' he heard Marias say. She held out a shallow bowl to him as he turned. He accepted it, breathing in the scent with pleasure.

'You must not call me that,' he said, sipping. 'I am Gabriel. I will kill you if you do not call me by my name.'

'I . . . I'm sorry . . . Gabriel,' she stammered, bowing her head.

'Do you hope to summon him, Marias? Is that why you use his name? He is not here. Believe me when I say I have searched for him.'

'I serve, master,' she said without raising her head. 'That is all.'

Gabriel felt a spasm of anger and yet he did not touch his sword. No one else had thought to serve him tea, after all.

'It seems these mountains cannot be crossed,' he said. 'If I am to remain here until spring, perhaps . . . perhaps I will need someone to serve me.'

He had felt the pulse in the air as he'd spoken. The call, if call it was, sounded more forcefully a thousand miles closer to Darien. Even the idea of waiting till spring made it beat, hard enough to stop the four returners in their tracks. Gabriel looked across the stable yard, where a huge black workhorse bowed over its door. Thomas had been stroking the animal, enjoying the velvet touch of its muzzle. The Fool still stared at the mountains as Gabriel had been doing, caught mid-step as he had crossed the yard. He'd felt it. So had Sanjin, who was sitting at a table covered in frost, staring into nothing.

Gabriel looked sharply back at Sanjin. As he watched, Sanjin grinned for the first time he could remember. Slowly, Sanjin stood up and leaned over the table, pointing.

'Look! Look, Gabriel, Thomas . . . come and see!'

Gabriel went closer, while Thomas came with his hand on his hilt, always wary of a trap. The man trusted no one, which had not saved him from death the first time. Gabriel felt his thoughts scatter as he saw crystals of frost retreat from the table. Where Sanjin laid his hand, whiteness blurred and melted away, leaving dark, wet wood.

'Can you heal yourself?' Gabriel said. The spite he felt was beneath him, he knew very well. Yet he had been the only one able to harness whatever power had brought them back. That unique status was vanishing in the awe of Sanjin's expression.

'I don't know . . .' Sanjin said. He closed his eyes. Lines appeared on his forehead as he frowned, but Gabriel could neither see nor feel any other change. Sanjin gasped as if he'd held his breath and shook his head.

'No, but I felt something. I reached out and I touched . . . something. And the frost vanished.'

'That's good, brother,' Gabriel said.

He did not say it wasn't quite restoring a man's eyes, but he could see that awareness come to Sanjin as he flushed. Gabriel turned to Marias and discovered once again that he could not leave her behind. He made a decision, though he felt his stomach knot as he spoke.

'Marias. Tell the village headman to fetch the best wraps and shoes and cloaks, enough for us all – whatever he would wear himself. We'll dig out the pass by hand if we must. We'll trust in the stone or die. Either way, we're not stopping here, not till spring.'

He and Sanjin tensed for another pulse, but there was nothing. They sagged, exchanging a glance. That silent beat wore a man down, no matter what drove him. Yet the choice to go on felt like no choice at all.

Hondo had refused to let the doctor rest for two nights, though the man dozed on his seat for most of the second day. They'd taken a great ham from the camp store, as well as bread and pickled vegetables that made Hondo's mouth pucker. He'd found Doctor Adams a somewhat surly companion, at least once he'd discovered he would be accompanying his patient.

The logging trails were wider and clear, leading right back to the city. The doctor said they wouldn't even be active at that time of year if not for all the construction going on in Darien. It seemed new walls were going up.

Entire streets were being flattened and rebuilt, or built higher inside. That winter, the city was a hive of activity, though Doctor Adams had no particular interest in the reasons for it. He whipped the two oxen whenever they slowed and replaced one at the village of Wyburn as they went through, with Hondo's silver greasing their passage.

Hondo came awake when the twin Je dug an elbow into his side. His brother lay wrapped and cold on the bed of the cart, with Bosin moaning alongside him. That seemed an almost familiar sound to Hondo's ear, though the big swordsman was delirious and hot with fever. His words made very little sense, which was a relief from the complaining they had known before.

Ahead of them, the city gate stood open, with a trail of carts stretching back along the road for the best part of a mile. The line ground forward slowly and yet Hondo realised their own road would cut right to the front of the queue. Adams made no attempt to slow, but called out for a doctor as soon as he was in earshot of the gate guards. They seemed to know him and waved him past, though Hondo saw them peer into the cart as they did so. His own attention was caught by a huge gold dog sitting with the gate guards. It turned its massive head to watch them pass. Hondo shivered. It seemed the sort of animal Bosin would appreciate. For his own part, he had never liked the creatures.

Some of the waiting carters called out in protest at their being let through, but Hondo ignored them as the doctor steered expertly around a narrow space and into the city beyond. It had taken just moments. Hondo looked for the first time at the inner streets of the foreign city that had given shelter to the king's uncle, the adulterer Tellius. He could hardly believe he was there at last, nor the sheer noise, filth and chaos that formed the roads within. It was impossible not to compare it with home. Shiang was paved in clean stone in all but the slave areas. It was a place of perfect order, beyond occasions such as the king's birthday when people were allowed more licence to drink and celebrate. Hondo shook his head in distaste. If the streets of Darien even had stone underpinnings, they were hidden by a thick layer of mud and manure.

Roaring at a startled wine merchant to make way for an injured man, Doctor Adams forced his way into a row of carts and horsemen trundling along a narrow road. Everywhere Hondo looked, there was a crush of men and women, all yelling at the tops of their voices.

Almost knocking against the wheels of the cart, Hondo saw a wrinkled man pushing a little hand-wagon, piled high with what looked like rags. As Hondo watched, the man stiffened suddenly and fell into the gutter, spilling the wagon and its contents. The swordsman leaned to stare as a small child tumbled out and sat bawling, holding up its hands. A passing woman stepped into the mud and swept the baby up out of the road, but the man who had fallen lay there still, blind and twitching, kicking his heels in some sort of fit. Hondo saw the woman purse her lips angrily as she was forced to wait, her good deed punished.

The sword saint blinked as he sat back, disliking the city on first sight and smell. If Bosin lived, Hondo suspected the man would find much to enjoy. Darien had a sense of chaos to it, much like Bosin himself. Hondo looked back at the swordsman who had groaned or wheezed constantly since being shot. The pallor of his skin was not good and he was wet with sweat despite the cold. Yet he was alive. That was all that mattered. As Hondo glanced back, he saw the twin reach down and pat his brother's corpse on the shoulder, as if encouraging him or to give himself comfort. Both the brothers had reached Darien. Hondo grimaced. What words could possibly help with that loss? He had said almost nothing to Je since the death. Yet he had witnessed a private moment of grief and he could not ignore it.

'He died going forward,' Hondo said. 'In courage and honour.'

Je bowed his head in reply, though his eyes gleamed. Hondo had to turn away, rather than shame him by noticing. He called instead to Doctor Adams as the man swore at another carter trying to edge in front of them.

'Which way now?' Hondo discovered he too had to shout, just to be heard over the arguments all around him.

The doctor pointed mutely to another road, leading away from the walls. Making that turn took an age and Hondo was tempted to draw his sword before they were through. Yet the change was immediate, the noise level half what it had been before.

The gates to a tavern yard lay open ahead of them. If they had been painted red many years before, it looked as if they had not been rubbed down or even closed after that first day.

'The Old Red Inn will have rooms for us,' Adams said. 'Basker owes me a favour, anyway. I can call a doctor from here easily enough – someone who'll know what to do with your friend.'

'He's not my friend,' Hondo said.

Adams raised his eyebrows.

'I heard he stepped in front of Vic Deeds, while that man's hands were on his guns. I'd say that qualifies him.'

The doctor reined in and dismounted, going inside to look for the owner. Hondo wondered at a city that would just let him enter without a search or even a question about his intentions. He supposed the doctor was well known to guardsmen who might occasionally need a wound tended. Perhaps, too, the sort of men who drifted into a logging camp were not always the most upright of citizens.

It was still a strange feeling, to stand in Darien at last. Hondo dismounted onto flat-cut cobbles, neat work by the look of it. The yard looked well kept, with a small fountain in the middle and a cup that was held by a piece of rope. Hondo used it to drink the dust from his throat, though he thought the water had a taste of iron in it. A few horses nosed from the stable doors, watching the new arrivals. Hondo and the twin exchanged a glance, though Je was blank with grief.

'Can you put your hurt aside for a time?' Hondo asked softly. 'I need to know you are able to finish the task we were given.'

The twin nodded.

'Find Tellius,' Je said in a whisper. 'Bring him home.'

It was not a command – he would not have dared give an order to a sword saint. The words were the last the young king had spoken to them. Je's eyes were bleak and utterly cold, but Hondo found the remembered words reassuring. The twins had not been sent west for their charm, but because they were ruthless killers. He needed that focus. No matter the death of one of their number, or whether Bosin survived or not, they still had the task they had been given.

Hondo wrinkled his nose as a faint smell of rot wafted out from the cart. The cold had helped preserve the twin, but the city was warmer around them and another need presented itself. They had to discover how the people of Darien dealt with the dead – and urgently.

Gabriel felt Marias huddle closer behind him. They'd all wrapped themselves in furs and blankets until they were just shambling figures, staggering onward and upward, step by step. The path had been clear at first, if cold. Gabriel had pushed the others on, though Sanjin limped and cursed, saying he'd lose the foot when it froze. Gabriel privately agreed that would be the case, though he was no longer sure. Sanjin wore an expression of bitter joy when he thought he was unobserved.

They'd rested where the headman had told them to stop for the night, in a cleft high up on the slopes that offered at least some shelter from the gale. The poor man had been almost in tears when he'd heard they were leaving, pleading with them to wait until spring. He'd offered to keep Marias and Lord Ran while the others went on, but Gabriel had refused.

In the darkness, snow had come whirling down upon them, burying the rocks that made their shelter, so that in the morning they had to kick and shovel snow just to get out onto a pristine new surface. There was no longer any path to be seen and the peaks were impossibly far. Gabriel knew the cleft he wanted was much lower down, but it was too easy to imagine missing the route to Horse Skulls pass.

The morning was clear enough, but the sky whitened above them and new snow fell as they trudged upwards, each step muffled in a hiss of flakes. It was near impossible to see where they were heading and yet they did not stop. At intervals, Gabriel would turn a full circle and then point in the right direction. He was not certain the pulse could be used in that way, but there was no other choice. The cold had begun to reach through whatever defences he'd won from the stone, so that he shivered and had to clench his jaw. Marias walked in his shadow with her eyes closed or her face hidden in the crook of her arm. Lord Ran . . . Gabriel had to admit the older man was failing. The nobleman fell often and it seemed to take longer and longer for him to rise. Lord Ran seemed to have lost any desire to live. Gabriel had even taken time to explain what he knew of the grey place that awaited them, hoping it would give the lord new heart. Yet the man was past caring.

Sanjin complained bitterly that the cold was ruining his leg, that he would find ice there and have to cut it before it rotted and killed him. The voice was a litany, but it did not grow weaker. It took Gabriel until the second afternoon to see the man was not suffering as much as he claimed to be. They were all panting by then, heading up a slope so steep they had to put their gloved hands to the ground and climb. Yet Sanjin was humming to himself as he went.

Gabriel waited for him to catch up. As the wind howled and snow whipped around them, he drew the sword he had taken from the hand of a dead king.

Sanjin looked up, sensing the stillness of the figure above him. His eyes widened when he saw the bare blade.

'What is it?' Sajin demanded. 'A bear? What?'

'You are not cold, Sanjin,' Gabriel said over the wind. 'You are not shivering.'

'What do you mean? I am freezing . . .' Sanjin gave up his protest and grinned. 'All right, Gabriel, what of it? I found a way to use what lies within me. Just as you did.'

'I gave Thomas his eyes,' Gabriel snapped. 'I did what I could for you . . .'

'Not enough!' Sanjin replied, instantly angry. 'I have not known a single day without agony since I returned. Without bleeding and stink and rot! And I could do *nothing*, while you . . .' His voice became a growl. '*You* made yourself a king, in a body you stole, just as I did.'

'And I have overreached, Sanjin! Do you understand? Whatever faults you see in me can wait for later. The cold, the wind – it is too much. We will not survive this place.'

'I will,' Sanjin replied, with a shrug. 'I can walk right over the pass and down to the plains beyond. Even on this half-foot, I can.'

Gabriel saw ugly triumph in the man, but he had another card to play.

'And what of Lord Ran? If he dies, how will you seek out the other stones that call to us? How will you use them if you find them? Lord Ran is the one who drew us back, Sanjin. There is no one else! Yet he is almost dead on his feet. I thought we could push through with our strength, but the pass is buried so deeply, it will take an age to dig it out. Lord Ran will not last another night up here. No matter what you feel about me, if he dies, you are done.'

Gabriel waited, though every moment of stillness brought cold further into his bones. He saw both Marias and Lord Ran were pale, with death riding on them. He would have prayed, but there had been no one in the grey land to hear.

Sanjin swore.

'Damn you,' he said. 'Very well.'

He closed his eyes and Gabriel felt the change immediately. Warmth washed over him and he cried out in surprise. It grew hotter, so that he was uncomfortable in instants, where before he had been freezing to death. He saw Marias open her eyes in wonder and stretch out from her crouch.

The wind still howled, but the snow melted under their steps. Sanjin was steaming with the flakes that landed on him, his eyes glittering as he pressed forward.

'Well? Walk then!' he said.

Thomas and the Fool brought up the rear, while Marias and Lord Ran fell in behind him, basking in a warmth that slowly brought life back to their limbs. Even the wind died around them then, so that they walked in perfect stillness, with only the sound of steps and panting breath. Thomas began to laugh, in something like awe. Gabriel watched as rock revealed itself beneath their feet, a flat place. Ahead, snow crumpled back to reveal a horse skull on a pole, the eyes empty. He nodded in relief, sheathing his sword and taking up a shovel as the way cleared before him and the storm swirled impotently overhead.

Taeshin felt himself shudder, though he was not cold. Nor was he hungry, though he had watched the battles on the plain for too many days to remember, over and over. At first, he had not dared leave the spot by the stone at the hill's peak. The others had trooped down and he'd seen them take up weapons and shields and join the lines of soldiers marching. He did not want to go with them and so he had stayed.

Yet as time passed, he'd crept forward to watch the battles, always afraid of some nameless pull that might tug him into the ranks, or steal away his sense of who he was. Yet he could not abandon Marias, not to the cruelty of the man who had killed him. Taeshin frowned at the thought.

He'd had nothing but time to think. He did not sleep or eat or do anything but watch the battles and dream of crossing a snowfield and a high pass in winter. He dreamed one of his companions walked with flame in his veins, so that ice melted before him. Another made the gale bend, the air itself bowing to his will. Taeshin felt the joy of it, even there, in the grey land. The sun he had seen was the only splash of colour in his entire world and Taeshin relished it.

When he looked up, he was standing at the edge of the battle. One or two of the men saw him there. They glanced over as they picked up their shields, ready to march.

'Come on, lad,' one of them said gruffly.

Taeshin's gaze dropped. At his feet lay a shield. He knew if he picked it up, he would be one of them. His fears would drift away like smoke and he would walk with friends against an evil foe. He would have purpose, with no more strange dreams, no more aimless sense of loss.

He bent low and his fingers brushed a surface of brass. The desire to let it all go was almost unbearable, but then he thought once more of Marias. He would not let them hurt her. He rose empty-handed as the lines made ready to march, rank upon rank stretching into the distance. Each man looked ahead, in hope, to the battle to come.

Taeshin watched as the king rode along the line. The horseman was a man in his prime, with a helmet set with a gold circlet, prickly as thorns. He carried a great sword in his hand and he was broad enough to wield it. Taeshin had seen the king make that same ride many times. Sometimes he was killed, while on other days the king was there to declare the victory. It never seemed to matter which it had been. Taeshin stared as the man rode to within a dozen yards of him.

'Highness!' he called, suddenly. 'Your Majesty!'

If the king heard, he did not look over. Instead, he raised his hand in the air and dropped it, while those behind crashed into movement. Before them, another army came out of the dust, ready to defend or to destroy, again and again, for ever.

15

The Red Inn

Hondo stood when the stranger entered. They had been given the largest room in the Red Inn, with clean sheets and hot water steaming in a bowl on the dresser. It seemed the owner had been a soldier in a previous life. Basker had seen injuries before and sent a boy running off down the street as soon as he saw Bosin dragged in by the other three.

Doctor Adams entered behind. He shut the door firmly and nodded to Hondo and the twin.

'This gentleman is Master Physician Burroughs,' he said.

Hondo noted the doctor to a logging camp was in awe of the newcomer. Hondo bowed to one of high status on instinct. As he rose, he saw Burroughs was slightly flushed, his hand still outstretched. Hondo took it, gripping too hard so that the man winced. He bowed again, embarrassed.

'And you are . . . ?' Burroughs said, a note of impatience in his voice.

'Hondo LuTse of Shiang,' Hondo replied. 'My companion is Master Je Saon. Thank you for coming . . . I . . .' He broke off.

'So this is the patient . . .' Burroughs said.

Without waiting for an answer, he crossed to where Bosin lay stretched out on a double bed. With Adams and a flustered Hondo looking on, the man cut through the crude wrappings with scissors and then eased the dressings away from the skin. Hondo watched him smell the wounds and nod. He tried not to think how close he had come to telling the doctor exactly who they were and why they were in Darien.

'Not terrible. Fair bit of pus, but clean pus,' Burroughs said.

Adams nodded, looking relieved.

'Master Burroughs was on hand in the hospital when Basker's lad came in. We're very lucky to have him.'

'All right, John, don't drown me in all that butter. How's my sister these days?'

'Very well. She asks after you.'

'There's always a place for her husband in the public wards, if he changes his mind. Or if she'd prefer to stop living in a hut in the middle of a forest.'

'We move with the loggers, Master Burroughs. And we have no regrets. Those men need someone to tend them, perhaps more than most.'

The physician looked over his shoulder with a wry expression, judging Adams with his eyebrows raised. He saw no weakness there and sighed, turning back to his task.

'As you say. Still, tell her I miss her and that she could visit once in a while.'

He went back to his probing, then frowned, turning to Hondo.

'Bring that lamp over, would you? I can't see a thing in this light.'

Hondo hesitated, but in that place, the man's authority was as absolute as that of any king. He had not missed seeing how Adams deferred to him. Hondo bowed and gathered up the lamp, feeling out of his depth. In a duel, or in the royal court, he knew his status and the correct manners without thought. Here, he was lost. He was aware he needed a wash and a shave, as well as new clothes and a good night's sleep. Hondo allowed the doctor to adjust his grip and the angle of the oil lamp, so that the light fell exactly as he wanted it to but the hot oil didn't spill.

'There, that's perfect. Can you hold it still?' Burroughs asked without looking up.

Hondo nodded.

'I believe so.' He had held a sword motionless for thousands of hours in his youth, building strength in his forearms. In comparison to that, an oil lamp was not so great a burden.

Hondo watched as Burroughs produced a set of tools from a case made of fine-grained leather. Each one was dipped into a glass of clear spirit. Hondo watched everything, determined to learn all he could. The man was not particularly fit, Hondo had decided, though his hands were steady and moved as if they belonged to another. They took up tools with a certainty of grip he recognised.

'Did you make the tongs yourself?' Hondo asked suddenly.

Burroughs was manipulating something beneath the surface and looked up in surprise.

'No, though they were fitted for me. I have had them since my first year of residency. I have a fascination for the finest steel.'

The doctor's glance dropped to the sword laid at Bosin's side, a scabbard of dark blue enamel topped in a long hilt that had been ruined by mud and blood. Hondo knew it would have to be replaced, though the hilt was nothing. Only the rippled blade mattered. He saw the doctor's interest and glanced at the twin, Je, who watched the exchange. Je gave an imperceptible nod, granting permission.

'This one is still owned, but if you save this man, I will make a gift of one that is its equal.'

'I would have treated this man anyway,' Burroughs said, 'but I won't refuse the gift either. Isn't it bad manners to refuse? I have never met someone from Shiang.'

Hondo blinked. The man missed very little, it seemed.

'Never?' he asked.

The doctor did not reply immediately. With a long pair of tongs in one hand and a rod of polished steel in the other, he reached deep into Bosin's side, right down the passage of a bullet. With a dull click, he gripped something in the flesh and slowly pulled it back to the air. He held up the bloody bullet to show to Hondo.

'There's one. Damn these things. Three or four years ago, I'd never seen anything like it. Now, they are too common. They are a pestilence – and one thing is always true. You have to get the bullet out or the patient dies. No matter where it is lodged or the damage you have to do to reach it. If it doesn't go straight through, we lose half our patients cutting deep enough to fetch it, or to the fevers that follow. It is a nasty business.'

He dropped the piece of lead and nickel into a bowl and began to press and tap Bosin's chest. Burroughs pressed his ear to Bosin's ribs and held up one finger for silence. Hondo held his own breath.

'There. It's still in him. There's infection already – you can hear it in the wheezing.'

'He had a cold before,' Hondo said. 'We were on the road for weeks without rest.'

'Something must have been urgent,' Burroughs said without looking up. 'If it's trade you're after, I have a few contacts. As I say, there are more legends than facts about Shiang. The consort keeps his past close to his chest, of course.'

'"Consort"?' Hondo said in confusion. It was not a word he knew.

'Tellius – your man, I believe. Isn't he from the east? I heard he was.'

The doctor was speaking while he worked on the patient, without looking up. He had no idea of the shock he caused. The twin rose to his feet, his hand drawing a knife from his sleeve that he would use to get whatever else the doctor knew. Hondo held up a flat palm to stop him.

'I would like to meet this consort, this Tellius of the east,' he said.

Burroughs chuckled as he smeared a dark yellow liquid all over Bosin's chest. As Hondo looked on frozen, the doctor widened the bullet hole with deep cuts, then attached a brass clamp with a steel screw to hold the unnatural lips apart. Blood flowed and Bosin stirred, groaning in pain to himself, though he did not wake. His skin had taken a pallor close to the wax stillness of death and Hondo wondered if he would ever wake again. In that moment, it seemed unlikely. When the doctor spoke once more, it jolted him from a stupor that was down to exhaustion.

'There isn't much that goes on in Darien without the consort hearing about it. If I had to guess, sir, I'd say you'll meet him soon enough. Men of Shiang? Arriving dead, half dead and shot to pieces? Likely as not, he'll come to find you.'

On the table, the unconscious Bosin suddenly coughed. Blood dribbled both from his open wound and down his unshaven chin. The twin dabbed at him, his face stricken. In the same moment, Burroughs nodded as something clicked in his tongs. After an age, he held up a second piece of shining metal, peering at it.

'Fine workmanship, though I am surprised it didn't go straight through your man. Even at his size, a bullet like this would pass through a shoulder blade and likely the man standing behind him.'

'He was wearing heavy layers of fur, leather and wool, doctor,' Hondo said. 'Will he . . . live?'

'He might now. The bullet looks to be in one piece, for which you can thank the gunsmiths of Darien. It didn't hit a bone and shatter, so I have it all. No, your worry now is infection – fevers. He'll need to be nursed. Now I, er, heard you'd be willing to pay. I could include the services of two nurses for a week, if you have the funds.'

Hondo held up two thick gold coins and the doctor's eyes widened as he accepted them.

'That is more than enough, sir. I'll have Basker bring up some of his chicken and leek soup – it's very good. And I'll arrange for new blankets and whatever dressings he'll need.'

The man hesitated for a moment, then pressed on.

'There is still the matter of the body . . . the, er, gentleman downstairs.'

He saw Hondo look to Je for an answer and the doctor's gaze followed that authority.

'Cremation or burial? I'm afraid the Families won't let you leave him in Basker's yard. There's too much fear of plague, especially these days.'

'I will bury my brother,' Je said.

Burroughs frowned uncomfortably. Where before he had been in his element, he was never quite sure what to say to the recently bereaved.

'I'll send the head of the city mortuary to you, sir. He'll arrange the plot, the stone, anything you need. It will be a ceremony of the Goddess, if that suits you?'

'The Goddess?' Je asked, confusion warring with grief.

'The service. Darien is a Goddess city, though we don't speak her name. The funerals will consecrate your brother to her.'

'That is not what he would have wanted!' Je said. 'If we were in Shiang, my brother would go into the family tomb.'

Burroughs tilted his head. He hardly needed to point out how far they were from Shiang.

'I am sorry,' he said. 'Perhaps if you took him out to the forests again. Three or four days from the city, I don't think anyone would know if you just buried him there. Or I could have him embalmed and made ready for travel, whatever you want.'

'I don't want any of this!' Je shouted suddenly.

He stood up from where he leaned against the wall and was in an instant, a dangerous presence in that room. Even Hondo sensed it and stood back, preferring not to interfere with raw grief. With a growl, the twin went out of the room and clattered downstairs.

'It is a recent loss,' Hondo said. 'He needs a little more time.'

Burroughs shook his head.

'I am sorry, but there are half a million people in this city. I won't be responsible for bringing some pestilence in. It should be cremation really.'

'Like a mad dog,' Hondo murmured.

Both Burroughs and Adams flushed.

'It is not meant to be disrespectful. Public safety comes high on the list of concerns at the moment. Half the city is training for some threat this winter. I won't be the man who brought it in.'

Burroughs was certain of himself once more and Hondo nodded when he saw there would be no compromise.

'Cremation, then. Send your friend of the mortuary. His brother will want the ashes returned. I advise you to call me when they arrive to collect the body, however. My companion is in the first throes of grief. It might take another mad dog to keep him calm.'

Gabriel came down the slope to a plain that stretched as far as the eye could see. The sun was setting ahead, smearing colours across the horizon. There was no sign of a road, or even tended fields. Scrub grass and wild streams dominated the landscape, with a dark blur of forests away in the distance.

His motley group looked ragged, somehow, after crossing the mountains. Lord Ran's beard had come in white, so that he looked twenty years older and was much thinner than the first time they had met. Gabriel reminded himself to feed the man, when next he had the chance. It was easy to forget and Lord Ran seemed not to care much for his own health.

Thomas scouted ahead, loping off and ranging for miles around them as they sought out some sign of a village or horses. He followed orders well enough, though there was something contained about Thomas that gave very little away. He had been the second of them to step through and he was almost as fast as Gabriel himself. Thomas certainly felt the pulsing thump as strongly, like blind bees turning to a queen. He had begun to raise his hands to it, as if in greeting or worship. Gabriel wondered if any of them were masters of their own fate. Had they even chosen to head west? Or had they been drawn there on strings they could not see? In his heart, he feared the answer.

Sanjin had developed a certain swagger since the high pass. The experience of walking with the heat of the sun and watching the drifts curl back and vanish had delighted him. Gabriel was not sure if he disliked the mage Sanjin more than the crippled swordsman he had been before. At least he still limped. For all Sanjin's ability to warm the snowstorm, he had not been able to restore his foot. Gabriel hid a smile at the thought, until his gaze drifted across Marias, talking to the Fool on his leash.

She tormented Gabriel, simply by existing. He returned to her again and again, but he had not dared order her to stay behind. He was uncertain what he might learn if he did. So she remained, proof of his fears.

Only the Fool seemed content, though Gabriel suspected he understood nothing. The poor devil who'd come through had found himself in a smaller room than he'd known before. Gabriel imagined the higher thoughts snipped off in the instant of arrival. A brain that had been ruined could not hold a man. Perhaps if the Fool had asked him to try and heal him, Gabriel would have, but he could not ask. There were times when Gabriel saw some awareness in his eyes, but they were few and more pitiful for existing at all.

Gabriel rubbed the bristles on his chin, still black, unlike Lord Ran's. They would not have looked like a formidable force to anyone who stumbled across them, but he had walked with just these few through the Mazer swordsmen of Shiang, right into the presence of the king himself. Gabriel touched the sword on his hip. It may not have cut as well as it had for the previous owner, but it remained a symbol of his throne.

Thump. He felt it, stronger than ever in the air. Each of the others froze for a second, and the Fool stumbled and hissed to himself. Gabriel clenched his fist. Perhaps he had no choice, but when he had gathered the stones, he would be able to go anywhere he wanted, do anything he dreamed of doing. He understood what they were in a way few others could imagine. Power called to power, he thought. He and Thomas and Sanjin and the Fool were all the Aeris Stone. It had dragged them from the grey land and it ran like white gold in their veins. He could feel its sisters in the distance, not quite as separate points, but the source of the call to him. Darien. He would fall on that city like an invading army.

Tellius watched as the body was cut apart. There were three mortuaries in Darien, but this was the only one owned by the Sallet family. It had taken a few quick moves and a bribe to have the dead Shiang swordsman brought to that place for cremation, but Tellius did not regret the loss of time or money. The furnace huffed and creaked in another room, heating the whole building, so that the mortuary was warm and comfortable while snow lay on the ground outside. Tellius felt knots in his shoulders ease for the first time in weeks.

The body on the table was as if he looked back in time. The hands bore sword calluses, while pale scars showed on the forearms and thighs – duelling cuts to show first blood, rather than any deep gash. There were only a few of them, which meant either the young man had been inexperienced, or that he had been very skilled indeed.

The king's physician, Master Burroughs, cracked the chest while Tellius watched, retrieving one whole bullet and two pieces of a second that had spiralled through the young man's gut. Whoever the swordsman had been, he had not had a chance. Tellius scratched his chin and considered how much he disliked the guns that were being made all over the city. Perhaps Lord Canis had been right that the things would change the city for ever, or at least the relationship between those who ruled and those who were ruled. Tellius realised he was biting the inside of a lip as he thought. He'd been doing that more and more over the previous month and made himself stop with an effort. There were different rules for peace and war, whether Lord Canis understood that or not. In peace, Tellius might even have agreed with him.

There were new bodies caught in the river lock gates each morning, dumped there by one of the gangs of the city. They had the same holes in them as the swordsman on the table. Tellius had heard a dozen complaints and private pleas to do something about the guns, but the problem was that he was spending another river of gold on vast orders of them.

Whether Lord Canis approved or not, or Lord Bracken or any of them, Tellius had seen the black wave crashing over the city. He would not deny the new militias the best weapons they could get. To make them stand and face an enemy with just cold steel would earn him only their contempt.

He winced as Burroughs began to sew up the chest once more. It was somehow more disturbing to see loops of thread drawn tight in the skin than it had been to see the breastbone chiselled in two.

'Same gun?' Tellius asked.

Burroughs nodded.

'As far as I can tell, yes. Same calibre of bullet, same location. Adams said it was Vic Deeds. We have enough to hang him, I'd say.'

Tellius chuckled.

'We're preparing for a war, doctor. I had enough to hang him when it was just a suspicion.'

'I don't believe I heard that announcement,' Burroughs said, his face stern. 'Is it martial law, then?'

'Very droll, doctor. You know what I mean.'

Burroughs finished his sewing and cleaned his hands in a bowl.

'In all honesty, sir, I do not. We are not a dictatorship and there are laws. The Twelve Families say they are above such things, but I think there are natural laws as well – and no man stands above those.'

Tellius blinked at finding rebellion in such an unlikely place. He might have replied, but three sober young men wrapped the body in the sheet on which it lay and bore it away to the furnace. Tellius shook his head in regret at the waste of it. That body had been built by years of labour into an extraordinary thing – and then made into meat in a moment. He turned to leave and then stopped.

'Why did you stitch him up, doc?' Tellius asked. 'He's going straight into the furnace, after all.'

Burroughs shrugged.

'For his dignity. I have a son about his age. It was a small thing to do for him.'

Tellius looked at the doctor for a long moment, then nodded.

'Good for you,' he said. 'Now I think I should meet his friends and see what brought them to my city.'

16

Assault

Loggers needed sleep or they tended to get hurt, so Moke wasn't exactly happy about being left to stand in the dark woods all night. Though he'd been a witness to Vic Deeds shooting those strangers, he didn't think it was worth setting guards like they were some sort of military camp either. They were woodsmen and loggers – almost the opposite of soldiers, when you thought about it. Moke would have abandoned his post and gone back to bed if the others in his hut wouldn't have beaten him black and blue in the morning. Some things turned a camp sour and the rest of them seemed to take their turns without too much grumbling. Moke swore under his breath. Nineteen years old and alone in the dark in the middle of winter. It was hard enough to stay warm in his bunk some nights, never mind out there, no matter how he stamped and blew on his fingers. They wouldn't let him have a fire, of course, saying it would make him blind in the darkness. They were bastards, is what they were.

He heard a rustling begin nearby and he shook his head, instantly angry with his bunkmates. He'd known they'd try something. It wouldn't have surprised him to find half a dozen of them creeping about, just to make him shriek like a woman in the night. It was a rough old crew, but the money was good and he liked not bothering to wash for weeks at a time. No one seemed to mind the smell and it wasn't too bad in the cold anyway.

'Come *out*, you sods,' he hissed into the darkness.

He had a torch of oil-soaked wool on a pole, but he'd been told not to light it unless he was actually under attack. The man from the timber company had said they would take it out of his wages if he lit it without good cause – and it wasn't cheap, either.

Moke heard footsteps and his nerve failed. The head of the torch rested on a serrated iron ring about the length of his hand. He found the flint that dangled from a cord and scraped it hard onto the slick wool. Sparks showered, revealing the trees around him in a flash. He blinked at what he'd seen, but held still as the flame caught and spread, so that the light grew.

Three men were walking towards him, with darker figures following along behind. Moke didn't know any of them.

'You're not . . .' he managed, before Gabriel put him down with a single stroke.

The torch fell from his hand and Thomas snatched it from the air, walking past the body without looking back.

'Hello, the camp!' Gabriel called to the silent wooden huts. He was hungry and cold, after walking so many miles. The forest had been endless and he'd followed an old track for an age before deciding it led nowhere and come back. He was tired and angry and in no mood to be baulked.

A few men stumbled out, rubbing their eyes and yawning. They did not seem unduly alarmed and Gabriel's patience frayed like rotten cloth.

'Fire!' he shouted. 'Treachery!'

It had the desired effect. The entire camp came alive at that and poured from the huts. Gabriel saw three other torches lit, revealing the positions of sentries around the camp. They came in with the rest and faced him, like schoolchildren before a master.

'Gentlemen,' Gabriel said loudly. 'I need food for six and directions to Darien.'

'Damn it! More of them,' one of them growled.

The logger's arms were powerful, though his belly strained against a shirt and a thick belt. He stood with a surly expression and black whiskers, glowering. Gabriel looked at him and smiled.

'No. You haven't met one like me before.'

The man reached behind him and raised a black iron pistol with a long barrel, pointing it at Gabriel.

'I saw one *just* like you. And I saw what put him down as well.'

Without another word, the man pulled the trigger and there was an almighty crack of sound. Gabriel took a step back in shock. It felt as if a strong man had swung a hammer against his chest. He could taste blood in his mouth as well as anger.

The man who had shot him gaped as the smoke cleared and he was still standing. Gabriel reached to a spot high in his chest and pinched the flesh there, as if to hold it closed. Before the eyes of that crowd, a shining bullet tip appeared slowly between finger and thumb. It eased out, bright in blood, until Gabriel held the whole thing. He was very aware of Sanjin's gaze on him in that moment.

'If we get the stones in Darien, I'll heal you,' Gabriel said. 'On my soul, I swear it.'

Sanjin nodded, the pact sealed.

The gunman stood wide-eyed in disbelief as Gabriel turned back to him. The man's hand quivered as if the weight of the gun was too much. Gabriel saw the moment he decided to keep shooting, when the tendons of the forearm tightened. The weapon was formidable, Gabriel had to admit. Yet there was only one. The others carried hatchets or axes and he was not afraid of those. They were not fast enough to bring him down.

With no warning, Thomas suddenly raised his hands wide, palms out in welcome. He looked like a priest about to bless his congregation. Wind swirled suddenly past them from the woods, dragging leaves and a smell of damp through the clearing. On Gabriel's other shoulder, Sanjin pointed slowly at one of the loggers. There was a moment of stillness, then the panicking gunman fired again.

Gabriel flinched from the crack of sound, but Thomas did not. He faced the loggers as if he stood behind glass. Gabriel gaped when he saw the shots made embers in the air, slowing before Thomas in orange trails of heat. When they fell, they sizzled in the leaf mulch and mud.

The man Sanjin had chosen boiled from the inside. Some of those standing closest began to retch when the smell of cooked meat began to steam from him. One eye popped white and the rest turned to run when they saw that. There was safety in the darkness and those who held torches threw them down.

Those who were quickest survived. The rest perished as Gabriel or Thomas walked amongst them. Twice more, pistols were brought out and levelled at the intruders. Both times, Thomas made the air thick, so that the bullets showed as fireflies in the night. It was not long before the camp was silent beyond the crunch of their steps on frozen ground. Sanjin found the food store and came out with a huge vat of ale held in his arms. Thomas was grinning at him as Gabriel came alongside. He asked no question, but Thomas grinned wryly and answered even so.

'I was behind you, brother, when we returned. If you can turn your hand to healing, I thought I should be able to do *something*. We had the power of that stone driven into us, like chips of dust under the skin. That's what it is, isn't it? The stone held an ocean – and we four were made to drink from it, or choke.'

Both men turned at the sound of laughter. The Fool was playing with a head, in the mud, kicking it back and forth like a football.

'The gift of the stone seems rather wasted on him,' Thomas said.

'Perhaps . . .' Gabriel said. 'I did think I might try to tap him, like a battery, or one of those spikes that dribble tree sap. If I can find a way to do that, he might yet be useful.'

Silence fell again between them, until Thomas broke it. Excitement bubbled in him, like a man drunk for the very first time. He could not be still, though there was darkness all around.

'I learned how to turn the wind away, up in the high passes. At first, it was just to lessen the sting of ice, but I found the trick of it, the concentration. I realised I was walking in calm, while the rest of you squinted. Then Sanjin started to melt snow.'

'The wind died down,' Gabriel said, in wonder. 'I

remember. What are we, Thomas? To be able to do such things?'

Thomas laughed and shook his head.

'I've practised every hour since then. It's more than I ever dreamed, to be able to do this, brother. I can make air as hard as iron.'

'Then I give thanks,' Gabriel said, feeling something like a parent's pride. He clapped Thomas on the shoulder. 'You will be my shield.' He thought for a moment. 'Darien has the power of many stones. I'd like to go in like a thief and steal them away, but if I have to, I'll break those walls down. I'll kill their king and sit a second throne.'

'Two seems a little greedy,' Thomas said.

Gabriel glanced at him and chuckled.

'It does. Very well, Thomas. I'll bend the knee to you in Darien, if you bend it to me in Shiang. How about that?'

'What are you two smiling about?' Sanjin said as he came up, dropping the cask of beer to the ground with a thud.

'The future,' Thomas said lightly. 'Now, if I can find a few jugs and cups, I will toast the stones of Darien, I think. On such a night, it would be bad luck not to.'

Marias listened to them talking. She stood with the Fool on his leash, away from the light of the torches. She knew Gabriel could turn and find her if he chose to. He always seemed to know exactly where she was. Those were the moments that hurt most, when she thought it had to be Taeshin looking so steadily at her. Then she would see him move with that unnatural speed, or speak so coldly she was amazed he had not killed her. Twice more she had

226

called him Taeshin without thinking, but he had not followed through on his threats. It was the only thing that gave her hope. The one called Gabriel did not know her, but he had still saved her from Sanjin's rough hand on her arm, back in the beginning. Was it by chance that Gabriel had walked just ahead of her through the high passes, shielding her from the cold? She did not think it was.

Marias shivered in memory as she stood there in the darkness, wrapping her arms around herself. What a strange group they were. The Fool was an innocent of sorts, too ruined to know sin. Sanjin was a man of petty vengeances and hatreds. She had even warned Gabriel about him, though he'd laughed at her.

She watched Gabriel smile at something Thomas had said, feeling love and misery. He was not Taeshin, not then. Sanjin came over to stand near them and Marias found herself edging away from his malice. Thomas seemed kind enough, though he too had killed without a moment's hesitation. He frightened her, but it was more like a storm. A storm could surely kill you, but it would take no pleasure in it. That was not much of a comfort, she thought. She was over a thousand miles from home and everything she had ever known. The bodies of working men cooled on the ground around her and she stood with a ragged imbecile on a leash. Listening to the creaks and hisses of settling death, she felt stained by everything they did. Yet she would not run from them, not while there was a chance some part of Taeshin remained. Gabriel called himself a king, but her Taeshin was strong, stronger than even he had known. If anyone could find his way home, it would be him.

Marias prayed in silence for a time, until Gabriel turned and looked directly at her in the darkness, as if he had known all along where she stood.

'There you are, Marias! Will you look in on the camp kitchen for me? My stomach is cramped with hunger.'

It is not your stomach, Marias thought as she went past him, her head bowed. The Fool went with her, smiling and blank as a mountain stream.

Hondo was asleep in a chair when the clatter of running men startled him awake. There was nothing quite like the sound of marching ranks for bringing a man from slumber. After all, those who woke tended to survive to have children of their own. Those who remained asleep had not survived all the dark centuries of history.

Hondo was still exhausted and a little confused. He yawned blearily, smacking his lips and looking around as he tried to see what had woken him. Dawn lit the room grey, with the street outside still pale and all colours washed out. Seated by the window of the room at the Red Inn, Hondo looked past trails of condensation onto the city of Darien.

His eyes widened as he saw soldiers in green livery taking station down below, with more of them vanishing from sight as they entered the building. They were trying to be quiet, but Hondo could feel the vibrations of men. Further off, more soldiers in the same colours were dragging sawhorses across the road and waving passers-by around that junction.

The swordsman came smoothly out of the chair. One glance at the bed told him Bosin was still deep in useless slumber. The big man's fever had worsened the night before, but the nurses were keeping him cool with cloths and fresh water, doing everything they could. The women Burroughs had sent were both middle-aged and sensible-looking. They saw Hondo's sudden agitation and stood by their charge with heads bowed.

Hondo looked further to where the twin still slept, stretched out between an armchair and a footstool. It would have been unthinkable at home to be found so deeply asleep, but the journey across winter mountain, plain and forest had left them all less than they had been.

Hondo rubbed his hand across his chin, enjoying the smoothness of oiled skin once more. The barber had cut him twice, which was actually not bad for a man working with Je's sword laid across his throat.

'Je!' Hondo snapped.

The twin was up and on his feet like a cat, his youth bringing him alert in an instant. Hondo tried not to feel a stab of envy. He still felt half-asleep. At least he had woken first, though he was twice the twin's age.

'Soldiers outside,' Hondo said, jerking his head to the window.

As he spoke, he knew it was hopeless. He was in his enemy's heartland, while he knew almost nothing of the local customs. He thought he could probably escape through the window and be off over the roofs before they came up the stairs, but where would he be escaping to? He hesitated, wondering if he could leave Bosin to whatever foreign cruelty they would dream up for one such as he. Would they put him in a cage, or make him fight wolves in an arena? They'd lose an awful lot of wolves if they did.

Hondo cursed softly to himself. He could not leave the big fool, any more than he would have abandoned the remaining twin. Some loyalties crept up on a man, whether he wanted them or not.

As Hondo considered how best to defend the room, the door opened and a man came through. The fellow was followed by others on his heels, all wearing green patches or armour tinged in that colour. Hondo's gaze remained on the first. He felt his mouth open, without any sound.

'So this is the big one, is it?' Tellius said, crossing the room and leaning over the enormous body. The mattress had proved too soft for one of his great weight. Bosin had sunk slowly into it, as if entombed by weak springs and horsehair. Tellius glanced up as Hondo dropped his hand to his sword.

'I'd appreciate it if you didn't draw that in here, Master Hondo.'

Tellius had learned the man's name and anything else he had been able to glean from Burroughs and the staff of the Red Inn.

'You are Androvanus Yuan-Tellius?' Hondo asked in shock. To have the man he had come to capture simply walk into his room was still too much to take in. Hondo saw the man's expression tighten, confirming his suspicion. The right age – and the resemblance to the young king of Shiang was written in his cheeks and lips.

'That is an old name. A strange name to use here,' Tellius replied. 'I have not heard it since I was a young man. It seems to me that anyone who might still use that name cannot possibly have a claim on me, not after so long. You came all the way from Shiang, Master Hondo!

I'm afraid I do not know of you. You must have become a blade after I left.'

'After you ran,' Hondo murmured.

Tellius smiled, though it was not a pleasant expression.

'I did have a number of angry swordmasters clamouring for my head at the time. Were you never young, Master Hondo? Young men make mistakes they live to regret, if they are lucky. Sometimes they make peace, as well. I have done so, though it is no business of yours. Now, if you came here for me, I'm afraid you will be disappointed.'

'I am the sword saint of Shiang,' Hondo said, standing straighter. The other soldiers looked unimpressed, but Tellius blanched, taking a step back as Hondo kept speaking. 'You cannot stop me, Yuan-Tellius. I have come far and seen the death of one companion and the wounding of another – all to bring you home for your crimes.'

'I slept with a woman, Master Hondo,' Tellius said indignantly. 'A woman who was not at all unwilling, by the way.'

'A woman who was queen at the time! Whose husband, your brother, was away at war! But this is no court, sir. I am not your judge. That lies before you. Now, I will take you back, or I will kill you here.'

'You did not abandon your friend, even when you saw soldiers close the street,' Tellius said quickly. 'Will you leave him behind you to die now?'

'My orders come before all other concerns,' Hondo replied. He tightened his grip on the sword hilt and the room became very still. Tellius stood in the centre, by the bed, with Je behind him and Hondo on the far side.

'Hellfire,' Tellius said loudly.

The result was a great hammer blow against the doorframe that caught Hondo by surprise as he drew his sword. For a single heartbeat, Hondo looked in astonishment at the huge green figure revealed in dust and broken plaster. The Sallet Green was somewhat more than an enclosed suit of green armour. Marked with sigils and gleaming with a green light, it stood taller than the man within and much faster. There had been six of them two years before. Only three were whole after that conflict, though Lady Sallet was working to restore a fourth. They were the greatest treasure of her house and each one was beyond price.

Tellius had a better idea of a sword saint's capabilities than anyone else in Darien. As he spoke the emergency signal, he threw himself down. He caught a glimpse of Hondo completing his draw and whipping a flash of light across where he had stood. Tellius felt a searing pain as the sword nicked his scalp. With a yelp, he crawled right under the bed. He had no idea where the other warrior was, nor his quality. One was bad enough. Tellius had forgotten the extraordinary grace of a Mazer swordsman. It was a little like seeing a bridge or a pasture of his childhood. It made him shake his head in delighted awe, even as blood trickled from the cut.

Under the bed was the safest place in that room. The Sallet Green went for Hondo and was attacked from behind by the second swordsman. The two Sallet guards who had come in with Tellius were outclassed, but they attacked the twin. Tellius could hear blades ringing against armour while the whole room shook and trickled dust. Basker would be furious, of course, even if they didn't bring the first floor down around his ears. The Sallet Greens were really heavy,

Tellius recalled. They were better suited to a stone street than bouncing around on wooden joists above a tavern, but he'd wanted an edge no Shiang swordsman could possibly have expected. The decision had saved his life, he thought complacently, looking up at the underside of the springs. A sword saint! The single greatest swordsman from a city that revered skill with the long blade above all other concerns. In any other situation, it would have been a great honour to meet such a man, to hear his stories or see him perform. Tellius shrank away from a sight of that blade as it was driven down from above, missing him by a hair's breadth. A great clang sounded after that and the sword was withdrawn. Tellius hoped the Sallet Green had really belted the man.

When there had been silence for some time, Tellius edged out from his hiding place. The two nurses had pressed themselves against the wall, visibly trembling. It was a little strange to see the younger swordsman lying unconscious on the floor. The twin was bleeding from a torn ear, but he still looked eerily like the one Tellius had seen examined in the mortuary. Two Sallet soldiers stood over him, both of them looking terrified he might leap up once more. Tellius had saved their lives by bringing the Green with him, he realised. Judging by their expressions, they seemed to understand that.

The Sallet Green had managed to disarm a sword saint of Shiang, Tellius thought in wonder. Perhaps he would find a moment to explain to the young soldier in the suit exactly what that meant. Not right then, though.

The monstrous armoured figure held Hondo in a chair, pressing down hard on his chest so that he could not escape or wriggle free. One of the massive green legs was dragging and Tellius felt his eyes widen when he saw Hondo had managed to pierce the knee joint, so that blood showed on the armour. In just a few brief moments of savagery, the swordsman had seen a weakness and struck with enough precision to get past the protective plates as they moved together. It was astonishing. Tellius was almost proud of the achievement.

The sword saint himself was panting hard, grazed and scuffed, with blood pouring from his nose. Yet Hondo was still alert enough to glare at Tellius as he stood up and dusted himself down. His sword lay beyond his reach, but he stretched for it in fury and frustration.

Tellius strolled over and picked it up, admiring the black and orange stitching on the hilt. With a twist of his fingers, Tellius removed the bamboo token that bound hilt and blade together. He tossed the hilt down and examined the maker's mark on the long tang he had revealed. The blade was a masterpiece, rippled in a thousand folds on the forge, impossibly strong. Hondo became very still and Tellius smiled at him.

'Don't worry. I would never destroy something so beautiful.' He picked up the hilt and fitted the pieces together again with expert hands. 'There. I will return it to you when you leave Darien.'

'I cannot leave without you,' Hondo said.

His teeth were stained in blood, Tellius saw. The Sallet Green officer had been forced to hit him really hard to put him down.

'I think you will. If I had more time . . . but it is what it is. Here is my offer. Your life, and that of your companions. I will keep you safe and warm in the cells of the Sallet

234

estate while your friend heals. I will hold your swords for you until you stand outside the walls of Darien, forbidden from entering ever again. Do you understand, or did my green friend here knock the wits out of you?'

'I understand,' Hondo grated. 'I think it is you who do not . . .'

'Excellent,' Tellius interrupted. 'How is my nephew, anyway? You know, I never even met him. He was born after I left.'

'King Yuan-Choji was delighted to find out where you had hidden yourself,' Hondo said. 'He blames you for his father's death, a man he adored. His *mother* took her own life to follow her husband, leaving a broken boy to rule with a regent until he was grown. The king considers you a traitor, Yuan-Tellius. He has never stopped looking for you, never. Consider that when you are telling me so proudly what you will do. If I do not return you to Shiang for punishment, you will see an army march against Darien. What will you do then? Can your single green warrior hold back a sea?'

Hondo saw Tellius grow pale suddenly, as if he had been struck. He could not understand why his words had had such an effect.

'Darien has other defences, Master Hondo,' Tellius snapped. 'And if you ever see them, it will be your last day.'

He calmed himself with an effort, putting his head out of the door to call more of the Sallet officers. The guard captain who entered looked intrigued. Hondo watched closely, seeing the king's uncle was treated with respect in that place. Tellius had risen far, it seemed, to command such forces. Hondo looked into the eyes of the green warrior who had moved like the wind. He saw only his own reflection. He wondered how Bosin would have fared against the thing.

'Tie these two well, Galen,' Tellius said. 'They will be deadly with any weapon. Treat them with enormous care and put them in the cells at the estate.'

He stopped and thought for a moment, pressing his finger to his lips.

'They are going to strip you now,' he said to Hondo. 'I'm sorry, but I cannot allow you to hide weapons you might use to escape. I'll have a blanket brought for you and another for your friend.'

Hondo swore at him and struggled, but he could not move.

'What about the big one on the bed?' Galen said.

Tellius shrugged.

'Thank your lucky stars he wasn't able to jump in and help the other two. By the size of him, I'd have needed more than one Green. Yes, though. Put him on a cart and bring him too. Oh, and you'll have to pay Basker for the wall. Be generous. He won't be able to rent the room until it is repaired.'

17

Breach

Gabriel first spotted the village by the pale streams of smoke rising from its fires. Night had come almost imperceptibly as he and the others had walked through another long day. Marias was limping badly, but he'd been able to resist the desire to heal her – a small victory that had raised his spirits. Lord Ran was skeletal. Gabriel suspected the man was willing himself to die rather than serve. He vowed to watch that Lord Ran ate properly from then on, determined to protect the one man who understood the stones.

The village was no more than three or four streets crisscrossing one another, with farmland all around it. Gabriel could smell the hot iron and embers of a smithy along one of the roads, with the sweetness of old beer marking a tavern on another. Under moonlight, he and his companion passed dark houses with shuttered windows, feeling as if they were the only ones alive in the world.

Sanjin strode ahead of them, confident in his own powers. Heat trailed him through the night air. Gabriel was caught between wanting to preserve a resource that could be vital to them and letting the fool exhaust his store. He had not enjoyed the Sanjin that had come out of the high passes. Some men were quiet and dignified in lesser positions, but tyrants when they had power. It seemed Sanjin was one of those. He wore his arrogance like a cloak and Gabriel saw the calculation in him, whenever he was asked to do anything. Could he be made to do it? No, that was beyond them. Gabriel thought he might perhaps manage to kill the man, but never force him to carry a shield, or scout ahead, not if Sanjin refused.

An owl hooted in the trees behind them and Gabriel heard the soft snort of a horse nearby. He breathed in relief. Marias could hardly walk another step. Gabriel suspected the only reason he remained well was that he healed himself of weariness as he went. If that were true, it was beyond his conscious control – and as much a waste of power as Sanjin torching dead trees in the woods, drunk on what he could do. The ocean could not be allowed to run dry – until he possessed another stone.

Gabriel stopped at a wide gate and unlatched it, stepping through into a yard lit only by a sliver of moon. The horse stalls were sheltered from wind and rain and in deeper darkness, so that he could barely sense the movement as horses put their heads out. They were such curious creatures, he thought, stepping over to one and stroking its neck. The animal seemed content just to snuffle against him, looking for food.

Gabriel was waiting for some alarm to be raised, but the house slept on and nothing came. He saw an oil lamp hung from a nail and looked around for Sanjin to light it. There was no sign of him and Gabriel had to search for a flint and striker, finding it on a shelf nearby. He smiled, imagining the stable owner putting it exactly where he could find it again, even in the dark. They were a long way from home, but people still thought about the same things. They still planned for hard winters and cared for horses.

They built a city like Darien and they didn't understand what they had, or that it could all be taken from them.

He cupped the wick in his hands and enjoyed the light that sprang up. There was no breeze in the shelter of the stalls, but he replaced the glass even so, as any careful owner would have done. This was a well-kept stable, a place of order. Gabriel raised the lamp and saw the nodding shapes of a dozen horses stretching away down the yard.

A dog began to bark, snarling and snapping madly. Gabriel cursed under his breath.

'Sanjin? Where are you?'

The light of the lamp didn't reach far enough to give him the answer, so he strode forward. In that moment, he didn't want to break the slumber of someone's home with more blood and violence. He just wanted to take horses and tack and ride away, leaving the people to their peaceful lives.

A dark shape came racing across the yard at them, a big animal driven mad with rage at the sight of intruders. Gabriel tutted to himself, but he raised the lamp with one hand and struck out with the sword as the dog reached him. The blade he carried may not have cut through steel for him, but it was still a four-foot razor and he made it sing.

The barking was silenced in that blow and he stalked forward, spreading the light of the lamp to reveal a long, low house at the other side of the yard. He understood the noises he had heard then, the thumps and muffled cries. His previous sense of peace disappeared like morning frost. Wherever he went, violence followed, Gabriel thought. Perhaps it was not something he could avoid.

Sanjin came out of the house, grinning to himself and

shaking his head. He saw Gabriel waiting there, with the dark shadow of Thomas coming up behind him. They faced the limping soldier as if they stood on one side and he on the other. They could see Sanjin felt their judgement as they looked at him. There was blood on his sleeve. He saw Gabriel's gaze rest on the stain and he raised it up, instantly defensive.

'I took care of the family. Don't worry about it. They won't be raising an alarm, not now.'

'"The family"?' Gabriel repeated quietly.

Sanjin either didn't see the warning in his stance, or more likely he didn't care.

'Father, mother, three daughters. A family. Oldest girl offered to do anything to save the others.' He chuckled in memory, flicking blood from his sword so that it spattered on the stone flags of the yard. 'I could have made her dance a lot longer than I did, but I knew you wanted to move on.'

He seemed to sense the anger or disapproval in the others and he bristled, suddenly angry.

'*Don't* thank me, then! You'd both rather they went running to the other houses, would you? How many would you have to kill then, if they came against us?'

'You are right, of course,' Gabriel said. He waited for the man's ruffled feathers to settle. 'Choose a horse, Sanjin. I will not rest in this place. The city is close and I am weary.'

'Fine,' Sanjin said. He had been expecting an argument and they hadn't obliged him. He still felt nettled, somehow, dissatisfied, but he walked to the horses. All along the stalls, a row of oil lamps lit without a touch to give him light, with only the one Gabriel held missing from the row. Sanjin looked back in triumph at the show of power. Gabriel inclined his head to the man, but when he turned away, he and Thomas exchanged a look that had his death written in it.

'We need him,' Gabriel murmured.

Thomas dipped his head a fraction.

'For the moment, yes.'

Like the dog that had come snarling across the yard, they would put him down as a danger to them all. When they had taken the stones, when Sanjin had used the ocean within him, when he was weak, they would send him back to the grey place without regret.

No one else from their group went into the house. Marias and Lord Ran stood in numb silence as horses were brought for them. Thomas checked the animals had taken the bits and each belly band had been tightened. He helped Marias to mount, cradling her boot in his hands.

'What kind of man kills children?' she whispered down to him.

Thomas winced.

'You'll lead the Fool's horse,' he said, ignoring the question. 'I haven't fetched a long rein for you to be led in turn. Call out if he falls or jumps down. If you run, I'll ride you down myself. Is that understood?'

She nodded, her eyes accusing. Thomas shook his head like a twitch and walked away to help Lord Ran to mount and tie his hands to the pommel.

When they were all ready, Gabriel led them out. Thomas and Sanjin followed side by side and the others trotted miserably behind. The oil lamps snuffed one by one as Sanjin passed through the gate, so that darkness and silence returned.

*

Tellius stopped the head of the Sallet household with a hand on her arm.

'Do not get within arm's reach of him, Win. Promise me. A sword saint is . . . always dangerous. A hundred thousand master swordsmen compete every twelve years – once a generation. The man in this room is the one who beat them all.'

'So you have said, dear,' Win replied. 'Honestly, you'd think I'd never met a dangerous criminal in these cells before.'

He chuckled, remembering his first glimpse of her, when he'd been chained to the table where Hondo now sat.

'Then try not to fall in love with this one, all right?'

Lady Sallet nodded, more serious. She saw genuine worry in the man the city jokingly called her consort. In its own way it was a compliment.

'I will be careful, I promise.'

He nodded and opened the door, stepping through before her. For any other door in the city, Tellius would have held it open, but he would not let her step before him into a room containing the sword saint.

Tellius looked over the chains holding Hondo in place. The Sallet captain had taken his warning seriously, it seemed. Thick iron links clinked at every movement, running through a massive shackle welded to the table. Tellius shook them hard, testing whether they were still solid. He drew both opposing chairs out from under the table and only then did he invite Lady Sallet to take a seat.

'There,' Tellius said. 'Master Hondo, I would like to introduce you to Lady Sallet. Mentor to the king and head of one of the first families in Darien.'

'It is a pleasure,' Hondo said. 'Excuse me if I do not rise to kiss your hand.'

His wry mood lasted as long as it took to speak and then he frowned at Tellius.

'I have had neither water nor food since my arrival. Nor have I been allowed to . . .' He glanced at Lady Sallet and Tellius repressed a smile. 'To bathe. If I am to be a prisoner, you should remember that you might one day sit in my place.'

'I will give the relevant orders, sir, the moment we leave this room,' Lady Sallet said.

Hondo looked to her, trying to gauge the relationship. Younger than Tellius, she was a striking woman. She wore a dress of green velvet cut deep at the neck over a white blouse. The effect was one of simplicity and he found himself admiring her. With an effort, Hondo turned his mind to more serious concerns.

'What of my companions?'

'The twin is kept in much the same conditions as these,' Tellius answered. 'We returned an urn of his brother's ashes to him and he has not said a word to anyone. Is he a mute?'

'No,' Hondo said. 'Though he does not waste words. Perhaps he has nothing to say to a traitor.'

Tellius stiffened and glanced at Lady Sallet. He cared for her opinion of him, Hondo realised. That was interesting. She raised an eyebrow, though her gaze never left the man she had chained in a cell far below her family estate. Hondo wondered how difficult it would be to make him disappear as if he had never come to Darien. As he looked into cold blue eyes, he suspected the answer would be not very hard at all.

'I am not a traitor, Master Hondo, no matter what you have been told. I made a mistake when I was a young man – and I regret it bitterly. I regret too that my nephew should be so concerned about the ashes of the past, long dead though they surely are, as to send four swordsmen to Darien. What, to snatch me off the street?'

Hondo shrugged.

'If it came to that, yes. My orders were to bring you back, to face your accuser.' He rattled his chains. 'If you free me, you could still come home.'

'I *am* home,' Tellius retorted. 'It is a shame you don't understand that.'

'What of Bosin?' Hondo went on without a pause. 'Has he woken? Did his fever break?'

'Doctor Burroughs says his lung was damaged,' Lady Sallet said. 'It is filled with poisonous muck and he has grown too weak to cough it out.'

Hondo looked at his chained hands for a moment. It did not sound like they expected the big man to recover. He was surprised how much the news dismayed him and he bit his lip in thought.

'Then he will die,' he said. He hesitated and then spoke again. 'You have magic – green warriors, strange glowing . . . stones in your walls. Can you heal him?'

'Lord Canis . . .' Lady Sallet began, leaning forward.

Tellius put his hand across, reminding her not to get too close to the most dangerous man in the city.

'No, we cannot heal your friend. The cost is too high and if we could ask this Bosin for permission, he would not be willing to pay such a price.'

'So you *could* heal him?' Hondo asked. 'But you choose not to. He is your prisoner now. If he dies and you could have saved him, his blood is on your hands.'

'That thought does not trouble me particularly,' Tellius

said. 'Do not believe these people are soft, Master Hondo. I have learned to love them in my years on this side of the world, but they can be a hard people. Pray you never have to learn the truth of that.'

'So I am to be held until Bosin has recovered or died, though you do not think he will live. Why not just kill him as he sleeps, Yuan-Tellius? If your new friends are so ruthless? At least then I could see if you will honour your promise and return my sword to me!'

He said the last as a shout and tried to rise from the table. The chains held, though they creaked. Tellius was up and ushering Lady Sallet out of the room in an instant, pulling the door shut behind him. He jerked his head to the guard in the corridor.

'Keep an eye on him through the window. At all times. If he escapes, he will wreak havoc in the city, understand? It took a Sallet Green to capture him the first time – and he came close to putting it down.'

The young man nodded and leaned against the door to see the man struggling with his chains within.

'And check the chains!' Tellius said. 'Take a group of three or four men, with no weapons he can grab, to test each chain and make sure he hasn't broken one.'

As he spoke, he walked Win away to the stairs that led to sunshine and the world above.

'Lord Canis can heal his friend,' she said softly.

'You know the cost,' Tellius snapped. He saw her expression of surprise and was instantly contrite. 'I'm sorry, Win. I just . . . I would not do that to anyone. None of the Canis family are right and it's all the fault of their damned stone. You know about his daughter?'

'Of course. That was sickening. I understand, but if you want these men of Shiang to stop hunting you, you have some hard decisions ahead. I merely wanted you to consider asking Lord Canis. There are other choices.'

Tellius shook his head.

'I won't kill them, Win.'

'That one back there would kill you. In a heartbeat. I can see it in him whenever he looks at you.'

'Perhaps, though he has a sense of honour. I will say then that I would prefer not to kill them. If there is no other choice . . .'

'Ask Galen to do it. He understands how valuable you are to me. If he has to remove three prisoners to keep you at my side, he will not see a problem.'

'No, my love, I don't think I will. If it comes to that, some things a man should do for himself, unpleasant as they might be.'

The sun had risen in the east as he and Lady Sallet came up the last flight of steps from the cells below. They'd passed through two barriers of iron and one set in the walls that opened only because Lady Win carried a cell token in a pocket of her dress. Anyone who tried to push through without such a token would be made a greasy puddle on the fine stone floor. Like her Sallet Greens, it was an old magic. She wondered if one day it would stop working and she or Tellius would be torn apart by whatever forces lurked in the walls.

'Yuan-Tellius?' she asked as they turned to the rising sun.

He sighed and closed his eyes for a moment.

'A family name. No longer a part of me. It was another life, my love.'

'Why then did he call you traitor?' she asked softly. As she spoke, she wound her hand into the cloth of her skirt, as a comfort.

'I had an affair with my brother's wife. It was discovered and I ran, rather than face him. According to our friend in the cell, things were not right between them after that. They tried for years to patch it up. They even had a son and heir out of duty, but after that, my brother took ill and died. His wife followed, while the king was still a boy.'

'They left their son alone?' she asked softly.

Tellius clenched his fist.

'Yes. It seems I am responsible for a great deal of pain and grief. The son blames me for the loss of his parents. Believe me, that does not make me proud. I thought I'd put it all a long way behind me.'

'The boy shouldn't blame you, though, not for all of it.'

Tellius rubbed his eyes, feeling them sting.

'If I am the cause of it all, perhaps he should.'

'I would not let them take you,' Lady Sallet said firmly. 'You are a man of Darien now.'

He smiled, but it was in sadness.

'Ah, love. I wish that were true, or the whole truth. Yet my memories go back a lot further, to a different time and place.'

The main gate of the estate opened to admit Captain Galen on horseback. As First Sword among the Sallet guards, he was one of the few outside the bloodlines of the Twelve Families with permission to ride a warhorse on the streets of the city. Galen made a fine figure as he dismounted and bowed to his mistress first. He and Tellius had grown accustomed to one another over the years. Galen accepted that the older man would never allow Lady Sallet to be harmed. On that subject, they were in perfect agreement.

'My lady . . . Tellius,' he said in greeting. 'You asked to be brought news of any other men of Shiang approaching the city. I have a report from the north gate. The guards there have stopped a party of six on horseback. They could not give a good account of themselves.'

Tellius' eyes widened.

'Call out your guards, Win. All of them. And all three Sallet Greens.'

'Is it an attack?' Lady Sallet asked.

'I'd rather be wrong than right. Galen, I need your horse. I must see that group.'

'I am not giving you my horse,' Galen said. He saw Lady Sallet look up and went on before she could make it an order. 'But if you mount behind me, I will take you.'

'Send to the other families, Win,' Tellius said. 'Get the militias out. If I'm mistaken, it will be nothing more than a drill. If I'm right . . . pray I am not right.'

Gabriel could feel heat rising around Sanjin, despite the very precise orders he had given. The sheer size of Darien was daunting. The walls rose a hundred feet in the air, so that they had been visible for miles over the roads that approached the city. The gates themselves were of huge beams and black iron, set in massive new fortifications, thick enough to resist an army. Gabriel had discussed the best approach with Thomas and Sanjin as they'd drawn close. The sun was rising and they were fresh. The city gates had been closed and a train of carter families rested asleep in their wheeled homes, waiting to be admitted.

Gabriel had ridden past them all and shown a hand's breadth of sword when a lone man protested. That had been enough to keep the others quiet. There were few laws beyond the walls of the city and not that many within. The traders might have defended their stocks with sword and axe, but they wouldn't risk their lives to punish the bad manners of such a rough-looking crew. When the gates had finally opened, Gabriel had been the first to ride through the widening gap.

He found himself facing a narrow road, with walls made of sandbags funnelling the entrants past some yawning soldiers. He could not see how the bags were meant to work. They seemed more a theoretical barrier than an actual one – he could have dug in his heels and jumped his mount over them in an instant. Yet he had agreed to speak softly at first. He, Sanjin and Thomas were predators who walked unseen amongst the sheep and goats. He would decide whether they should tease out what they needed, or just put a sword through the heart of the city. Peace or war. The choice tugged at his sleeve.

'What is your business in Darien?' the first guard said.

The man wore enamelled plate armour that overlapped in strips across his chest and down to his thighs. The material clacked and creaked with every movement. A dagger was there to be drawn in a sheath across his chest and a long sword sat his hip. It was rather odd, Gabriel thought. He was a man dressed for battle, not to question feed merchants and farmers.

The guard was beginning to show subtle signs of alarm as he took in the group before him. The man's eyes flickered to Thomas and Sanjin – and, of course, Sanjin was leering around him like a savage. Then there was Lord Ran, his hands bound, looking beaten down and miserable. Last through the gate were Marias and the Fool, who still wore his collar and leash. He looked around like a child, hissing softly to himself.

'We are mercenary soldiers,' Gabriel said. 'From Shiang. I heard the city is hiring.'

A boy near the gate suddenly took to his heels and sprinted away down a main road. Gabriel watched him go, waiting for the guards to relax.

'Mercenaries? You might find work, right enough. That one has his hands tied, though,' the guard said. 'How does he fit in?'

Two more of the guard's companions had stirred from brewing their first cup of tea to come out and see what was holding up the line. As Gabriel frowned at them, a huge dog padded out of their little guardhouse. His heart sank. He had never liked dogs. Sure enough, the animal began to growl as he glared at it, sensing a challenge.

'That's a nice dog,' Gabriel said, forcing a smile.

The guard nodded.

'He don't like *you* much, though,' he said, looking Gabriel up and down.

The man seemed in no hurry to let them past, though the merchants behind were already being waved through on a different lane. Gabriel felt himself flush as those families watched in delight, thinking the ones who had pushed in were in trouble.

'Why are your hands tied, son?' the guard called to Lord Ran.

The man looked up blearily and shook his head.

'Run,' he said in a croak. 'Just run.'

The guard stepped back and drew his sword in the same moment. In an instant, there were half a dozen armed men doing the same and the great gate began to close behind them. Gabriel didn't care about being shut inside the city. They should be concerned about being shut in with him. The light darkened as the gate was wound shut and a sort of silence descended on that part of the wall, as everyone in range peered over to see what was happening.

'Where are the stones?' Gabriel asked in exasperation. Despite his patience, the moment had still slipped away from him.

'I think you should dismount, sir,' the guard said. 'Moving slowly, so as not to alarm anyone.'

Gabriel sensed movement overhead. He was far enough inside the gate to be able to look back to where half a dozen men stood with crossbows aimed at his heart. Slowly, he raised his head and smiled to them. Heat was coming off Sanjin as if they stood too close to an oven. Thomas was watching Gabriel, ready to move. Lord Ran crouched over and began to moan in fear.

'Thomas?' Gabriel said. 'I think we'll do it your way now.'

Thomas nodded and all hell broke loose around the gate.

18

Contact

Lord Bracken came out of sleep as if he'd been punched in the gut. He rose with a huge inhalation, then turned the rising tone into a shout of anger. The two great dogs that slept at the foot of his bed leaped up and snarled, looking for an enemy. The bedroom door slammed open an instant later as the night guard kicked it in and entered with a drawn sword.

'Hold!' Bracken snapped before the dogs could take the man off his feet. Beyond the room, the clatter of paws approaching could be heard. He had very few servants, though the Bracken estate in Darien had better defences than any other.

'What is it, my lord?' the guard asked, peering around for any threat.

Lord Bracken stood up and rubbed his face.

'One of my dogs has just been killed – the one at the gate.'

He turned to the two animals watching him as they sat in silence. The guard was not surprised when the lord spoke to the pair watching him.

'Go to the gate and watch, but do not get close. Be my ears and eyes.'

The dogs pushed out past the guard. Bracken's expression became colder once the animals had gone.

'Bring me mail and my sword. The city is under attack. It seems Tellius was right.'

The sun was barely up when Tellius and Captain Galen skidded to a halt at the end of the road looking onto the north gate. Half the city was still waking, yawning warm and safe in their houses while the market traders and bakers were already out. Yet on the streets around the gate, the air shook and thumped. Tellius and Galen shared a glance as screams grew louder and a crackle of gunfire echoed back from the roofs nearby. Tellius dismounted, staring in fury at the flickering light and sounds of battle. He could smell gunpowder on the air. The light of flames flashed yellow shadows on every wall and the ground trembled.

Tellius swore, then raced up a flight of outside stairs. At the top, he leaned out over an iron balcony to see what was happening. He and Galen were some twenty yards away, one street clear and protected by houses on the corner. Tellius muttered under his breath as he squinted. His eyes were not as sharp as they had once been. The action by the gate looked like bees swarming around a single point, rather than massed ranks forcing an entrance. He ducked instinctively as something whined past him and cracked a tile above his head.

'Militia coming!' Galen said, looking back down the street.

The city had not been caught unprepared and Tellius thanked the Goddess and Lady Forza for that. If this was the wave, they had half of Darien in arms.

His jaw sagged as he began to understand what he saw.

Soldiers with crossbows and pistols on the high walkways were shooting and reloading as fast as they could. They did not seem to be having any effect at all. As he peered across the street, Tellius saw those men begin to scream, beating at themselves as if they were on fire. He realised that was exactly what was happening. He hadn't seen anything like that since Nancy, two years before. There was no sign of her threads in the air, but the men still burned. Magic was being used and Tellius could not see the source, nor think how to counter it. Except through force. When in doubt, send in men with iron.

The plan had never been to let an enemy into the city before dealing with them. Like everyone else, Tellius had expected an army, not a tiny group on horses who looked as if they would be swept away at any moment.

Yet they were not. As he watched, the twitching bodies of the crossbowmen collapsed, burning with greasy black smoke above the gate. Tellius leaned further over the rail and froze, suddenly, as if he'd been made into glass. It lasted an instant, then he turned and ran down the steps and out onto the road, heading towards the gate. He heard Galen curse behind him, but Tellius had to confirm what he'd seen.

Three men stood at the heart of chaos, not a dozen yards away. The air itself seemed to move around them, and as Tellius watched in astonishment, spears and arrows arced in and came to a stop, burning to ash.

He heard the clatter of hooves behind as the man in the lead spotted him standing alone. Tellius saw the man laugh, showing neat white teeth. It was a Mazer swordsman. Tellius could tell that from the almond eyes and the way the man moved. Tellius shook his head, his mind whirling. He glimpsed Galen come between them and took the arm that reached down to him, allowing himself to be dragged up.

Tellius felt a wash of heat on his back as the horse galloped clear. Galen had been forced to take another road and they found themselves cantering down a street filled with marching men, all heading to the gate. Tellius waved the officer to a halt.

'Five men and a woman,' he gasped.

Information was vital in the first moments of an attack, when everyone was asking the same questions. The officer listened with grim concentration.

'Three seem to be leading. They have some sort of offensive magic – heat, certainly, I don't know what else. We need help here. Sallet Greens, Regis shield, De Guise sword. Try to hold the position, to keep them close to the gate, but, corporal, fall back if you have to.'

'Thank you, sir,' the man replied. Not a month before, he'd been a baker in a small hotel, but he saluted crisply and waved a hundred men on as Tellius and Galen pushed through.

'Take this next road on the left,' Tellius said.

Galen half-turned.

'I need to get back to the estate, sir. I'd like to get the Greens out – and the main force. It's my job to be there.'

'You will be, but I need Lord Canis first,' Tellius said. 'Don't make me dismount, Galen. There's not enough time to run there. No more half-measures. I need to do this.'

Galen clenched his fists on the reins, but he knew Lady Sallet was safe in the estate. He went around the corner without slowing down, so his horse almost lost its footing on slick stones.

'Without breaking my neck, ideally,' Tellius added, tightening his grip.

The Canis estate was a mile away across the city. With the streets still light on traffic, they crossed it in minutes. The roads there were peaceful, with no sign of panic or even awareness of the threat in anyone they could see. Unless they brought the attack quickly to a stop, that would surely change. Tellius slid off the horse's haunches.

'Go on, Galen. I'll come as soon as I can. Take the news back to the estate. Get someone else to Regis and De Guise – and remind them they were not to be found two years ago.'

As Galen galloped away, Tellius approached the black iron gate of Canis House. He was immediately brought to a halt by guards stepping out to meet him, already bristling at all the commotion in the public street.

'You know me, or you should,' Tellius said. 'So one of you run to your master and tell him Androvanus Tellius begs his pardon and requests his permission to use the Canis Stone on a man.'

The older of the guards nodded to the youngest, who raced off, disappearing down the drive. The Canis estate house could be seen from the road. It was some six storeys tall and much more a city residence than some of the others. Tellius admired the look of the place, though he preferred the larger grounds of the Sallets or the royal estate.

There was nothing to do for a time and Tellius waited in the morning sun. The street was oddly quiet, he realised, as if the local people sensed something was off. Those who did walk past him went quickly, hurrying away.

'Is Lady Sallet hurt, sir?' one of the guards asked.

'I would not come to your master if she was,' Tellius snapped. 'No, the city is under attack. North gate.' He saw the man pale.

'I have family there,' the man said, suddenly shaking.

'It's not an army. If they stay inside, they should be safe.' Tellius had no idea if that was true, but he needed the man to concentrate.

They both saw Lord Canis at the same time. The head of the house wore a long black coat and was dressed in dark grey trousers and a white shirt under a black jacket. His shoes were as polished as a servant could make them. The lord carried a leather bag and looked more like a royal physician than Burroughs ever had as he crunched out across the gravel. The guard ran to open the gates and a black coach came around the side of the house, drawn by two horses.

'Well? I don't imagine you would waste my time, Master Tellius,' Lord Canis said. 'Get in. Explain on the way.'

Tellius bowed his head in relief. He could not like such a cold man, especially once he had understood the source of that coldness. Yet he still thought it was the right decision.

'Sallet estate,' Tellius told the coachman. 'As if your life depends on it.'

He slapped the side and sank back into soft leather seats, dark as the coach itself or the horses that pulled it.

'I imagine you could always hire this out for funerals,' Tellius said, looking around him.

Lord Canis did not smile. He sat stiffly on the seat across from Tellius. His black bag rested on his knees, with both of his hands keeping it safe.

'I have met you more than halfway, Master Tellius. You called and I came, with my family stone. I lent my aid to your preparations, just as I promised I would. Tell me then, what is so urgent and so desperate that you call on Canis?'

'The city is under attack, my lord,' Tellius said. It was hard not to respond in kind, with emotion repressed. Yet there was no matching the icy stare that weighed all it saw and found the entire world wanting.

'I see. Is it the attack predicted by Lady Forza?'

'I don't know, my lord. Not yet. I saw great forces at play. I would be a fool not to take the threat seriously.'

'Still, be wary, sir. Our enemies are capable of mis-direction.'

Tellius blinked for a moment, but they were coming up fast on the Sallet estate. He had the door open to leap down before they had come to a halt.

'Open the gate,' Tellius shouted. He saw Galen's face appear on the walkway and nod to those below. The gates swung wide and the black coach rode into a yard busy with soldiers running everywhere.

'Captain Galen!' Tellius called to him as the gates were closed once more. 'See that Lord Canis is offered tea, would you?'

'Where are you going, Master Tellius?' the lord said. He had climbed down from the coach and stood waiting impatiently. 'Will you play games with me? Where is the patient?'

Tellius knew the man was quite capable of turning the coach round and leaving. He did not want Lord Canis to lose his patience, famously short as it was. For that matter, Tellius didn't want to discover what other defences the head of one of the Twelve Families of Darien might have on his person. He drew to a halt.

'My lord, I beg your indulgence in this. Give me a few moments and I will know whether I need the gift of your stone or not.'

Lord Canis' expression could not have become any stiffer. He dipped his head the tiniest fraction of a degree, deeply displeased to be left standing in the open yard like a tradesman.

'Given the nature of this morning's news, I will give you leeway, sir. Do not test my patience further than you must.'

'You have my word I will not, my lord,' Tellius said. He broke into a run then, heading for the entrance to the cells that lay under the main estate house.

Hondo came awake, though he was not sure if it was day or night. It seemed an odd thing never to dim the lights, just as they never seemed to tire of staring through the small square of glass at him. He'd watched the faces change half a dozen times, learning the shift patterns to keep himself from going mad. They'd fed him like a child and then escorted him to the toilet wrapped in so many chains he could barely move. He shuddered at the memory of that particular experience. Their fear of him was a compliment in its way, but no man should have to endure being wiped by another, not while he had his strength.

He watched with interest as the guard suddenly looked away and spoke to someone. Hondo could read subservience. Not a rescue then, he thought. It would have been unlikely, but small hopes of that sort helped him to endure.

He had a strong suspicion he would be made to disappear when Yuan-Tellius decided he could be of no more use to him. They had extraordinary magic available, and yet they waited for Bosin to choke to death without lifting a finger. That was the true measure of them. It had confused Hondo to witness the obvious affection between Tellius and the lady Sallet. The man he had thought of only as a traitor had seemed rather ordinary then. Not a monster at all.

Hondo sat up straight when the door to his cell came open, his chest straining against the bonds that held him. Tellius walked in with a bunch of keys held in his hands. He grabbed the first lock and began slotting them into it, one by one.

'What are you doing?' Hondo asked.

'The city is under attack, Master Hondo. By men from Shiang.'

The news rocked Hondo, though he tried not to show it. He waited as Tellius found the right key and tossed a padlock aside. Hondo felt the first chain give, but three more needed to go before he could stand up.

'What is that to me? Why free me now?' he said.

Perhaps because he had been alone for so long, he found it hard to resist the urge to speak. Tellius removed a second lock and Hondo felt the links by his ankles fall loose. If he'd wanted, he thought he could have stood and grabbed Tellius by the throat at that moment. Was it a trap? A test? Either way, each lock removed was one step closer to freedom. The third lock fell away.

'Are you not afraid I will kill you?' Hondo asked softly.

Tellius paused and looked him in the eye. His face was grim.

'Not any longer. One of the men wore a sword with a dark red scabbard and a gold band. A very particular sword, Master Hondo. It used to be worn by my brother, and when he died, it would have been worn by his son.'

He saw the blood drain from Hondo's face as he understood. Tellius nodded bitterly.

'That blade is beyond value, Master Hondo. It would never – never – be given to another. If this man carries it, my nephew is dead.'

'That is a lie . . .' Hondo said, though he believed the manner of the man he faced as much as the words. Tellius was pale with anger, but also grief, as if he could barely speak.

The last lock dropped with a rattle and Hondo stood slowly, stretching his limbs. Tellius placed the bunch of keys on the table.

'Why would I lie?'

Hondo rubbed his wrists.

'Because it suits your cause. If the king is dead, my orders are null. I have no reason to complete the task given to me. For the price of a single lie, you would have me ride away.'

Tellius shook his head, looking old and tired.

'You haven't thought it through,' he said. 'You told me the king had no brothers and no sons. If he is dead – and by his sword, I know he is – who does the throne fall to then?'

Hondo stood very still as his world crashed down around his ears. After an age, he spoke again, though his voice shook.

'You cannot expect me to accept this on your word alone.'

'I do not. My city is under attack. When you see the sword, you will know – and in that moment, I will order you to defend me, to defend Darien.'

'You do not have the authority,' Hondo said immediately, though his voice trailed away as he said the words. If Tellius spoke the truth, the man he had come to bring home as a traitor had all the authority he needed. Hondo ran a hand over his jaw as he thought, suddenly uncertain.

'Have you spoken to Je? What of Bosin?'

'I came first to you, Master Hondo. You can explain to your companion. As for Bosin . . .' Tellius winced. 'I have brought the Canis Stone to this estate. It can heal him.'

'You lied before, then,' Hondo said, anger rising quickly in him.

'No. I said the price was too high – and in time of peace that was exactly right. In war, everything else goes to hell. A man who can take the royal sword from the king in Shiang will not be easy to stop, if we can stop him at all. Perhaps he is the black wave, I do not know. I do know that we'll need every master swordsman, including your friend. With your permission, I will have Lord Canis restore him.'

'And the price?' Hondo asked.

'You will see when you meet Lord Canis. His father used it on him when he was a boy, when his leg was crushed. It saves, but it takes . . . warmth. I would see that thing ground into dust if I had my way, but if this Bosin is anything like you, I would be a fool to deny his skill to my city, just when we stand against men of Shiang. Do you understand? If your man loses his soul, I would still do it.'

'Bosin vowed to serve,' Hondo said. 'He dedicated his life and all his strength to the king.'

'Dying is easy enough,' Tellius said. 'This? It might be better to leave him.'

'No,' Hondo said, making the decision. He had seen Bosin's strength and the man was right. Bosin unconscious was useless.

'Do whatever needs to be done,' Hondo said.

Tellius struggled with himself. He began to turn away and then spat the words that needed to be said.

'Lord Canis strangled his own daughter, years ago. She had cut herself on a thorn-bush and she was crying. When they asked him later why he had done it, he said he'd asked her to stop and she had not. That is what they are like, those healed by the Canis Stone.'

Hondo looked at him in something like awe. Slowly, in the cramped space, he dropped to his knee and bowed his head.

'You are a good man,' he said. 'I didn't know.' He hesitated, still reeling from what he had learned. Then his jaw set and his eyes shadowed. 'But before you do anything you cannot take back, I would like to see the one who carries the royal sword. If I see that, I will allow Bosin to be healed by this stone.'

Tellius nodded, but it was to confirm his own conclusion, not in agreement.

'There is no time,' he said unhappily. 'Lord Canis is here now. Trust me – or do not.'

He waited while Hondo thought over everything he had said. The man stood absolutely still and Tellius did not try to rush him. He was asking for a fine judgement, but Hondo didn't have enough information to make it. Trust or not trust. In the end, it always came down to instinct. After an age, the sword saint dipped his head.

'Thank you,' Tellius said in relief. 'Very well then. Come with me. The twin is in the cell next to yours. One of those brass keys will open his door. Bosin is further along. I'll have the guards bring him into the main house.'

He rushed out, leaving Hondo to stare in amazement. He had risked everything, but the proof that mattered most was that he had been trusted in turn. He looked at the keys to the cells and the open locks in amazement, still reeling from the change in his status. King Yuan-Choji was dead? Hondo clenched his jaw at the thought, feeling himself tremble. If the one who had murdered that young man was in Darien, his duty was clear. He was the sword saint and he would not fail.

Thump. Gabriel took a sharp breath. Was it a call or a warning? It felt close, as if he could almost see the gleam of the stones. He did not doubt he could find them, if those around him gave him just a moment of peace. Yet they would not – and they were dying because they would not. Sanjin in particular seemed to delight in the violence he could achieve. He made men scream like children, and when Thomas pulled the air from their throats to give them a quick end, Sanjin had glared at him with such rage Gabriel had thought he would turn on them. The man was running mad – and yet Gabriel could sense something coming. It felt like a brightness in the air, a purple heat approaching that point around the north gate. It had to be a stone – what else could evoke such longing in him? Power called to power. He and the others *were* the Aeris Stone. Perhaps that was why the things had clustered in

Darien, brought into proximity by ancestors who never truly understood what they had created.

Gabriel looked back to where Marias and Lord Ran cowered, hearing her voice cry out even through the screams and crashes of fighting all around him. Thomas had thickened the air, but something had come through in his moment of inattention. Gabriel cared more for the sense of heat building ahead. If he could snatch just one more stone, he would not need Sanjin or Thomas.

He saw Marias hold up her arm where a bolt had pierced her. He could not let her be killed, but at the same time he knew very well that the thought was not his own. The air itself swirled with broken pieces of wood and sparks of flame, while another stone approached him – and all the time, he fought an unnatural urge to get Marias to safety. Yet she stood with Lord Ran. If the old man was killed, who knew if a dozen stones would be any use?

Gabriel cursed and turned back to the pair of them, his steps crunching on mud dried to dust by Sanjin's wild heat. He put out his hand to Marias as she sank to her knees, blood pouring from her arm. Around them, bolts and spears burned. It was almost beautiful.

'I am here, Marias,' he said.

Somehow she heard him. He took her by the other arm and plucked the bolt from her flesh with a single movement, making her take a breath in sudden pain. She still held the leash. The Fool watched them without any sign of understanding, unaware of the danger that surrounded them.

'There, it is better now,' Gabriel said, touching his hand to the wound.

She looked at him in wonder.

'Taeshin?' she said.

His smile hardened.

'Take Lord Ran and the Fool to safety, Marias. It is too dangerous for you to stand with me.'

He glanced aside at one of the houses that edged the street. Sanjin was advancing against the ranks of militia attempting to engage them. Gabriel saw Thomas widening his stance, trying to keep them both covered.

'Quickly,' he said.

He took short steps and kicked a door right off its hinges, revealing a kitchen and a cowering family. Marias fell to her knees as he pushed her inside. He could feel the thickened air moving away as Sanjin pressed on, drunk on destruction.

'Gabriel!' Thomas called to him.

'I'm coming,' he said.

He pushed the Fool in behind her. In his haste, Gabriel plucked too hard at Lord Ran, so that the man's shoulder was cruelly wrenched and he cried out. Gabriel swore, bundling him through the doorway even as fresh gunfire sounded behind him.

He turned around at that. Gabriel wanted to walk towards the new line of men that had appeared on the wall. Their iron pistols offended him, as a swordsman and as a king. Yet he saw shots spark off the stones around him. The protection Thomas gave was fading in his wake and he did not want to waste the tides within on merely healing his own wounds.

Gabriel turned his back on Marias and felt the resistance vanish in him as he did. She was safe and whatever shadow of Taeshin that remained in his flesh was satisfied. He was quite alone as he walked back to the others.

In the grey land, Taeshin roared out his displeasure. He stalked the battle lines like a hunting leopard, haranguing them, calling to them, but never daring to pick up one of the swords or the shields that lay scattered on that field. He knew he would be lost if he did, but equally, he knew in despair that he would take a weapon into his hand in the end. There was nothing else in that place. Each morning, he walked down the hill and shouted and sang and capered – anything he could do to catch the attention of the soldiers. Some of them turned to look at him, but they never seemed to understand. Then the horns would sound across the field and they'd all look forward, like dogs called to the hunt.

He had watched the king brought down by knights. He had seen him cut down in single combat against a champion. More times than not, Taeshin had seen the man win, against the odds. He'd come to understand this king doomed to battle for eternity was not a weakling, whatever sins had damned him to that place. The man was a rare fighter and he looked after those who followed him. More than once, the only reason they'd won was because he'd avoided actions that would have bled them dry on the field. A warrior king did not have to be a good man, but he had to lead – and his men had to want to follow him. Taeshin could see it in their faces as they watched him and smiled, the way a son might smile seeing his father coming along a path in the woods.

Taeshin watched them march on and this time he did not go with them, but stood, utterly defeated, as they went to death or glory. He'd seen Marias pressed through a doorway, kept safe from the barrage of missiles and stones. The thought made him look down, to where his boots rested on the grey ground. He nudged a stone there and his eyebrows rose in surmise.

19

Bracken

Lord Canis had not moved from the spot when Tellius returned. He stood with no expression at all, though his eyes followed Tellius as soon as he appeared.

'Where is the fellow who is to be healed? Are you wasting my time, Master Tellius?'

'He is being brought up, my lord. There was no room below, for you to tend him. There is also a small chance he will be . . . hostile. I could not guarantee your safety in his room. If you'll follow me, I will lead you to the main house.'

He spoke as if he was reciting a poem and the result seemed to please Lord Canis, who bowed his head a touch further.

'Lead me wherever you wish, sir, but be quick. I cannot dawdle here. This is the limit of my favour, Master Tellius. Neither should you assume your gates hold me here. My will alone holds me here.'

Tellius bowed deeply, feeling old muscles stretch and ache. He led the way to the estate house of the Sallets, away from the huge doors where the Sallet Greens were being readied to go out. He thought the lady of the house might not appreciate Lord Canis seeing those preparations. Tellius smiled to himself as he entered through the main door into a hall. He had found love, but also loyalty to the lady who shared his bed. It seemed he would bleed green, if the worst happened.

Bosin had been laid on a litter, his weight borne by four big guardsmen. They were red-faced and dusty from efforts Tellius could only imagine. The narrow stairs from the cells had been designed to make a rush of prisoners almost impossible. Manoeuvring Bosin around those corners had left the men perspiring but triumphant, as they placed him on a long table in the day room.

Hondo and Je took station on each side of their companion. Tellius thought he had never seen a less comfortable pair in all his life. If the situation hadn't been so serious, he would have laughed at them. Instead, he approached Je confidently, as if the man had not intended to capture or kill him only recently. Tellius watched the young man's eyes widen as he walked over from the far end of the room.

'Has Master Hondo explained the situation to you?' he said as he came. 'About the sword that is now in the hands of one of the men entering this city?'

Je nodded, resembling a child caught stealing rather than the fearsome warrior he actually was. Both men were nervous as cats, Tellius saw.

'I was sorry to hear you lost your brother,' he said.

There was a beat of silence then in the awkwardness between them. Tellius shook himself mentally. All that mattered was that neither of the men of Shiang would attack him. He had blustered his way through a difficult situation, forcing them to take positions before they truly had time to think it through. So far, it had brought Bosin to that room and kept the peace. Tellius had tried to think of every objection, but he knew sooner or later Hondo would ask for his sword to be returned. That would be the true test. With his blade in his hand, Tellius knew very few things could stop a sword saint. The twin pistols concealed beneath his jacket might be one of them, however. He eyed the man who had reached the top of a pyramid made of a hundred thousand swordsmen. He hoped he never had to find out.

Tellius felt his expression stiffen as Lord Canis examined the enormous swordsman on the table. The man Hondo called Bosin looked swollen around the face and neck, as if fluid had gathered beneath the skin. He had groaned as the Sallet guards brought him in, but there was no sign of life then. His eyelids were bruised and dark and the chest hardly rose or fell. Tellius winced as Canis probed with long fingers, pressing and sniffing as he circled, like some spider that would eventually lay its eggs in the man.

'Master Tellius? Shall I begin?' Canis called to him.

Tellius shook himself free of the trance that gripped him. He looked to Hondo. To his credit, the sword saint hesitated, pressing his lower lip between his teeth.

'He will be changed?' he said.

Lord Canis raised his eyes to the ceiling, clearly impatient to get on. Tellius wondered how many times he had heard some variant of the same question.

'He will be better,' Canis said.

Tellius waited, though the city was under attack and he wanted nothing more than to run from that room and watch the defences brought down like a hammer on the intruders. He thanked the Goddess for Lady Forza, but the enemy had come through their new walls. Whatever

270

lay ahead would be settled by steel and guns and the arte-facts of Darien. As it should be, he thought.

Hondo dipped his head and Lord Canis decided he had waited long enough. He reached into the black bag at his feet and withdrew a stone of similar colour, though Tellius thought it was flecked with gold in the depths. It was the fourth stone he had seen – the Sallet, the Forza, the Bracken Stone its lord wore as a bracer and then this, one he had hoped never to lay eyes on. Tellius imagined every noble family in the city had whispered the name of it at some point. They would all rather see it gone. Yet if a choice had to be made between a life marked by that stone, or death without it . . . It was all too easy to imagine a child lying there. Lord Canis may have been cold, but someone had loved him once.

With care and concentration, Canis set the stone into a glove of leather and gold wire. Tellius watched the man use one hand to ease the other into the exact position. He could no longer close his fist. The stone was held against his palm like a tumour, polished and gleaming. Canis adjusted a couple of tension bands to his satisfaction, fix-ing it in place in complete silence. No one in that room dared to speak while he did so. It was as if they had stum-bled onto some horrible ritual. Tellius cleared his throat twice as it seemed to swell shut. He tried to remember every detail and at the same time prayed he would never consider using the thing on himself or anyone he loved. He made himself swear he would not, but when death stood in the shadows, who knew what oaths would hold or be broken?

Lord Canis pressed the stone and his hand hard against

Bosin's chest. Tellius saw him smile, as if he had returned to a lover. There was something deeply unpleasant in the expression and Tellius raised his hand to call out in warning, to stop whatever he was seeing. It was too late.

There was a thump in the air that seemed to sweep past all those watching, as if just for an instant the room had rippled like water. The effect on Bosin was immediate. Hondo and Je stepped close in astonishment as colour flooded through the big man on the table. As they watched with open mouths, the swelling around his face and neck fell back, while his flesh lost the waxen yellow look it had worn before. The wounds on his chest had been raw and pink, standing in mounds above the skin. They sank back and closed. Hondo leaned right in, unable to believe what he was seeing.

They were all startled when Bosin suddenly groaned, the first noise he had made since the process had begun. Lord Canis took the stone away from him then and removed the fastenings that bound it to his hand and wrist. He flexed his hand in obvious relief as soon as he could. The man looked weary and Tellius understood it had cost him something as well.

'Thank you, my lord. Is it . . . done?'

He assumed that was the second question Canis heard more than any other, but the man nodded without any of his previous irritation. He seemed spent somehow, washed out and weary. The bearer of the Canis Stone would endure hope and grief whenever he was called, Tellius thought. Still, he remembered the story of the man's daughter. That might be the third question he was asked, but Tellius decided he would not. Some things were too terrible.

'I will return to my carriage now, sir,' Lord Canis said.

Tellius bowed to him and led the way back to the street side of the estate house. The carriage waited, the driver wordless. Tellius wondered if he too was one of those who had been healed by the stone. The idea made him shudder.

By the time Tellius returned, Bosin was sitting up, shaking his head as if he'd been punched, and was trying to gather his thoughts. Tellius saw the man crack his neck and suddenly stand. He had not realised quite how large Bosin was. It was not just a matter of height, but width and depth. There were slabs of muscles there that Tellius had never seen on any anatomical chart. The stomach stood out to a surprising degree, though there was no fat on the man.

Bosin shook his head again, then again, looking more like a dog with an itch in its ear it could not shake. He made a growling sound to himself as he did so, then rubbed his chest with his clenched fists.

'There is a man in Darien who carries the personal family sword of the Yuan,' Tellius began. 'By that proof, your king is dead. My name is Androvanus Yuan-Tellius and I command you to defend my city.'

Bosin looked down at the man who addressed him, then across at Hondo and Je. They stood as men might stand while a tiger pads through the room. He nodded. His thoughts cleared, becoming chill and simple.

'Is he telling the truth, Hondo?'

'I believe so,' Hondo replied.

'Where is the other twin?'

'Dead,' Hondo said.

Bosin took that in.

'I see.'

He frowned for a moment, as if he could not quite understand his thoughts. After a while, he shrugged.

'I will need a sword,' he said.

Hondo watched the man he had found more irritating than anyone he had ever known. There was a solemnity to Bosin he had never seen before. Hondo felt a sense of having done something terrible, that he could not take back.

Gabriel felt the air thump and gasped at the power of it. The citizens of Darien had not run from that gate. No, they had gathered. Having guns seemed to lend them an unnatural confidence, so that they leaned from every window and peered round every corner Gabriel could see, pouring on shot after shot. As far as he could tell, Thomas was holding them off well enough and Sanjin – he walked with death, so that his sword blurred. Yet if Gabriel understood anything at all of the stones, it was that the ocean could be drained to nothing. He felt a nagging sense of doubt, but he strangled it and pressed forward towards the stone he sensed closer than all the rest, closer still with every step. He opened his arms to welcome whoever would stand against them, striding ahead of Thomas and Sanjin and the trail of burned and dying that stretched right back to the gate.

Lord Bracken walked out onto the street, his face stern. Two dogs trotted at his side, their attention on the maelstrom around the three men of Shiang.

'Do you see him, Thomas?' Gabriel called, pointing.

Thomas nodded and Sanjin too turned to focus on the

stranger. Gabriel could sense a sort of purple presence in the man. He had a stone. He actually wore one. Somewhere . . . there, on his right arm, under a sleeve. Whoever the man was, his arrogance had brought him to the front. Gabriel smiled, feeling his heart beat faster. Power called to power. Perhaps he had been drawn to them, as they had been called across mountain, forest and plain to Darien.

'Be wary, brother,' Thomas called. 'He carries a stone.'

Gabriel dipped his head. When he closed his eyes, he could still see the thing as a hole in the darkness. It looked a little like the golden eye that had dragged them all forth from the grey land. Yet whoever the man was, he merely wore a stone. The men of Shiang actually were one.

'Take him,' Gabriel ordered. 'Before others come.'

He saw Sanjin grimace at being given an order, but they stepped forward together. Ahead of them, the man watched without fear and Gabriel felt a chill come to the base of his stomach. The dogs watched them come and he realised they should have run, from the heat that licked around Sanjin, from the strange movement of air around Thomas, from the fact that Gabriel was a predator, with their deaths written in his every step. Yet they stood their ground. One moment they were walking alongside their master, then at a signal Gabriel did not see, they sprang, coming at him in silence.

Sanjin burned one where it ran; Thomas rammed air down the throat of the other, so that it spun end over end, choking. The man who commanded them inclined his head. He was separated from Gabriel by no more than thirty paces or so, the distance across the road. He did not seem afraid, not then. Gabriel was pleased to see that. If the man had run, they would have had to chase him. Gabriel wanted him to come close enough for them to snatch the stone from his dead body. It was an ache in him, like a sweetness in his mouth as he stalked forward.

Lord Bracken folded his arms, which allowed him to rest one hand on the stone of his family, that had remained as symbol and writ of their authority for centuries. Other families had artefacts of great power, like the Regis shield, or the Herne box. Perhaps every family of the Twelve had once owned both a stone and an artefact. Over time, the strong had separated from the weak. The Sallets had risen to stand at the right hand of kings, while the Aeris family had become generals and officers for the city, their vote worth almost nothing in council. He knew Forza, Woodville and Saracen had only their stones. Whatever wonder of the world that had gone with it had been lost, or stolen, or destroyed.

Bracken smiled at the three swordsmen approaching him. The house of Bracken had only the one stone as well. The difference was that they knew what it was and how to use it.

From behind him, the street filled with hounds. Hundreds and hundreds of them poured around their master and arrowed in at the three swordsmen. They came in deathly silence, without a single bark or growl. Bracken chuckled at the expressions of the foreign mages who had dared to come into Darien, who thought the city was just a plum to be plucked from a branch.

'Tear them to pieces,' he said softly, though his voice reached them all.

The stone pulsed on his forearm. As one, his dogs

began to howl. Those in front accelerated, scrambling to tear and savage the three men.

They were met with fire, and air, and iron. Gabriel moved, his sword already a blur as it took the head off the first dog to reach him. The problem was the sheer number of them. He heard Sanjin swearing as the man tried to focus. Dogs evoked an almost childish fear in the three of them, as swordsmen could never have done. Both Sanjin and Gabriel hesitated, unsure. It fell to Thomas to keep them back, yellow teeth straining inches from Sanjin's face as he steadied himself. He raised a hand as if to stroke the struggling animals leaping and straining, trying to reach him.

'Sanjin,' Gabriel snapped.

He was rewarded by a bloom of heat washing over him, as well as a stench of burning fur. Gabriel nodded as a ring of fire spread out, consuming the hounds as fast as they could race in. Animals could scream, it seemed. Gabriel put down half a dozen as they reached him, though half were already blind and burned, driven insane and beyond even their master's control. Gabriel took note as the worst wounded animals lost that peculiar drive that forced them in, so that they wandered off, backs curved and tails tucked up between their legs. The man who was their master was driving them all.

Gabriel advanced on him, though he had to wait when he felt the air thin. Thomas pushed through dozens of the dogs, flinching from their snarling faces even as he choked them with sharp gestures, or broke their backs, so that they fell to crawl away. He shuddered as he did it, though Sanjin was grinning as he swept them aside in flame. The fear of that fire showed in all their eyes, but their master's control was too great and the animals kept coming.

Gabriel saw the man take a step towards him, then another. The Darien lord raised his hands and the entire sky went dark. Gabriel looked up at the noise of birds. These did not come in silence, but shrieked as they fell.

'Thomas!' Gabriel called in rising panic.

He had dogs coming at him below and what looked like crows above. They began to fall as Sanjin dragged flame through them. The air filled with an appalling stink of burned feathers to go with the fur and blood and faeces on the ground. Birds fell by the thousand, but Gabriel had to flinch as some beaked and clawed thing raked his face and tore a gash from his forehead to his nose. He heard Sanjin cry out in pain, howling. Black feathers rained down through streamers of fire. The air was thick with wings.

Gabriel turned his head without taking his eyes off the Darien lord.

'Thomas? Sanjin? Protect me and I will take his head. He controls them all. Make me a path and I can reach him and stop whatever he is doing.'

He felt blood dripping down his face as he spoke and dashed another bird away as it clawed at his hair. Crows were carrion birds, with long black beaks and cruel claws. They were both strong and clever, and it seemed there was no end to them. Despite the heat and the shield of air, all three of them were bleeding and furious.

'On my mark, then ...' Thomas called. 'Ready ... mark!'

A path opened in the pack and the sky above. Thomas went down in the same moment, struck or bitten and curling as he fell. Sanjin sent a blast of fire along the edges and then he too yelled in pain as something reached him.

Gabriel went forward, fast as a shadow, towards the man who wore a stone. He hungered for it as he raced over the stone road, his sword ready for a single blow that would bring the storm to ash and feather and mindless hounds.

He did not see the thing he struck. It lay across the road as a filmy barrier without substance or thickness. Gabriel ran hard into it and felt it give before him, but hold. He looked left and right to where two bronze staffs rested on clawed feet, like enormous candlesticks. Men in blue livery stood to attention there, with fear on their faces at the violence of moments before.

Quick as thought, Gabriel struck whatever protected the lord of wolves and crows. His sword rebounded with such violence it almost broke his wrist, as if he had struck a wall. Yet he'd felt it move when he'd run full tilt into it, he was certain. He saw the men on either side of the road grin at one another, relieved the Hart Blue Border had held.

Gabriel hesitated, suddenly unsure of himself. He heard Thomas snarling like one of the dogs, struggling back to his feet. The path he and Sanjin had forced open had closed once again, so that Gabriel stood in a sea of the animals, barely kept from his flesh. He killed with abandon, but there were too many of them. Without Thomas, he would have been brought down, his throat torn out.

'What is happening?' Sanjin demanded. 'Kill him and be done with this!'

'I can't reach him,' Gabriel roared back. 'There is some sort of barrier. An artefact.'

In his anger, he put out his bare hand and pressed his fingers into it. He saw the Darien lord smile grimly at him beyond, but he might as well have stood in Shiang.

'We are the stone, brother,' Thomas called to him. There was desperation in him and he was bleeding from a dozen wounds. 'Go through it, or we are done.'

Gabriel leaned against the barrier he could not see. He reached out to it and summoned the ocean that lay within him. It was there, driven deep, but of such an essence as to make a man immortal. He took up the Yuan sword and this time when he touched it to the barrier, it cut through. There was a sound like a bell or glass breaking, and it was gone. One step brought him to the astonished lord. Gabriel took Bracken's throat in his hands and crushed it, letting him fall. At his back, the cacophony of snarls and howling ceased and the hounds fell still.

Above them, crows reversed their dives and clattered away as one, so that winter sunshine fell across the street once more, after an unnatural darkness. Gabriel smiled. He reached down and took hold of the Bracken Stone, ripping it free. He saw it was set in gold and bound to the man's wrist with leather and golden discs, like coins. Lord Ran would be fascinated, Gabriel thought.

He turned to his companions and saw how spattered in their own blood they were, how weary and dazed. Gabriel tutted. Plans changed, he thought, turning to the men in blue livery.

'You – where is your master's home?'

They gaped at him and he killed one in a blur. Still they shook their heads, so that he raised his eyebrows in surprise.

'Really? So loyal?'

Another turned to run and Gabriel swept his legs out before he could take more than a pace, so that he fell, white with pain, as blood pooled under him. Moving deliberately slowly, Gabriel advanced on him.

'The Bracken estate is just over there – not a hundred yards down this road, my lord. No one is inside, not now anyway.'

The man looked down at the broken figure of Lord Bracken. One of the dogs had returned to sniff the man. It growled as Gabriel glanced at it, but the animating drive wasn't there any longer. It was just a dog nuzzling the hand of its dead master.

'Show me,' Gabriel said.

The Bracken Stone was warm against his hand. It felt almost alive.

20

Stone

Hondo came to a halt at the sight of the Sallet Greens waiting in the yard. He remembered only too well the one he had encountered at the Red Inn. To see three of them turning to watch him was an uncomfortable experience. One still bore the mark of a sword where Hondo had dug the tip into the knee joint. That one watched him with particular intensity, he thought with satisfaction.

'We had six once, but some were damaged a couple of years back,' Tellius said.

He would have said more, but Lady Sallet came out then with the captain of her guards. Though her sleeves were white and a long skirt reached almost to the ground, she wore a shimmering green panel across her chest, like fish scales, though each piece was layered in iron and enamel. Tellius knew it would withstand a pistol shot. He had tested it himself. Men trooped beside her from whatever barracks lay beyond a great door, so that a hundred and twenty of them took station facing the gate to the street, ready to protect their mistress and the city.

Hondo frowned as he saw the way some of the men moved. To his eye, it was as if they carried a banner with 'Mazer steps' picked out on it. They had clearly been trained in techniques and methods that were guarded as faithfully as anything in Shiang. Hondo caught Tellius watching him.

'It was within the scope of my orders to make an end to anyone you had taught,' Hondo said.

Tellius raised his head a fraction.

'I see. And are those orders behind you, Master Hondo?'

'If you say so, they are,' Hondo replied. 'Though if you would have me defend my city, I will need a blade.'

It was hard for Hondo not to smile at the tension in those ranks when three swords were brought out, carried by a single house servant with less than perfect respect. Hondo's gaze was drawn to his own scabbard and hilt in black and orange, as it would have been to a daughter, looking for any signs of ill-use or improper care. He ignored those around him as he accepted the sword and felt the familiar weight. He knew that blade as well as his own hands and, despite all that had happened, he felt his spirits lift with its return. He did not respond to any of the fools who let their own hands creep towards hilts as he did so, ready to draw if he made a move against their master or mistress. Whatever training they'd had, they could not have stopped him.

'So. Are you ready, Master Hondo?' Tellius said. 'Master Je?'

The old man seemed to be amused, though his expression was a little manic. Hondo bowed to him.

'I am,' he said. 'I have given you my oath. Of course, if there is no royal sword, I will not consider myself bound by our agreement.'

'Yes you will,' Tellius said.

Hondo showed none of the surprise he felt. The man

was correct. His oath stood, even if he had been fooled, or lied to. Shiang's history was full of stories illustrating that exact point.

Before he could reply, Bosin came out. He had the same physical presence as before, so that laughter died and grown men shrank back, preferring not to challenge this particular warrior.

Bosin wore his own trousers and boots, with a new shirt and mail under a chest-plate. Steel armour encased his arms and legs, making him clank as he walked. It looked uncomfortable. Bosin did not call out or grin as he sighted Hondo and the twin, nor comment on any part of the forces waiting to go out to defend the city. The fact that he did not made Hondo breathe in sadness.

'This armour . . .' Bosin said, 'was made for a smaller man.'

He tugged the breastplate away from where it pressed against his neck as he spoke. They all heard the metal protest as it stayed bent.

Tellius looked up at him. He trusted Hondo – and through Hondo, the twin. He was not quite sure what to make of this man. The Canis Stone had healed Bosin, but that same coldness made him something else, perhaps something to be feared. Tellius glanced at the third sword, waiting for Bosin to take it up. His glance went further then, to the largest doors opening onto that yard. He chewed a corner of his lip in thought.

'You were to be my reserve, Master Bosin. Perhaps, though, if your armour is too small, I might find you something better.'

The big man stared and Tellius felt cold hands walk down his back.

'You have better armour?' Bosin said.

Tellius nodded. The city was under attack, he reminded himself. Bracken should have engaged by then and sent a dog back with a report. Tellius had seen no sign of those hounds, though it was still early. He had time, he thought, rubbing his jaw. He did have a set of armour that might do.

'Galen and I will take the men out, Tellius,' Lady Sallet said suddenly. 'Join us when you can, would you?'

'Yes, dear,' Tellius murmured. He glanced at Captain Galen and saw the man nod – his private promise to keep her safe.

The gates opened and Tellius watched the forces of House Sallet go out to the street beyond. He could smell burned feathers on the air and he wrinkled his nose. Tellius turned to the huge man beside him, waiting patiently to be given some instruction. He wondered who Bosin had been before, what he had been like. Tellius sighed to himself. It didn't matter any more.

'Come with me, Master Bosin,' he said. 'I believe I have something better than iron.'

Gabriel felt the lock snap as he pushed open the iron gates to the Bracken yard. The drive stretched around the house in a swathe of ancient yellow shingle, though green patches of dandelion and thistle showed wherever he looked. Brambles ensnared the black iron railings that marked the boundary, untended for years in thick loops and thorns. The whole place was overgrown, he noticed, with an air of decay. The building itself was squat, but not unattractive – a porch of sandstone pillars and three main storeys, with a fourth revealed in gable windows along a roof of ancient slate. Perhaps the garden gone wild was some reflection of the family name, or simply because Lord Bracken lived alone with his dogs and cared little for such things.

'I need to rest, brother,' Thomas called behind him. 'There are marching ranks coming. There . . . and over there. More of the militia and who knows what else.'

Gabriel reached the front door and, on impulse, tugged the bell that dangled there. Bullets struck pieces of stone from the porch. He heard steps approach, though Thomas began to swear weakly behind him.

'When you are ready!' Thomas growled.

Gabriel glanced at him and chuckled. The door opened and he yanked out the servant standing there, sending a middle-aged woman sprawling onto the gravel. She struggled to stand, but a stray bullet snagged her leg and knocked her down again. She opened her mouth to scream.

Gabriel passed into the gloom of the interior, with Thomas and Sanjin coming in together at his back. They slammed the heavy front door closed on the wailing woman and then waited to see if it would withstand the shots from outside. One or two sounded like hammer blows, but nothing came through, so they relaxed.

'That gives us a respite,' Gabriel said cheerfully. 'It was hot for a while out there. I could use a drink and something to eat.'

He rubbed his hands together in anticipation. The hall was clean, for which he was grateful. It smelled strongly of too many dogs, but Gabriel imagined Lord Bracken had at least ordered them into the garden at intervals. The man's use of the stone had been extraordinary, Gabriel thought.

He brought it out and ran a hand across its surface, very aware of the gaze of his companions.

'Come on,' Gabriel said. 'There must be a kitchen around here. We need to decide what to do next.'

'Well, we can't stay here,' Sanjin replied.

He looked up at stairs leading to a greater gloom above, clearly uncomfortable in the house. Their feet clattered on a polished stone floor in black and white. Perhaps that was to avoid carpets and rugs getting clogged with dog hair, Gabriel thought. He liked the clatter, personally – and the echoes.

'Why not?' he said, as they walked further into the house. 'We wanted stones – and we have one. If we stay in this house, won't the others come to us?'

There was no sign of any other servants, but Gabriel followed the smell of herbs and found the kitchen after a couple of false starts. It was a long way from the front door and he wished for more eyes, to place around the house and perhaps on the roof. The three of them could never defend a sprawling property in the heart of the city.

They carved thick, feathery slices from a ham and Thomas found some bread and mustard in cupboards. The result was delicious and silence fell for a time.

'That stone belongs to all of us,' Sanjin said. 'I did as much as you – more probably.'

Gabriel held it up for them to see. Golden wires dangled from it.

'Of course,' he said. 'Though without Lord Ran, I don't know if I can use it, do you? Would you put this on your arm?'

'In a heartbeat,' Sanjin replied, gesturing in the air. 'Give it to me, I'll show you.'

'I think I should be the one to take the risk,' Gabriel said easily. 'You see these discs, though, like coins? They touched both the underside of the stone and the skin beneath. I think the gold is more than just a clasp or a bracer. I think it linked him to the stone somehow.'

'To control animals,' Sanjin said with a sneer.

'Animals which nearly took us all down, remember,' Thomas snapped. 'And that was just one stone.'

He turned to Gabriel, leaning forward on his elbows.

'If we stay here, they'll gather. They'll surround this place. Just one of these was nearly too much! How will we handle two, or four, or five at once? Fair enough to take stock for a moment, but we should go out the back way and keep moving. Let's try and capture one more stone by tonight, say, then more tomorrow.'

Gabriel shook his head as he examined the Bracken Stone and the gold that spidered around and across it.

'You and Sanjin can't keep thickening air and boiling men. You'll run dry – and then I'll be vulnerable. I'd rather try to use this stone, here, while we have a moment of quiet. They may have controlled beasts and birds with it, but I should think that was just the desire of some ancestor. The stones are . . . pools. And I should be able to use one as I see fit.'

'What about Lord Ran?' Thomas asked. 'If we wait till dark, I could go across the roofs, back to where we came in. I could fetch him.'

'Yes . . . if it comes to that. We could barricade this place till nightfall.'

Without warning, Gabriel pressed the stone to his fore-arm, exactly where he had torn it from Lord Bracken. The straps of the bracer hung loose and broken, but he arranged the gold discs between the stone and his arm. He could feel them, warm against his skin.

He closed his eyes and emptied his lungs, becoming still. In the distance, dogs began to howl.

'Ah,' he said, his chest rising and falling once more. 'There you are. Oh, they have no idea what these things can do. Dogs and crows! Madness.'

Gabriel let an ocean wash against his mind, purple waves lapping golden sand. He sensed the Aeris white surging within him, but they mingled at the edges, staining white and purple together. With a deep and shuddering intake of breath, sitting in the kitchen of the Bracken estate, Gabriel drew it in.

When he opened his eyes, he saw the kitchen and the two exhausted men watching him in new colours, as if they had been muted before. Gabriel felt strong. He smiled with the sheer pleasure of being alive.

'I don't think we'll be needing Lord Ran,' he said. 'Gold works. Lord Bracken knew. I wonder if the others do.'

He flexed his hand, enjoying the play of muscle and bone. It was so fragile and wonderful, in the same moment. When Thomas laid his hand on the table and bared his forearm, Gabriel frowned at it. Did he need the man? If he trusted Thomas with the stone, he would have to give it to Sanjin as well, or see blood splashed across that kitchen. He clenched his jaw as strength surged in him, certain in that moment that he could murder the other two and walk out. The power of the stone was intoxicating and he wanted to keep it for himself.

'Now me, brother,' Thomas said, his voice low and serious.

Gabriel nodded. They had come a long way together and a whole city was armed and warned against them. He made his decision and reached over to adjust Thomas' arm. With a wrench, Gabriel removed the stone from his skin and placed it on Thomas, prodding the gold discs into place with his thumbs.

'It is more than just the touch,' Gabriel said. 'Close your eyes and draw on it. Seek the colour and pull it into you.'

He pressed the stone down, holding it steady. Suddenly, Thomas slapped his hand over Gabriel's, crushing it as he heaved in a huge breath of air. Gabriel watched the man's exhaustion vanish, the dark circles smooth away under his eyes. Thomas seemed to grow younger and larger of frame, and Gabriel could not pull back from him.

'My turn,' Sanjin said, eagerly.

Thomas opened his eyes and Gabriel knew the gaze he rested on Sanjin had death in it. The perspective of a god was a cold one. Yet Thomas came to the same conclusion and allowed Gabriel to remove the stone.

'That was . . . the most extraordinary moment of my life,' Thomas said. 'I want a stone of my own, Gabriel. I sense them around us. No more of this dipping of beaks. I want the ocean.'

Gabriel kept his hand pressed over the stone as he applied it a third time. Sanjin closed his eyes and wrinkled his brow, seeking the connection. Heat built around them and Gabriel swore softly as his skin blistered, but he did not let go. He could heal himself as fast as the blisters formed and he did not want to leave the stone in Sanjin's control, not even for an instant. They needed each other, but he did not trust the man at all. Gabriel smiled through pain at the thought, while his hand sizzled as if he held it in a fire. Sanjin seemed oblivious, but who knew with him? Some always seemed to be unaware while others cleared the way and did their work for them. Sanjin was one of those, Gabriel thought. He would take special satisfaction in cutting his head off, when he had the rest of the Darien stones.

'Nearly . . . I can see the colour. I can . . .'

'Quickly, Sanjin,' Gabriel murmured. 'You are burning me.'

'Nearly there . . .' the man said. He tugged hard at arm and stone together, as if trying to snatch them from Gabriel's grasp. Sanjin's eyes were still closed and it could have been a twitch or an unconscious move, but Gabriel held on grimly.

The change began at last, the shaking breath taken in, the marks and tiredness vanishing. Gabriel yanked his hand back. The stone remained in his grip, so that the connection was broken. Sanjin opened his eyes in confusion and something like pain. He looked at the other two in sudden suspicion.

'Why did you pull away? I had only begun . . .'

In response, Gabriel held up his burned hand, though it was healing as he did so. At the same time, they all heard hammering outside the house.

'There was no more time,' Gabriel said. 'And you were burning me, without realising it.'

'I had no idea,' Sanjin said, though there was something spiteful in his expression.

Gabriel wrapped the stone in a cloth. He was brimful of a power Lord Bracken had never known, or could not have used even if he had. As Gabriel stood, he pushed the wrap inside his shirt, over his heart.

'I think we should go out, Thomas, as you say. We don't need Lord Ran. Marias is safe.' He paused, furious with himself for speaking the last, when he didn't care if the slave lived or died. Perhaps he wasn't free even then of his silent passenger. 'Before they bring too many . . .' he finished.

Thomas rose in turn and Sanjin came with him. They had been bruised and bloodied when they'd entered that place. The Bracken Stone had brought back strength and confidence. When Thomas grinned then, it was a wolf's smile, with little lambs to play with.

'Shall I go first, brother?' he said.

They walked down the corridor back to the front hall and the great door at the end. Their boots clacked on the stone floor and Gabriel straightened and stood tall.

'Each time they think they know us, we change. Let me look at them. I am not afraid of Darien.'

Gabriel flung back the door and the winter sun streamed in, bright and cold. He had an instant of time to see the triple rank of black barrels arrayed through the iron railings of the yard, all pointed at him. A massed fusillade punched him from his feet an instant later. As he fell, one of the sandstone porch pillars cracked right along its length, sending chips of stone-like bullets through the air.

Thomas had dropped to a crouch, while Sanjin had thrown himself aside in the moment it took for the lines of militia to open fire. Gabriel had taken the worst of it. Thomas could see bullet fragments like drops of lead and silver rain all over the porch as he struggled to thicken the air ahead. It was hard to do it while the guns crashed on and on and thick smoke obscured the gates.

When the air was an iron band in front of him, Thomas leaned out, intending to drag Gabriel back to the shelter of the house. As he touched his leg, Gabriel made a growling sound and stood up. His clothes were tattered and he reached inside his shirt to see the Bracken Stone was still whole. He blew air in relief at that.

'Are you hit?' Thomas asked. Bullets still whined, but they dragged to a halt in the air, turning orange and giving off a trail of white smoke. He could see no blood on Gabriel, though there were burn holes in his shirt.

'Yes,' Gabriel spat. 'But I am not hurt. They cannot bring me down, brother, not now. I have power to burn. Power . . . to *burn*.'

He raised his hands and flame filled the air, scorching the ranks who had gathered to save the city and bring down the three mages. Men twisted and coughed in the blast, taking their last choked breath. Dozens more fled, beating out flames in their hair and clothes.

Gabriel smiled.

'I can be their saviour, or I can be the angel of death. Come, Thomas, Sanjin. See what they have brought to greet us.'

Three huge green figures had come through the ranks of men, untroubled by flame. They stopped at the gates to the Bracken yard, looking through the railings at the men of Shiang standing there. Each of the massive warriors stood taller than the iron points. Gabriel narrowed his eyes in wonder and delight. Darien was an extraordinary city, he realised. He wondered if he had made the right choice to remain in Shiang and give Darien to Thomas.

As he watched, the Sallet Greens exchanged some silent

communication. Working together, they tore through briars and railings in an orgy of destruction, smashing bricks and iron into rubble. They cleared the ground while the men of Shiang watched in awe and made no move to stop them.

When there was no longer a barrier between the Bracken grounds and the city, the three huge warriors were as still as the statues they resembled. Then they drew green swords and came on as a blur. Gabriel laughed and went to meet them.

Lady Win Sallet held position on the other side of the road to the Bracken estate. She had seen the three invaders withstand a massed volley, without blood or apparent loss of strength. The swordsmen Tellius had such faith in were standing in stunned disbelief at what they had witnessed. The younger one had covered his ears, she'd noticed. It did not fill her with faith in them.

As Gabriel stood up once more in the doorway, she turned to Captain Galen. Grey smoke drifted across the porch of the Bracken house. The news had flown that Bracken himself had been killed. It was more than she could take in.

Galen wanted to lead the others in a charge, but both he and his mistress could see it would achieve nothing. They needed an edge against those men – and the Sallet Greens had always been that edge. They stood to one side, gleaming like hunting hounds ready to slip the leash.

Out of the corner of her eye, Lady Sallet watched another messenger being roughly searched. No matter what colours they wore, they were never allowed within knife range, but she was desperate for any news. This one wore Regis red tabs on his tunic, she saw. She waved him in as soon as her man nodded.

'My lady . . .' he began, before his words were lost in the sound of flame.

Galen stepped protectively in front of his mistress as heat passed over them. It had been directed at the massed ranks of gunmen. Lady Sallet could hear them dying and she felt herself shiver.

'Report,' she said to the messenger.

He hesitated, unable to drag his eyes away from the burning militia. She slapped him hard and he blinked, rattling words out.

'The royal forces are on their way, my lady. Lords Regis and De Guise are coming. They ask that you contain the threat as best you can. That you hold them here. You may pull back as they arrive, if you are still able.'

Lady Sallet pursed her lips. She could hear the arrogance of Lord Regis in every word and nothing of the king's in whose name he acted. Arthur would never have addressed her in such terms, she thought. Yet it was no time to insist on proper respect.

'Very well,' she said. 'I will do what I can. Return to your master. Tell him not to waste time.'

She saw the messenger startle and wondered if he would dare say that to Lord Regis. Probably not. As the lad sprinted away, Lady Sallet turned to Galen. She watched as the armoured warriors smashed down the iron and stone that separated the Bracken estate from the city. Her city.

'Send in the Greens,' she said.

21

Greens

Marias sat in the front parlour of a home belonging to a family who would not leave merely because their front door had been kicked in and three strangers shoved into their midst. Lord Ran had gone to a window seat, where he rubbed his injured shoulder and wiped the glass at intervals, peering out at the street. The Fool had beamed when he saw a baby playing with wooden blocks. Though the mother snatched her child away from him, the Fool sat on the floor and stacked them in different colour combinations. The baby had started to wail then at the sight of someone else using his blocks. Marias felt the sound could not possibly grow more shrill, until it did. The baby clawed the air with tiny hands, struggling to get away from its mother and back to the blocks.

The woman watched the strangers who had invaded her house with big, dark eyes. The old man who sat in a chair and stared unblinking at them might have been her husband, but Marias thought he was more likely her father. Not a word had been said since they'd arrived. They watched each other in mutual fear.

Marias saw a kettle was being warmed in the embers of a small fire. It began to whistle and the mother looked at it and frowned, but did not dare move. It was Marias who moved slowly to take the kettle off the heat, holding out her hands.

'We will not hurt you,' she said. 'All we want is to save our friends and to go home.'

Lord Ran snorted at that, but he did not turn from where he sat, staring out of the window.

'Do you understand me?' Marias lifted the kettle as she spoke, so the whistling died away. She looked for cups. The mother's gaze drifted to a cupboard and Marias put the kettle on the bare bricks of the hearth and gathered a handful of chipped mugs.

'Do you have any tea?' she said softly.

The mother nodded.

'Of course we have tea. But this is my home and I did not ask you to break down my door and walk in here. You should go, before my husband comes back.'

'They'll kill us if we do,' Marias said.

To her irritation, Lord Ran sniffed again.

'What?' she said.

He stared dully back, but she kept her gaze on him until he was forced to reply.

'They might kill me, or the one they call the Fool, but not you. Haven't you noticed? Gabriel watches you whenever you are around him. What can possibly be so special about you?'

He spoke with scorn and Marias coloured as anger flared in her. Lord Ran had said almost nothing for weeks, but the moment they were alone, he found his courage?

'I am here to try and bring back my . . . man.' She'd almost said 'master', but she did not want to admit to being a slave, not to him. Anyway, were there even slaves in

Darien? Perhaps she breathed free air in that place, the same as anyone.

'He's gone, dear,' Lord Ran said.

She looked at him as if she'd been stung, but he shrugged. A blanket lay loose on one of the chairs and he picked it up and wrapped it around his shoulders.

'It was my mistake, to use the stone like that. Whoever you think he is . . . well, he is gone, as I say.' He wrapped the blanket tighter. 'I will take tea, yes, if there is a cup going,' he said to the mistress of the house.

To Marias' astonishment, the woman dipped her head and began bustling around. She had accepted the tone of his voice as much as the words. Marias shook her head in irritation.

'If Taeshin is truly gone, it's your doing, you useless, feeble old bastard,' Marias said clearly.

The Fool stopped playing with his blocks. Lord Ran turned to her and wiped a shining bead from the end of his nose.

'Yes,' he said. 'I started this, all of it. I wanted to make them better – faster and stronger. Instead . . . well, you've seen what they are. Mourn your man if you must, but don't expect him back.'

'If he's gone, completely gone,' Marias said, 'why did they bring me? You, I understand. The Fool is one of them, though his mind is gone. So why me? If there's no trace left of the one I love?'

She paused as she realised what she'd said. It was true, though a slave's love was a path to misery and humiliation. There were a hundred stories about such things and they always ended badly for the slave. Lord Ran didn't seem to have noticed that slip, or perhaps he just didn't care. He frowned as he considered.

'He brought you a long way . . . and he put us out of harm's way the moment he came under fire. This is a new science, dear. Perhaps there is some remnant in him, I don't know. I am cold and tired and afraid. Thank you, yes, two spoons.' He said the last to the woman, who had held up a tin of sugar as he spoke.

Marias raised her gaze to the ceiling.

'If there is even a whisper of Taeshin in him, I will call it out.'

Lord Ran sipped his tea and nodded approvingly to the woman, who seemed pleased.

'If you try that, Gabriel might not kill you,' he said. 'But the other two will.'

'Perhaps,' Marias replied. 'You stay here with the Fool, drinking tea. I am not a coward. I am going out.'

Lord Ran sighed. He was truly weary, in a way that the young woman would not understand until she had seen at least sixty winters. Assuming she lasted even one more.

'My dear girl, I did not say I would not come with you. But could I please finish my tea first?'

Marias nodded and thanked the lady of the house when she put a second cup in her hand. The heat and sweetness were more than welcome. As she drank, the Fool beamed at them both.

Hondo suddenly understood that he would die in that street, in a city he did not know. The forces at play were vast, far beyond mere mastery of a sword. It would be like a couple of hares attacking lions. He looked at his fellow hare, Je, and made himself smile in encouragement. Flames still burned on the scattered bodies of militia soldiers. It was no place for a man.

Hondo wanted very much to walk away. He had tested his courage a thousand times. There was no need for a sword saint to challenge mountains. Yet he had seen the blade the man of Shiang carried. The scabbard was dark red with a gold band, the hilt patterned red and black, in dyed sharkskin. It was the Yuan family sword and Tellius had been right – it had to have been taken from the king's dead hand. The three who stood in defiance in that Darien yard were all enemies of the state in Shiang. They were traitors, as well as murderers. Hondo thought back to his oath of allegiance to the throne and chuckled bitterly to himself. *To defend or avenge with my life the person of the monarch.* If he walked away, he would leave his honour in a foreign city.

Je drew his sword, still looking to Hondo for a decision.

'Are you sure?' Hondo said to him. He heard the lady Sallet take note of their exchange. She began to call orders, but it was not her concern how a man chose to end his life. He saw Je nod and salute him with the blade.

'It would be my honour to fight at your side,' the twin said.

Hondo nodded. That was true.

'Stay low, use the Greens as distraction. Keep moving and work with me,' Hondo said, stalking across the road. He heard more voices roar for them to come back, but both men ignored them. They reached the rows of rubble and burned bodies and brought their swords low, ready to strike.

*

Gabriel had the measure of the armoured creatures attacking him, he was sure of it. He needed just a few moments to catch his breath and take stock of the situation, but of course they would not give him that. He, Thomas and Sanjin were being battered and there was no time to consider tactics, only to react and react again. Flame seemed to have little effect on them. Sanjin had been backhanded flat to discover that. Only the intercession of Thomas had saved him as the thing stepped on his chest and brought all its weight to bear.

They were not immune to the sword, Gabriel was certain. He struck a dozen times as they came at him like a building falling, but the armour was sound and there was no obvious slit to see or breathe through, as he might have aimed for in a man's helmet. Still he kept striking, over and over, as if he was trying to sharpen his sword on them. The Yuan blade could be trusted not to break, even if it didn't cut for him as it once had. More, his attacks kept them off-balance and spoiled a dozen moves. Yet every time he batted one of them away, bullets would whine around him from fresh militia men gathering across the road. Gabriel could not take a full breath and he was growing furious.

They tried to use the suits as a weapon, of course, just as he would have expected. Two of them focused on him and Gabriel fended off elbows, knees, even the helmet of one as he sidestepped. Armoured warriors were hard to fight at the best of times, but they tired easily and they were slower. Not these green men. If they were even men. Gabriel could sense intelligence in the way they reacted. He thought there were trained soldiers inside them – to fight a man is to know him, as his father had once said. He blinked as sweat stung his eyes and a bullet ripped through his chest, a skilful shot at that distance. The pain was appalling, but he sealed it with one hand.

Gabriel just needed a little quiet to find the knack of the air shield Thomas used. It was a more subtle thing than flame or speed, and he could not do it. Without any let-up in the attacks, he could not make proper use of what he had dragged from the Bracken Stone, though it surged in him like a storm wave. Perhaps if he'd managed to bind the stone to his arm . . .

He stopped a punch from one of the monstrous suits with his free hand and struck automatically across the elbow joint with his sword. His speed and strength made his response a savage blur. To his delight, the joint buckled. Liquid gleamed from it, mingling red and green as it dripped down the massive arm. Gabriel smiled through bloody teeth. He thought he heard a cry of pain from whoever hid inside it.

'Come out and face us,' he called to the thing, gesturing with his sword.

The one he had injured stepped back in perfect balance as it examined the damage. The arm was locked straight, Gabriel saw. He brushed his hand past his face as bullets whined like flies around him. More of them struck and pain restored his focus. He looked past the green warrior to the men who shot from the road with shaking hands and wide eyes.

Gabriel witnessed Hondo and Je clambering over the broken remains of the estate wall. He frowned at two swordsmen daring to step into that place of fire and destruction. If the green warriors noticed them, they gave no sign. He looked back to the one he had injured and saw a green sword coming at him, faster than it had any right to be.

'Strike the joints, Thomas,' he roared as he ducked and came up again. 'Sanjin! Fire has no effect. Hit the elbow!'

He shouted the last just to make the one in front of him react. As he had hoped, it turned to shelter the undamaged arm. Gabriel lunged then for its knee, driving down through the joint. His sword had his unnatural strength behind it as it broke through layers – and the leg collapsed. More blood and green fluid spurted and that time he was certain he heard a cry of agony.

In a great spasm, the green warrior launched off its other leg and tried to grab and crush him. Gabriel stepped left as he might have done in his first life. He didn't try to block the lunge, just let the wounded opponent surge past and struck at its back, to wound. It was the wrong move against armour, the product of years of training to fight men. His instincts had to be rethought and *still* they would not allow him a moment of reflection.

Before he could turn, he found himself under attack without magic. The man he faced was of Shiang, which was strange enough in itself. The swordsman carried a blade the mirror of Gabriel's own, with a hilt of black and orange. Gabriel's astonishment almost got him killed. Hondo wore a simple tunic and leggings, but he moved with a fluid grace and he struck half a dozen times before Gabriel had come to terms with it. He needed to face the green monster that was surely rising at his back, but for a few vital instants, he had to defend in desperation or lose his head.

When he managed to beat the sword aside and strike

back, the man read his intention and was not there, so that all his speed came to nothing. It did not matter how fast Gabriel moved, the man seemed to know where he would aim. Gabriel began to add blows no ordinary man could have produced, his temper fraying. As the swordsman blocked his blade, Gabriel hammered his elbow into the man's face, staggering him. He did so twice more, at such a speed it would have been like being hit by a thrown brick. The swordsman's face was bloody and he stood dazed and helpless. As Gabriel raised his sword to kill him, he heard the grate and creak of armour at his back. His thoughts scattered like frightened birds.

Behind him the Sallet Green had risen up with an iron gatepost in its hands. It swung with appalling force, so that Gabriel crashed a dozen yards over the surface of the road, skidding to a stop with blood pouring from his mouth and his back broken. His sword tumbled through the air, disappearing into the rubble and the burned dead.

He had never known pain like it before. He began to heal himself as fast as he could, but he had been torn inside, with vital parts wrenched. Gabriel felt the world pulse in and out, and he knew fear then: of the grey land, of dying once more. He thought he could hear the grating footsteps of the green giant dragging itself through the rubble after him. Gabriel tried to breathe and discovered he could not. Blood poured from his mouth and steamed as it struck the cold ground. All he could do was try to crawl away.

Thomas shouted in anger and frustration. He was being engaged by one of the Greens and a grim young swordsman who seemed unnaturally skilled. Thomas used the speed he'd been given to match the man's attacks and dodge the green warrior. He kept his air shield around Gabriel for a time, before he was forced too far back. He was barely holding his own when another of the damned green things broke Gabriel almost in half with an iron post.

In shaking fury, Thomas closed one hand in the air, so that a band tightened on the neck of the armoured Green that faced him. He concentrated on just holding it in place as he struck out at the young swordsman. Divide and conquer was the key, he was certain. He was rewarded by a stripe of blood as he broke through the man's defence. The response was blistering and Thomas felt the sick pain of a gash in his hip as he swayed aside from a plunging strike that would have impaled him. He fell back on his defence, where his speed could counter the rattle of blows. Whoever the man was, he was too skilful and too determined to take on.

As he defended, Thomas concentrated on the green figure clawing at its throat a few yards away. With a vast effort of will, he began to twist the armoured head in a band of air that was as unyielding as an iron collar. His concentration took him almost outside his own body as he defended sword attacks and even bullets from the perimeter. All the while, he turned the massive green head, so that it was forced to look left, then further. The green warrior began to panic then, Thomas could feel it. He pressed even harder and his blade moved with a life of its own. Power poured out of him and he thought he would have been dead if not for the torrent he'd received from the Bracken Stone.

With a crack, the green warrior dropped bonelessly to the ground. Thomas opened his mouth to shout in triumph, but was tackled by another Green moving like a train. He went down under its weight, seeing the young Shiang swordsman loom over him, looking for a killing blow.

Thomas pushed back. They'd caught him by surprise and the green warriors were both fast and powerfully protected. Yet he had their measure. All things needed air – and all men stood in it. He rose to his feet not through the strength of muscle and bone but his own will. His body was weak and bleeding, too battered to stand on its own. Yet air settled too around the green warrior straining for him, pulling it upright. The young swordsman danced in and Thomas held him still. Bullets slowed to orange trails as he made a circle of silence around them.

'Now then, gentlemen. You've had your best shot – and here we are, still. So, what shall I do with you?'

He glanced past them as the last of the Greens moved. It had been damaged and it limped, reminding him of Sanjin. Gabriel was still lying wounded, though the man was already trying to sit up. Thomas smiled at the sight. They were hard to kill twice.

Sanjin came from the side, pouring flame at the young swordsman, forcing him to breathe what killed him. Held in place by Thomas, Je could not turn away from the furnace. His life was gone in a single beat, though Sanjin kept burning him and yelling in ugly triumph. Thomas saw Sanjin bore a brutal gash from forehead to chin, so that his face was almost in two pieces. He was red with his own blood and pain and rage. In relief, Thomas let the burned swordsman fall and turned to look at the green warrior.

When Thomas was sure the thing was watching him, he closed his hand slowly to a fist. The result was terrible, as the Sallet Green was crushed by forces no one could see. Green panels crumpled and blood poured from the joints and plates. Someone screamed within until it was suddenly choked off. Thomas smiled. His fists were shaking in the air as he broke the green warrior. When there was no life left, he relaxed his grip and let it drop. The green armour faded to grey as he watched.

He looked at Sanjin, as survivors of a disaster might have looked to one another. A bullet whirred past them in that moment and Thomas frowned, thickening the air. The effort made him grunt and he realised he had broken ribs. He felt his neck and winced – his clavicle had also been snapped. Every step and breath would be painful until it healed. All he wanted was to find a place to rest and recover. He doubted the people of Darien would allow them that luxury.

'Where is Gabriel?' Sanjin asked. His voice was hoarse and his lips were torn and still swelling obscenely. As he spoke, he pulled a piece of glass out of his arm with a growl. Something from the house had smashed or exploded in the battle and Sanjin had taken the worst of it. He was panting and wild, standing half-bent as his wounds made him weak.

Thomas saw the last of the Greens had clambered over the rubble, despite dragging one leg and one arm. Gabriel was sitting up by then, but the other swordsman had seen him and was staggering towards him as well, though clearly wounded. As Thomas stared, he saw the strange swordsman pause and reach down to something on the ground.

*

Hondo could see the man was recovering. He had never before witnessed the sort of power he had seen used in that yard on that day. He was astonished to have survived even to that point. Men were fragile when great forces moved. Hondo had no illusions about his own skills. He had been the best of a hundred thousand. He was said to be the greatest swordsman Shiang had ever produced. But he had not been able to match the speed of the one who carried the Yuan sword. It had been all he could do to read the man's muscles and stay out of the way of his blade. Even that had not been enough. Every time he had blocked, the bastard had struck out like a hammer. The world had swung upside down and Hondo could see blood wherever he looked.

He had made his peace. Hondo knew Je was dead. He had seen it happen and been ashamed at the manner of it. No warrior should be held and burned like an animal. Whoever they were, the three men of Shiang had no honour. Sadly, Hondo did not expect to live long enough to teach them the cost. He advanced slowly on the broken figure, squinting to focus, wondering if he could take the man's head off before he passed out.

As Hondo came to within a dozen paces of Gabriel, he saw the Yuan sword lying on the ground. The blade was still perfect, though it had been flung across shingle and rubble. Hondo hesitated. He could not leave the royal sword of Shiang in the dirt.

As he bent down and closed his hands on the hilt, he saw soldiers running at their position. Hondo had no idea how long he had been fighting, but it seemed Lady Sallet had decided to commit her reserves. Yet instead of engaging the enemy, they formed a defensive line, with shields facing the Bracken house. The last of the green warriors was gathered in amongst them and moved back.

Hondo shook his head in confusion. He saw the big officer shouting at him, but his ears rang and he could not hear him at first.

'. . . back. Fall back, sir. Please. We can't hold this spot.'

'He's down,' Hondo said, trying to point. 'One of them – the leader. He had this sword.'

He held it up to Captain Galen to show him, but the world swayed and Hondo staggered. Galen took him in his arms then and bore him backwards. The Sallet soldiers retreated in good order, leaving chaos and flames to take hold behind them. There would be no saving the Bracken estate, that much was clear. Thick smoke poured from the windows from whatever had caught fire inside.

Hondo saw the two who had killed the twin walk across the yard. He watched them as if through glass, understanding that he had been battered witless by the leader, but unable to make his thoughts settle. He was being carried away with armed lines retreating before him. Without warning, Hondo wrenched out of Galen's grip to vomit. He felt his mind grow a touch clearer as he saw Lady Sallet. She met his eyes and her expression was terrible. Hondo shook himself, trying to stand on his own. He felt both swords prised from his grasp and did his best to help as one of them was placed in the scabbard on his hip, first the wrong way and then with much fumbling, sliding home with a satisfying click. Both twins were dead. Bosin had been ruined. Hondo could not understand why he was still alive.

'Fall back in good order,' Lady Sallet said. 'Let Regis and De Guise have the street.'

Hondo looked to where she was glaring and saw ranks of red and black marching down the main road to that position. Cheers could be heard from some of the windows all around.

'Come with me, Master Hondo,' Galen said to him. 'You have a broken jaw. I'll have Burroughs look at you.'

'Not Canis,' Hondo said. He realised then why his words were so strange and not what he heard in his head. Yet Galen seemed to understand.

'Not Lord Canis, no,' he said, leading Hondo away.

Taeshin advanced along the line. He held a big stone in his fist and he knew the path the king would take to encourage his men. He had watched it many times and the pull to join them had grown to a great ache. Only the dreams of his old life kept him apart – and perhaps his desire to keep Marias safe. He would not let her down. The thought of giving up and just sinking into the ranks tugged at him, as blissful sleep calls to a weary man. He longed for it, but he could not give in, not then.

The king was looking over the army as he rode. He showed no awareness of Taeshin standing in his path as he cantered along the line. A ton and a half of armour, man and mount was a frightening thing to have bearing down at speed, but Taeshin had tried everything else.

He waited as long as he could and threw the stone in his hand. It flew true and hard, striking the king on the helmet and rocking his head back. The man looked for what had struck him in puzzlement and it seemed he would ride on even then. Taeshin swore and leaped at him, yanking hard. He brought his full weight to bear on the king, wrenching him over to one side. The man's boot stayed in its stirrup, but the other flailed in the air, so that he hung upside down. For a few breathless instants, Taeshin hung on, terrified of going under the hooves. Then something snapped and they crashed down together. Before the eyes of the astonished army, Taeshin bounced to his feet and watched as the king rose up, his eyes like flint. As Taeshin opened his mouth to speak, the king drew a great sword.

'Oh, son, I'll have your head for that,' the man growled, advancing on him.

22

Regis

Gabriel staggered as he made his way back across the broken gates and twisted ironwork surrounding the Bracken estate. Flames and smoke poured out of every window by then, so that he joined Thomas and Sanjin with the world on fire at their backs.

Ahead of them, they could see roads filling with marching men. Gabriel looked at Thomas, who seemed wild, his eyes gleaming. Sanjin was a different matter. His wound was terrible.

'Let me heal you,' Gabriel said to him, though even the thought brought a wave of sickness. He'd used almost everything he had just to keep himself from death. For the first time since entering the city, he felt they were overmatched.

Sanjin sidled up to him, his gaze on the streets around the Bracken house. Despite his own pain, Gabriel placed his hand in the bloody mess that was Sanjin's face and concentrated. He felt the flow of blood ease and the gash seal itself. A scar appeared under his hand, as if he drew it with a finger. With a grunt, Sanjin pulled away.

'Little bastard tagged me while I was distracted. Those green things . . .'

He did not need to explain. Gabriel unwrapped the

Bracken Stone as Sanjin spoke. They all looked to it as it was revealed, seeing the depth of purple, flecked in gold.

'Can you take more?' Gabriel said.

Sanjin put out his forearm in response and he pressed the stone to it, edging the gold discs into place with his fingers until Sanjin gasped and closed his eyes, breathing like a woman in labour.

'There it is . . .' Sanjin whispered.

Gabriel and Thomas watched the ranks assembling. The last of the green warriors had been borne away by its owner. He could not sense another stone in the area.

'We could get away,' Gabriel said.

Sanjin's eyes opened and he removed the Bracken Stone, fixing it like a leech to Thomas in turn.

'To where?' Sanjin said as Thomas stiffened. 'They know this city better than we ever could.'

'I don't know – to hide, to heal. Somewhere. We came for more stones and we have this one. I can't feel another . . . wait . . . over there.'

He pointed to the right of the assembled ranks, to the rear. He could see a man dressed in black, carrying a leather bag as he climbed down from a carriage of the same colour. For Gabriel, it was a smudge across his vision, as if a spot of grease had appeared on the lens of his eye. He could feel the presence of a stone, as perhaps it was aware of him.

'Power calls to power,' he murmured. 'They'll come to us.' He had no desire to see what other artefacts the city of Darien had created for its defence. All he wanted was the stones themselves.

Thomas waved his hand and Gabriel pressed the

Bracken Stone to his own arm once more. He had only closed his eyes for an instant when he felt it pouring into him, filling him with light and life and raw power, to be turned any way he wished. His healing accelerated, so that he felt bones knit and muscles grow where they had snapped. He breathed more easily.

'Tie it on, brother,' Thomas said, looking at him.

Gabriel raised his eyebrows.

'You are sure?'

'You can use it – better than the man who had it before. All three of us have the Aeris Stone in our blood. We can call on the others, but I want to survive long enough to see the rewards.' He looked at the soldiers marching down the road towards them and shook his head. 'We are not meant to be in this world, Gabriel. I think to stay here, we have to fight, to cling on with teeth and nails and everything we have. So spend it all. Let there be no limit. We stand here and we break these people. Or everything we've done is for nothing.'

Gabriel put out his hand and Thomas shook it. Sanjin laughed, cracking his neck in his hands.

'I know my choice,' Sanjin said. 'I will burn this city to ashes before I go back.'

Gabriel tore a piece of shirt and wrapped it round his arm. He felt the stone against his skin, trickling power into him. He nodded to Thomas.

'Very well. Let's take them on.'

Walking with a Sallet Green had its advantages, Tellius thought. The armoured warriors were legends in Darien. Marching ranks got out of the way for one of the massive

Sallet artefacts. Even the patchwork one. The workshop men of the Sallet estate called it that for the shifting colours of green and grey. Ever since it had been drained and then burned two years before, the suit had been too badly damaged to use. Yet with two others fit only for scrap, it meant that Lady Sallet's people had ruined suits to work on, for the first time. They'd understood so little of how the suits were made that at first they'd been like children in a workshop, not daring to touch the machines for fear they'd destroy them. They had learned a great deal from taking them apart. The patchwork suit was not as powerful as the others, but the day green had bloomed again along its panels had felt like a victory.

Tellius looked back to the thing following him, feeling like a child himself as it towered over anyone else in the road. He did not know who Bosin had been before his healing. The man he was at that moment was utterly focused on the task at hand – learning how to use the armour. Tellius had thought he would have to persuade the Shiang swordsman, but Bosin showed no indecision or fear of the thing. From the first moment he'd seen it waiting for him, he'd been coldly appreciative.

As Tellius looked back, he saw Bosin rotating the wrists and lifting the legs high, so that he stamped and twisted at the waist, a hundred different movements to mimic his own. The green panels flickered, so that he sagged for an instant. Before Tellius could do more than curse, the man was up once more, jumping in place with enough force to crack the stones of the road. The green sword on his back was still there. In one huge gauntlet, he carried his own sword, the long blade of a master.

Tellius could see flashes of light and drifting smoke ahead of them. He fretted as he walked. The street was full of the militia forces, all pressing forward. There was no sign yet of Sallet guards, nor the only one he wished was nowhere near that place. If he could have forbidden her presence, Tellius would have done it. Yet Win was the head of the house and her guards, even sensible men like Galen, would not refuse her orders for those of her beloved companion, regardless of him being constantly, continuously right. It was infuriating.

Tellius breathed in relief when he glimpsed Sallet colours ahead, though his expression became sickly as he saw the Bracken house burning. The sun was going down and the short winter's day was coming to an end. Yet flames and heat bathed them all. He caught his breath when he saw Lady Sallet standing with Hondo and Captain Galen. Tellius went forward in a rush then, relying on the presence at his back to clear the path.

Lady Sallet glanced up with all the others. Her eyes widened.

'You brought Patchwork?' she said.

Tellius smiled tightly. He did not like her using the term as a pet name for the thing. The Sallet Green may have been damaged, but it was not a faithful hound, nor a child's toy. It was still an artefact of extraordinary offensive ability – and if it had its weaknesses, well, he had put a Mazer swordsman inside it, a man trained from childhood in every aspect of combat. He'd worried Bosin would be too big to get inside, but the suit had adjusted as it had for others, settling ten thousand rounded metal heads against his flesh. As he moved, they moved, and the suit amplified it all.

Tellius felt his eyes widen as he took in the carnage around the Bracken estate. Two Sallet Greens were down and the one nearest him was still leaking blood from the man inside. As he watched, Galen's men brought a flatbed cart and began loading the armour onto it. They made no attempt to remove the man within, not then, with too many eyes around to report their secrets.

Facing the street, Tellius saw the same three men he'd seen entering the city. As he watched, they stood close together, clearly discussing tactics like any team about to face another assault. He reached back and patted the patchwork armour on its arm, not that the man inside could have felt it. The huge figure at his side seemed to lean forward and the armour creaked threateningly.

'Hold here,' Tellius said. 'Wait for my order.'

Bosin stood like a statue then, peering over the flames and scattered bodies. Tellius kept a wary eye on him as he looked for Captain Galen and Win.

Hondo came through the crowd of Sallet soldiers. They parted for him as they would have done for Bosin, and Tellius understood why as the man stopped in front of him. Hondo was marked in blood and soot from head to toe. He'd rolled and dodged and been struck hard any number of times. Tellius saw he held two swords and he gaped as Hondo bowed and presented one of them to him.

The hilt of the Yuan sword was filthy, the red and black sharkskin ruined. Yet the blade was perfect, a silver length unmarked. Tellius raised it in awe.

'I saw this last . . . when my brother wore it. Can you believe that? Before his son. It is like looking into the past.'

'Stand back, salads!' a voice came.

Tellius looked to the source and raised his eyes as he saw Lord Regis approaching, surrounded by a hundred or so of his soldiers in dark red. The man carried the Regis shield on his left arm and wore a short sword on his hip. Tellius was interested in the shield, but he found the man himself unbelievably irritating.

'Be polite, Tellius,' Lady Sallet murmured at his shoulder.

'There you are,' he replied as quietly.

He reached over without looking and touched her hand for the briefest of moments before they let go. Lord Regis was bearing down on their position and Tellius braced himself. Win never seemed to notice the barbs Regis managed to include in every exchange. 'Salads' was just one example.

'Evening, master consort,' Regis said. He frowned at the patchwork armour looming over them all and bowed to Win. 'Lady Sallet. Bit of a fracas! Thought I'd help out.'

The man was red-faced, broad of chest and loud, but Tellius was convinced he only played the part of a brash and stupid man. No actual idiot could have managed to get under his skin so effectively, he was almost certain.

'Defending the city, my lord, yes, as you agreed you would, in council. You are very welcome, of course. I . . .'

'Brought De Guise here,' Regis said over him, as if he'd wearied of Tellius already. 'Old Geese and his sword. Your fresh salads can stand down, I should think.'

'These men are very powerful,' Tellius said. As much as he would have enjoyed seeing Regis brought to his knees, the shield was an asset that could be useful, even if the man who carried it was a moron.

'Those three dear young maidens?' Regis said, peering

into the flame-light around the Bracken estate. The evening darkened further every moment and Tellius wondered how he would prevent the invaders just disappearing into darkness.

Regis did not look particularly impressed at what he saw.

'I'll block them with the shield. De Guise will bring up the sword in my shadow and that should be about it. Anything else I need to know?'

Regis seemed to be preparing himself to attack. He edged away, glaring at the three enemies. Tellius spoke quickly before the lord could rush off.

'Hondo, you've fought them. Advise Lord Regis, would you?'

Tellius was furious at the sense of rush that had been forced upon him. Regis gave the impression of being the most impatient man alive, as if everyone else was just kicking their heels against a wall, while he was the only one who wished to act.

Hondo bowed and Regis raised an eyebrow at the state of him. The sword saint had bandages wrapped right around his head, supporting his jaw. Every part of him that could be seen was scraped or gashed. One eye was almost completely red and he had lost some of his teeth. He spoke carefully, slurring the words.

'One uses air somehow – to choke and tighten. Or as a shield. Two of them seem able to produce fire without fuel. I think they burn the air, though I could not see how it was done. They are all fast – faster than me, or any other man I have ever fought.'

He was panting and took deep, ragged breaths as he

stopped talking. For once Regis was silent, perhaps out of respect, or awe at the man's injuries.

'They are not particularly agile, nor skilled as swordsmen,' Hondo went on. 'I would say they are merely competent, though their other gifts make them hard to engage. Nor are they invulnerable. I saw one of them shot with your guns, more than once. He bled, though he did not fall and seemed to heal himself. They are clearly . . . allies and will rescue or defend one another if they are overmatched. Yet the one who stands in the centre now is the leader and commands the others . . .' He trailed away, rubbing grit from one of his eyes as it streamed.

Some of the bounce seemed to have gone from Regis at the exchange, Tellius noted. Those marching to battle never enjoyed the sight of those coming away from it. Yet even as Tellius had the thought, he saw the lord's chest swell, his confidence return. Regis didn't learn from the experiences of others. How could he, when he was always proved right in the end? It was infuriating, but they still needed his shield – and perhaps a fearless man to carry it.

As Tellius watched, Regis clapped Hondo on the shoulder.

'You kept them busy while we gathered, sir,' he said. 'The house of Regis thanks you. Well done.'

Regis brushed past them all. His moustache seemed to jut further forward in his eagerness to reach the enemy. When he turned and filled his chest with air, Tellius put one hand over an ear.

'Regis! On me, Regis!' the man bellowed.

His voice was like a crack of thunder close to, and his men pressed in around him. Every one was of powerful frame and many of them had the same auburn hair and pale, freckled skin, as if they were cousins or bastards of the lord they followed. Tellius turned from them as Regis bellowed instructions.

'Can you go in again, Master Hondo?' Tellius said. 'I would not ask, but the shield and the De Guise sword are the greatest weapons of the city. If they fail, we all go down.'

'If you order it, I can fight,' Hondo said.

Tellius saw the acceptance of death in the eyes of the other man. He said nothing for a moment as he failed to find words. In the end, he merely nodded.

'I put your companion in the last set of armour, the one we call the patchwork. It isn't as fast as the others, but I thought, with him in it . . .'

'Yes. Bosin is a fearsome opponent,' Hondo said. He looked up at the armoured green giant standing behind Tellius. 'Can he hear me?'

'Of course,' Tellius said.

Hondo bowed his head in reply. The effort to speak clearly cost him, each word wrenched from ruin.

'Master Bosin, Je is dead, gone to join his brother. You and I alone remain. And . . . and I am sorry for what we did to you.'

The gaze of the green and grey armour was like glass as Hondo stood before it. Regis was already moving and Lord De Guise had swung across to join him. Tellius could not wait any longer.

'Galen! Take Lady Sallet out of danger,' he said.

Lady Sallet snapped her head around.

'Captain Galen will do no such thing,' she said.

'He will, Win, because you need to live through this. Who else can . . . counsel the king? Go with him, please.'

He heard his love swear under her breath and almost smiled. If Lady Sallet refused, he would not go in with the others, but instead remain at her side.

'My lady?' Galen said.

He and Tellius had discussed any number of scenarios over the previous months, ever since the Forza prophecy. One was simply what might happen if Tellius feared Lady Sallet would be killed, when there was a threat so great he thought they would not win against it. He had made Galen swear he would disobey her orders in that event, that he would risk his own neck and smash his career to pieces rather than allow her to be hurt. In that, he and Galen were in perfect accord.

Lady Sallet saw the determination in Galen's face and understood what it meant.

'I will not go far, Tellius,' she said firmly. 'Just out of this crossroads and up to the roof of one of the buildings. Do not presume further on my good will.'

Galen waited for Tellius to nod in agreement, which would cost the man later, if they survived. Tellius saluted with the sword he held, bowing slightly to her as she walked through the ranks of men, her head held high.

'Good man,' Regis called back to him. 'Keeping the lady safe. Geese and I have the measure of these three.'

Tellius blanched, hoping Win hadn't heard that bit.

'Sallet guards!' Tellius called. 'Advance on those three men. Ready guns for step volleys. We will advance on my mark and hold position at the boundary of the yard while Regis and De Guise engage the enemy. On my mark! Advance!'

A hundred green-coated men tramped forward towards the Bracken estate. Alongside them came Regis soldiers in red and De Guise in black and grey. They approached the strewn rubble and bodies around the Bracken estate yard, while flame poured like liquid from every window, lighting the night. Huge cracks had appeared across the front of the house, showing gold within. It looked like it could fall at any moment.

The three men who stood watching all their preparations seemed unafraid, for all an entire army had come to that place to destroy them. Tellius marched with Hondo on one side and Bosin's massive steps shaking the ground on the other. Tellius carried the sword his brother had worn and that was an intimacy of a sort. He swept the air with it as he walked. If there was the slightest chance to bury the thing in the neck of one of the three men who threatened everything he loved, he would take it.

Regis rather enjoyed the company of De Guise. The chap admired him, which was always gratifying. Young dog, looking to the old one for how to bark, sort of thing. The current head of the De Guise family was twenty-two and was delighted by the world he'd found around him. Of course, in private, Regis thought the man he called 'Geese' was as ruthless a killer as his father had been. The line ran true, as it had to when it came to the Twelve Families. They had not floated gently to the top of a city like Darien by feeding orphans and whatnot. No. Regis and De Guise had been two of the twelve founders of the city on the river, so it was said. According to the family records, the first men of that name had been friends for thirty years.

Perhaps that sort of thing meant nothing to some, but Lord Regis believed in tradition as an almost holy thing. In time of war, when a De Guise called, a Regis always answered – and vice versa. He could never have been the first to let the side down, after Goddess knew how many centuries. That sort of infamy survived a fellow. Far longer than bothering other men's wives, or arranging murders. Being shy in the face of a threat was about the worst thing Regis could imagine.

'These are tricky sods, as I heard it,' he called behind. 'I'll be ready to block whatever they throw, Geese. Use me as cover and take one of them off his heels. Dealer's choice which one.'

He felt the younger man's hand rest on his shoulder and they went forward as a pair, with the long red shield held before them. It gleamed as if alive, shining with the colour of war, rage and blood. Regis did wear a sword, but the shield was his first care and greatest weapon. He hadn't even drawn a blade and didn't expect to.

'Company in good order!' Regis bellowed. He'd always had a fine voice for the field. In that place, it echoed back from the houses around the crossroads. 'Now do keep up, lads. I can't do everything.'

His men grinned as they readied weapons and shields of their own. Regis was utterly against the idea of the common citizens of Darien being armed with the new pistols. That did not mean he rejected their use. Each of his lads carried two guns in a belt or in holsters, as well as sword, shield and dagger. Most wore mail or limited armour that protected chest, back and neck and left the arms and legs free to move quickly. They clanked as they ran. Regis chuckled at the sound. He saw the three interlopers cease their private chat and turn to face the threat.

'Ready, Regis! Ready, De Guise!' he roared at them. 'Clear shots only, gentlemen. If you can't see the enemy, don't take the shot. Do *not* shoot me in the back.' They'd lost a few men in training before that rule was well established, unfortunately.

Regis raised his shield a little higher as he went forward. The three men didn't look like much, he thought. Yet he could see the broken remains of two Sallet Greens lying on the rubble, one of them in pieces. For all he'd always disliked those green monsters, it was hard to imagine anything that could take them down.

'Ready, Geese?' he said over his shoulder.

One of the three was gesturing to the green armour, as if . . . Regis swore. Limbs or panels of green metal were rising into the air, spinning in silence with a cloud of rubble.

'Hit him, Geese!' Regis yelled.

A hail of metal and stone accelerated towards their advancing line. Regis sensed the crack in the air as De Guise did whatever he did to trigger his black sword. He roared as the leader of the three was smacked flat by the impact. Rubble and armour dropped as if strings had been cut. Only a few rattled against the Regis lines.

'I can do this all day, son!' Regis yelled. 'Gunners! Supporting fire!'

He held position as the ranks of guns swept up, rather than risk wandering across the line of fire from those behind. It was unnerving, even so. The thought that just one of his men with a grudge would mean being killed or crippled always crossed his mind and made him sweat, though he did not show it. A nobleman had to lead, his father had always said — and a leader had no fear, no weaknesses. No crisis of faith in the middle of a battle. Regis could imagine the old man's derision all too easily. He had experienced it many times before putting him in the cold ground.

The front rank knelt to fire, so that bullets poured out in a rolling hail from two ranks. They swept the Bracken yard with shot. Grey smoke billowed, making De Guise curse.

'Stop shooting! Hold position!'

With only three targets, the young lord cursed the smoke that drifted across. He needed to be able to see, to hit. De Guise caught a glimpse of a shadow and stepped out of the cover of the shield with his sword held straight before him. Something black and impossibly fast smashed across the yard from that blade, as if an eclipse had sprung out in a single line. Rubble sprayed into the air and then the young lord De Guise sensed someone standing by his shoulder. He began to turn, but Gabriel cut his throat in one swift move. The De Guise sword fell to the stones with a clang that reverberated a long way.

Regis turned in shock. They moved so fast! He was still bringing his shield round as the man flickered his sword out to kill again. The Regis shield rang like a bell, but Gabriel vanished backwards and Regis was up and after him in an instant. He'd known what would happen — the shield reflected blows, doubling their force. No normal swordsman could . . . He felt the air thicken around him, so that suddenly the sounds of the yard died away. Sound was carried on air, he remembered weakly. When the air became still, it was as if the entire city had been muffled. He tried to turn the shield to face the furious mage coming slowly closer, but he was held like a fly in grease, for all he struggled.

Thomas dragged one leg, where it had been broken. The pain and sense of sickness was appalling, but he recognised the shield-bearer and swordsman as the main dangers in that place. Gabriel had been sent tumbling and some sort of black bar had knocked Thomas head over heels into rubble. He'd seen his ankle catch and his leg twist until it snapped. It was not even a clean break. Shards of bone were already poking through to the surface and blood leaked in spots along his shin. He needed Gabriel to heal him quickly before the pain made him pass out.

Thomas saw the Sallet Green coming, turning to it in dismay as it clambered over rubble and bodies to launch itself against him. He saw its panels flashing grey as well as green, and yet it was still horribly, sickeningly fast, like a spider that could jump.

As the patchwork Green reached him, it swung a silver sword. Thomas dropped his control of the red shield to protect himself, thickening the air so that the monster was trapped and held. His leg was jolted by the turn so that it sent a fresh spike of agony, like white light through him. He felt dazed and ill, but they would not let him rest. With a grunt, he began to turn the flickering grey head slowly round as if he held it in a vice, waiting for the crack.

23

Patchwork

Marias walked the path the others had taken since coming through the gate. She saw the bodies of thousands of crows littering the street, with children picking them up in armfuls and dogs fighting over them. Some of the golden animals wagged their tails as Marias passed by with Lord Ran and the Fool. It was not hard to know where to go. As darkness descended on the city, Marias could hear gunfire down one street and see the light of a burning house. Thick orange embers floated through the air and house-holders were already throwing buckets of water onto doors and roofs wherever she looked. They were a determined people, she thought.

'You said it was just to look, Marias, remember?' Lord Ran wheedled, sniffing.

He had been offered a sword by the woman who had given them tea. He held it awkwardly, an archaic-looking thing with a curved blade, more suited to hanging above a fire in a tavern than actual use. The Lord of Trade in Shi-ang still clutched his blanket around his shoulders with his other hand and rubbed a dripping nose. Marias did not answer him. She wanted to see Taeshin again, even if it was to watch him die, even if she would die herself in that moment. She was not sure if what she felt was love, or exhaustion, or just the sense that she was so very far from home and would not see it again. Yet she knew she could not just watch Taeshin snuffed out for ever and go back to whatever life she had waiting. She would not be sold again, not in Darien. The woman who had given them tea had confirmed that much. Marias knew she could find work, but she hadn't crossed mountains simply to wash clothes or scrub floors in a strange city. She'd come to see that Taeshin survived, no matter what the cost.

Despite the darkness, the street was thick with soldiers, talking and laughing together, secure in the knowledge that some other poor sods were in the thick of it at that moment. Armed men in a dozen different colours blocked the road. Marias saw two officers almost come to blows as they argued over the order of march. With Lord Ran and the Fool in tow, she took alleyways around two of the closed positions, working always towards the cracks of gunfire and flickering lights. No one questioned them. The soldiers had no orders to stop those behind coming through. Unnoticed, the three of them slid along walls and twice through a tavern, excusing themselves as they went. The Fool beamed the whole time and something about him calmed what angry glances came their way.

Marias held her hand to her mouth as she saw massed ranks across the road ahead, made black against the glow of forty windows, all hissing flame. In that destructive light, dark figures lunged and struck, too fast for the eye to follow, so that they seemed to flicker. She had reached the heart of it, and the city trembled around her, with good reason.

She jumped as another fusillade of shots rang out,

followed by furious orders to hold fire. Smoke rolled over broken stones and dead men, obscuring the open ground. At her side, Lord Ran sniffed miserably once more. When she went to go closer, he put his arm across her chest, thin and weakened by fever as he was.

'You said you only wanted to look! Whoever he was to you, he's gone. You can see that now, surely?'

'Take your hand off me, Ruin,' she said, using the name she'd heard on the docks of Shiang. 'You said he can't kill me.'

'I meant . . . don't!' he said, but she was moving towards the flame-light before he could grab her.

The Fool looked back at him and smiled, following Marias. Lord Ran rubbed his nose hard, almost angrily, then stepped back, leaning against a wall in shadow. He knew the Returners rather better than most. He would not have gone into that maelstrom for a crown and an estate on the river.

Regis gasped as he found he could breathe again, recovering slowly. The air had been like porcelain in his throat. It was not that he'd been choked, but that he hadn't been able to move his lungs at all. He knew he had begun to die in the first moments, and to feel that awful constriction shatter to pieces around him was almost an ecstasy. He heaved in breath after ragged breath, but as he did so, he could see the Sallet Green being held in place in the same way. Panels flickered grey amidst the green and the thing clawed the air, trying and failing to reach its tormentor.

Regis didn't want to face a man who could thicken air into something he could not breathe. He had never known such helplessness in his entire life and the prospect of encountering it again was hard. He thought of his father's scorn then and grinned weakly. Perhaps it helped to imagine that. The old devil had never found much to praise in his son, except when he battered one of the guards unconscious in training.

Regis stood up and raised the red shield. Smoke drifting thick all around, two threats nearby – Goddess alone knew where the third had gone. The one before him stood on a broken leg and was the weaker of the two he'd engaged. The one the shield had sent flying moved like a damned hummingbird – and he had killed Geese. Regis heard himself growl and shook himself.

He had built a frame of muscle and hard bone on the training field and in sparring, every day of his life. He had done so for just such a moment. He raced forward, driving on with the red shield held before him. Most men thought of a shield only in defence, to hold a line or fend off an enraged enemy. Yet when the thing reflected and magnified impacts on its polished surface, it brought an entirely different effect to the battlefield. Regis was a heavy man, with powerful legs. He drove himself to accelerate, running at an enemy who could steal even breath.

Thomas was engrossed in his torture of the patchwork armoured figure. He'd already crumpled one of them that day – and broken the neck of another. Of all the Returners, he was the most experienced in dealing with the armoured green things. He had the patchwork figure up on its toes as he strained to break its grip on life. This one seemed to resist with greater strength, so that Thomas had to focus and double his effort.

He raised one hand and slowly turned it, as if he held a lever only he could see. With satisfaction, he heard a grunt from the warrior inside as the strain made his neck creak. The stillness in the air spread around the green and grey armour hanging in his grasp.

With no warning, Thomas heard running steps and caught a flash of red coming at him. He let the Sallet Green drop and tried to duck, expecting a sword blow. Yet his broken leg betrayed him and Regis hammered the red shield into him at a sprint, the lord's shoulder braced against the inner curve. Thomas flew back with a clang, tumbling over the rubble with his broken leg flopping horribly. When he lay still, he was on his back and he took a breath only to scream.

The patchwork armoured warrior settled into a crouch and stretched its neck. It raised one hand to Regis to halt him, rolling its shoulders like an athlete limbering up. Its gaze was fixed on Thomas. When Regis gestured for it to go ahead, the thing jerked into movement, loping the dozen yards between them and the fallen man.

Regis heard a light, pattering step behind him, like a man sprinting over sand. He turned in time to raise the shield to block Gabriel's blow and roared in triumph as the man was knocked through the air by his own attempt to cut him down from behind.

'Hurts, does it?' Regis said with savage glee. He had knocked the man into the ranks of De Guise soldiers. They had seen their own master killed just moments before and they fell on Gabriel with extraordinary savagery, battering at him with everything they had.

Regis turned from one side to the other, unsure where

best to use the shield. As powerful as it was, it had its flaws in battle, which was why his family had formed such a close bond with the De Guise. The sword they carried was not his to use. It rested by the body of a young man who had been in the prime of his youth. There would be no new heir from that line, no more partners to stand with a Regis on the field. He picked up the sword for the first time in his life. For the first time in a hundred generations, a Regis held the De Guise sword. His shield seemed to ring with it and the dust of the ground trembled beneath his feet.

Thomas felt tears come into his eyes as he struggled to stand. Every man was confident before the fight began, when they were fit and whole and strong. It was only after injury that the struggle changed, when a torn gut or a broken bone made every movement agony. That was when courage mattered. All men believed themselves immortal as they took the field.

His leg did more than throb or ache: it screamed at him. The pain was so intense he wanted to cut it off his body as a traitor before it killed him. He remembered feeling the same once with a childhood abscess, when he'd pleaded with his mother and a dentist to just yank the foul thing out with pincers. The smashed leg brought insanity and weakness. It had betrayed him and he could not see to fight, when he needed every ounce of control.

The Sallet Green scrambled into an attack with greater grace than the ones before. Whoever the man was within, he seemed tireless, so that as Thomas waited for a breath, a respite, it did not come. Instead, blow after blow slammed down on him from all angles. He held a shield of air against them all, but the armoured monster threw its entire weight against it, so that he lay back and could not rise a second time.

Thomas cried out as the Sallet Green clambered right on top of him, for all the world as if it straddled a glass ball. He could see it there as the shield of air began to fail, thumping crazily at him with sword and armoured fist. As he stared, he saw the thing make a spear of its fingers and try to jam them through the barrier it could not see. The attempt reminded him there was a man inside the armour, an enemy, yes, but just a soldier, not some terrifying creature of legend. Thomas tried to restore the choke hold he'd had on it before, but the pain was too great and it was all he could do to prevent it collapsing onto him.

He saw his own death in that moment and, to his surprise, it gave him strength. He had died once, after all. He had no illusions about what it meant. Other men might have given up under such an onslaught, but Thomas knew where he'd wake if he did. He could not bear the thought of the grey land stretching around him once again. He would rise, he told himself. Somehow, he would stand. Gabriel or Sanjin would come and set him free.

Sanjin startled awake, gasping aloud. Something had struck him in the first volleys of gunfire, before grey smoke rolled across the yard. Thomas had failed to keep his shield ready, or more likely he'd looked after himself and Gabriel, leaving Sanjin to be shot. He felt anger bubble like acid in his gut. His foot was bleeding again, of course, so that he left red prints and the bandages were crusted with brown muck. Gabriel had promised, but Sanjin understood very well why he had not finished the healing. It gave Gabriel power over him, that was all it was. It kept a leash on Sanjin, just like the one they had used on the Fool. He would have done the same. Gabriel was afraid of him, which showed he had some sense.

Sanjin sat up on his elbows, understanding that he'd gone down so fast in the darkness that none of the attacking companies had seen where he lay. His head throbbed and seemed twice its normal size, but he was alive and there was no one coming at him in that moment.

He pressed a hand to his forehead and felt the groove in the bone that had put him down. He blinked at the sight of bright blood on his hand, feeling suddenly ill, so that he turned to vomit into the bricks and twisted iron around him. That made his headache even worse and he found his anger growing. A great ocean rose within him, but he could not heal a graze, nor make a breeze blow.

He had seen Gabriel use fire. The man had been drunk on all he'd drawn from the Bracken Stone and he'd sent a torrent of flame, spending power as if it would never run dry. Sanjin frowned. They had come back together from the grey land, but it had been Gabriel who sat on a throne, Gabriel who took a young woman as his queen. Gabriel who led them to Darien for more stones.

There were dead men lying all around that yard, Sanjin realised. In the darkness, he would be invisible amongst them. Perhaps he could just walk away. He could leave Gabriel and Thomas to whatever fate they had brought down on themselves and just disappear into the city. His foot throbbed, reminding him. Half a foot. The cauterised spots had not held for long. He knew he could have it removed and sealed by a decent surgeon, but Gabriel could bring it back.

With a growl of frustration, Sanjin stood up. He was *sick* of this city. All he and the others wanted was the stones! Why did the people have to keep fighting them? It was a kind of collective madness, perhaps.

He saw Marias walk from the dark street into the flame-lit yard, the Fool trailing her like a faithful dog. Sanjin showed his teeth at the sight of them. Marias was Gabriel's weakness. The man made no formal claim of his own on her, but it seemed she was still too good to be given to a man like Sanjin, too fragile to endure his rough touch. He looked around him, taking in the ebb and flow of the battles going on across the yard. He saw Thomas struggling with one of the armoured green warriors and Gabriel lit by a bloom of flame further over.

They were surrounded; Sanjin understood that much. Perhaps there was a way out around the back of the Bracken estate. Or perhaps he would find more soldiers waiting for him there if he tried to creep away. He flexed his hands. The moment he moved, he would be back in. That was clear enough. He'd been granted a chance to just walk into the night and never be seen again. Perhaps the stones would cease their pulsing call to him if he stayed in Darien.

The thought was dizzying. A normal life. Not stolen thrones, or facing armies in battle, but eating lunch and walking in a park. Working for a wage and even finding himself a wife and a little place above a shop. Near a tavern, obviously. Perhaps that was all he had wanted.

Marias had not seen him, Sanjin thought. He crouched amongst the shadows and the dead, but she would pass just a few paces from where he was. He relished the fear and shock he could cause. He could come out of that black stillness and snatch her. Gabriel would never even know she had been there.

Only the presence of the Fool made him hesitate. That poor, ruined man stumbling along with her seemed to understand nothing. They had never even learned his name. Yet it was all too easy to imagine him pointing and hissing and weeping that Sanjin had hurt Marias, making a mush of the words.

Sanjin slowly raised his head. For a few moments, he'd dreamed a different life, something ordinary. That was not truly what he wanted. He had been given the power within him to use. He had not come back just to live like some farmer or tradesman. He had despised such people in his first life. No, that was not for him. He had come back to rule.

Marias was walking closer, beautiful in the gleam of flame. The whore had struggled when he'd taken her by the arm, as if his touch appalled her. So he would allow himself one moment of spite in the midst of battle, and then he would fight alongside Gabriel and Thomas – his brothers in arms – to wherever their fates took them.

He opened his hands like a flower and flame bloomed between them. He saw her turn to the light and then he flung a rope of it, a stream of gold and white that struck Marias and enveloped her.

Sanjin poured it out, then breathed more gently, the ground around him steaming with heat. As his eyes adjusted, his smile died as quickly as it had come. The Fool stood with his hand resting on her shoulder. Marias was untouched, unburned. The Fool beamed and cackled and Sanjin's temper surged. He advanced out of the darkness, but a crackle of gunfire held him back. His flame had alerted every soldier with a pistol. He shrank down and Marias and the Fool passed by, untouched by the violence whining in the air about them. Sanjin saw one or two orange trails as bullets slowed and he heard the Fool hissing laughter. The little bastard had been learning the whole time, Sanjin realised. He cursed to himself and made a decision. It was time to enter the fray. He would burn the air itself if he had to. He took a single, deep breath and began to walk across the yard. Apart, they were too weak to stand; together, Darien would fall.

Thomas felt his will crumble. The horrible figure of the armoured warrior was still gripping his sphere of air as if trying to lift it, hammering all the time with ceaseless energy. Thomas knew he was seeping blood, and no matter how he told himself to rally and stand, he could feel himself getting weaker. Sanjin had run off somewhere like the coward he was, but Thomas expected to see Gabriel still.

Gabriel would never run. Whatever some men had that made others want to follow them, he had. Part of it was that private oath, that bond. I will not run, when I see you fall. Gabriel had called him brother and Thomas had heard the promise in the word. Yet he was failing, and the spidery monster of green and grey was getting closer as the sphere shrank. Thomas could look into his own reflection on the helmet and see he was filthy with dirt, blood and fear. He bared his teeth at that green version of himself – and pushed back, trying to roll the monster off him.

Thomas almost sobbed when Gabriel appeared, standing to one side. The man took hold of the armoured green warrior by neck and leg and just threw him across the yard. Thomas felt his shield collapse and he lay there, breathing in relief, tears slicing through the dust on his face. He sensed Gabriel kneel. The first touch and the sudden cutting off of pain sent a shiver through him.

'My leg . . .' he murmured. 'Do what you can, brother . . .'

Gabriel began to reply, but the patchwork green warrior belted into him, snatching him from sight as it hit him at full speed. Thomas was left looking up at stars and floating embers. He found the strength to stand, though the bones of his leg broke again the moment he put weight on them, making him shout long and loud in his frustration.

To one side, Gabriel rolled with Bosin, punching and striking with appalling speed. Thomas thought he could not take a single step to help them, not and remain on his feet. All his promises were drawn apart, ruined by loss of blood, by too much pain. He wanted to sit down, to sleep. He could not fight any more.

He turned to see a man as marked in soot and filth as he was. Lord Regis hit him with the De Guise sword, knocking him onto his back. Without hesitating, the man leaped on top and brought the shield down. Thomas raised one hand to fend him off, but the impact was like being hit by a falling wall. It drove the air right out of him so that he could not take a breath. He was too weak to save himself and Regis gave him no time to harden the air, no time to breathe. He punched the shield down over and over, each blow doubled in its impact, until Thomas did not twitch and just stared, unmoving. Even then, Regis kept up the assault, grunting with each blow. He had never been afraid in his entire life until air had been made into glass in his mouth. That fear played itself out as he crashed the Regis shield down with all his strength, until the man beneath was bone and blood and cloth and Regis could barely raise his arms. He sat astride the body of the dead mage, panting so hard he thought his heart would burst in his chest.

'Majesty, please! Listen to me,' Taeshin said. 'I was not sent here. A man named Gabriel left your ranks with three others. Thomas and Sanjin – and one more whose name I never learned.'

The king used an old style of attack, Taeshin saw in relief. The man was tireless and strong, but he telegraphed his blows so that Taeshin could bat them aside or duck under them.

'Gabriel stands in my ranks,' the king growled at him. 'With better men than you, boy. Should I listen to a traitor? Who sent you?'

'I am not part of this battle, this grey place!' Taeshin yelled at him. 'Point Gabriel out, if you can, Your Majesty. He went back and dragged me here in his place.'

'No one goes back,' the king said with a sneer.

He turned to the ranks making ready to march that day. Taeshin held his breath as the king peered up and down the lines, a frown appearing.

'You see?' Taeshin pressed him. 'Gabriel has gone, with three others. Can you call him back to his place?'

'No one leaves this field,' the king said, though with less force. He closed his eyes for a moment. 'If there was a way home, don't you think I would go through it myself? It would take the power of a stone to open a door.'

'There was one. I saw it. There was a white stone,' Taeshin said. He was desperate. He had not spoken to anyone since arriving in that place an age before. He was close to weeping just to have the king hear him. 'Please. You are a king. Can you at least call them back?'

The man sheathed his sword, while his army looked on and another gathered on the fields beyond. He tapped a horn that rested on a thong around his neck, but there was only sadness in his expression.

'I can call them, boy. And they must come. That is my part to play – and theirs.'

Taeshin stood with his mouth open and wide eyes.

'Then . . . that is all I want! Please. Send me back. I am not meant to be here.'

'Oh son, I am sorry. I can call them, as I said. But do you see a morning stone, here? I can't send you home. Take up a sword and join the ranks. There is still time to fight today.'

Taeshin felt hope shrivel and die, so that he looked with new eyes around him.

'Call them, even so,' he said.

The king nodded.

'If you wish.' he said, his eyes shadowed. 'Where did you find the door?'

He looked to where Taeshin pointed and the king began to walk with him, climbing the slope away from the battlefield.

'What about your horse?' Taeshin said.

'The horse is what holds me, son. As when the new souls take up a sword or a shield. You pulled me from the saddle and so I was free, for the first time in . . .' He shook his head. 'I do not know.'

'Will you go back to the battle, after?' Taeshin asked him. 'When you call Gabriel and the others?'

'Where else would I go?' the king said, sadly.

24

Grey Land

The hill was gentle in its rise, though the effect was deceptive. Whenever Taeshin paused to look back at the plain, he was astonished how far they had come. The king too seemed awed at what he could see.

'I thought, so many times, that I would like to walk up this slope to the top, just for the view. Yet somehow . . .' His expression became darker. 'Somehow there was never enough time. There was always a new battle to fight, or I had to rest and prepare for the start of another day. And I never came, though the view is worth the climb.'

Taeshin wanted to keep the man on his side, his one chance to put right what had gone wrong – in a grey land that stole all hope. He feared asking the wrong question and seeing the blank expression return to the king's face. So he spoke carefully, trying hard not to give offence.

'I have been here for months . . .' he said. 'I've watched you fight more times than I can recall. Do you know you fight each day? That those who have been killed rise up once more and take up arms? Do you remember the battles?'

'Some. Those I win, more than those I lose,' the king replied. 'When I was . . . before I died, I loved to fight. Can you believe that? I felt I was never truly, completely in the world unless I could smell iron and oil, unless there was a sword in my hand, with regiments marching across the hills around me. You move like a fighter, son. Do you understand what I am saying?'

Taeshin nodded, feeling the man's gaze. The grey land was not a place of life or light, but the lies men told themselves had no place there.

'I understand. I have . . . felt the same at times. All I ever wanted was to test myself, my courage, my skill. I trained every day, looking for . . .' He trailed off. 'Honestly, I don't know what I was looking for. Fame? Admiration? It doesn't seem to matter as much now.'

'We all die,' the king said. 'In the end, regardless of whether we spent our lives selling fish or fighting and laughing.'

'Selling fish?' Taeshin asked.

The king shrugged.

'My people were fishermen, long before we were kings. Perhaps this is meant to be heaven, for soldiers and generals, I don't know. I am sure a heaven for fishermen would have boats.'

'I was not meant to be here,' Taeshin said softly.

They had climbed as they talked and the crest of the low hill was not far off. Taeshin saw a shadow move and he reached for a sword he did not have. The king looked up and they both saw a dark figure appear. At first, it raged and spun on the spot, then as they drew close, it crumpled and began to keen softly to itself.

'Thomas,' the king said. He went to the man and rested his hand on his shoulder. 'Go down, son. Take your place in the line. I'll need you to watch my back today.'

Thomas stood and nodded, wiping at tears no longer there as he broke into a run down the hill. Taeshin and the king watched him go.

'He was one of them,' Taeshin said.

The king sighed and shook his head.

'What of that? How did it profit him? He has more regrets now than before. They come wounded to the line, son. They come broken and weeping. I've seen it more times than I can say.'

On the plain, the battle began, with great squares marching and

343

slicing into one another. It seemed less real over distance, though it held the king rapt. He stared in wonder at something he had only ever known in the midst of the fighting.

'I should be down there, in the fray,' he said, dreamily. 'Not here on the hill.' He took a step down, then another.

'Please,' Taeshin said. 'Call Gabriel and Sanjin back. Even if you cannot send me home, undo that wrong first. Nothing is right until they are here.'

The battle was not going well without the king to lead them. It was a slaughter, with entire regiments vanishing from view as they were cut down and routed. In all the variations Taeshin had seen, he had never witnessed such a colossal defeat.

When the king turned to him once more, anger darkened his gaze.

'I should not have come with you. My place is down there, with them, to live or die each day.'

'And to do it again, over and over, without end or purpose?' Taeshin said in frustration. 'This is not heaven, Majesty. It must be hell, it must be. You can see that, can't you?'

The king was very still, watching his regiments scattered and broken. The slaughter would have been appalling in life. The other king rode the grey waste, up and down, up and down.

'The battle is lost,' the king said, despairing.

'Then win it tomorrow, when you do it all again!' Taeshin snapped. 'But call back the men who escaped first. Call back the ones who took my life from me and put me here. Do as you said you would, if you remember anything of honour in this place.'

Gabriel brushed dust from his coat, gun smoke drifting like fog around him. The armoured warrior had gone down hard under his blows and Gabriel had staggered away, desperate to save Thomas. He shook his head. He did not know if Thomas lived. He did not even know how many men he had killed that night. It was strange how Darien differed in so many ways from Shiang. In the royal precinct, he'd slaughtered Mazer swordsmen and royal guards, spattering himself with blood until he left red footprints on the marble. Yet in the end, as he'd taken the royal sword and sat the throne, the rest of them had surrendered. The city had fallen into line in days, without rebellions or riots.

It seemed the lords of Darien were more stubborn, or perhaps it was simply that he had not gone straight for the king. Symbols mattered, Gabriel thought with disgust. Once more he was covered in fluids and filth, with dust and pieces of flesh stuck to his face. If he and the others had not been challenged at the gate, perhaps they would have made their way to the royal estate and cut just one head from the wolf.

He snarled, sending flames sputtering in a ring around him to force the soldiers back.

'How many more of you need to die?' he snarled at them. 'I swear, if you . . .'

'Taeshin?' he heard.

He knew the voice in an instant, of course. Something in him leaped closer to the surface, terrified to have Marias appear in that place of savagery. He had not mastered the shield of air and he could only stare as she walked towards him with the Fool at her side.

'Go back!' he shouted, though it was not his own voice. Gabriel roared, trying to clear his throat of the one who had made words come. He would not share this body, not after all he had done to keep it. The Bracken Stone pulsed on his skin and he drew more from it, goosebumps rising all along his arms.

'*Marias! Go back! Before you get yourself killed!*' *Taeshin shouted suddenly.*

The king tilted his head and looked at him in confusion. A breeze began to blow and the king almost staggered as he realised he had never known one before, not in that place. He waited until Taeshin's focus seemed to return and rest on him.

'*You are bound to the world, still,*' *the king said, in wonder.*

'*Then send me home,*' *Taeshin pleaded. He could feel the night air of Darien, cold on his face. He could hear the crackle of gunfire and smell burned powder as some part of the world he had known drifted into the grey land. The king smelled it too, filling his lungs. After so long without, even that bitterness was intoxicating.*

'*If I could, son, I swear I would,*' *the king said.* '*But can you see? The link is getting weaker, even now. This is a place of death. If some part of you still lives, I do not think it can survive for much longer.*'

'*But I can feel the cold air! I can smell burning!*' *Taeshin said.* '*Please. I am just a word away from going home.*'

The king shook his head.

'*Stars burn bright in their last moments. Close your eyes and reach out, Taeshin. Perhaps she will hear you say goodbye.*'

Taeshin stepped forward and wrapped his hand over the lip of the king's breastplate, drawing him in. He spoke in a low growl, his temper surging in the air of Darien that swirled around them both.

'*Call them,*' *he said.* '*Gabriel and Sanjin. They are your men. You are responsible. Call . . . them back.*'

Gabriel slaughtered four men who charged suddenly out of the darkness, cutting them down as if they bent their necks on purpose to his blade. He paused as the last one fell, watching the entire facade of the Bracken estate fall into the yard. It struck with a rolling thunder, scattering stones and revealing a greater inferno. Gabriel smiled at the sight. He had thrown the armoured warrior of grey and green to that part of the yard. He loved flame for its destruction, though the sword was cleaner.

Freed, he moved again towards Marias. If a bullet found him, he sealed the wound. The flames had caught houses on either side of the little square and there were screams in the dark and women crying for help. He let his lips slide back in a feral expression. If this was hell, perhaps he was its master. He had brought light to Darien, after all.

He raised his hand in warning to Marias, but the presence within him was fading. He had not known how completely it had made a home, like some curling vine grown through all his joints and along the marrow of his bones. He knew it only when he felt it wither and grow soft, weakening as he grew strong. He smiled at Marias. In that moment, he knew he could kill her. Gabriel thought he would do it, just to show his contempt for the lover who had tried so hard to claim back his flesh. More, he would do it to demonstrate his control to that dying spirit, that pitiful failure. To make his last memory of the world a cry of despair.

Gabriel loped forward. To those watching, he seemed to skitter across the ground like some fearful insect, at a clattering, blurring speed. Bullets chipped stone around him as he attacked her, seeing her expression change to shock. He brought his sword down across Marias' neck — and came to a halt, trembling, while the Fool smiled.

Gabriel began to curse as he understood. He readied fire, drawing deeply from the stone on his arm. The Fool had challenged him, one of his own. One of the Returners. It would not stand.

'You should not have done that, brother,' Gabriel said.

Gabriel heard the scrape of a step behind him and whirled round. He almost laughed when he saw only Tellius there. He had feared the patchwork green warrior, or the maniac with his red shield. In desperation, just one old man had crept up on him in his distraction. Gabriel readied himself to burn the skinny old devil to ash, but then he recognised the hilt of red and black.

'Give me that sword,' Gabriel said. 'You have no idea what it is. It is mine. Give me the blade and live, or I swear I will kill you.'

'No. You are not worthy to carry it,' Tellius said. He lowered his stance a fraction, perfectly balanced between front and back leg, so that he could move to attack or defend in any direction. The Yuan blade rested in the air, ready to strike.

Gabriel wanted to laugh at him, at his pitiful defiance.

'I see you were a Mazer swordsman once,' he said. 'When was that, though? I can almost hear you creak, old man. Will you make me kill you? For what? Just give me the sword and go back to your nurse, would you?'

Tellius struck: a step forward and a straight lunge that might have come from the first page of any combat manual for swordwork. He was quick for one of his years, though compared to Gabriel, it would always have been too slow. With a sneer, Gabriel brought his own sword up, flicking it across to knock the attack straight up and away from him. The blow was a hard one and he thought it might break the old man's wrist.

To Gabriel's astonishment, his sword slipped past the Yuan blade in two pieces, so that the lunge passed straight through and sank into his chest. Gabriel gaped as his mouth filled with blood, unable to understand how it had happened. Had his sword snapped off at the hilt?

He fell backwards and Tellius went with him, keeping both hands on the Yuan blade and pushing it further in, pinning him on his back.

Gabriel began to heal himself, though the blade had pierced a lung and cut his heart almost in two. Whenever he managed to stop the bleeding, the old man wrenched it back and forth, torturing him. Blood surged in his throat and he tried to spit and speak.

'Someone else!' Tellius shouted without looking round. 'I can't hold him like this for much longer. Take his head off. Bosin! Hondo! Galen! Where are you?' He recalled he had sent Galen away to protect Lady Sallet. In that moment, he wished he had not.

Gabriel reached up, his fingers bloody and shaking. The blade had sunk so far through him that it grated on earth and stone, deep in the ground. It would surely be ruined. He put his hands over the old man's on the hilt and began to draw from the stone strapped to his forearm. He had to keep healing or die, but he needed to burn hot.

With so many fires lighting the night, the air was already warmer in that place than anywhere else in the city. They were at the heart of an inferno and yet Tellius felt something sting his cheek as embers began to drift towards the struggling pair. He could not believe the monster still lived. He had felt only satisfaction when the Yuan sword went in, but that was quickly curdling and becoming fear. Tellius was over sixty years of age and his arms were weakening, while the man he leaned on seemed only to grow in strength.

The woman was pleading with him and shrieking, Tellius realised. He pressed down on the sword, putting his whole weight behind it. Yet the woman began pulling at him like a wild thing.

'Get away from me! If I let him up, he'll kill us all. Sallets! On me, Sallets!' Tellius bellowed.

He could feel a worm of panic uncurling in his stomach. He'd had one move to make – one move based on the fact that he was of the blood of the royal house of Shiang. He'd known the sword would be alive in his hand, as it had never been for Gabriel. Yet it hadn't brought an ending. His arms were shaking. The woman was actually scratching him with her nails and Tellius swore as she raked his cheek. Looking into Gabriel's face, Tellius saw bloody teeth as the man smiled up at him and began to push back.

Sanjin clenched his fists. He saw Gabriel intercept Marias and the Fool, though Gabriel turned to whip the life out of some soldier creeping up on him. Sanjin's eyes widened when he saw the sword pierce Gabriel's heart. He began to lurch into a run as Bosin scrambled from under the stone of a broken wall and turned his head, spotting Sanjin. The armour was more grey than green and Sanjin saw in delight that the thing could not stand up. He darted at it, ready for a quick blow. He'd cut the monster's head off first.

As he closed, another man Sanjin recognised came and hunched down in front of the patchwork Sallet Green, still struggling to free itself from the rubble. He carried a red shield and a black sword that looked more like glass than metal.

Sanjin sent fire ahead of him. He thought it would have no effect on the green warrior, but perhaps he could scorch the air hot enough to kill the shield-holder. He closed the gap at the speed that marked all the Returners, the legacy of the Aeris Stone in their blood. His half-foot made him ungainly, but he was still a match for any ordinary soldier, hard even to see.

Sanjin came through his own flame and struck the Regis shield hard enough to cut it in two. He lost consciousness in the impact, hearing only the sound of a bell as he crashed into rubble and a great stone fireplace that stuck out of the ground.

Sanjin opened his eyes to see the green-suited monster lurching towards him, the shield man alongside. He closed his eyes again, feeling his mouth full of blood and sharp pieces of broken teeth.

When he opened his eyes for a second time, they were both peering down at him.

'Welcome to Darien, son,' Lord Regis said.

He made a sharp gesture and Sanjin struggled as the massive armoured figure took his head in its hands and twisted until they heard a great snap. They waited then to be sure he was truly dead, then dropped him and walked away.

Taeshin jerked round when he saw another shadow form on the crest of the hill. He recognised Sanjin from the glimpses he'd had of

Gabriel's dreams and horrors. He heard the shade wail as he looked around him and understood where he was. Taeshin watched as the shape became more solid, but kept scrambling around the hilltop, looking for a way to return.

'Did you call him?' Taeshin asked the king.

'It was time for him to return,' the man said.

Taeshin frowned at that, but he walked over to where Sanjin dug at the grey ground.

'I must get back,' Sanjin said as he sensed Taeshin standing there.

Taeshin lifted him to his feet. He was tempted to knock the wind out of him, though he knew enough of the grey land by then to know it wouldn't cause the man pain, not really. Those who died in the battle never cried out. Even the ones who lost a hand or sat with their guts spilled in their lap didn't weep or wail. The grey waste was a place outside life, perhaps even outside death. Yet the man had tried to hurt Marias, so Taeshin hit him anyway, battering him to his knees and then kicking him down the hill until Sanjin found his feet and ran the rest of the way.

'What was the point of that?' the king asked him.

Taeshin raised an eyebrow.

'If I'm to spend eternity here, I want him to know I have his measure.'

Taeshin turned to face the king. A breeze blew more strongly and he thought he could hear Marias calling his name. The real world was like a window, with his face pressed against it. Yet he could not go back. He struggled to remember every moment of his life – and Marias herself. The smell of her hair, the way she had laughed. He understood then that he had wasted years.

'Call the last of them, Your Majesty,' he said. 'If you have any power at all, bring Gabriel back.'

25

Gabriel

Hondo answered the call. He fell into step with Bosin and the lord who had been so brisk on their first meeting, who carried a red shield and a sword of black glass. They had all taken a beating, though Hondo looked the worst. His face had swollen to an extraordinary degree. Black bruising spread all the way down his neck. He still tried to smile when he saw Bosin nod to him.

'Just one of them left,' Regis said.

His voice had lost the brashness from before and Hondo could see he had been worn down. Every part of him was scuffed or grazed or bruised. One of his fingers stood out at an angle that meant it was broken. Yet he still winced when he saw Hondo's face.

'You look like a horse trampled you,' Regis said.

Hondo stared at him. They walked together to where Tellius pinned a writhing Gabriel to the ground like a bird with a maggot. A woman was heaving at Tellius, her hands deep in his coat. Hondo reached to push her away and found he could not touch her. His hand slid clear as if she was coated in clear glass. He saw a man crouching at her back, hissing like a snake. Hondo drew his sword, the sound attracting the gaze of each member of the tableau.

Marias stopped clawing at Tellius, though her face was marked in tears and dirt and she was too spent to do more than stand there and weep. Hondo eyed the Fool, but saw no threat in him.

'Orders, my lord?' he said, forcing the words out with huge difficulty past his swollen tongue.

'Take his head off,' Regis replied. 'Or stand back and let me do it.'

'I believe he was asking . . . me,' Tellius growled at the red-headed lord. He was so relieved to see them standing in support that he began laughing weakly.

'With respect, Tellius, you're no lord,' Regis said. 'He's . . . not . . . a lord, son,' he went on, slowly and clearly, in case Hondo did not understand the ranks and ways of Darien.

Bosin chose that moment to fold back the helmet of the Sallet Green they called Patchwork. It clicked and whirred open, half-sticking in the process before he was able to breathe in the night air. Regis watched him in amazement.

'I knew there were men in them,' he said. 'I knew it. It doesn't matter what magic can do – you always need someone at the tiller. Damn me, I wish my father was alive. I'd make him eat his words.'

'If you have finished your discussion, I agree with Lord Regis,' Tellius said. 'He won't die.' As he spoke, he wrenched the blade back and forth like working a lever, cutting pieces out of the heart within. Gabriel gasped in fresh agony, snarling at him.

'Let me stand,' Gabriel gasped, 'and I'll show you how it's done. I don't think you . . .' A confused look crossed his face like a shadow. 'No . . .' The hands holding the hilt fell back, splayed wide. The eyes went dull and life fled from him, leaving just blood and bone. Marias fell to her knees and wept at his side.

The king drew his sword, stung to act at last by Taeshin's scorn. He swung the blade wide, though it touched nothing. Then he reached and gathered folds of a shadow in his hand.

'Come to me, brother,' the king said.

Taeshin heard a voice cry out in fear or despair and then the king dragged the shade back. Taeshin didn't know the man's face, but he had no doubt it was Gabriel. Somehow, in his moment of triumph, it was hard to raise either anger or hate. He suspected the reason was that the grey land had taken hold in him, so that nothing mattered as much as it had once done. Taeshin stood uncertainly as the king spoke to the newcomer.

'You were missed in the lines, Gabriel,' the king said. 'We lost badly today, the worst I remember. Thomas and Sanjin have already gone down. Will you fight alongside them? Will you take the field for me tomorrow?'

Gabriel raised his head as life and taste and touch faded.

'Go to hell, you tin-pot beggar,' he said. 'I too was a king. You should take the field for me.'

For an instant, his gaze flickered across Taeshin. Gabriel knew well the face he had worn. A spasm of rage showed in his eyes. Without another word, he walked down the hill, but not towards the battlefield. His feet took him away from it, out alone across the plain.

Taeshin looked to the king as he sheathed the great sword once more.

'I should not be here,' Taeshin said. 'Please let me go.'

'I cannot,' the king replied. 'I'm sorry. Come, I'll find you a place in the lines. There is a battle to fight tomorrow, one we must win.'

Together, they began to walk down the hill to the grey plain. Taeshin felt he might weep, but no tears were ever shed in that place.

Tellius withdrew the Yuan sword. He held it out to Hondo and the sword saint of Shiang took the blade and bowed over it, then began to clean it with a pained expression. The blade needed to be ground and repolished by a master – and he did not imagine such a man resided in Darien.

No one attacked them, which took time to understand. Regis walked away without warning, to see the body of De Guise was properly tended and laid out with dignity. Bosin remained, as much a statue as the armour he wore, so that Hondo saw no spark of the travelling companion he had known. Tellius called one of his men across to summon Lady Sallet back to the battleground. Around them, the citizens fought the fires that still threatened to spread right across the city from that burning heart.

Tellius didn't know who the woman was, though he was wary of interrupting her grief. He eyed her still-beaming companion with suspicion, but crouched at Marias' side.

'You knew this man?' Tellius said. 'I would like to hear your side of the story if you did.'

'You killed him,' she whispered. 'No, I knew the man he was, before he was . . . lost. The one who attacked this city was nothing to do with me. Gabriel and the others . . . they were terrible men. They brought us here, from Shiang.'

'Us?' Tellius said.

He saw she had pressed her hands into the crook of the dead man's neck. It was a pitiful gesture and he could not quite make it fit with all the cruelty and power he had witnessed. Tellius reached out and gripped the body's right arm, ready to place it gently across the chest. He felt the hardness of the stone under the cloth as he did so. His eyes widened as heat sprang from it.

'There is a stone here!' Tellius cried out.

The response was immediate. Soldiers rushed towards him, ready for whatever threat had caused the shout.

Tellius tore at the ragged shirt, exposing the purple Bracken Stone. The flecks of gold gleamed bright in firelight and shadow. Tellius frowned at the sight of gold discs peeping out from beneath. There had always been rumours about the Bracken Stone and its master's constant contact with it. Only Bracken and Canis wore the stones of their families. He wondered . . . As he reached for it, it gleamed, suddenly too bright. He turned his face from the light, but still tried to reach out and snatch it in his blindness.

The stone crumbled under his fingers, becoming dust as fine as flour, that dribbled almost like liquid. The light died away and Tellius panted hard in fear, unable to explain what had just happened. His fingers snagged on gold wires and he crumpled them into his palm as he pulled back. The great wound in the chest had closed, leaving a scar like an eye.

On top of the hill, a golden eye opened. Taeshin felt its warmth and spun round, his jaw sagging in astonishment. Not far away, Gabriel too looked back, while on the other side, Thomas and Sanjin exchanged a feverish glance. All three began to run to the peak.

Taeshin looked at the king in wild hope. The man shrugged and took position on the hillside, raising his sword.

'Go on, boy. I'll hold them, "tin-pot beggar" or not. And I'll keep a place, for when I see you again.'

Taeshin didn't have time to reply. Without a word, he scrambled back to the sole bright spot in the whole of the grey wasteland. As he ran, he prayed it would not close, with every step and breath. He did not look back at the others, even when he heard the clash of arms and the king bellow in challenge. Taeshin threw himself into the brightness.

Taeshin woke to see strangers all around him – and one who was not.

'Marias,' Taeshin said, coming to his feet.

The reaction to that simple movement was terrifying. Swords came up and Taeshin saw a massive figure in green armour turn to face him.

'Please stop!' he shouted. 'I am not him! Whoever you are, please let her go.'

'Taeshin?' Marias said.

When he nodded, she began to sob. She threw her arms around him, pressing her face into his neck. That act was strange enough and Tellius raised his hand to halt Bosin before the man hammered them into the ground together.

'How can we be sure?' Tellius murmured to Hondo.

Taeshin heard the question and his eyes widened at the sight of the sword saint of Shiang.

'Master Hondo?' he said, in astonishment. 'Forgive me, I have missed a great deal.'

To Tellius' surprise, the young man knelt to Hondo, putting one knee into the ash and dirt. A strange expression crossed his face and Tellius saw him rub a bare hand along his side.

'I am healed, Marias,' Taeshin said.

Tears filled his eyes to match hers and Tellius was suddenly weary of them all.

'Right. You are all under arrest. Hondo, take them into our custody. Return them to the Sallet estate – this grinning one included. I will hear the tale from them.'

'Who are you to give orders to the sword saint?' Taeshin said indignantly.

In reply, Bosin cuffed him over the back of the head.

'King Yuan-Choji is dead. Long live the king of Shi-ang,' he said stiffly.

A few paces away, Lord Regis heard and fumbled his shield, dropping it with a clang before he had it up and on his arm again.

The fires burned for three nights, killing more than a thousand people and laying waste to great sections of the city that would have to be rebuilt. One of the architects who submitted designs in the spring referred to the fires as a great dark wave of destruction. Tellius hired him without looking at his plans.